US THREE

Ruth Jones

BLACK SWAN

TRANSWORLD PUBLISHERS
Penguin Random House, One Embassy Gardens,
8 Viaduct Gardens, London SW11 7BW
www.penguin.co.uk

Transworld is part of the Penguin Random House group of companies
whose addresses can be found at global.penguinrandomhouse.com

Penguin
Random House
UK

First published in Great Britain in 2020 by Bantam Press
an imprint of Transworld Publishers
Black Swan edition published 2021

A CIP catalogue record for this book
is available from the British Library.

ISBN
9781784162238

Typeset in 11.25/15.25pt Sabon by Jouve (UK), Milton Keynes.
Printed and bound in Great Britain by Clays Ltd, Elcograf S.p.A.

The authorized representative in the EEA is Penguin Random House Ireland,
Morrison Chambers, 32 Nassau Street, Dublin D02 YH68.

Penguin Random House is committed to a sustainable
future for our business, our readers and our planet. This book
is made from Forest Stewardship Council® certified paper.

1

For my bold and beautiful bad-weather friends

Omne trium perfectum
Every set of three is perfect

PROLOGUE
2017

The shoes were a big mistake. Her toes had gone numb and every time a stiletto heel crunched on to the unforgiving surface of the pavement, it set her teeth on edge. Once again vanity had taken precedence over comfort. *Nice one, Lana.*

She was tottering up Bessemer Place, which ran along the side of St Theodore's. Decades earlier the lane had been a teenage haunt for them, a place for slurping sweet cider and smoking in secret. She sighed, heart heavy, weighed down by loss and the searing pain of grief. All exacerbated by the discomfort in her feet.

Approaching the corner where Bessemer Place met the main street, she saw several figures dressed in black heading for the church – some solitary, some in couples, some in groups, all united in their loss. The service would no doubt be packed and Lana's heart lurched like a stalled engine at the prospect of what lay ahead: the funeral of her most wonderful friend.

'Lana.' A voice behind her.

Cautious. Sad.

It was Judith.

Inevitable that they should see each other – today of all days. Uncertainty fizzled between them, and they hesitated on the verge of a hug before both deciding against it.

'Can't believe it's happening, can you?' asked Lana, her voice shaking as she fumbled in her bag for a small bottle of Rescue Remedy and swigged back its contents like whisky.

'The family wants us down the front,' said Judith.

'Oh Christ, I'm not sure I can handle that . . .' replied Lana, panicking. 'So close to the coffin and . . . I'm just not very good with—'

Judith trampled over her words. 'Today's not about you though, is it, Lana? It's about Catrin.'

Lana bit her lip and refrained from reacting as the awkwardness between them grew. Then, without warning and with the worst possible timing, Lana felt the familiar surge of heat spread across the back of her scalp and down her neck as if she'd been plugged into a wall socket. 'Bloody hot flushes,' she mumbled, and pulled off the black silk wrap that was draped over her shoulders before flapping the neckline of her dress.

'Here y'are, borrow this,' said Judith, reluctantly rustling in her bag for a Spanish-style fan.

'Cheers,' said Lana, flicking it open with flamencan flair and cooling herself in its welcome breeze. A minute later the flush had passed.

'Shall we go in then?' asked Judith, a tad more gently.

'Yes,' said Lana as she held Judith's gaze. 'We can do this. Can't we?'

PART ONE
1986
Thirty-one years earlier

1

Catrin

Catrin's father was doing his Sensible Face. This was the face that forty-eight-year-old, half-Welsh, half-Irish Huw Kelly adopted whenever Catrin or her brother were about to embark upon any kind of trip without their parents.

Catrin had first encountered Sensible Face aged five, before her school visit to Coed Celyn museum in Mrs John's class. After that, the Face appeared before all hockey, netball and swimming tournaments, Guide camps or youth-club jaunts to Belgium, church pilgrimages to Lourdes, and sixth-form skiing trips to Austria. Sensible Face was also known as Here-Are-the-Practicalities Face and What-To-Do-in-an-Emergency Face. But underneath it lurked the precariously hidden face of Terrified Dad, looking down at this precious cargo, which grew more valuable with every day that passed, and who was currently thinking, *If anything happens to you, my life will be over.*

Huw had reason to worry, because Catrin was about to head off on the Big Trip – island-hopping for a month in Greece, accompanied by Judith Harris and

Lana Lloyd, her best friends since she was five. The three girls were as different as chalk, cheese and chocolate. But they knew and loved each other inside out and were as close today as they'd been in the first week of infant school. During their thirteen-year friendship they'd barely spent a single day without seeing each other and all three knew that when they returned from the Big Trip, they'd be heading off in very separate directions – Catrin to study medicine at Cardiff, Judith to read economics in London, and Lana to train as a musical theatre actress. So what lay ahead was more than just a holiday. It was their final hurrah, their last chance to stock up on each other's company before beginning the next chapter of their young lives. Deciding where to go on the Big Trip had been far from easy: backpacking in Australia? Campervanning in New Zealand? Fruit picking in France? Judith had suggested interrailing – drawn to the history and might of great European cities like Hamburg and Nice – whereas Catrin longed to see Paris and Rome. 'It's so romantic,' she said wistfully.

'It is if you're loaded!' Lana had warned, instantly dampening her friends' enthusiasm. 'But us three are on a budget of ten quid a day. And I'd rather wash in the sea and sleep on a beach than spend a month in a manky train full of horny stoners.'

'Classy,' Judith had said sarcastically and Catrin sighed.

'Look,' said Lana, softening. 'What about island-hopping? There's shed-loads of history and stuff in

Greece, so that's *that* box ticked for you, Jude. And Cat, if you want all the romantic bollocks, then what's more idyllic than a sunset on Skiathos? *I'll* be sorted with a beach and a bar, so Bob's your uncle. What d'you reckon?'

They had begrudgingly agreed. Both of them were used to Lana getting her own way, but frustratingly she was usually right.

'Excellent!' Lana had said with a smile. 'Island-hopping it is.'

'Now you're to keep it on you at *all* times, d'you hear? Even when you sleep!' said Huw as he held out a highly unattractive khaki-coloured money belt.

'But I can't wear it swimming, Dad, or in the shower. All the travellers' cheques and cash will go soggy,' Catrin replied.

'She's got a point mind, Huw,' said Liz, Catrin's mother, who was peeling a price tag off the sole of a new flip-flop.

'We've discussed this, Elizabeth.' Huw always used his wife's full name whenever he was trying to be serious. 'Catrin is to locate the nearest safety deposit box at every location – be it an Athenian youth hostel, or a taverna in Kos, whatever . . .'

'I don't think they have safety deposit boxes in crack dens mind, Dad,' said Catrin's twenty-one-year-old brother Tom as he sloped sleepily into the kitchen in search of Shredded Wheat.

'Not helpful, Tom,' sighed Huw.

'Weren't you meant to be in work at nine?' asked Liz. She loved the fact that her student son had a summer job at the bakery – he brought home all sorts of lovely treats.

'Taken the day off, haven't I? To say goodbye to Frog Head.'

'Oi!' Catrin laughed and threw a toast crust at him. Tom had called her Frog Head ever since she was brought home from hospital at one day old. Aged three, he'd stared at her in silence for ten seconds, then announced to the world that she looked like a frog.

Catrin Kelly couldn't look less like a frog if she tried. She'd inherited her grandmother's pale Irish complexion, 'which *must* be protected with Factor Fifty when you're out in that sun,' Liz had warned her, over and over again. She'd also inherited Nana Kelly's laughing green eyes – which she liked – and her strawberry-blonde hair – which she didn't. Mainly because it stubbornly grew in an unruly abundance of corkscrew curls. They'd appeared when she was two and had never left her since, defying gravity and copious amounts of hair-straightening products. 'I wish I had your hair!' people would say. And Catrin would smile politely, thinking, 'No you bloody don't – it's like walking round with a Highland cow on my head.' Catrin had a catalogue of complaints when it came to her physical attributes: she thought her nose was 'pixie-ish', her legs were too short and her knees turned inwards – none of which anyone else could see, of course. She was also blind to her other endearing features – such as her open-heartedness, her massive capacity for compassion and her staunch loyalty to those she loved. But Catrin's parents thought she was the most beautiful girl in the world, both inside and out.

'Just think – we may never see you again, you go fallin' in love with some Greek hippie!' Tom continued.

'Nobody is doin' no fallin' in love with no hippies,' said Huw, without conviction. 'And stop throwing food at your brother.'

'Do they even *have* hippies in Greece?' Liz wondered in all honesty.

'Will you *please* take this seriously, the lot of you!' Huw exploded in frustration, the Irish accent of his childhood creeping through as it always did when he was even mildly upset. He passed Catrin the money belt. 'Now try it on so I can demonstrate adjusting the width.'

'OK.' Catrin did as she was told. She'd learned over the years that it was easier to just go along with her father when he was anxious like this. It would at least put his mind at rest, even though she knew she'd be hiding the belt under her bed before she left, with no intention of ever using it.

'Thanks again for last night,' Catrin said as she placed the belt around her waist. 'Everyone had a crackin' time.'

'Ah, it was a pleasure, wasn't it, Huw? You've got such lovely friends.' Liz smiled.

'Aye,' mumbled Huw, whose head was still a little fuzzy from the farewell bash they'd thrown the night before.

'Judith didn't stay long,' said Tom through a mouthful of breakfast. 'We were gonna have an arm wrestle an' everythin'.'

'Arm wrestle!' exclaimed Liz. 'Dear God, is it any wonder you've not got a girlfriend, you go arm wrestling with young women at parties!'

'She had to get back early,' said Catrin. 'You know what her mum's like – Oww! Dad, calm down, mun! Don't be so rough.' Huw was tugging at the money belt with such enthusiasm, Catrin nearly lost her balance.

'I'm just testing it for strength,' Huw said, more to himself than anyone else.

'Judith will be glad of a break from that woman, you ask me,' said Liz. 'How she puts up with her I will never know.'

'Her dad's all right though – had a game with him down the club the other day,' said Tom. 'Don't say much, but he's a demon with a pool cue.'

'Yeah, well don't go saying anything to her today now, OK?' said Catrin. 'It's been enough of an ordeal getting Jude to come in the first place. Lana's worked really hard persuading her that Patricia will manage without her. Dad, that's actually digging into my flesh. I think you're drawing blood.'

'Sorry, sorry . . .'

The doorbell rang and Catrin's parents exchanged a look. 'Ah, that'll be Father O'Leary,' said Huw with forced breeziness as he made his way into the hall.

'What's *he* want?' said Tom.

Liz looked sheepish and turned to Catrin. 'Well,

your father thought seeing as you didn't make it to Mass on Sunday . . .'

'Mum – seriously, how many times?' said Catrin. 'I don't go to Mass any more!'

'She's a fully fledged atheist now, like me,' said Tom. Liz flicked his arm with a tea towel, whispering through gritted teeth, 'Hush your nonsense, Thomas Kelly! Sayin' things like that with a priest standing just outside the door!'

And suddenly in a Jekyll and Hydeian attitude switch she became all smiles and grace, turning towards – 'Father O'Leary!' – as he walked into their kitchen. A short, squat, solid little man, who looked like he could handle himself in the ring, never mind the pulpit, was nodding enthusiastically at them all.

'Alrigh', Liz? 'ow's it goin', alrigh'?' Father O'Leary was from Cardiff, and his broad accent and chippy, high-pitched voice always took anyone he met by surprise. He somehow sounded too urban for a man of the cloth.

Huw stood behind him, glaring at his children and daring them to misbehave in the presence of Christ's Representative on Earth. 'Catrin Mary, will you make Father O'Leary a cup of tea now?' said Huw with fake jollity – his accent becoming positively Corkonian. This often happened when he was anywhere near churches, vicars or nuns.

Catrin, still wearing the khaki money belt, stared back at Huw defiantly. 'Sure now, dear Father, I will, to be sure!'

13

The priest was putting on his liturgical stole and didn't seem to notice Catrin's sarcasm. She headed for the kettle.

Catrin loved her parents dearly, but this kowtowing to the Church did her absolute head in. She wasn't actually an atheist like Tom, she was *something* – she just didn't know what any more. When she was little she'd loved all the drama of going to Mass, the dressing up for her first communion, inventing sins to take to confession and repeating endless Hail Marys in quick succession like a lucky mantra. But as she'd grown older, Catrin's faith had begun to crumble. Sure, she liked the *positive* side of Jesus – he seemed like a nice man with good values: kind, compassionate, forgiving. But the rest of it? No, thanks. All that guilt and retribution. So they came to a family compromise: Catrin would continue to go to Mass until she turned eighteen, but after that it was only fair she should be allowed to make an adult decision. Seeing as she was now, well, an adult.

She'd never told anyone, not even Judith and Lana, but the first week she didn't go to Mass, she lay on her bed and cried. Was she tempting Fate? Was something awful going to happen to her now that she'd become . . . actually, what *had* she become? A heathen? A God-less monster? The Catholic guilt with which she'd grown up was not going to be easy to shift. Her parents never once tried to persuade her to join them on Sunday mornings, and she appreciated that. But then when

Christmas came, she couldn't stay away from Midnight Mass. 'I feel such a hypocrite,' she'd said to Judith, who couldn't understand why.

'I don't see what the big deal is. Can't you just go to church as and when you feel like it? You know, a bit like Aerobics?'

'Maybe,' Catrin had said. But it didn't sit comfortably with her.

The kettle clicked and Catrin made the tea. 'So, it's this afternoon you's off then, is it, Kate?' Father O'Leary had never got her name right in eighteen years.

'That's right, Father,' Liz answered on her daughter's behalf.

'Actually, my name's Catrin,' she mumbled pointlessly, as Liz jumped in over her.

'Huw's taking them to Bristol airport at one and they're flying straight to Athens, would you believe!' Since Catrin had 'abandoned the Church' her mother was presumably nervous of letting her answer the priest of her own accord, in case she began spitting blasphemy in an *Exorcist*-inspired tirade.

'Ah, Athens. Crackin'. Well, now, here's the thing . . .'

Catrin was bizarrely fascinated by the way Father O'Leary spoke. As if he was jabbing them all on the arm with his Cardiffian-accented utterances. Short, staccato and stilted. Like a series of dotted quavers on a music manuscript. He carried on, taking his crucifix out of his bag as he spoke and placing it delicately on the kitchen table. Liz surreptitiously removed Tom's

15

box of Shredded Wheat. 'Your mum and dad – they wants me to say a little prayer for you, alrigh'? Just to send you on your travels, like . . .'

Tom glanced at his sister, desperate to laugh. She returned the look with mortification.

'So, let's all bow our heads a minute, is it?' And his voice changed gear, sinking down an octave, becoming intense and mysterious, yet still delivering words with machine-gun-like rapidity. 'Lord-Jesus-Christ you are the light-an'-th'-hope. Deliver oh Lor' our servant Catherine—'

'It's Catrin, it is—'

'Ssh,' hissed Liz, her eyes firmly closed.

'. . . that she may stay safe-in-yer-care, as like Sain'-Chris'pher the patron saint of travels she travels herself to the far'way lands of Greece, an'-that.'

Tom couldn't control himself and exploded in a snort.

'Amen.'

Huw and Liz in unison said, 'Amen.'

'Sorry, can I ask something?' Catrin interjected.

'No. Ssh,' said Huw. The priest had turned to his bag of tricks once more and was rustling around inside.

'But how can the prayer work if he got my name wrong? I mean, did he even say my name right when I got baptized?' Catrin pleaded in hushed tones.

By now Tom was having to stifle his hysteria with his mother's Tower of London tea towel, stuffing almost half of it inside his mouth.

'Ta dah!' announced Father O'Leary, producing a

16

small blue box. Catrin noticed the vinyl was peeling on one edge. He opened it and nestled inside on a cushion of grey plastic sponge was a gaudy-looking silver-coloured necklace.

Catrin looked closer and realized it was a tacky St Christopher charm, the kind they sold in the dusty cabinet at the back of the church.

'What d'you think of that then?' said Father O'Leary with gleaming eyes, as if he was showing her the Koh-i-Noor diamond.

'It's to keep you safe on yer hols!' announced Huw.

'Lovely!' declared Liz. 'Now let's get it on you, shall we? Let it start doin' its job!'

Catrin looked at her mother in disbelief.

Tom had tears streaming down his face. 'It's absolutely beautiful, Karen,' he announced. And nobody detected his sarcasm. Except Catrin, of course. Who stood there resplendent in her khaki money belt and nickel-plated St Christopher charm that looked more like an SOS medallion, only not as subtle.

'Hey now doesn't that look the real deal!' declared Father O'Leary.

The phone rang in the hall.

'I'll get it!' Catrin screeched, desperate to get out of the kitchen. She leapt into the hallway and grabbed the phone. '5-0-6-5?' she said.

'Cat, it's Lana.'

'Oh, thank God! Look, the sooner you get here and we bugger off to Greece, the better. My family is actually deranged. My mother has only gone and—'

'Babe, we got a problem.'

Catrin caught her breath.

'What's going on?' she asked, worried.

On the other end of the phone, Lana sighed.

'It's Judith. She's not fucking coming.'

2

Judith

After checking her bedroom for anything she may have forgotten, Judith picked up her bulging rucksack to test the weight and heaved it on to her shoulders. She couldn't wait to leave. Focusing on the trip had buoyed her up through the pressure of exams. A little beacon in the otherwise murky mass of revision timetables, instant coffee, late-night cramming and nervous stress. But now she could put all that behind her: soon she'd be flying to Athens for the adventure of a lifetime with her two best friends.

A loud banging from the back yard disturbed her reverie. Going to the window, she watched as her father called the cats over for their food, clanging a spoon against the tin bowl. He did it with the same rhythm and velocity every single morning. He loved those cats. 'Betty! Betty! Come on! Twister! Breakfast!'

She watched him stretch and look out over their modest back yard, sighing deeply. *I know you're unhappy*, she thought, and a sudden lurch of sorrow clutched at her heart: would he be all right without her? As if sensing she was there, he turned and looked up. 'All packed?' he called.

'I think so!' she replied, injecting as much jollity as she could to stop him feeling sad.

'Got time for a game before you go?' he said with a smile.

Twenty minutes later they were sitting in the sunshine on two nylon-backed camp chairs, sipping strong Glengettie tea: hers made with three sugars and top-of-the-milk cream, his black with no sugar. The backgammon board was laid out in front of them on an old coffee table he'd once rescued from a skip. Whenever in use it had to be stabilized with a folded-up beer mat. Judith threw the dice and made her move, the two of them sitting in comfortable silence like they always did when they played. Betty and Twister lay on the warm paving stones near their feet, indulging in a post-breakfast nap.

As Judith moved the checker around the board she stole a glance at him: the father she had loved as her own since she was six years old. To any onlooker she could easily pass as his flesh and blood. Her thick dark shoulder-length hair, scooped up now and pinned back with a tortoiseshell clip, was the same colour and texture as his – at least, his when he was younger. And her brown Bambi eyes and gentle frown could give her a very serious look, just like him. Though when she smiled, her joy was infectious.

Adopting the voice of a sports commentator, she whispered, *'It's getting tense now, ladies and gentlemen.*

World backgammon champion George Andrew Harris is worried his crown is about to be nicked!'

He laughed, picked up his own dice and threw.

George wasn't her stepdad's real name.

Nor was Andrew or Harris. But when he'd arrived in Wales from Cyprus in 1973 he'd quickly discovered that nobody could pronounce Georgios Andreas Charalambos. Even though they'd had no problem getting their tongues around Rhosllanerchrugog or Llanfairpwllgwyngyllgogerychwyrndrobwllllantysiliogogogoch. Judith had always loved hearing how Georgios became George: how the foreman at the building site where he'd first found work had told him, 'You're gonna have to change it, mate. People are funny round 'ere with foreign names an' that.' And so overnight he became good old George Andrew Harris. And whenever he told the tale, he said it with a laugh in his voice, making it into a joke. But Judith knew her father secretly missed his real name. On more than one occasion she'd heard him saying quietly to the cats, 'My name is Georgios Andreas Charalambos. Pleased to meet you!'

They finished up the game. He had 'allowed' her to win – Judith knew this but she didn't let on. As she started packing the board away, he picked up the red set of dice – *his* dice – took out a small hand-carved box from his pocket and placed them carefully inside.

'Where d'you get that from?' she said, admiring its craftsmanship.

'Ha, I found it when I was clearing out the shed.' He snapped it shut. 'I must have made it years ago when I was bored.' He handed her the box. 'I want you to take it with you. Who knows – you may play the back-gammon on your travels, eh?'

She knew by this he meant, *You may play the back-gammon <u>when you visit Cyprus</u> on your travels*. It was strange how they never really talked about his homeland. She'd often tried to, but her questions were always met with one-word answers or an abrupt change of subject.

From the snippets of information she'd gathered over the years, she knew he was from a place called Kako-petria, and that he had no family over there any more. He was an only child and his parents had died before he'd left. He'd said it was all so long ago, it seemed like another life. 'I'm a Taffy boy now, isn't it?' he'd joke.

She held the little box in her hand, feeling its smooth edges that she knew he'd have lovingly sanded. 'But if I take your dice,' she said, 'you can't play when I'm not here.'

'Who else 'm I gonna play with?' he laughed. 'No one else is as good as you!'

It was the strangest of moments. Anyone watching would have said he was sharing a simple little joke with his eighteen-year-old stepdaughter, making her feel good about herself before she went off on her milestone holiday. But she knew there was more going on. She just couldn't pinpoint what.

He reached out and held her hand. 'You are going to

have such an adventure, Judi-moo,' he said, using his pet name for her which he'd used for as long as she could remember.

'We're gonna pack in a ridiculous amount, I know that.'

He paused, then smiled. 'Not just on this holiday. In life!'

She frowned. 'Dad, are you OK?'

His lip trembled and he looked as if he was about to say something more. Then came an urgent knocking on the back gate. The cats leapt up in defence.

'Hello? Mr Harris, are you there?' said a voice neither of them recognized.

George got up and walked to the gate, undoing both bolts. Standing on the other side was a female police officer.

'Oh, thank goodness. I don't think your doorbell's working . . .'

'What's happened? What is the matters?' asked George. His English always faltered when he was distressed.

'You *are* Mr Harris, I take it?'

'Yes,' Judith and George answered simultaneously.

The police officer took a deep breath. 'Right, sir. Well, I'm afraid it's about your wife.'

3
Lana

Eighteen-year-old Lana Lloyd looked good on the back of Gareth Metcalf's Honda 500. And she knew it. Frequently described as a 'surfing chick' – even though she'd never been near a surfboard in her life – she was tall and willowy, with blonde, layered hair, painstakingly crimped in homage to Stevie Nicks. She had hazy, hazel eyes, a dazzling smile and was perfectly at home in her own skin.

The two of them had gone for one final spin before she left for the airport, taking their favourite route, over the Heads of the Valleys Road. She'd clung on to him tight, thrilled as ever by the speed and power of the bike as it navigated the winding road that offered breathtaking views of the Welsh valleys. It was one of the best feelings in the world.

Lana and Gareth had met almost a year ago when she'd taken her new old banger of a Fiesta out for its second run. She'd saved and saved for this car, scraping together every penny she'd earned from her Saturday job at the sweetshop and Sunday-waitressing at the pub. It was more than her pride and joy – it was her ticket to freedom, and it – no, *she* – was called Diana, because she was such a princess. Having learned from an early age to be independent, and not wanting to bother her poor dad, who was always up to his eyes either in nappies or shift work, Lana decided it'd be a good idea to learn some basic car maintenance. Because she didn't want to rely upon anyone should Diana ever break down.

So she'd headed over to Whitley's Garage on the little industrial estate just outside town. Pulling into the workshop area at the back, she was greeted by the sight of three mechanics of varying ages, beavering away, either bent over, lying under or sat inside three different vehicles. Radio 1 was blasting forth in the background, and Simon Bates was telling the woeful tale of a tragic couple on his *Our Tune* slot.

She slammed the door for attention and shouted a little too loudly, 'Boys, may I introduce you to Diana? She's getting on a bit and needs a good seeing-to!'

The guy underneath the white van quickly rolled out on his mechanic's creeper and whispered, 'Be with you in a minute, it's nearly finished.' Then rolled back under the van.

Lana stood there, confused, as Simon Bates drew his story to a melodramatic finale. '*The crematorium curtains slowly closed . . .*' he declared over the opening bars of 'Against All Odds' by Phil Collins, '*and Jessie knew she had finally lost him for good. It was time to say one . . . last . . . heart-breaking . . . farewell!*' The music got louder and the lyrics kicked in:

How can I just let you walk away?
Just let you leave without a trace?

The mechanic fixing the Maestro cassette player whooped, cheered and applauded, and the older mechanic bending over a blue Cavalier lifted his head and wiped tears from his eyes. 'Oh, that was a good one! Fair play!' And finally the guy under the van reappeared on his trolley. 'Yep, got to give it to him, never a bad story with Bates!' Then he rolled off, leapt to his feet, wiped his oily hands with a rag and smiled at Lana. 'Sorry 'bout that, only we listen to it every day.'

Lana stood there, speechless.

'*Our Tune*,' he explained. 'Now, what were you after?'

It took Lana a while to work out why she was lost for words. Was it simply the shock of witnessing three grown men moved to tears by such sentimental tripe, or had she in fact been stupefied by the gorgeousness of the sight before her – this tall, tanned, smooth-skinned, toned-armed, *Our-Tune*-loving mechanic? He looked a bit older than her – early twenties, maybe? – with his oil-covered but beautifully shaped hands, thick dark locks and grey eyes. She was mesmerized until he interrupted her reverie.

'You want me to take a look?' he said, indicating her car and still wiping oil from his hands.

'Yes, please,' she bleated.

I sound like a sheep, she thought, and tried to pull herself together.

But then he smiled. And she wished he hadn't, because she could feel herself blushing. His was the most bewitching and captivating smile she'd ever encountered.

'Open her up then,' he said, heading for the car. 'I presume you know how to do that?'

'Umm, no, not really.'

'Handle under the steering wheel. Pull it towards you.'

'OK.' She followed his instructions and heard the satisfying *thunk* of the hood latch as it opened. She watched him deftly seek the second latch and lift the bonnet, securing it in place with the hood prop. 'D'you mind if I write stuff down?' she said, brandishing a notebook and pen.

'Go ahead,' he answered, evidently impressed. 'So, who bought you this then? Present from Mummy and Daddy, is it?'

'Hah! You're kiddin', aren't you? We're a family of seven. My birthday, I'd be lucky to get a five-pound Boots voucher!'

'Oh, right,' he said, and began checking out the engine. He showed her how to clean the dipstick before measuring the oil – 'but do it when the engine's cold, OK?' – and how to fill the screen wash and the water. He explained the fuse box and how to use the jump leads. And finally, how to change a tyre.

'Blimey, I hope I never have to do that!' she said, finishing off drawing a complex set of diagrams.

'Tell you what, pass us that,' he said, indicating her pad and pen. She handed them over and he scribbled down some details. 'That's the number here at the garage. Keep it somewhere safe – glove compartment maybe – and you can always call us if you ever break down.'

'Ah thanks.' And then she watched as he tore out a sheet from the pad and wrote down another number. Next to a name. *Gareth*.

'And that's me.' He held the pad out to her and she took it, their fingers momentarily touching. 'If ever you want to take her out for a spin, just give me a call. Play your cards right, I'll show you how to do a handbrake skid and a jump start!'

Their eyes locked and she smiled.

'Or we could just skip all that if you like, Gareth,' she said, 'and go the cinema tonight?'

Ten months later they were what her father would call 'going steady'. Was it love? She didn't know. What she *did* know was that she felt a secret smugness that Gareth was her boyfriend. Unlike the other girls in school dating other *boys* in school, Lana loved the fact that *her* fella was a proper *man*. Older – albeit by only three years – and oh so, so much sexier.

'You *do* like a bit of rough mind, don't you, Larn?' Catrin had teased her as they'd ambled home from their end-of-school party in June.

'Yeah I do, as it goes,' she'd answered, matter-of-fact, as if she'd just been asked if she liked sugar in her tea.

'God, remember that bloke Cormack from the waltzers down the fair,' Catrin continued, 'with the pierced tongue and that snake tattoo up his leg?'

'Shut up!' Lana retorted, smiling. 'You could hardly call him a boyfriend! I only saw him for a week.'

'Whilst simultaneously seeing the assistant manager of Dixies Grill,' Judith chipped in.

'Yeah, and *he* was no spring chicken, let's be honest!' added Cat.

'Hey, what's this?' Lana had laughed. 'Have-a-go-at-Lana Night? Dennis was twenty-five! And I don't remember you complaining at the time, Catrin Kelly – gave you your fair share of free onion rings, didn't he?'

'Oh yeah, that's true.'

'She just likes to keep her options open, don't you, Larn?' Judith had carried on. 'I mean why settle for one bad boy when you can have a handful?'

They'd all had a few drinks by that stage and Lana knew that if she didn't laugh this off it could turn into one of their silly rows. So she didn't rise to the bait and changed the subject.

There was an ongoing antagonism between Lana and Judith when it came to boyfriends. It was no secret that Judith hadn't taken to Gareth when he and Lana started going out. But by the same token, Lana hadn't ever had time for Judith's ex-boyfriend, Matthew Price, who was deputy head boy at school and, in Lana's eyes, boring, safe and distinctly dull. Though admittedly Lana could see the physical attraction, him being on the chunky side and playing rugby for the county. When Matthew broke up with Judith the previous Christmas, Lana wasted no time in telling her it was a blessing.

'That bloke was so far up himself it's a wonder he never got vertigo.' But instead of appreciating Lana's support, Judith snapped back, 'Huh! You're dating a mechanic with two O-levels and an addiction to Hubba Bubba. You're hardly in a position to comment on *my* taste in blokes, Lana Lloyd!'

Catrin had had to intervene at that point, before things turned nasty. 'Come on, girls. Look, we might not always like each other's boyfriends, but we mustn't let it come between us, OK?'

Lana and Judith both privately thought this was rich coming from Catrin, who'd never had a proper boyfriend in her life. But they knew it would be cruel to point this out. Dear Catrin. Always the diplomat. And at least *she* thought Gareth was OK, even if Judith found him annoying.

Lana thought Gareth was OK too – and she was really going to miss him over the forthcoming weeks. But she was also going to miss the sanctuary of his little home. His two-bedroomed flat above the ancient launderette in Coed Celyn, which was pronounced *Koyd Kellin* and literally translated as Holly Wood. The flat was a world away from her own household, which was bursting at the seams with an ever-growing family.

Just before Lana's fourth birthday, her mother had suddenly died. Lana could barely remember her, but she did remember that for three years after that it had been just the two of them – Lana and her dad, Keith. Then, seemingly from nowhere, Janis had appeared and two became three. Janis was great. She'd always been patient and kind with her little stepdaughter and treated her as her own. But before long there was a baby sister on the way, followed by another, then another, until Lana's status as an only child had become very much a distant memory, finding herself the eldest of five girls.

These days she shared a bedroom with her fifteen-year-old sister, who was incapable of *not* talking. And everything in her family home was *noisy* and *messy* and *dramatic*. It wasn't that everyone was always arguing, but everyone was always SHOUTING. And sometimes Lana hankered for peace like iced lemonade on a dusty bike ride. Which is why she continually sought solace in Gareth's little two-bedroom flat. She loved it. Yes, it was shabby and the décor was grim; there were no radiators, just an old gas heater that they dragged from room to room when it was cold, and there was never enough hot water for a proper bath. Condensation trickled down the windows in winter, and in summer, when they opened them, they were frequently made queasy by the overpowering smell of washing powder floating up from the launderette. But she loved it.

Arriving back in Coed Celyn, Gareth took a shortcut down Victoria Road. That's when they saw the police car, parked right outside Judith's house. He slowed the bike to a standstill. 'D'you wanna go in and check?'

'I dunno – it's probably their neighbours. Judith said they're always fighting.'

But just as Gareth was revving the engine to move off again, a policewoman came out of the house, followed by Judith and her dad.

Lana called out, 'Jude?'

'It's my mother,' she said quietly, her face ashen. 'She's in A&E.'

'Bloody hell!'

'They think it's a heart attack, but they're doing tests.' Judith's father was standing a few yards off, looking eager to get away. The policewoman held open the car door. 'Look, I've got to go.'

'D'you want us to come with you? To the hospital?' said Lana.

'Don't be daft. You've got a bloody plane to catch!' Judith attempted a smile.

It took a moment to sink in, before Lana exclaimed, 'Jude, we're not going without you, you silly cow!'

'I'm not coming, Lana.' She sounded almost annoyed. 'How can I?'

'But we can get a later flight, or go tomorrow . . . next week, even!'

'Babes, don't you see?' Judith carried on. 'My mother's gonna need looking after. There's no way I can leave her.'

Lana sighed. 'It just feels so . . . I dunno . . . *final*.'

Judith hugged Lana tight. 'You and Catrin, you're gonna have a brilliant time. And I want at least ten postcards, OK?'

Lana nodded, too choked up to speak. The trip they'd been planning so meticulously for a year had been smashed apart in a matter of minutes. It was all so unfair.

'Come on,' said Gareth quietly. 'You better let Catrin know.'

There was no point in saying any more. Lana nodded and climbed back on to the bike, clinging to her boyfriend even harder now, for comfort.

4

Judith

According to the ambulance team who'd brought her in, Patricia Harris had been found collapsed on Coed Celyn high street at ten o'clock that morning. Walking home from her shift in the kitchen of the Sandringham Hotel, she'd 'felt this overwhelming pain in my arms and chest and thought oh God it's happening again.' The ambulance arrived within minutes of a passer-by calling 999 from the shoe shop outside of which she'd fallen, and when the paramedic did the usual medical-history interrogation, Mrs Harris had explained she'd suffered three cardiac arrests over the past ten years. So the chances were this was no ordinary fainting or low-blood-sugar incident.

'Stay with me, darlin', will you?' Patricia had begged Nolly, the student nurse. 'Just until my family get here.'

Nolly hadn't dared say no. She found Mrs Harris to be both terrifying and fascinating: a fifty-one-year-old white female, a little below average height at five foot three and a little above average weight at ten stone two, attractive in a jaded, defeated sort of way – with a face that had definitely seen better, sexier days. The grey roots of her far-from-natural auburn hair were defying the home-kit colour she so rigorously applied each month, peeping through her scalp as if to say, *You can't escape us, lady!* Her make-up was dated: a heavily shaded top lid and false eyelashes that appeared to have been recycled several times. Her lipstick looked like it had started the day a frosty peach, and the deep-red varnish on her nails was tired and chipped. She reminded Nolly of the 1960s lampshade in her grand-mother's best room.

But her main fascination with Mrs Harris came from the fact that the doctor could find nothing wrong with her, even though the patient *insisted* she was dangerously ill. After carrying out an ECG, and checking her blood pressure and oxygen levels, there was no sign whatsoever of any problems with her heart. So Patricia was told to take it easy and visit her GP if she felt unwell again. She complained that she couldn't stop shaking and would someone please find her a wheelchair as she feared she may collapse if she tried to walk.

'There they are!' she exclaimed with a faint smile when George and Judith arrived an hour later. 'My husband, my lovely daughter, thank God!' and she choked back the tears. 'Oh George, I've had such a fright!' she cried out as they approached. 'This little one has been an angel,' she said of Nolly, who smiled at them politely and began to explain the diagnosis. But before she could get her words out, Patricia interrupted. 'Darling, don't let me waste any more of your precious time!

Come here!' And in a flamboyant show of gratitude, she kissed the nurse firmly on both cheeks before thrusting a pound note into her hand.

'Oh, we don't accept tips,' said Nolly.

'Take it!' Patricia urged, with the tiniest hint of a threat.

The nurse did as she was told and said goodbye.

Judith and George stood there staring, not really sure what to do next.

'You took your time,' Patricia said in a low voice, a far cry from the weak, emotional, tip-thrusting patient she'd been just seconds before.

'The police came,' George said. 'We didn't know you were—'

'I was lying on that pavement for a good ten minutes – another five and I'd have been dead! That's what the ambulance man told me!'

'How come they're not keeping you in?' asked Judith.

'You're a doctor now, are you, Missy? A medical expert!'

Judith opened her mouth to answer but was interrupted by Patricia hissing, 'Just get me home, will you, for God's sake. I'm to have twenty-four-hour bed rest for at least a week.' She didn't look at either of them when she said it.

'I'll go and call a taxi,' Judith offered, and exchanged a sad smile with George.

As she approached reception she saw the student nurse putting Patricia's pound note into a charity box on the desk. 'To make sad children happy . . .' it said along its base. Judith picked up the handset of the dedicated taxi phone-line and waited for a reply. 'Excuse me,' she said to the student nurse, 'can I just ask . . . my mother – did she have a heart attack?'

Nolly smiled back. 'Er . . . no. Didn't she tell you? We think it was something hormonal . . . We only checked the heart because of her previous history.'

'What previous history?'

Nolly glanced around – she was still very new to this. Was she breaking patient confidentiality? Surely not – this was the woman's daughter, after all. 'Well, she told the ambulance man she's had three previous heart attacks,' she said quietly. The look of confusion on Judith's face undermined the nurse's confidence. 'So . . . that's why we checked?' she said slowly, and it came out as more of a question than a statement.

'My mother's never had a heart attack in her life,' Judith said.

Celyn Cabs. Where to you goin', please? The voice of the taxi operator came crackling down the line.

'Er, yes, Victoria Road, please,' said Judith, shaking with what felt like rage. 'Three passengers. Name of Harris.'

The nurse gave her a sympathetic smile and watched as Judith replaced the handset and headed back to her parents.

In the taxi on the way home, Judith didn't speak. Not that she ever said much in the company of her mother, but this time she remained completely silent. As did her father. Patricia was oblivious, chatting away – some would say flirting, even – with the driver from Celyn Cabs, divulging the drama of her morning, and explaining she'd had a mild heart attack and would have to go back for more tests but *they'd treated her like royalty there, thank God for the NHS.* The driver was completely taken in. He thought Patricia was charming. They always did.

Sat in the front, Judith struggled hard with her anger, wanting to scream out loud at the injustice of having a mother like hers. A mother who would purposefully sabotage her daughter's much-longed-for holiday. A mother who would so shamelessly lie in order to prevent her daughter finding any kind of happiness.

I hate her, she said inside her head, over and over like a mantra, twisting the little box of dice in her hand from pure frustration. She'd kept it in her pocket like a lucky charm since George had given it to her that morning.

They pulled up in front of the house and George got out, paying the driver and opening the door for Patricia.

Reverting to victim mode for the benefit of any watching neighbours, Patricia took her husband's proffered arm and let him lead her slowly indoors.

Judith went ahead of them, wanting to put as much distance as she feasibly could between herself and her mother. She walked straight through to the kitchen. Her rucksack sat by the fireplace, waiting patiently to leave home for its big adventure, like an eager puppy longing to be walked. She went to the sink and poured herself a glass of water from the tap. Through the window she could see the backgammon set in the yard outside, half put away as it had been when the police had come knocking.

From the living room, she heard the familiar sound of her mother chipping away at George: *Don't do this ... Make sure you do that ... nip, chip, nag, sneer ...* The well-worn soundtrack of Judith's home life. She took a deep breath, steeling herself to go back into the other room.

'I'll put the kettle on,' George said, passing Judith as she came back in. Her mother, slumped now in an armchair, had her eyes closed, her head back.

'So what happens now?' Judith asked her quietly.

'Going back next week, see the specialist,' Patricia mumbled, monotone.

Judith nodded. Biding her time. 'And they said it was a heart attack, did they?'

'George, bring me in some Alka-Seltzer, will you, love?' Patricia called out to the kitchen. Sometimes her mother could sound so sweet and normal. 'And a couple of Veganin. I've got a migraine coming on.' The dexterity with which she could avoid an unwelcome question was remarkable.

'You'll need to get on to Beryl at work for me. Tell them what's happened ...'

'And what *has* happened, Mother?' Judith asked, her voice level.

Patricia avoided the question. Again. 'Course, *you* could offer to do a few shifts instead of me. Ring Beryl now, sweetheart, and tell her. I'll be off for a good couple of weeks, the doctor reckons.'

George came in with the Alka-Seltzer and painkillers and handed them to Patricia, who took them without thanks. She swallowed and sighed. Then stared at her daughter, challenging. 'Well, what are you waiting for? Sooner Beryl knows, the sooner she can organize cover for me.'

Judith steadied her shaking hands and launched straight in. 'Mum, you do know I'm meant to be on my way to the airport right now, don't you? To catch a plane. With my friends. For the holiday we've been planning for the last two years.'

Patricia looked at her. Cold. Unsympathetic. 'And what d'you expect me to do about it, Missy?' she asked. 'I can't help it if I had a bloody heart attack in the middle of the town centre! Oh excuse me for being ill, excuse me for being at death's door!'

'Yeah, but you weren't ill, were you? And you didn't have a heart attack. Nor have you had three previous heart attacks, like you told the doctor you had!'

'What's she talking about, Pat?' George asked.

'I have absolutely no idea,' Patricia answered. 'Now will you please phone Beryl before it's too late. I don't want to mess the woman around.'

Judith looked at the wall clock above her mother's head.

And made the decision in a demi second.

She took two strides towards the fireplace, picked up her purse and her passport from the mantelpiece, and heaved the rucksack on to her back.

'What the hell d'you think you're doing?' Her mother was incredulous.

'I'm going on holiday.'

Patricia, suddenly match-fit again, was on her feet, attempting to pull the rucksack back on to the floor.

'You are not leaving this house, young lady!' she shouted, but Judith's defiance and determination had made her strong. Patricia didn't stand a chance.

'Oh, but I am,' Judith replied, striding towards the door. 'You've ruined enough things in my life, Mum.' And she turned to make her way through the small hallway, difficult with the cumbersome luggage on her back.

'Well don't just stand there, George, for Christ's sake!' Patricia screeched, and George made his way towards Judith.

'Don't, Dad, there's no point in—'

But George wasn't attempting to stop her leaving. He was opening the door to let her go.

'Oh I see, like that, is it?' Patricia laughed, the sneering laugh Judith knew so well. 'As usual – ganging up on me! You should both be ashamed!' she cried, and in the same breath turned on the tears.

Judith looked at George, fighting back the temptation to cry herself. 'Bye Dad, I'll see you in August, OK?'

George threw his arms around her, speechless,

holding her like his life depended on it, looked her directly in the eye and finally let her go.

'You walk through that door, Judith Harris,' Patricia hissed, 'it'll be for the last time, you mark my words.'

'Good luck at the doctor's, Mum! Get well soon!' Judith shouted, bordering on hysteria as she stepped outside. And as she took a few steps away from the house she heard the sound of the Alka-Seltzer glass being hurled at the living-room wall.

'DON'T YOU EVER COME BACK, D'YOU HEAR?' Patricia screamed.

Judith headed off down the street, feeling like she'd just been punched. She was crushed, defeated and very, very alone.

Fifteen minutes later she was standing at the bus stop, staring in shock at the timetable, tears streaming down her cheeks. Suddenly a voice called out, 'How's your mum?'

It was Gareth on his motorbike, the car behind him beeping impatiently at the hold-up. For some reason she felt irritated seeing him there. He pulled into the bus stop.

'I've just missed it,' she said, her voice shaking. 'The bus, I mean. Could've got to Cardiff in time and a train to Bristol centre and then, I dunno, a taxi maybe, but now I've missed the whole bloody . . .' and she started crying afresh.

'Oh. Right.' He paused. 'But I thought . . .'

'Look, what d'you want, Gareth?' she snapped, standing there bereft, the rucksack and her wet clothes weighing her down in solidarity with her heavy heart.

He unbuckled the spare bike helmet usually worn by Lana. 'Jump on the back an' I'll take you,' he said, revving the engine, ready to go.

She didn't know what to say. She and Gareth barely ever spoke on the rare occasions they were in each other's company. And now he was offering to do her a massive favour. She remained silent. Unsure.

'Well, hurry up then,' he said. 'We ain't exactly got all day!'

Within half an hour, they were on the M4 heading east towards Bristol airport.

5

Lana

As only two of them were now being taken to the airport, it meant there was a spare place in the car. And Liz Kelly didn't need inviting twice to fill it. She told Lana she'd been desperate from the get-go to accompany her daughter to the airport, but Huw's Ford Sierra wasn't the roomiest of cars, so she hadn't been allowed to come. 'I even toyed with the idea of getting the train there, then travelling back to Wales with Huw, but my entire family told me I was being dramatic!' she laughed. 'So I won't lie, sad as it is that Judith isn't coming, at least I get to say goodbye to my daughter properly. At the actual departure gate. Like in all the films.'

Catrin rolled her eyes.

The journey to Bristol airport from Coed Celyn was a good two hours, but seemed longer due to the fact that Mr and Mrs Kelly spoke for the entire duration. Lana sat in the back with Catrin, exchanging weak smiles at some of the ludicrous comments coming from the front of the car, but for the most part the two girls were glad to sit and listen, or just switch off. They were still reeling from the news that their best friend wouldn't be joining them on their much-anticipated trip.

'She've never struck me as someone with a dicky ticker,' Huw said, glasses firmly on his nose, hands firmly on his steering wheel as they trundled conservatively down the M4, two miles an hour under the speed limit.

'Well, exactly,' said Liz. 'I mean, she's hardly fat, is she, Huw? I wouldn't call her *fat* . . .'

'Noooo, not fat as such – but not skinny neither. I'd call it . . .' He struggled to find the right word. He didn't want to be too complimentary in his description of Patricia Harris, because if truth be told he'd always found her quite attractive. In a dirty, sluttish, Jackie Kennedy-esque kind of a way. 'I'd say she was . . . well-proportioned.'

'*Pfffff*, makes her sound like a sideboard!'

'Er, OK . . . *comely*?'

'*Comely???* What, like a comely wench?' Liz laughed.

'Let's say *curvaceous* then!' Huw finally conceded, regretting it instantly and going bright giveaway red.

'Oh my good Lord, do you fancy her, Huw?'

'Excuse me, this conversation is hideous,' Catrin interrupted, much to Huw's relief. 'That's Judith's mother you're talking about!'

'Sorry, yes, sorry,' said Liz, crossing herself. 'God rest her mean-spirited soul.'

'And she's not dead!' Catrin exclaimed. Her parents were unbelievable sometimes.

'The point is,' Liz continued, 'all your father is sayin'

is that Patricia Harris don't look like your *usual* candidate for a heart attack, do she, Huw?'

And once again they were off, discussing various people they knew who *had* suffered heart attacks and comparing their physical stature with that of Patricia Harris, before launching in to discuss numerous diets, Liz fixating on the merits of the F-plan when it came to shifting the pounds. 'I'm telling you, Huw, it's baked potatoes morning, noon and night and the woman lost three and a half stone!'

An hour later, Catrin and Lana were sat in the airport lounge, miserably drinking their second coffee, staring at the information board and waiting for the revelation of a gate number. Lana suggested there was no point in *all* of them waiting, and maybe Mr and Mrs Kelly would like to be heading home. But Huw wouldn't hear of it. 'And what happens if the flight is cancelled and me an' Liz are merrily wending our way back over the Severn Bridge, leaving you stranded on some airport bench?'

Lana wondered if Catrin's parents would be happier if the whole trip *was* cancelled. But more than that, she wondered if Catrin herself wished it was cancelled. 'It just all feels wrong, Larn,' whispered Catrin forlornly. 'Like it's doomed or something.'

'Don't be ridiculous,' Lana said, though without much conviction.

But suddenly she was interrupted by a familiar voice. 'Girls!'

They looked up and were met by the strangest of

sights: walking towards them was . . . Gareth! And walking alongside him, passport in hand, rucksack on back, beaming smile on face, was *Judith*.

'Oh my God, Jude! You came!' screeched Catrin.

'Babes! I don't understand . . . what about your . . .' stammered Lana.

'Long story,' interrupted Judith.

'Found her at the bus stop by Lipton's, I did,' said Gareth, with a hero's grin. 'Bit hit and miss gettin' here, like. Probably got a few points on my licence, but it'll be worth it.'

'Well, good God!' declared Huw.

'Cheers, Gareth,' said Judith quietly, standing there in awkward gratitude as Lana planted a massive kiss on Gareth's beaming face.

'Haven't I just got the best boyfriend in the world?' she said.

'Gate Twenty-Three!' shouted Liz hysterically, who'd been watching the departures board like a hawk. 'Gate Twenty-Three! Come on! Go you!'

Judith and Lana screamed with excitement and grabbed their bags. Catrin, seemingly stunned that they were actually, finally leaving, hurriedly hugged her parents and followed her two best friends as they made their way towards the gates. They'd not gone far when Catrin stopped in her tracks. Lana and Judith had gone several steps before they noticed. 'What's up?' Lana called back.

'I can't do it,' whispered Catrin, her voice drowned out by the airport noise.

'What you on about?' asked Judith, ducking out of the way of oncoming passengers.

'I just . . . I'm homesick already. You two are braver than me.'

'Bollocks we are,' said Lana. 'You're much better travelled than me an' her. You've been to Majorca!'

'And Yugoslavia,' added Judith, who'd made no secret of the fact that she'd always envied Catrin's family holidays.

'Furthest us two have been is that crappy youth-club trip to Belgium,' said Lana.

'And Bristol Zoo, to be fair,' said Judith with a wry smile, and Catrin managed to smile back.

Final Call for passengers Harris, Kelly and Lloyd booked on to flight AF369 to Athens, came a tinny, nasal announcement over the PA system. *Please make your way immediately to Gate Twenty-Three, where boarding is about to close.*

All three ignored it.

'Aw Cat! Come here,' said Judith. 'Lana! Group hug, come on!' And the three of them huddled together amidst the throng of holidaymakers. 'We are going to have the *best* time, OK?'

'Yes, she's right,' said Lana.

'Sorry,' sniffled Catrin. 'I'm being silly, I know . . .' and a sob caught in her throat; she felt like a tired four-year-old.

'OK, so you know what we need to do?' asked Lana, a wicked smile in her eyes.

'No, Lana,' said Judith, laughing. 'We are *not* singing the song. Not here!'

Catrin started laughing through her teariness. 'We've got to get on the plane!'

'Not before we sing the song. You know you want to,' said Lana. 'It always works!'

Back in 1973, when the girls first met in Mrs John's class, Catrin's father had invented a silly song, which he'd sing to the tune of 'She'll Be Coming Round the Mountain'. Ever since then it had been their anthem. And as they stood, arms around each other's shoulders in a group hug, the trio of best friends – two of them reluctantly at first – launched into their well-worn theme tune.

Catrin Kelly, Judith Harris, Lana Lloyd!
Fell into a muddy ditch and got annoyed
All their clothes they were a-smellin'
So they went back to Coed Celyn
Catrin Kelly, Judith Harris, Lana Lloyd!

'Here's to Greece!' shouted Lana.

'To Greece!' shouted Judith and Catrin, and off they ran, towards Gate Twenty-Three.

6
Catrin

Catrin need not have worried. Three weeks later, her anxiety about leaving home had vanished without a trace into the hot Aegean. She couldn't believe she'd ever doubted coming – she was having the time of her life. The three of them had soaked up the sun to saturation point and were living on a diet that largely comprised ouzo and olives.

At Skiathos they'd landed unwittingly on a naturist beach, where they were reprimanded by a naked Scot with a droopy moustache for not being nude enough, and on Kos they'd naïvely accepted the offer of a bed for the night from some friendly young men who turned out to be Armenian terrorists. They'd dressed up in togas for a Greek-themed night on Paros and watched the royal wedding of Fergie and Prince Andrew in a beach bar on Mykonos, where Lana had sung the Welsh national anthem at the top of her voice in an attempt to express her republicanism. And now, with eight Greek islands under their belts, they'd finally landed in Crete.

The Samaria Gorge had been at the top of Catrin's must-see list for this entire trip. She'd read about it in her dad's *National Geographic* magazine and was mesmerized by the photos of this ancient gorge, snaking its way between the Lefka Ori and Mount Volakias. The daytrip wasn't cheap, but Catrin promised Judith and Lana that they wouldn't regret a single drachma of the eighteen hundred it was costing them. Despite protests from Lana the night before about wanting a few beers at Lexi's Bar, Catrin had put her foot down and insisted they had an early night. 'We'll need to be up at six, and then it's at least an eight-hour hike. You'll thank me in the end.' And she'd poured them each a glass of Sprite and shuffled the cards for canasta on the balcony.

The bus was parked by a row of cafés on the north side of Chania Harbour. Angelina the tour guide was ticking off names on her clipboard, smiling a *kalimera* at every passenger. Those clambering aboard were a mixture of ages and nationalities and Catrin was impressed at how lively everyone was, considering it was only seven a.m.

Checking the final head-count, Angelina looked at her watch – and, tapping a hand-held microphone to check it was switched on, she explained that although there were still two more passengers to arrive, they couldn't wait any longer.

Mikos the driver closed the doors and started the engine, accompanied by some enthusiastic cheers.

Just as they began pulling away there was a frantic banging on the side of the bus and Mikos put on the brakes. The doors opened again and a young guy, mixed race, late teens, climbed aboard, breathless, in shorts and a vest with a small rucksack on his back. He looked like he'd been running for hours. 'Sorry, so sorry.' He could barely speak.

Angelina smiled sympathetically. 'And you are Mr . . . Cook? Or Mr . . .'

'Blythe. Mr Blythe,' said the guy. 'Eddie couldn't make it. He's the Cook. Well, no, he's not a cook, he's gonna be a vet, I just mean he's *the* Cook, on your list. Mr Cook.'

Angelina looked thoroughly confused. She ticked off his name from her list and invited him to find a seat. He headed up to the back of the bus. Catrin, who had been momentarily distracted by the kerfuffle, returned to reading in her guidebook about the abandoned village of Samaria, which it said they would reach halfway into their hike.

Suddenly a voice.

'Can I sit here?' It was the latecomer.

'Er . . . yeah!' She moved her sunglasses and cardigan to make room for him, inwardly disappointed that she no longer had two seats to herself on which to stretch out.

He put his small rucksack in the rack above them, along with the sweatshirt he'd had tied around his waist, and sat down hard into the seat.

He took several glugs from his water bottle and sighed with relief. 'That's better,' he said to no one in particular.

Hidden behind her guidebook, Catrin watched

curiously as a drop of sweat scurried from the guy's forehead, trickled down his nose and loitered uncertainly on the top of his lip. He wiped it away with the back of his hand, then turned to her.

'I'm Solomon,' he said.

And Catrin was completely floored by his unexpectedly beautiful smile.

They'd ended up chatting for the whole journey whilst Judith and Lana both slept in the seats in front of them. She was fascinated by his faint Geordie twang and the way he lit up when talking about stuff that excited him. They had a huge amount in common. A startling amount, in fact.

He, too, was on his travels before going to university – spending a gap year seeing the world with his mate Eddie. 'The no-show Mr Cook?' Catrin smiled.

'That's the one,' said Solomon, smiling back. 'And he was meant to be coming today, but the stupid dork got so drunk last night he couldn't even move this morning. He went to this bar called Lexi's?'

Catrin laughed, thinking how Lana could so easily have been Eddie, had she not put her foot down the night before. 'Yeah, I know it,' she said.

'I should probably have stayed with him this morning just to make sure he was OK – he could be dead now, for all I know! But the thing is, I've been looking forward to the Samaria Gorge for almost the whole trip.'

'Me too,' she said.

'And Eddie knows that! Like, I first read about it when I was, like, ten.'

'*National Geographic?*' she asked, catching him off-guard.

'Yeah! How d'you know?'

'Me too!' she replied.

There were a lot of 'me too' moments in the conversation, both from Catrin and from Solomon. Two lifetime summaries crammed into a forty-five-minute bus journey. They both had an older brother called Tom, a love of Elvis Presley and an allergy to cats. 'And yes, the irony's not lost on me,' said Catrin.

'Sorry?' Solomon looked confused.

'That my name is Cat and I can't go near them!'

'Oh yes!' And his eyes lit up as they carried on discovering common ground: neither was remotely artistic, both were good swimmers, and they shared a passion for maps and globes. But weirdest of all – *really* weirdest – was that they were both left-handed lapsed Catholics who were off to study medicine in October.

'Cardiff. What about you?' she said when he asked which medical school.

'Cambridge, actually. Trinity,' he said, a bit embarrassed.

'Wow – brain box then,' she laughed.

'No, not really. Just lucky. I had a cousin went to Cardiff,' he said, changing the subject. 'He had an amazing time.'

'Yeah, I'm looking forward to it. And it's far enough away from home for me to feel like I'm doing my own thing, but near enough if I run out of food or can't afford the launderette.' Catrin smiled.

It was like discovering a long-lost friend. When he was talking she'd steal secret glances at him. Not in the way strangers look at each other when they're engaged in polite chat on a bus journey to a Cretan gorge. These glances felt almost voyeuristic: she was absorbing him, taking in the texture of his cropped, black hair and the way he ruffled it when he was trying to remember a name; taking in the deep brown tones of his laughing eyes, which she noticed were flecked with hazel. She'd just begun following the contours of his lips when she realized he'd asked her a question.

'Sorry?' she asked, feeling caught out.

'The Agia Irini Gorge?' Just wondered if you'd done it,' he said. 'It's much shorter than the Samaria – like, three hours? And loads quieter, 'cos less people know about it.'

'Oh right – well, to be honest I had to persuade the girls to come today, so it's doubtful they'd do a second gorge. I suppose I could always go on my own . . .' she mused, aware that she was hinting for him to join her. Ridiculous – she'd only known him half an hour.

'Yes, why not? You'll be perfectly safe,' he replied. Her hint had clearly been too subtle. But then he took her completely by surprise. 'I'd have offered to come with,' he said, 'but we're going home tonight. Eleven p.m. flight. Squeezing this trip in, to be honest.'

'Oh!' She couldn't help showing her disappointment. And thought she detected his, too.

Before she could find out, their conversation was brought to an abrupt end by Angelina announcing their arrival at the entrance of the National Park. Lana and Judith stretched and stirred. 'Aw, I was having an amazing dream,' Lana mumbled sleepily. 'There was this dog and it was wearing my shoes!'

Solomon stood up and pulled down his rucksack from the overhead rack. Catrin sensed he wanted to carry on talking, or maybe even ask if he could join them on the hike, but the people behind him were impatient for him to move on, eager to get off the bus.

So they had a jagged and awkward farewell. 'Nice talking to you!' he said cheerily as he set off down the aisle.

'Yeah, you too. Enjoy the hike!' Catrin knew she sounded hysterically enthusiastic.

'Who was he?' asked Judith after Solomon had disappeared from earshot.

'Oh, no one,' she replied. 'Just some guy.'

Lana complained for almost the entirety of the initial two and a half miles. She was cold. She was hot. She was tired. Her feet hurt. Her head hurt. She was thirsty. She was hungry. When they arrived at Neroutsiko, the first natural spring en route, a long queue of thirsty travellers had formed, desperate to refill their water bottles. 'I wanna sit down,' Lana declared.

'Oh Larn, you've got to change the record, mun!' said Judith. 'You're worse than a three-year-old.'

Sensing a potential row, Catrin stepped in. 'Tell you

what, if you can bear to walk a few more minutes we'll reach the little chapel of Agios Nikolaos, which is a kind of resting place. And there's more water there.'

'As long as we can have a snack,' Lana mumbled petulantly.

'Of course.'

'*Are we nearly there yet, Mum?*' said Jude mockingly. Lana flicked her on the arm and they carried on walking.

Fifteen minutes later they reached the little chapel and quenched their thirst at the spring.

'Come on, let's find somewhere to sit,' Catrin said, in an attempt to jolly them along.

Behind the chapel they found a little patch of dusty grass next to a cluster of magnificent cypress trees. Catrin took some Greek bread and tzatziki from her rucksack and cut an apple into six pieces. She shared it all out like a patient parent and felt the tension instantly dissolve.

'Amazing what a bit of food and drink can do,' she said, and lay back with her eyes closed for a couple of minutes' rest. Gently dozing in the sun, she felt soothed by the sounds of nearby traveller chat and singing wood larks.

'Tallest cypress trees in Crete, y'know!'

Catrin opened her eyes and squinted upwards. Solomon was standing there, admiring the view.

'Oh hello,' she said, caught unawares by how pleased she was to see him again and worried that she might be looking a bit sweaty.

'Alrigh' mate?' said Lana. 'You were on the bus, weren' you?'

'Yes, I'm Solomon,' he said. 'Call me Sol though if you like.'

'You been inside yet?' asked Judith, pointing to the ancient building.

Entering the cool stillness of the Agios Nikolaos chapel, the four of them marvelled at the delicate beauty of the icons on the wall. Catrin read aloud from her guide-book, adopting a slightly posh and eager-to-impress voice. She informed them that 'this tiny chapel is built on very sacred ground, where Apollo once was wor-shipped.' They all stood in respectful silence, the air heavy and pensive.

'Hey Sol, we got a nightclub in Coed Celyn called the Apollo,' said Lana, unintentionally ruining the moment. 'Bloke got stabbed there last year. Danny Rhys. Borrowed a strimmer from Eryl the Smack and never gave it back.'

Catrin glared at her.

'Oh yeah!' said Judith, oblivious to Catrin's awk-wardness. 'And it's weird, 'cos you wouldn't think Eryl the Smack would own a strimmer, y'know.'

Catrin was mortified by the impression her friends were creating. She looked at Sol. What must he be thinking?

'I dunno, Jude,' he said, straight-faced. 'Just 'cos someone's a heroin addict doesn't mean they're a bad gardener.' There was a pause, then he smiled. Lana and

Judith burst out laughing, unexpectedly warming to him. And Catrin felt her skin tingle.

As they set off on the rest of the hike, Sol and Catrin naturally put distance between themselves and Lana and Judith, who were not the fastest of movers. But Catrin was glad. Because all she wanted to do was walk with Sol along the gorge, talk to him, stumble on another rock so she had an excuse to lean on him, and talk to him some more.

When they reached the abandoned village of Samaria, they walked around its ruins and stroked the curious Kri-kri goats who'd made the place their home. There were benches and shade there, so Catrin chose a seat and took out her packed lunch. 'You not hungry?' she said to Sol, who sat, hands in his empty lap.

'Absolutely starving,' he said. 'But I didn't have time to buy anything.'

She smiled, and placed her share of the picnic feast between them. 'Dive in,' she said, and he began devouring the Greek bread before she had time to say 'taramosalata'.

An hour later, they passed a place where people were building little pyramids out of small stones, as they whispered their secret wishes and prayers. Not wanting to miss out, Catrin and Sol built their own, though neither of them shared with the other what they were wishing for, both confessing that their Catholic guilt still made them feel weird about doing anything vaguely pagan like that. They were seven hours into the hike and Catrin knew this would soon all be coming to an end.

Walking through the narrow cutting known as the Gates, they stretched out their arms laughingly to prove how little space there was between the two megaliths. 'They're like two giant security guards,' Catrin said, 'escorting us off the premises.'

'That's so true!' Sol laughed. 'Hey, pass us your camera.' And he took several shots of her posing – the filling in the mountain sandwich. But before he handed it back, he stopped a fellow hiker and said, 'Excuse me, mate, will you take one of the two of us?' Just hearing him say *the two of us* made her melt and she never wanted that photographically snatched moment to end, as the joyous image was captured on film, their arms thrown around each other's shoulders in a display of newly discovered friendship.

When they untangled themselves from the pose and Catrin took back her camera, there was a tiny and silent exchange between them. It was only a look. But in that look pulsed a million heartbeats. And they both knew this was so much more than just friendship.

They'd reached the other end of the gorge, walking in silence towards the once-flooded village of Agia Roumeli and the lazy, turquoise sea. Catrin had arranged to meet up with Lana and Judith at a café called Irene's when they'd all finally finished the hike. Sol said he could wait with her for half an hour, but then he'd need to get the ferry to Sfakia. 'I wish I could stay,' he said. 'I'd like to see your friends again. They seem like a good laugh.'

'Is that the only reason?' she teased, slightly scared that it might be.

'I think you know it isn't.' And he looked at her, his eyes gently chiding.

They ordered an Orangina each and the waiter swiftly brought them over along with two ice-filled glasses. Sol asked him for a pen and a piece of paper, and quickly scribbled down his phone number. 'I'd really love it if we could stay in touch, Cat,' he said.

She looked at the small sheet torn from the waiter's order pad. A flimsy, cheap sliver of paper. Insignificant, yet bearing so much. 'Write your name down too,' she said. 'I might have forgotten it by the time I get home.' They laughed. Truth was, she wanted something more to remember him by than just a series of digits on a page.

He took back the piece of paper and wrote something else, shielding the words from her with his hand, before folding it and placing it under her glass. He glanced at his watch. 'I'm so sorry, but I'm going to have to go,' he said, clearly annoyed that he did. 'If I miss this ferry I'll miss the plane. Eddie's already gonna be wondering where I am. I said I'd be back at the hostel an hour ago.'

'What?' She laughed. 'You told him you could walk the Samaria Gorge in five hours?'

'It has been known.' He smiled, reaching across the little café table to take her hand. 'I have loved today,' he said quietly, his forehead leaning gently against hers, their fingers interlocked.

'I have loved today too,' she whispered, too scared to speak in case her voice might break.

People were playing on the beach nearby, splashing in the sea; the scent of sweet tobacco drifted in the air, mixing with the smell of suntan lotion and coffee and freshly squeezed lemons; a baby was laughing and Greek music spilled out from a tinny speaker in Irene's café. It was the perfect summer-holiday day.

And the perfect backdrop.

To the perfect kiss.

He didn't say goodbye. She watched him walk to the ferry, get on board and wave. She waved back and didn't stop watching till she could no longer see the ferry's wake or hear its tired engines growl. And when she knew he had finally gone, she took the precious piece of paper from under the glass, opened it and read. Beneath his name and number, he'd written:

Today when we built our pyramid of pebbles, the wish I made was to see you again. And I think that will happen.

She took a sharp breath, completely floored by his words.

In the distance, her name was being called. Looking up, she saw Judith and Lana making their way towards her. Quickly she refolded the paper and put it deep inside her pocket. 'How are your feet?' she shouted, finding it impossible not to smile.

7

Lana

The bustle of Nicosia was a far cry from the sleepiness of the Greek islands, but Lana secretly welcomed a bit of metropolitan buzz. They'd been in Cyprus for two days and today they were heading to Kakopetria, the home village of Judith's dad George Harris. 'D'you think this thing will actually get us there?' Lana had joked as they boarded the ancient green and yellow Bedford bus at Plateia Solomou, gearing up for a two-hour journey to the Troodos Mountains.

Lana had sat with Catrin on the journey, because Judith had opted to sit on her own down the front. She said she wanted time to think: this was a big deal, going to her father's home village, even though there was no one there for her to visit any more, George's parents being long gone and George himself an only child. No actual reason to go. Except that Kakopetria was where he'd apparently grown up. And Judith wanted to see it. There was something so heartbreaking about George, though Lana could never work out what it was.

As they pulled into the little square in Kakopetria, Judith turned to them from the front of the bus and smiled. At least the journey seemed to have lifted her mood. The three girls dismounted and looked around them. So much quieter than busy, noisy Nicosia. They breathed in the fresh mountain air and stretched.

'I am bustin' for a pee,' Lana said.

'You're *always* bustin' for a pee,' laughed Judith. And they headed towards a prettily painted restaurant called Taverna Lenia.

Underneath the shady trellises of lemon verbena, and sat around three tables all pushed together, a sprawling Cypriot family was enjoying a late Sunday lunch al fresco. The adults were laughing and chatting, whilst various children perched on the knees of their parents or aunties or uncles, swapping laps intermittently like a game of musical chairs. One woman was discreetly breast-feeding and a boy aged about six was trying to master a Rubik's cube.

A tired-looking waiter in his forties came out, carrying two large dishes of *kouba* and whitebait, placing them wherever he could find room on the table and clearing any empty plates. As the girls approached, Lana felt like they were gate-crashing a party. But when the waiter turned to them and smiled, his face was transformed into a kind welcome.

'*Yassas!*'

'Hi,' said Judith. 'Table for three?'

'*Tria!*' Catrin chipped in, holding up three fingers. '*Parakalo.*'

'Oh, and the toilet please,' said Lana, who was on the verge of wetting herself.

'Come! Please,' he said, and they followed him indoors, where he seated them at the bar. Lana headed off to the loo, but when she returned, Catrin and Judith were nowhere to be seen.

'They are out of side,' said the waiter. 'With new friends.'

The girls had been invited to join the large family group on the verandah, and were installed at the table with children crawling all over them and their Zivania glasses being filled. Lana found this unusual Cypriot tipple strangely soothing and soon dived in for seconds.

One of the party, Maria, spoke superb English and acted tirelessly as translator, explaining that they had this family reunion several times a year, and the occasion this time was a christening the next day, it being a feast day at the local church. An icon of the Saviour would be carried in a procession around the village, and baby Katerina would be baptized too.

The family were fascinated by the girls – they'd not heard of Wales. Though one of the older men, Themis, who Lana thought looked very wise, seemed to have heard of Richard Burton. There were big nods of approval that all three were going on to higher education in the autumn, and they were particularly impressed that Catrin was going to be a doctor.

'*Ey! Giatros!*' they cheered.

Uncle Leonades said something that made the whole table laugh and Maria translated, saying he had trouble with his bunions if Catrin would like to take a look.

The afternoon turned into one of those unexpectedly delightful gatherings, unplanned, unique and unforgettable. Once the savouries had been cleared away with cheers of thanks for the chef, the waiter brought out several platters of mouth-watering Cypriot desserts – baklava, *galaktoboureko*, and a kind of custard dish called *mahalepi* made from cornflour and served with rose water.

As they all tucked in, Themis whispered something to Maria.

'My uncle wants to know why you choose Kakopetria when you could be in the nightclubs of Limassol?'

They all laughed, and tentatively, feeling confident now in the bosom of her new-found friends, Judith explained her connection with Kakopetria: how her father had grown up here before he moved to Wales in 1973. There was much joy when the party realized that Judith was in fact a Cypriot! But she was quick to clarify. 'He's my stepfather,' she said, 'so I'm not really.'

'Ah, *patriós*!' Maria explained and everybody nodded a little awkwardly. Lana sensed that step-parents weren't a common occurrence in Cyprus. 'What is your father's name? Perhaps we will know his family,' asked Maria.

'Well, that's unlikely,' said Judith. 'He was an only child, and his parents died when he was about twenty. I'm not exactly sure – he doesn't talk about it much.'

Maria translated for the others, but Lana sensed that their curiosity had been piqued and they wanted more information.

'Er . . . he's known now as George Harris – his middle name is Andrew. But that's because he changed his name when he came to the UK.'

'Yeah, 'cos we're all too bloody lazy in Wales to learn how to pronounce foreign names!' Lana interjected, a bit tipsy now thanks to the Zivania.

There was delayed laughter in response to Maria's translation.

'But his real name – his Greek name – is Georgios Andreas Charalambos,' Judith said, clearly proud of her perfect pronunciation.

But rather than the mild applause Judith had anticipated for her efforts in Greek, a shocked silence descended. And then a collective mumbling stirred around the table. Except from the children, who had more important things to think about, like how to snaffle another helping of *mahalepi* when no one was looking.

'Sorry, can you say the name again?' Maria asked.

'Yes – Georgios Andreas Charalambos. Actually, I've got a photo of him here,' she said, taking out the photo-booth picture of herself and George that she always carried in her purse. 'It's from about ten years ago – we were on a daytrip to Dan-yr-Ogof Caves.'

The family passed it round, accompanied by gasps of shock, followed by a sequence of fiery exchanges amongst them; concerned looks, raised voices, shaking heads and car keys being sought. One of the women started crying, and was comforted by another, who crossed herself and handed the photograph back to Judith.

The girls looked at each other, confused.

'What's going on?' asked Lana, sensing that whatever it was, wasn't good.

Nobody answered her, everyone still lost in the chaos of their reaction.

'Look, maybe we should go,' she said, more to Judith and Catrin than to anyone else.

'No,' said Maria. 'Wait. Please.' And her husband, who was now getting into his car, shouted something back to her.

'*Entáxei! Naí!*' she replied, and turned to Judith. 'We think . . .' Maria looked around the table, at the family – all waiting on tenterhooks for Judith's response to what she was about to learn. 'We think that your father, Georgios Charalambos, may be the brother of a friend.'

The three girls tried to process what they were hearing.

'What?' asked Lana, Judith clearly too shocked to speak.

Maria continued, 'My husband Nico, he has a friend, Iannis, who has a wife. She is called Sofia.' Maria paused, allowing the information to sink in. 'Some years ago, Sofia's brother – Georgios – he left Kakopetria to go to England for one year. But he never came back. We think—'

And Lana finished the sentence, 'You think that Sofia is Judith's aunt!'

8
Judith

Fifteen minutes later, a woman in her thirties – with the same straight nose and kind brown eyes as Judith's father – got out of Nico's car, followed closely by two confused and awkward children, along with a man who Judith presumed was the woman's husband. Neither of them could say anything at first, so Nico stepped in, his faltering English not as good as his wife's but certainly good enough. 'This is Sofia, sister of Georgios,' he said quietly.

Judith stared at Sofia and fought the urge to laugh. Was it some kind of hysterical reaction? In contrast, Sofia – *Aunty Sofia* – was shaking and weeping like a baby.

'Hello – I'm . . . I'm Judith,' she said, unsure of what to do next. Her world had just been turned inside out. Her father wasn't who she thought he was and she'd inherited an entire Cypriot family in the space of ten minutes. Nervously she held out her arms to Sofia, who needed no encouragement to return the embrace. Judith had never been hugged so tightly in her life and there followed a long sequence of tight embraces, face-holding and loud weeping, until eventually Sofia calmed down. The unsuspecting family who'd only come out for a regular Sunday lunch had found themselves spectators to a real-life drama, applauding from their ringside seats. They were joined by Catrin and Lana as the happy-ever-after unfolded before their eyes.

At least, Judith hoped it was going to be a happy-ever-after.

Realizing they couldn't stand there for ever, Maria took charge, encouraging Judith and Sofia to go inside the taverna, sit down and talk. Catrin gently apologized and pointed out that it was now five o'clock and they still had nowhere to stay. 'So whilst Jude catches up with Sofia, me and Lana will go and find somewhere, yeah?'

When Maria translated this, Sofia became animated again. The subject wasn't even up for discussion. 'She says you must stay with her,' said Maria. 'All of you.'

'Seriously?'

'Of course! You are her family!' said Maria with a smile.

And so within an hour of discovering a brand-new aunt, uncle and two young cousins, Judith was on her way with Catrin and Lana to Sofia's smallholding, a mile or so out of the village, where they'd been offered a bed for the night. Maria had agreed to come with them and translate, which Judith thought was bloody kind of her considering she was meant to be attending her own family party. But then on reflection, as Lana said, 'I bet she's gagging to know about George!'

They were greeted in the yard by a handful of chickens and a goat with two kids, who came running over to see what all the fuss was about. Heading inside, Iannis, Sofia's husband, invited them all to sit at the kitchen table whilst he made coffee and put out glasses of water. Sofia produced a large platter of cookies called *koulouraki* and a dish full of *glyka* or 'spoon sweets' – pickled figs, and cherries and walnuts.

'I am going home the size of a whale!' Lana mumbled to Catrin, who didn't care and couldn't wait to get stuck into the treats.

When they were finally all settled around Sofia's kitchen table, they began – with Maria's help – to unpick the mystery of Georgios Andreas Charalambos.

'You may have heard about the war,' said Maria.

'What, like with Hitler an' that?' asked Lana and Catrin discreetly kicked her under the table. Obviously not *that* war.

'No, you mean here in Cyprus, don't you?' said Judith. 'In the mid seventies?'

'Yes, 1974. The Turkish Army, they invade the north of the country and many families they have to leave. It got very bad.'

'*Papagálos*,' said Iannis, who was sitting next to Maria, smoking nervously.

'Who's Papagálos – like a priest or something?' asked Judith.

Maria smiled sadly. 'No, *papagálos* means parrot – his family they had a pet parrot and they left it behind because they thought the fighting was just for short time and soon they would go back home. But they never went back. This happen to many, many families. They lose everything.'

'That's so sad,' said Catrin, sucking furiously on a spoon sweet.

'But I don't understand,' said Judith, trying to calculate dates in her head, 'George, my dad – he wasn't living here then.'

'No,' said Maria with a wry smile. 'Because Georgios he is a clever young man, and he sees a long time before the war that there is trouble coming between the Turks and the Greeks, and he thinks it will be dangerous to stay in the North, and so he says to his mother, *We must leave, let's go to our Theíos Nicolaous, our uncle in Kakopetria, where we will be safe.* And in 1971 that is what they do – they move from Petra in the north and they come here and live in this house. Long before the war.'

Judith glanced at Lana, who was smoking one of Iannis's cigarettes, clearly mesmerized as Maria continued to translate Sofia's tale.

'They live here for nearly two years. Georgios he had good job as a clerk with local government. Some days he travels to Nicosia—'

'Blimey, I hope he didn't go on that Bedford bus,' Lana chipped in. 'You need to be made of strong stuff for that!'

'Shut up!' hissed Catrin.

'I can't imagine my dad as a civil servant,' Judith mused. 'He works in a factory now. Electronics.'

Maria translated for the others and Judith thought she detected a hint of disappointment on their faces. Then she continued Sofia's story.

'But then Cyprus is becoming more troubled with the fighting, and everything is . . . how you say, *uncertain*? . . . and Georgios he worries that he will lose his job. And so he decide he will go to England for work – for one year maybe, get money and come home.'

Maria put her hand on Sofia's, checking that she wanted to carry on. She nodded.

'That was in the summer of 1973. He left and she never saw him again.'

'Bloody hell! It doesn't sound like George to just disappear like that. He's always been such a decent bloke,' said Lana, and Catrin glared at her again.

'At first he would write to them,' Maria said. 'They did not have telephone then, so it was only letters. And presents!' Maria smiled as Sofia talked of the gifts her brother had sent home – a snow-globe with Big Ben inside it, some Yardley soap for their mother, a tin of Walkers shortbread, even a pair of wellington boots! 'All the time he was sending presents.'

'And did you know where he was living?' asked Judith.

'No, he kept saying he would give an address when he settled, but that he was moving around so much there was no point.' Sofia took a sip of water before she continued. 'And then he writes and he says he has job,' said Maria. 'He is labour on building site and the pay is good. He say he will stay for eight more months and then he will come home, with money for them all.'

'Except he never did . . .' Judith said.

'Except he never did,' Maria repeated, and they sat in silence, taking it all in.

'Right, so obviously that was because he met my mother and got married . . .' said Judith. 'I would've been about five or six then.'

'I remember her coming to school to say she'd got a new daddy,' said Catrin. 'D'you remember that, Larn? We were in Mrs Owen's class.'

'God, yeah,' said Lana, turning to Judith, her face lighting up. 'And I was so jealous 'cos you got to be a bridesmaid and wear a nice dress.'

But Judith ignored her friends, trying to piece together all the information.

'I know they got married really quickly after they met because they'd fallen head over heels in love,' she said, looking over at her friends. 'Hard to imagine now.'

'Head over heels?' Maria asked, confused by the idiom.

'My mother, Patricia, she said she and George were very much in love and that's why they got married so soon.'

When Maria passed this on to Sofia, she gasped and shook her head.

'But I don't understand why that stopped him

coming back to Cyprus with her – with us!' said Judith. 'We could have met you all back then! Had a whole lifetime of knowing each other as a family!' Her voice began to falter. 'All this time I had cousins and an aunty . . . it would've helped. A lot.'

Catrin squeezed Judith's hand to comfort her, but the impact of her father's lies was beginning to register. 'Why didn't he tell me about you?' she said, anger creeping into her voice. 'And why didn't my mother ever mention you? I'm sorry, I don't think I can handle this.'

'It's all right, babe,' whispered Lana. 'It's a shock, I know.'

Sofia then spoke quietly to Maria, as if divulging something, and they all watched as Maria challenged Sofia, unsure whether she should tell them the next part. 'Sofia wants me to tell you about Cleoniki.'

'Great!' said Judith sarcastically. 'So there's more!' And Catrin threw her another sympathetic look.

Sofia got up and began searching in the dresser as Maria continued.

'In Cyprus we have something called *proxenia*. Like a make match? For son and daughter of two families.'

'Bit like *Blind Date*!' Lana chipped in.

Maria looked at her, confused.

'It's a show on ITV with Cilla Black,' she mumbled. 'Never mind.'

Maria nodded and carried on.

'Well, Georgios had *proxenia* with Cleoniki before he left and they were a very good match – they were, as you say, "head over the heel". And so they were betrothed.

75

Cleo said she would wait for Georgios to come back from England after one year and then they would get married.'

'Oh my God!' Judith couldn't believe what she was hearing.

'But one day, Georgios he write to Sofia a short letter – *this* letter.' Sofia nodded to Maria, passing her a faded envelope bearing a British stamp. She took a few moments to translate the contents.

Dearest Sofia – I cannot explain to you why I must do what I do, but please believe me that it is for the best. I cannot return to Cyprus. Never. And I cannot contact you again, nor my dearest mother. With all my heart I am sorry for hurting you, and for hurting Cleoniki, who surely deserves a man much better than me. I wish for you a peaceful life. I am sending you some money which can never make up for what I have done. Please forgive me in your heart and forget that you ever were cursed to have such a cowardly, weak brother. My love to you always, may God keep you safe, Georgios x

Judith noticed Lana look at Catrin, raise her eyebrows and slowly whisper, 'F-u-c-k-i-n H-E-L-L!'

Curiosity outweighed her anger now. 'OK, so obviously he'd married my mother, so he couldn't come back and marry Cleoniki,' she said, frustrated. 'But it's not the crime of the century, surely? People change their minds, don't they?'

'Yeah, like my cousin Lenny,' Lana piped up. 'He got jilted at the altar by his fiancée Meryl – she ran off with his own brother!' They all stared at her. 'Terrible, it was. Mind, they went ahead with the buffet 'cos it would've been a waste not to.'

'Hush, Lana,' said Catrin.

'They had an ice sculpture an' everything.'

'I mean surely,' said Judith, ignoring Lana, 'you'd have understood? You'd have forgiven him?'

When Maria translated this, Sofia began to cry.

'She says of course! There would have been anger maybe at first, but eventually there would have been forgiveness. All this time, Sofia believed and so did her mother that Georgios had done something bad. That he was maybe in prison. Or worst of all, that he had ended his life. They had no idea what could be so terrible to make him cut off from his family like that, and his country. He loved Cyprus.'

'*Ítan gálos anthrópos,*' Sofia wept. '*Gálos anthrópos!*'

'She says he was a good man,' whispered Maria.

Judith took Sofia's hand and sighed. 'He still is,' she said.

The shame had obviously been too great for George. To have come to Britain to better his prospects and save money for his family in Cyprus, fully intending to go back and marry Cleoniki. But instead he had met Patricia, fallen in love with her and started a brand-new life in Wales, becoming father to little Judith. Sofia simply wished he had told them. Just to know that he was still alive all these years would have spared them from so much heartache. But the saddest thing was that their mother, Alathea, had died in 1984, believing her son was no longer alive. It was all too too sad.

Looking directly at Judith, Sofia said, '*Thélo na ton do! Thélo na tou milíso! Aderfós mou.*'

'Sofia wants to know when she can see her brother – when can she talk to him?' Maria said.

Judith panicked at the thought of orchestrating such a reunion. It was too much for her. Feeling like she was six again, she just wanted her dad to make it all all right. 'I don't . . . I don't know . . .' she stuttered. 'Tell Sofia please to be patient. I need to go home, and I need to think and work out what to do, but it will happen.'

Maria nodded, understanding.

'I promise she *will* see her brother again.'

As she lay on the small camp bed that night, Catrin and Lana out for the count on the sofa, Judith stared up at the ceiling. So many thoughts raced around her head. How much life she'd wasted ignorant of the existence of her Cypriot family; how she wished she could stay here longer and not leave tomorrow – and how on earth could she hop, skip and jump her way through the rest of the trip, all jolly hockey sticks, knowing what she now undeniably knew?

How could her life ever be the same again?

Worse than that, how could she break it to her father that she knew who he really was? And what else could he be hiding?

9

Catrin

'*If they could see me now, that little gang of mine* . . .' she sang quietly to herself as she rinsed out the last of the shampoo. This had to be the most bizarre experience of the holiday so far and yet she was loving it: washing her hair, leant over an old tin bath in the middle of a barn in the Troodos Mountains, using two buckets of warm water, an empty tin can for pouring, and a bottle of Vosene. And all of it observed by a curious nanny goat and her kid, who stood watching in the corner.

Doing the 'squeak' test with her fingers to check her hair was clean, she squeezed out the excess water and reached over for the faded towel. She wrapped it tightly round her head and tucked it in at the back. Catching sight of herself in an old cracked mirror, she smiled. Her smile was different now. Had been ever since Sol. Though only *she* realized that.

It had been a whole week. A whole seven days living with the painful and ecstatic knowledge that *he* existed in the world; that *he* was somewhere right now – probably in his bed in Bayfield, sleeping, breathing, this human being of whom she'd been blissfully unaware until that fateful day in Crete and who had now taken up permanent residence inside her head. She still hadn't told Judith or Lana about Sol. Keeping him a secret somehow kept it magical.

When she'd made her weekly phone call home a couple of days earlier, she'd felt the most peculiar sensation – like she was somehow defrauding her parents. Keeping from them her big beautiful secret, knowing that the daughter they'd left at Bristol airport a month ago was not the same daughter who'd be coming home.

'Now tell me, are you getting enough roughage?' Her mother's voice on the crackly line had crashed into her thoughts. 'Because it seems to me – and your nana agrees – that over there it's all meat this and meat that, with your souvlakis and moussakas and kebabs and what have you—'

'A souvlaki *is* a kebab, Mum,' Catrin had said, only to be ignored.

'I mean I'm sure they're all very nice people, the Greeks, but I do worry about their diet. And the last thing you want is to be getting constipated!'

'Mum!' Catrin had felt herself redden.

Suddenly her brother's voice had come hurtling down the line as he shouted into the receiver, 'Nana wants to know if you've opened your bowels yet!' And she heard him scurry off laughing – he knew how to make her smile. This frequently used expression of their nan's had always entertained them: the idea of 'opening a bowel' sounded like something a local celebrity would do by cutting a ribbon with a pair of golden scissors and getting their photo on the front page of the *Gazette*. Bodily functions were readily discussed in the Kelly household, which her father said was healthy. Catrin just found it mortifying.

'We eat a lot of salads,' she'd mumbled, noticing that the coins she'd fed into the phone were almost used up.

'Oh, well that's something, I suppose. But do make sure you wash the lettuce—'

'Mum, I've not got much left on the phone – let me talk to Dad.'

'Hold on, I'll get him for you now.'

They always went through this rigmarole where her mother pretended to fetch her father, but Catrin *knew* he always listened in on the extension in the bedroom.

'Hiya Dad!' she said.

'How's my little pumpkin?' he asked brightly, and instantly hearing her daddy's voice made her want to cry.

She wanted to tell him all about Sol – *'I've met him, Dad!'* she wanted to say. *'I've met the man I know I should have babies with. He's perfect. You'd love him. And he reads the* National Geographic*!'* But instead she cleared her throat and asked him about his tomato plants.

'Ah Cat, I've got a bumper crop this year. And there'll be plenty here for you when you get home, although your mother's threatening to make a chutney!'

Catrin smiled, the digital display on the telephone unit warning her the call was about to end. 'I love you, Dad,' she said. 'We're gonna get cut off in a sec!'

BEEEEEEEEEEP. And the line had gone dead.

Speaking to them had made her homesick for the first time during the holiday. Only two more nights and they'd be flying back. Apart from the obvious, all-consuming joy she felt at the prospect of speaking to Sol again, there were other more domestic reasons for wanting to go home. Firstly she'd get to sleep in her own bed. Secondly she wouldn't have to live out of a rucksack any more – no matter how many times she shook it out, she always found sand in her clothes, especially her pants. Thirdly she'd get to eat her mum's shepherd's pie again. And finally she'd be able to have her films developed so she could see that long-awaited photo of herself and Sol taken at the Samaria Gorge. She hoped beyond hope that her eyes wouldn't be closed in the shot – she never looked good in photos. 'Well, I can always cut myself out,' she thought. After all, it was Sol she wanted to look at.

She checked the barn for a place to drain the waste water but couldn't see anywhere. So she grabbed the handles on either side of the bath and dragged it towards the entrance – blimey, it was heavy! Realizing she was being watched, she looked up and saw twelve-year-old Andreas and his ten-year-old sister Danoulla sitting on two empty wooden barrels, kicking their heels. They stared at her, both blowing huge, impressive, pink gum bubbles. She smiled at them, trying out an under-confident '*Kalimera!*'

Nothing.

Suddenly there was a screech and they leapt from their perch as their mother Sofia approached, berating them in Greek for failing to help their house-guest. Before she knew it, the bath handles were being eased out of her hands by Andreas and Danoulla, who staggered away with it. Sofia was left apologizing, smiling, entreating Catrin to come indoors. '*Éla! Éla!*'

Inside the cool of the modest kitchen, Lana was sat pouring Turkish coffee for everyone as Judith cut deep into a large watermelon. On the table Sofia had laid out a breakfast feast comprising hunks of fresh halloumi, the delicious sesame-seeded bread to which they were all now addicted, slices of juicy, over-ripe tomatoes and a terracotta bowl full of yoghurt. Next to it was a little jug of honey harvested from their own bees.

'Sofia made that halloumi herself,' Judith said, impressed. 'And the bread.'

'*Naí!*' Sofia obviously got the gist of what they were saying, nodding furiously. She took down a large pan from a rack above her head, ready to start frying the eggs she'd just collected from their hens.

'You are so kind, Sofia,' said Lana.

Catrin grabbed her phrasebook and attempted to translate into Greek: '*Eísai evgenikós!*'

Sofia smiled back, urging them to tuck in. 'Andreas! Danoulla!' she shouted and within seconds her children came scampering in like hungry puppies, dispensing with their gum and sitting at the table.

After breakfast, they walked to the little village church to visit the grave of George's mother.

'Alathea Kassia,' read Catrin. 'The Greeks have such pretty names,' she mused. She watched as Judith leant over and touched her grandmother's photograph, framed in gold on the headstone. Alathea's sun-kissed face cheekily smiled back at them, full of vitality. 'That's what Catholics do – put photos on the—'

'Will you zip it, Catrin Kelly!' whispered Lana. 'Judith's meant to be having a moment. She doesn't need you wittering on.'

'Sorry,' said Catrin.

Judith knelt by the grave and planted a pink cyclamen from Sofia's garden, lovingly patting down the soil around its base. In amongst the stems was a little card on which was written '*Gia ti giagiá mou*' – 'for my grandmother'. Catrin felt a lump in her throat as she silently observed her sad friend, and when she took a sideways look at Lana, saw that she was moved too. For both girls, the enormity of what Judith was going through was overwhelming for their tender years.

Afterwards, they went inside the church, where they lit candles in private solemnity. Catrin had always loved doing this in her own church when she was younger. There was something so simple and traditional about it, and yet so moving and symbolic. She watched the tiny flickering of the flame and closed her eyes, before offering up her own silent prayer.

It was a prayer of gratitude for the secret and magical meeting with Sol – *Please God, let me see him again* – but also for her two beautiful friends and the incredible time they had spent together. 'I think we have all three been blessed to know each other,' she whispered. 'I really, really do.' And she crossed herself out of Catholic habit, before brushing away a stray tear that was tumbling down her cheek.

10
Lana

Iannis insisted on taking them to Larnaca airport to catch the flight to Athens. Saying goodbye to Sofia and Danoulla and Andreas was hard. The two children had grown fond of their funny-sounding guests, even in such a short space of time, and they'd made presents for all three girls: some pretty little *komboloi* beads and a small hand-painted mountain rock, each bearing a big red heart. In return, Catrin gave them her copy of *Pride and Prejudice*, which they were inexplicably excited to receive, and Lana donated her Welsh rugby top, which she often slept in and which she couldn't remember ever washing. They were a bit more confused by that. But when Jude gave them the little backgammon dice-box that George had given *her*, they were beside themselves. And so was Sofia. She said Georgios had always been good at making things . . .

Sofia's own gift to Jude was a little Greek icon, which she said would protect her, and an 'evil eye' on a silver chain to ward off unfriendly spirits. Catrin said she didn't really like the sound of this, though admittedly it was much nicer to look at than her tacky St Christopher.

The most moving gift, though, was a beautiful plaited gold ring that Sofia took from a small box in the dresser. It had belonged to George's mum and Judith wouldn't accept it at first – but Sofia wouldn't let her leave until she had agreed. It fitted her finger perfectly.

Sofia sent them on their way with repeated hugs, buckets of tears and two big Tupperware boxes full of home-made food: one sweet, comprising baklava, *galaktoboureko* and *koulouraki*, and one savoury – olives, *koukouras*, dolmades and slices of halloumi, along with two loaves of delicious sesame bread.

'I tell you what, Cat,' whispered Lana as they climbed into Iannis's car. 'I'm not half gonna miss that woman's cooking!'

They arrived in Athens mid morning and booked themselves a room each as a treat in a cheap and cheerful hotel called Maxine's, where they dropped off their stuff before heading to the Parthenon and the Acropolis for their last round of sightseeing, sustained all day by Sofia's never-ending Tupperware feast. By six p.m. they'd showered and dressed up in their only remaining, vaguely clean clothes.

'Right, come on, ladies. Let's hit Athens where it hurts!' Lana announced. 'We're gonna end this holiday with a bang.'

A few hours later they'd landed in a tequila bar called Demetri's. Lana had drunk more than the other two and was well and truly wired.

'She frightens me a bit when she's in this mode,' Judith yelled over the music to Catrin, whose face dropped as she looked over her friend's shoulder towards the bar.

'Oh my God, look!'

Judith turned around and was horrified to see Lana dancing provocatively on a table, cheered on by some lively Irish guys.

'I think she's gonna strip!'

The two friends ran over, pushing their way through the crowd.

'Lana, get down!' shouted Judith, but Lana laughed back, ignoring her, and continued the routine.

It was Catrin who managed to get through to her. 'Lana Lloyd!' she yelled. 'Stop showing off and come down from that table right NOW!' And with that she grabbed Lana's arm and pulled her off the improvised stage.

The Irish guys booed and turned back to their beer.

'You are a bloody spoilsport, Catrin Kelly!' Lana sulked.

'Come on,' said Judith. 'I think you need to eat something. Soak up all that tequila.' And between them, Judith and Catrin wrangled their drunken friend out of the bar and along the busy tourist-filled street, till they happened upon a quiet little taverna.

'Table for three, *parakalo*,' said Catrin to the kindly owner, who couldn't have been more welcoming.

They shared a big bowl of *makaronia* and stuffed peppers and gorged on an endless supply of Greek bread until Lana was several degrees more sober, though still pretty merry. She'd reached the 'emotional' stage that the girls always recognized in her after she'd consumed a certain amount of booze. She insisted on their singing 'Calon Lân' and 'I Bob Un Sydd Ffy-ddlon', including the harmonies, and they knew there was no point in objecting.

Stavros the owner found it delightful, as did the other customers, who heartily applauded when the girls had finished their performance. Lana ordered them each a Metaxa, despite Judith telling her she shouldn't drink any more.

'Oh don't be such a boring old cow,' said Lana. 'Tonight's our last night. Who knows when we'll get a chance to do this again?'

And Judith relented. 'To Us Three!' she exclaimed when the drinks arrived, and they clinked their glasses in a toast.

Moments later, Catrin suddenly fell very quiet.

'What's up?' asked Judith.

Catrin took a deep breath and launched in. 'Girls,' she said nervously, 'there's something I need to tell you.'

Judith and Lana exchanged looks.

'Go on,' said Lana, intrigued.

'OK, well . . .' she hesitated. And then she said it. 'I've fallen in love.'

'What?' stammered Judith.

'Is it with a woman?' Lana slurred. ''Cos that's fine, y'know, babe, and I've been wonderin' for some time if—'

'Shut up, Lana,' Judith snapped. 'Go on, Cat.'

And both she and Lana sat mesmerized as Catrin relayed the story of the Samaria Gorge and how she'd kissed Solomon Blythe.

'He's beautiful,' she whispered, her eyes brimming with tears. 'He gave me this.' And she reached into her purse and took out the fragile piece of paper bearing Sol's words and telephone number. 'Look!'

They stared at it for a moment before Lana interrupted. 'Well, well, well, Catrin Kelly, you dirty, dark horse!' And she reached forward and hugged her friend, as did Judith.

'Babe, I'm so happy for you,' said Jude, emotional herself.

'Me too,' said Lana, beaming.

Catrin went on to tell them her plan to phone Sol the day after they got home. And how every time he wandered into her mind she experienced a terrible churn in her stomach. 'So God knows what I'll be like when I actually get to speak to him,' she said.

'How on earth have you managed to keep it from us for so long?' said Judith, smiling.

'I think I needed time for it to sink in. It still doesn't feel real, to be honest.'

'Right,' said Lana drunkenly, gathering up her things. 'Well, technically you're still single, and the night is young, so let's get back out there and strut our stuff.'

'No, Larn,' said Judith. 'We're taking you home.'

'But we're eighteen years old. We should be partying!'

'Sorry, but Judith's right,' said Catrin. 'We need to

get *some* sleep, otherwise that flight tomorrow is going to be horrendous.'

Lana sulked all the way back to the hotel, trying her hardest en route to drag her friends into every bar they passed, including Demetri's, outside which the Irish guys from earlier were sitting. They recognized Lana and called out to her to finish what she'd started. But Judith quickly pulled her away before she could engage in any conversation.

Back at the hotel, they helped Lana into her room, took off her shoes and put her to bed. She mumbled that they were 'both a pair of boring bastards' before falling fast asleep.

But as they shut the door quietly behind them, Lana opened her eyes again, waited as the footsteps of her two friends faded away, then promptly sat up.

Eight hours later, she was aware of a boxing match going on in her head. *Bam, bam, bam, thud*. Without opening her eyes, she reached out desperately to the bedside table, where she was sure she'd left half a can of Diet Coke the evening before. When she'd been getting ready. Getting ready for a night out.

Last night.

Oh God.

Her hand lighted upon the can and she brought it, shaking, slowly to her lips as she lifted her head from the pillow. The flat, sweet mix of chemicals and cola was like nectar in her parched mouth and, in that moment, the most beautiful drink she'd ever tasted in her life. She hauled herself up in bed and tentatively opened her eyes, daring to look.

He wasn't in the bed. She breathed a huge sigh of relief. But she knew she wasn't out of the woods yet. Clearing her throat, she called, 'Hello?'

Nothing.

She couldn't remember his name. 'You still here?'

Nothing.

And finally, when she was satisfied he'd gone, she moved to the edge of the bed, preparing herself to stand up. She'd have to do it in stages. No sudden movements or she was likely to throw up. Jesus, who invented tequila?

Hideous, hideous.

She tried stretching her arms in front of her, gradually easing herself on to her feet. 'That's it,' she whispered. 'You can do it.' She padded slowly over to the window and cautiously pulled back the cheap, brushed-nylon drape, letting daylight intrude.

Outside, Athens was gently coming to life. A sun-kissed summer morning, in a beautiful city, in a beautiful country, on the final day of her holiday with her two best friends, and she should really be feeling on top of the world.

Instead she felt as if she'd fallen into the deepest pit of dark and disgusting despair.

What the fuck had she done?

11
Judith

'Can I have a break for a minute?' Lana said after swallowing another mouthful.

They were sitting in the shade outside Paulina's café next door to the hotel, and Catrin and Judith were feeding omelette and chips, very, very slowly, to their very, very hungover friend.

Satisfied that Lana had eaten enough for now, Judith moved her plate away and Catrin handed her some tea.

'I just can't believe it,' Catrin said.

'It's tequila. It makes me lose the plot.'

'You can't blame the drink, Lana,' said Judith, aware that she was being far harsher on her friend than Catrin was. But she was annoyed. She couldn't help it. When they'd left Lana the night before, they'd both been convinced she was out for the count. Only it turned out that, far from enjoying golden slumbers, Lana had sneaked out again, back to the tequila bar, where the party was still in full swing, in search of the Irish guys, in particular Damian or Dorian or whatever his name was – Lana wasn't exactly sure. She'd then brought him back to her room with a bottle of Metaxa and had sex with him all night.

'Did you use a condom?' Catrin asked, ever the sensible one.

'Apparently.'

'What d'you mean, "apparently"?' snapped Judith, irritated by Lana's nonchalance.

'I saw a couple of used ones in the—'

'OK, OK, don't need the details,' Judith sighed, regretting the question.

'I dunno, there was just something about him . . . Y'know, like when a guy is confident and funny and . . . it's a real turn-on, isn't it?'

'Is it?' asked Catrin, confused.

'And he had this Northern Irish accent. And he was really fit – he's a builder. Did you see his pecs?'

'Lana!' Judith scolded her. 'You've got a *boyfriend*.'

'I know. I *know*, all right?' Lana looked down.

Silence descended and the three of them fell into deep thought. The waiter was chatting with some customers nearby, laughing, clearing plates and glasses, unaware of the tension on table five.

'Oh my God,' Lana said, breaking the mood as a sudden memory reared its shameful head. 'I've just remembered something . . .'

'What?' said Catrin, intrigued.

'When he was . . . y'know . . .'

'What?' asked Catrin, eyes wide open.

'Oh shut up, Lana,' said Judith. She was always a

step ahead of Catrin and knew that Lana was about to say something gross.

'At the end, when he . . . y'know . . .'

'Go on,' said Catrin naïvely.

'Well, I remember every time he . . . "finished", he'd say . . .' and she adopted a spectacular Belfast accent, 'he'd say, *"The Irish are comin', the Irish are comin'!"* and then do a sort of *Yee-hah!* like a cowboy!'

Thankfully the waiter interrupted Lana's recollection by replacing their ashtray and asking if they wanted more tea. They didn't. 'Just the bill, please,' said Judith.

'I think it was because I was missing him,' Lana said mournfully.

'Who? Gareth?' Catrin was having trouble keeping up.

'Oh that's nice,' said Judith. '"Sorry, Gareth, I was really missing you, so I went and shagged a builder from Dublin."'

'Belfast, actually,' Lana mumbled.

'Well, that makes *all* the difference!' Judith said sarcastically.

More silence.

Judith knew exactly why she felt annoyed with Lana. For starters, it wasn't meant to be that kind of trip. They'd all agreed before they left that this was about *them*, the three amigos *Catrin-Kelly-Judith-Harris-Lana-Lloyd* having a good laugh, and seeing things, and discovering things, and spending time in each other's company. Because they may never get the chance to do it again! Before they knew it they'd be back home, then off to uni, and the life they'd been accustomed to for all these years – seeing each other almost every day, like they had done since they were five – would come to an end. And now, not only had Catrin fallen in love with some random guy on a day-trip, but Lana had had a one-night stand with some bloke in a bar. Was she jealous? She didn't think so. Just disappointed.

Because this trip was meant to be about friendship. It wasn't meant to be a sex fest or a quest for holiday romance. If they'd wanted that kind of trip they could have just booked a fortnight in Shagaluf like Becky Williams and her gang. But they were better than that. At least, she'd thought they were.

'He had a massive—'

'Stop it!' Judith interrupted. 'I seriously do *not* want to know.'

Catrin looked like she *did*. But knew better than to ask.

'Look, girls. I've messed up, OK? I will hold my hands up and say I've been a complete and utter twat. I shouldn't have drunk so much, and if I hadn't I wouldn't have done it, OK? I wouldn't have shagged Danny or Donny or whatever the fuck he's called. So if you want me to feel bad, well, I do, OK? And I'm sorry.'

There was a pause, then Catrin said, 'It's not us you should say sorry to, though, is it?'

'Hey, hang on a minute, I'm hardly gonna tell Gareth, am I?'

'No, come to think of it, that would be a really bad idea,' said Catrin.

'Obviously,' snapped Judith and Lana together. Catrin wasn't always the full ticket.

'But please, girls . . .' Lana continued. 'Promise me that you will not tell a soul about what I did – and in exchange, I will give you my word that I will never, ever let it happen again.'

Judith sighed and begrudgingly nodded.

'Of course,' said Catrin, and she picked up an empty red Marlboro packet from the table. 'Let's swear,' she said.

'What you doing?' asked Judith, still irritated.

'Like we did when we were kids. When we swore on the Curly Wurly wrapper to always be friends, re-member? Let's swear on this fag packet never to tell. I know it isn't a Curly Wurly, but it will have to do. Say after me . . .'

'Sorry, but I'm not in the mood,' said Judith with a sigh, softer now. 'You're right, Larn, you were an idiot, but we all make mistakes.' She put her arms around Lana. 'So let's just forget it, yeah?'

'Not too tight, Jude, I might be sick down your back,' Lana mumbled.

The waiter handed them the bill and Catrin reached into her rucksack for her purse. Lana threw a handful of drachmas from her pocket on to the table, and Judith followed suit.

'What's the matter?' she asked Catrin, who had now begun emptying the contents of her rucksack on to the table.

'It always ends up right at the bottom,' she said, smiling, as she took out a pair of sunglasses, a book and a bottle of insect repellent. But the more she took out, the more her smile faded, until panic crossed her face. 'It's gone!' she said. 'My purse! I had it with me less than an hour ago!'

Judith emptied the rucksack, systematically checking the pockets again before fruitlessly searching under the table and the surrounding area. But no joy. They had to admit defeat: Catrin's purse was definitely gone.

'What a bummer,' said Lana, trying her best to sound supportive whilst battling the urge to throw up.

'Who'd have bloody nicked it?' said Judith sympathetically.

'From right under our noses. Bastards,' added Lana unhelpfully, her hand shielding her eyes from the sun.

'Look, don't worry,' said Jude. 'At least today's our last day, and me and Larn can pay for your omelette.'

'I don't care about the sodding omelette!!' Catrin screeched, hysterical now. Other customers turned and stared. 'My purse,' she wept. 'It had Sol's number in it, didn't it?'

12

Catrin

Huw had been ... e to greet them at the airport and
Catrin w... wh... he saw him.

'... look at the three of you!' he declared,
fight... ... emotio... ns at the sight of his little girl.
'Bro... wne ... Uncle Tim when he's been on the
sun... bec...

T... ... ...e had been a mixture of hysterical
laug... ... ...ve silence. They'd all belted out
'MA... E ... ...D FY NHADAU' as they crossed
the ... ... les, and shared with Huw some of
the ... ... stories from their trip, carefully
avoi... ding ... such as the Cyprus Scandal, the
Buil... ... st and, of course, the sorry tale of
Solo... ... nd they'd tentatively discussed the
A-le... ...iting them the next day – a subject
they... ... banned for the entire holiday, but
whi... ...t be avoided.

The ... ...a off first. Her sprawling family all
stoo... ...w, her dad Keith with a toddler in
one ... ...child clutching his knees and two

others waving madly, excited by the return of the native. They all waved back, including Huw, and the three girls launched themselves into an emotional group hug by Lana's front gate. Wiping away an errant tear, Lana whispered, 'I fucking love you two!' before turning and heading up the path to her front door. From the doorstep she blew them both a flamboyant kiss, and disappeared, swallowed up by her screaming sisters.

Judith was next to be dropped off, silent and worried about what awaited her at home. Catrin squeezed her hand as she got out of the car. 'You know where we are, babes,' she whispered. And watched as Judith let herself into the house, *her* welcome party nowhere to be seen. At nearly nineteen years of age, Judith Harris was still a latchkey kid.

Conversely, when they pulled up outside the Kelly house there were balloons and a massive banner – of course there were:

WELCOME BACK CATRIN MARY THERESA

She didn't really understand why they had to put her middle names up, but presumably it was to add to the drama. There were also seventeen members of her family all waiting to celebrate her safe return, including both sets of grandparents, her five cousins, two aunties and three uncles. 'We kept it intimate,' her mother said, 'because I know you don't like a fuss.'

Tom rugby-tackled her to the ground the second he

saw her. 'Welcome back, Frog Head!' he yelled, and Nana Kelly doused her in a dozen Hail Marys. Despite the mad energy, there was something so comforting about being back with her crazy, lovely family once again, especially as she nursed her broken heart.

An hour into the welcome-home celebrations, when her mother was just about to serve her famous Baked Alaska, the doorbell rang.

'Will someone get that, please?' Liz yelled. 'I'm about to goldenize the meringue!' ('Goldenize' was a term her mother had invented, and it made Catrin smile to hear it again.)

Tom said, 'Ah, that'll be Father O'Leary.'

'You are kiddin' me,' Catrin said. 'Surely to God she didn't invite him?' She peeped into the hall and watched her father striding to the door.

Standing on the other side of it, surrounded by all her worldly possessions and trying desperately not to cry, was Judith.

'I'm really sorry,' she stammered. 'Could I borrow two quid for the taxi?'

Catrin's mother abandoned the Alaska (thankfully rescued by Aunty Treen) to see what was going on. In between sobs, Judith told them how she'd arrived home to an empty house and gone upstairs to her bedroom to find all her things packed up, 'Like the whole room had been stripped!' And that on the bed lay a note from Patricia, which Judith held out for them to see:

Take your stuff and leave your key.
You are no longer welcome in this house.

Quickly assessing the situation, Liz Kelly launched into Supermum mode, taking control and instructing Tom and Huw to carry Judith's stuff to the spare room. She told her she could stay with them as long as she needed – 'Tia castle mia castle' (Tom whispered *casa* under his breath, but Liz was oblivious) – and gave her an all-encompassing hug. She insisted Judith come and join the party and Grampa Lewis thrust a plate of sausage rolls under her nose. When it came to over-whelming love, there was no escaping that of the Kellys.

The next morning both girls were downstairs by six a.m.

Catrin had hardly slept. Which wasn't surprising, given the amount of traffic zooming around her head as she desperately tried to recall the digits Sol had written on that piece of paper. She'd stared at it long enough. Why couldn't she bloody remember? And when she hadn't been thinking about Sol, she'd been worrying about her A-level results – what if she'd messed up?

Judith made them each a cup of strong tea, which they both decided was the most-missed thing from their time abroad.

Taking a big slurpy gulp, Catrin broached the subject of Judith's family situation. 'What you gonna do, babes?' she asked gently.

'When I've got my results, I'm gonna go and find my

dad. In work or whatever. 'Cos where the hell was he last night? He could've come here looking for me. He *knew* when I was due home and, I mean, it's obvious I'm either at yours or Lana's. Plus – he'd have seen my stuff was all gone.'

'Thing is though, Jude, who knows what pressure your mum has put on him?'

'You mean *Patricia*. I'm not calling her *Mum* any more. She's lost the right to be called that.'

Catrin noticed that Judith's hands were shaking as she raised the mug of tea to her mouth. She reached out, trying to comfort her friend.

'I'm gonna make a success of my life, Cat, even if I fail my exams, or don't get the grades—' she said.

'Which you *will*,' interrupted Catrin, but Judith ignored her.

'Whatever the outcome, I am gonna pull myself out of this pit. I'm not gonna be a victim of my own sorry upbringing any more.'

Catrin nodded. She'd never seen Judith like this before.

They were interrupted by Liz coming down the stairs in her dressing gown, picking up the newly delivered post en route. 'Well now, who's got their exam results today then?' she said in a cheery voice, too loud for the time of day. Liz had a penchant for stating the obvious.

'Morning,' said Judith, and Catrin could tell she was glad of the subject change.

'How did you sleep, Judy love, were you . . . ?' But

something stopped Liz in her tracks as she looked through the mail. 'Oh, this one's for you,' she said, surprised, as she held out a pink envelope addressed to *Judith Harris, c/o the Kelly Family*. Even Catrin recognized the handwriting straight away. It was from George.

Catrin and Liz both watched as Judith slowly put down her mug and opened the card, which had the words 'GOOD LUCK' emblazoned on the front, framed in a rectangle of four-leafed clovers. Inside, two fifty-pound notes had been paperclipped to the card. Judith said nothing. Then passed it to Catrin to read.

Dear Judi-moo
I have had to go away. There are too many things
to explain in this card but please be patient – until
I get the chance to tell you everything. I know that
today will be a big day for you. And whatever the
results, please never forget how proud of you I
am. Here is some money towards whatever you
decide to do next. I'm so sorry, my Judi-moo.
I hope one day you will be able to understand, and
to forgive.
I love you always, Dad x

Liz, for once, was lost for words.

Catrin handed back the card. 'Oh my God, Jude.'

She expected her friend to cry, but Judith continued sitting there, gulping down the rest of her tea as if she was in a tea-drinking race. Suddenly she stood up. 'Is it all right if I have a shower, Mrs Kelly?'

'Of course it is, love. Clean towels in the airing cupboard. Help yourself.'

'Thanks.' And she headed out of the door. 'And then we'd better get going, Cat!' she shouted over her shoulder, as if her life hadn't just been turned upside down. Again.

Liz stared at Catrin and whispered, 'Now you give her the spare key from the rack. I don't want any friend of yours ever feeling she's not got a home right here with the Kellys.'

Catrin felt a sudden rush of love for her mother and her big, generous heart.

Two hours later Catrin was at the school, holding a green computer print-out in both hands and staring at three tiny grey triangles standing atop each other's shoulders like acrobats in a circus.

BIOLOGY	A	BIOLEG
PHYSICS	A	FFISEG
CHEMISTRY	A	CEMEG

She had to blink to make sure she was seeing properly; the world had suddenly slowed down. Three As. *What?*

Looking up, she realized her two best friends were just as joyous. Lana was shouting, 'I got a bloody B in English! *Me!*'

And Jude had burst into tears. 'A and two Bs! I don't believe it. I got an A in Economics!'

The three of them looked at each other's results, threw their arms around each other in a three-way cwtch and jumped up and down, screaming, laughing, over the big bloody moon. They'd done it. They'd worked and searched and found the key that opened the door to the next instalment of their young lives.

After rushing home to tell her parents the good news, Catrin headed to Balkwill's to collect the photos she'd put in earlier for one-hour developing. Coed Celyn being Coed Celyn, she knew pretty much every shopper she passed on the way – all of whom wanted to know her results, which meant patience (because people were just being kind) and repeating the same words over again. 'I know! It was a real shock! . . . Yes, Cardiff. To do medicine . . . three As, yes! Cardiff . . . to do medicine.'

Eventually she was able to nip down the alley between Milza's café and the ironmonger's and into Bessemer Place, where she could furtively open the glossy folder containing her prints. As she scoured the matt-finish, seven-by-five photographs that charted their trip in thirty-six captured moments, panic set in: what if she'd put the wrong film in for developing? But then she found a shot of herself and Judith and Lana, stood at the entrance of the Samaria Gorge. So she knew that what she was looking for was just behind it . . .

And there it was, two prints later.

She and Sol, beaming between the walls of Lefka Ori and Mount Volakias, their arms around each other like they'd been friends for a lifetime. And her eyes weren't shut, and they both looked so happy. She thought it was the most wonderful photograph she'd ever seen in her life.

Next, she headed to the phone box on Highfield Road. She took out a pen and her little address book. For nearly two weeks she'd imagined making a phone call from here. On this day.

But not to this number.

She'd imagined calling him directly, hearing his voice, hearing him shout, 'Oh my God, Cat, that's *brilliant*!' But instead she was putting fifty pence into the slot and pressing just three digits.

'Directory Enquiries, how may I help you?'

'Hello, yes, the name is Blythe. And it's a village in Northumbria called Bayfield.' Her heart was beating so fast she had to force herself to take deep breaths.

'How are you spelling that, please?'

'B-L-Y-T-H-E.' Her mouth had gone dry. She could hear the tapping and clicking of the keyboard as the number search got underway.

'I have just one Blythe coming up in Bayfield – a Doctor E. Blythe?'

Catrin nearly screamed. 'Yes! Yes! That's him! His dad's name is Edward!'

'I'm sorry, but this number is ex-directory.'

She thought she'd misheard. 'What? WHAT?'

'I'm afraid I can't give you the number as they've chosen not to be listed.'

'No . . . NOOOOOOOOOOO!'

'That's often the case with doctors,' the operator said, trying to be helpful. 'Is there anything else I can assist you with?'

Catrin wanted to say, *Yes! Track him down! Tell him I'm an idiot for losing his number! Tell him to phone me! Mend my stupid broken heart!*

'Er, no. That's fine, thanks.'

And the pips went, and the call ended.

Along with Catrin's hopes of ever seeing Solomon Blythe again.

13
Lana

Six weeks later

Lana had arranged to meet Judith that first Sunday for lunch. Seeing as central London was less than an hour's train ride from Guildford, it seemed mad not to get together and offer mutual moral support after their first week of student life. Lana found Judith patiently waiting outside the Hippodrome, absorbed in a textbook about globalization and oblivious to the West End weekend that was going on around her.

'So sorry I'm late!' Lana flustered and dived in for a big hug.

'Only fifteen minutes!' laughed Judith. 'That's pretty good for you. Flippin' heck, you've had your nose pierced?' Judith stared curiously at the little silver sleeper encircling Lana's left nostril.

'Nah, it's fake, look.' And she unhooked it to show her friend.

'Don't need a demonstration, thanks,' said Judith, giggling. 'Come on. I'm starving. I've seen this cute place.'

They linked arms and set off in the direction of a

tiny basement wine bar on Leicester Square called the Hope and Castle.

'Oh my God, it is so good to see you,' said Lana as they settled themselves at a corner table. 'I've got a *load* of news!'

Judith picked up the menu. 'Let's share some garlic prawns, yeah? Cheapest thing on here.'

'And a large glass of house white for me,' added Lana.

'Bloody hell, Larn, drinking at lunchtime?'

'Well, we're celebrating, aren't we? Surviving a whole week . . .'

'I'll stick to ginger beer, yer big soak!'

The waiter came and took their order.

'Right,' said Lana, 'I want to hear *everything* from your end, but first things first: Catrin Kelly.' And she took out from her bag a letter addressed to Lana at her Guildford house.

'Snap!' said Judith, who produced an identical envelope, addressed to *her* at the LSE halls. Both of them had been relieved to hear that their friend was in such good spirits, hoping that the excitement of med school would help counteract the heartbreak of losing Sol so quickly after finding him.

Catrin had written pretty much the same thing to both her friends: Freshers had been brilliant – she'd done something called Bavarian Stompers, which 'basically involved dressing up in Bavarian costume and chucking beer over each other'.

'Classy,' laughed Jude and carried on reading. Catrin's course looked like it was going to be majorly difficult, but she said she was still glad to be doing it. She'd already been thrown in at the deep end with Anatomy and had been allocated a cadaver who she'd named Gwynnie, 'because she's so white and because *gwyn* means white in Welsh'.

'I mean seriously, Larn, can you imagine that?' said Jude, looking up from the letter.

'I know!'

'Anyway,' continued Judith, 'she knows we're meeting for lunch and she wants us to call her at two thirty.'

'There's a phone by the door, I noticed. Let's keep an eye on the time.'

The waiter then set down a cast-iron dish full of sizzling garlic prawns and handed them two forks.

'Ooh, fabulous!' said Judith.

'Right. You next, Judith Harris,' said Lana as she pronged a prawn and popped it into her mouth. 'What's it like? Are there any fit men on your corridor? Or sexy tutors, for that matter? Or are they all boring-as-fuck economists?'

Judith laughed at her friend's outlandishness, and proceeded to tell her how much she was loving her life at the London School of Economics. How every minute had been bliss: her new room that still smelt of fresh paint, the communal kitchen on her corridor filled with smiling faces, continuous cooking, different accents and daft conversations; how at the Freshers' Fayre she'd joined the Greek society and the swimming team, and on top of all that she had a timetable of fascinating subjects that she woke up every morning desperate to learn more about. It was as if she'd just discovered colour for the first time in her hitherto black-and-white life.

'Oh Jude, I am *so* happy for you,' said Lana softly, squeezing Judith's hand. 'You deserve this, mate.'

'Yeah, I think I do,' said Judith, and confided that she felt her place at LSE was some kind of reward. For being so tolerant of her dysfunctional home life. She'd heard nothing from either of her parents since arriving in London – but then why should she? George had quite happily disappeared off the face of the earth, or so it seemed. And Patricia had no interest in or knowledge of where her only daughter was now living.

Lana was bursting to tell Judith about life in Guildford. She told her she was living 'in this wild house' with an 'amazing' bunch of people – Linzi the African American Buddhist, who had 'the voice of an angel'; Clint, who was from Merseyside and 'like, has these really exciting ideas about politics – I *love* him!'; and Gerard, who was doing stage-management and could be a bit moody, but she respected his honesty. And then the course – well, the course was everything she'd ever dreamed about – she'd signed up for clowning skills, stage combat and Shakespeare sonnets on top of the main musical-theatre module, which was obviously her favourite.

'We're doing *Guys and Dolls* as the end-of-term show!' Lana said, her eyes filled with excitement.

'OK, hang on,' teased Judith, 'I think you're mixing me up with someone who knows about musicals.'

'It's fantastic! And I'm playing Adelaide, who is, like, the *best* female part in it. And I want you and Cat to come and see it. First week of December. You will, won't you?'

'Of course! And Gareth, presumably?'

'Well yeah, if he's speaking to me by then,' Lana said grimly, her enthusiasm waning as she beckoned for the waiter to bring her another glass of white.

'What? But I thought he came up on Friday?'

'He did. And he was meant to stay Saturday night too, but we had this big row.'

The waiter arrived with the wine and Lana went on to tell Judith what had happened.

Within two days of arriving in Guildford, she'd read an advert on the college noticeboard: auditions were being held for burlesque dancers at an exclusive club in the town centre. Lana had gone for it and been offered the job. 'I mean, it's brilliant – because it's performance-based. So I'm earning money – fifteen quid a show, Jude! – for doing something that will better my career.'

'*Burlesque?* But isn't that, like, y'know, *stripping*?'

'Jesus, Jude, you're as bad as Gareth. No! It's an age-old art form, thank you very much. An established performance tradition.'

Judith raised a cynical eyebrow and listened as Lana went on to explain that Gareth had been put out that their Friday night was being taken up partly with her having to perform, and how he'd only managed to stay

113

for the first twenty minutes of the show. 'He walked out! Can you believe it? Said he couldn't bear watching me "get my kit off for a load of drunks". I was furious.'

'Sorry, Larn, but he's got a point,' said Judith, venturing on to dangerous territory.

'But I didn't get my kit off! Anyway, it wasn't just that. When I introduced him to the rest of the housemates, Clint asked him what theatre he'd seen recently and he said *Jack and the Beanstalk* when he was ten!'

Judith nearly spat out her ginger beer laughing, though Lana was not amused. 'He was just being deliberately difficult. And we had sex and it was rubbish. Like Chinese takeaway. Y'know, good in the moment, but ultimately unfulfilling.'

'Oh poor Gareth,' smiled Judith. 'And you're still not speaking?'

'Kind of. He left yesterday morning, then I rang him last night. Y'know what he's like.'

'Well, not really,' said Judith, spearing the final prawn.

'He's not a sulker. He'd spent the day taking his bike apart, so I think that took his mind off things.'

'Well, maybe it was too soon for him to come up and see you. I mean, you'd only been gone a week.'

'Exactly. Anyway, it all worked out for the best, because . . .' and Lana's face lit up again, 'I went to this incredible performance-art class yesterday morning, which I'd have missed if Gareth had stayed, so swings and roundabouts.'

Judith looked a bit out of her depth as Lana described

the class. It was run by a woman called Belle, who Lana thought was 'the most amazing woman I've ever met'. Belle had asked them all to share with the group a personal and intimate life experience that would invoke in them some strong emotion, the idea being that they could 'bank' this and 'use' it later on when playing a part. One girl on her course, Lydia, had told them all about how she'd been cornered in a barn by a herd of cows when she was twelve. The next day she'd started her periods. Lana had thought this was funny, but apparently was the only one in her class who did. Belle told them it was a significant milestone for Lydia, the herd of cows symbolizing 'the feminine', and that Lydia being cornered by them reflected her resistance to puberty. She'd asked Lydia to stand in the middle of the circle and re-enact her experience. But without using words.

It was electrifying. At least, that was what everyone else said at the end of the class, and Lana didn't want to be the odd one out. So she'd agreed with them all, 'even though inside I was thinking, *What a load of wank!*'

'I have to say I couldn't agree more!' said Jude, but Lana carried on.

'Yeah, but wait, so then it was my turn to share with the group. I told them I couldn't think of anything, so Belle said she'd help me by asking a few pertinent questions about my childhood, my upbringing an' that. And before I knew it, I was talking about when my mum died . . .'

There was a pause; the moment left hanging between them. Judith looked surprised. It was a subject Lana never mentioned even to her and Catrin, let alone to a group of strangers.

'That's a bit much, isn't it?' she said.

Lana took a big gulp of wine. 'I dunno, Jude, it was . . . it was kind of . . . cathartic, you know?'

'So what did you tell them?'

'Exactly what happened, I guess. One day she was there, the next she wasn't. And I remember being given a load of presents and people around me crying all the time and me clinging on to Dad wherever he went, not really knowing what was going on.'

The two girls fell silent as the bustle of the wine bar carried on around them. Lana wasn't used to being vulnerable. She carried on, her voice quieter, gentler, the usual bombastic Lana having left the scene. 'I think I liked it, y'know, when it was just me and Dad. Christ, I can't remember much, Jude, I was only four. But me and him, we'd go places together – Griffin Park and up Brecon – well, I *think* it was Brecon, I remember a mountain, anyway . . . but then it was over, that bit.'

'When Janis came along?'

'Yeah, I guess.' Lana was pensive again. She knew that neither Catrin nor Judith ever thought of Janis as her stepmother, just her mum. She'd been part of Lana's life for as long as her friends had known her – just like George had been for Judith. 'I do love Janis, y'know.'

'Well, of course you do,' said Judith, who had never doubted it.

'But then there was a baby, and then another one, and suddenly Dad wasn't *my* dad any more, he was *our* dad. Janis was like a machine – popping them out like one a year, it seemed!'

Judith smiled, relieved that Lana was bouncing back.

'And so I told them – the other students, I mean – I said, now I'm like *surrounded* by siblings! I mean seriously. They're coming out of my ears! Five kids. It's disgusting,' she said, exaggerating her Welsh accent because she knew this made her sound funnier. 'And like *everything* is rationed. Because, y'know, when you're a family of seven, there's just *never* enough to go round. So it's each man for himself . . .'

'And what did Belle think of all that?'

'Oh, I dunno, she reckoned I was probably permanently on the lookout for someone to replace my dad, that I'd never got over losing him to Janis after Mum died.'

'That's absolute bollocks,' said Judith, in defence of her friend. 'Christ, I hate it when people start analysing . . . bloody pop psychology. At the end of the day she's a drama teacher, for God's sake.'

'Yeah, maybe. Anyhow, next thing she's telling me to get on my feet. "*Show us the pain, Lana,*" she says, "*the heartache of being starved of attention. Let's see you desperate, Lana, and clawing . . .*"'

Judith started laughing, enjoying Lana's impression of Belle, and the more she laughed, the more Lana played up to it, always loving an audience.

'"*You're trying to call out, but you have no voice . . . you cannot be heard . . .*" Honestly, Jude, I looked round at the rest of the group and they were so eager to see me turn myself inside out, emotionally, like . . . so I thought, *Right, I've either got to dive in with this one hundred per cent, or get the hell out of here.* And within seconds I was improvising this piece of performance art, with a pained expression on my face like the painting by that Edward Monk fella . . .'

'Munch, you mean. *The Scream,*' said Judith, becoming hysterical now as Lana re-enacted her performance.

'That's him. And I was stretching my arms out, begging, yearning, whilst Belle watched on, banging a drum.'

'Oh my goodness! You, Lana Lloyd, are one in a million,' said Judith, tears of laughter streaking her cheeks. 'Only you, only you!'

'Thing was, Jude, I quite enjoyed myself once I got going.'

'Sounds like it!'

'Oh hell,' said Lana, looking at the clock on the wall. 'It's nearly half past. Come on. Caterina will be waiting . . .'

Judith looked up Catrin's new number in her address book and the two girls made their way over to the pay-phone at the entrance of the wine bar. Lana loaded it with two ten-pence pieces and Judith dialled the Cardiff number, turning the receiver earpiece so that they could both hear their friend on the end of the line. It only rang once before a breathless Catrin picked up.

'Jude? Larn?' she said.

'All present and correct,' said Lana a little too loudly, buoyed up by white wine and the excitement of being in the company of her two best friends.

'She's a bit pissed, Cat,' yelled Judith down the phone.

'Outrageous!' said Lana. 'I haven't even started yet!'

'I am *so* glad you're both there. I've got something to tell you,' said Catrin, a hundred and sixty miles away, the tension in her voice undiluted by distance.

'What's happened?' said Judith, serious now.

At the end of the line they heard Catrin take a deep breath before diving in.

'Oh my God, girls. You will never believe it in a million years . . .'

14
Catrin

Moving into her room at New Hall had been a major drama. Mainly because, underneath it all, her parents were so devastated that their second child was leaving home, they were on edge the entire time. Tensions were running high and Catrin knew she'd have to handle the situation with kid gloves. Which wasn't easy, considering she was nervous herself at this new world into which she'd been plunged. She hated herself for being embarrassed by her parents, but she knew they could be a liability. Her only hope was that none of her fellow hall of residence mates would witness any Kellyisms.

Between the three of them, they managed to carry Catrin's boxes and cases into her room in one trip, which included a large tin, full of cake. 'There's two bara briths in there,' Liz said, as usual turning to food to distract from emotion, 'and your Nana Kelly made you a sultana sponge.'

'Aw, I *love* sultana sponge. Thank you!'

'Now, shall we start unpacking?' said Liz, reaching for Catrin's case.

'No!' said Catrin, reaching out to stop her mother a

little too eagerly – inside that case was the now-framed photo of herself and Sol taken at the Samaria Gorge. She'd managed to keep it out of sight and away from her mother so far: the last thing she wanted was to invite unwanted questions.

It had probably been a mistake framing the photo – it only served to remind her of her heartbreak at failing to contact this most wonderful human being. Two days previously she'd written to him at Trinity College, Cambridge – a last-ditch attempt in her quest. She knew it was early days yet – term probably didn't even start at Cambridge for at least another week, so she would just have to be patient. In the meantime, she had her parents to wrangle.

'Tell you what I'd like to look at,' said Huw gleefully. 'The union!'

She couldn't really say no, but she told them it'd have to be a flying visit. It was funny seeing this student hangout through the eyes of her parents. If she hadn't been with them, she probably wouldn't have noticed the grimy layer of spilt beer and ancient burger that seemed to coat every surface. All the tables and chairs had an indefinable stickiness about them, even though they were ostensibly clean. But Catrin was pleasantly surprised to see that her parents were actually in awe of the place, not disgusted by it.

'You go find us a table and I'll get the coffees,' she said.

Her father immediately thrust a pound note into her hand. 'I don't want you paying for a thing today.'

Catrin smiled and took the money. There was no point in arguing.

Five minutes later, she was balancing three polystyrene cups on a tray. She picked up some plastic stirrers and sugar sachets and turned to head over to the table, when she noticed her father walking towards her.

'We need another one, beaut. Milk, no sugar. It's for your friend.'

'What friend?'

'I didn't catch his name . . .'

Catrin looked over to the table, where she could see her mother chatting animatedly to a young guy who had his back to her. Then, as if sensing that she was looking at him, he turned round.

Staring straight back at her was Solomon Blythe.

She stood there like a wild deer, interrupted mid-graze.

He smiled first. 'Hey, Cat.'

She dropped the coffees.

And then they both laughed.

'Seems like you two have got a lot of catching up to do,' Huw said a few minutes later, when it was clear that he and Liz were gate-crashing a long-overdue conversation. They said their goodbyes, and as they watched them go, Catrin turned to Sol. 'So . . . you're sat in front of me. In Cardiff. Sol, seriously, what the hell?'

She listened in bewilderment as he told her why he was there, her heart racing, her brain still unable to compute that she was actually looking at him.

'When I got home from Crete,' he said, 'I was a mess. I mean, a *good* mess, but still a mess . . . couldn't eat or sleep, I was continuously nervous, felt sick all the time and was generally useless for days!'

'Glad I had such a positive effect,' said Catrin, secretly pleased.

'And I thought, *Right, get a grip, Sol, as soon as you hear from her everything will calm down.* I knew you wouldn't be home for a couple more weeks, so I just decided I had to be patient.'

'But then you didn't hear from me . . .' said Catrin forlornly.

Sol smiled. 'No . . . so obviously I started to think you must've changed your mind.'

'I didn't! I didn't change my mind!'

'But I didn't know that, did I?' he laughed. 'I reckoned you just weren't interested, otherwise you'd have got in touch.'

'Oh God, I can't bear it!' she said.

'I had to accept it, didn't I?'

'I'm so sorry,' said Catrin.

'Plonker. It wasn't your fault. Anyway, about a week before I was due to set off for Cambridge, I just had this . . . *epiphany*, would you call it? Or moment of insanity? Only time will tell, I suppose . . .'

He paused, gathering his thoughts. 'Trinity College, Cambridge. It's stunning. It's this rarefied existence – I knew how extraordinarily lucky I was to be offered a place there. But the thing was, Cat, there was always this nagging feeling that, no matter how amazing it

123

was, I would still always be in the wrong place. Because I wouldn't be with you.'

She drank in the glory of his face and wanted to lean over and kiss his eyelids.

He went on to explain how he knew straight away what he had to do. He contacted the medical school at University College Wales, who replied within forty-eight hours offering him an interview. They told him that it wasn't unheard of for students to want to change universities, and they'd certainly be happy to meet with him and discuss it. He'd driven down early one morning the previous week, and by lunchtime he'd met with the Dean and been offered a place.

Catrin thought she might faint. 'What? I don't understand? You're coming *here*?' she said. 'To Cardiff?'

'Well, that depends,' said Sol, 'on how you feel about it . . .'

She tried to put him off. Not because she didn't want him to come, but because she felt she should. 'We can commute! We can see each other at weekends. You really don't have to give up Cambridge for me . . .'

'I know I don't *have* to, but I *want* to.'

And then he told her about his brother, who had been so in love with a girl called Amy before he went to university. They'd made all these promises, all these vows to stay in touch, and they'd tried to begin with – thinking that their love would withstand the distance. But in the end it failed. And Sol didn't want to run the risk. 'I want to be a GP, Cat. Mrs Jones from Pontypony or Major Briggs from Little Whipley or whoever from wherever isn't gonna care if the fella sat in front of them writing a prescription for Lisinopril spent his five years in Cambridge or Cameroon. As long as he's qualified!'

Catrin laughed and stroked his arm.

'I just need to be where you are. I can't explain it. And it isn't what I was looking for. And I promise you, just say the word and I will sod off. But I've got a feeling you think the same.'

She was silent for a moment. And then she looked up at him and smiled. 'Your parents are gonna be so cross.'

She wasn't wrong.

The following day when he'd broken the news to them, he said his mother had laughed and his father had remained silent. 'Normally I love my mother's laugh,' he told Catrin. 'I call it her glorious Jamaican cackle. But when she laughs sarcastically, it's really unsettling.'

'Oh my God, what did she say?' Catrin was already terrified of Sol's parents. She wondered whether she'd ever get to meet them and how different they would be from her own. Both his mum and his dad were doctors, for a start.

Sol launched into a well-practised impression of his mother. '*You are giving up a place in Cambridge. CAMBRIDGE now. To go to Cardiff! Hah!* I said, *But Cardiff's good, Mam* and my dad said, *It's not Cambridge though, is it, son?*'

'And what did you say to that?'

125

'I just told them that it was something I have to do. And that they will love you. Because you are . . . well, you're astonishing.'

He reached out across the table and held her hand. 'So what d'you reckon, Catrin Kelly?'

By the following Monday, Sol had moved into a house-share in the Cathays area of Cardiff. For the rest of that term, he and Catrin would see each other every single day.

15
Judith

A tiny window in her life, it had been – where she saw who she could be and what she could become. How naïve of her to think it wouldn't be taken away from her.

Everything was always taken away from her. Within three weeks, the rich rug of education and London life was pulled from beneath her so abruptly she could hardly believe it had ever existed.

It was during a lecture on the Common Market that her personal tutor had come in at the back of the hall. She'd watched as he approached the lectern and whispered something to the Professor of Economics. Her heart sank. Even before she heard her name, she knew it was bad news.

'Judith Harris?' the professor said into the microphone. Heads turned and she felt a hundred pairs of eyes staring at her.

They claimed it was a suicide attempt. She couldn't voice her own doubts about its authenticity, because of how it would look – the hard-hearted daughter who didn't believe her own poor mother: her own poor mother who'd two months previously been abandoned by her cruel heartless husband (so it was claimed) and left alone, despairing and depressed. A neighbour had found her – in a crumpled heap at the bottom of the stairs, having ingested (so it was claimed) over thirty paracetamol. There was also a note, stating that she simply could not cope any more.

There'd been a psychiatric referral after the X-ray showed a broken hip. And it was believed Patricia would be discharged in a couple of weeks, as long as there was care for her at home. No rush for Judith to come straight back – she should take her time, her mother was being perfectly well looked after in St Luke's hospital for now. The university understood. They said they would keep Judith's place open or she could defer for a year if she wanted.

She waited till the following Sunday to come home. One of the tutors had a cousin in Chepstow and offered to drive her back. The students on her corridor sent her a card – one of those giant ones, with twenty-three signatures from people she barely knew, all saying how sorry they were. Judith wanted to weep at the kindness that some people in the world so naturally displayed. Why wasn't kindness equally apportioned? she wondered. Why didn't she have a kind mother – like Liz Kelly or Janis Lloyd?

Because she no longer had a key, she had to knock on the neighbour's door to ask to borrow theirs – yet another humiliation inflicted by Patricia from a distance. Judith let herself into the silent house and the familiar smell hit her straight away. Warm dust and stale cooking mixed with cigarette smoke, doused in Patricia's ubiquitous Chanel No. 5. She walked into the living room, the scene of her dramatic departure nearly three months previously. Only the heavy ticking of the mantelpiece clock was there to welcome her home.

Two days after moving back, she headed to the job centre and applied for a casual post at the Welsh Office. Judith was nothing if not practical. And her mother could be in St Luke's for weeks.

She was interviewed by a nice lady in the Economic and Statistical Services Division of the Welsh Office and was appointed as a temporary administrative assistant. The job itself was a lot less glamorous than the title suggested – the very lowest rung of a very tall ladder. She answered phones, photocopied, filed, and spent long hours in the mail room, but the fact that she was working somewhere that contained the word 'Economic' in its name made her feel somehow that she hadn't completely sold out, that she was still holding on by a thread to the notion of a career. And when she finally returned to LSE next term or even next year, at least she would feel that she hadn't totally wasted her time away.

There were three other 'casuals' signed up at the same time as her, and she was relieved that their backgrounds were all very different. There was Lyndon the Welsh-speaking trombonist, Glenys, who was in between teaching jobs, and Rachel, a biology graduate.

She didn't tell any of them her story. As far as they were concerned, Judith wanted a career in the Civil Service, and relentless photocopying or sorting out mail was a foot in the door. So they knew nothing of her short-lived university life, her strange mother or her runaway Cypriot dad.

She fought the temptation to get angry with George for leaving, because deep down she championed him for finally finding the courage to escape. But on a practical day-to-day level, she was pissed off that all this mess had been left to her to sort out. At nineteen years of age. Cheers, Dad.

One thing that reassured her was knowing there was no mortgage to pay on their little house. A small but not insubstantial win on the football pools for George when Judith was ten had ensured this. Patricia had been furious at the time – thinking the windfall would mean fur coats and diamonds and flash holidays abroad. But in a rare show of mettle, George, without discussion, had gone to the bank and paid off the mortgage. It meant security for them all, he'd said. So at least that was something. But she still had to eat, didn't she? And pay all the other bills. So getting a job was her only option. Which is why every morning and afternoon she'd find herself sitting on the Number 67 bus from Coed Celyn, which took her to Cardiff and back again, five days a week.

The first time she had visited Patricia at St Luke's she'd been met with 'I want no help from you!'

'Well, you've got no choice,' said Judith quietly. ''Cos I'm all you've got.'

The hospital was in Cardiff itself and Judith could walk there after finishing work at four p.m. On a couple of occasions the gang from the Welsh Office had tried persuading her to go out for a few drinks or to see a film – and she wasn't blind to the fact that Lyndon was actually a bit sweet on her. And yes – she was tempted. He seemed like a lovely guy. But Judith always said no, solid in her loyalty to Patricia and committed to those daily hospital visits. She hated herself for it, but she knew she'd hate herself more if she abandoned her narcissist of a mother.

Patricia seldom spoke when Judith visited. She was confined to a wheelchair whilst her broken hip healed, and would spend most of the hour staring out of the window.

Because Cardiff University was just down the road, sometimes Catrin came with her, coursework and timetable permitting. And on those occasions Patricia would be sweetness and light towards them both, telling Catrin how grateful she was that Judith had given up uni to come and look after her. 'I don't know where I'd be without this daughter of mine!' she'd say, and Judith would worry about her own sanity, especially when Catrin whispered to her afterwards, 'She seems to have mellowed, Jude, don't you think?' It took a lot of willpower for Judith to resist screaming. Maybe she was paranoid, but part of her wondered whether Catrin actually believed her when she described how different

Patricia could be when Jude visited alone – so convincing was her mother's performance.

One Wednesday afternoon as she was leaving St Luke's for home, Mr Sharma the consultant told her that her mother could be discharged at the weekend. He smiled when he said it. And she smiled back. Though they both knew they were putting it on. 'She'll need help till she's back on her feet again,' he said. 'But in terms of her mental health, I'd say she's coming on in leaps and bounds.' The idea of Patricia leaping or bounding anywhere was complete anathema to Judith, but she said thank you and promised she'd be there on Saturday morning to collect her. She would try and get a lift from someone (maybe Catrin's dad would help) and, if not, a taxi.

Finally, Patricia saw fit to speak to her loyal daughter. 'Make sure you're not late,' she said and turned away.

As she travelled back to Coed Celyn on the bus that evening, Judith realized how much life was going to change now that Patricia was coming home. She'd taken the solitude for granted, luxuriated in having the house to herself. But come Saturday the whole scenario would be different. She'd have to make a bed up for her mother downstairs – there was no way she'd be able to get up to her bedroom till her hip was completely better. She looked out of the bus window and sighed, rain pelting against the glass in sympathy.

'Shift over.' A voice disturbed her and made her jump. She looked up. It was Gareth Metcalf.

'Oh, hello,' she said, slightly irritated by the interruption. 'Didn't know you used the bus.'

'Bike's bein' serviced,' he said, sitting himself down, legs akimbo, with apparently no thought for Judith's personal space. 'Normally they've got a courtesy car in work, but it's out till tomorrow.'

'Right,' said Judith, not really knowing what else to say, which was always the case on the rare occasions their paths crossed. Certainly since Gareth had come to her rescue on the day of the Athens flight he'd gone up a bit in her estimation, but she always felt slightly uncomfortable in his company. Was it because she knew the secret about Lana and the Irish builder on their last night in Greece? Did she feel somehow culpable – even though it had been nothing to do with her? Or was it because she knew that he and Lana had been quarrelling a bit lately, Lana feeling the need to write Judith letters sharing all the ins and outs? She wished she didn't – it really was none of Judith's business.

'When's the old girl coming home then?' he said, and Judith flinched. Absolutely nothing wrong with the question – it was just the way he called Patricia *the old girl*.

'Um, Saturday as it goes,' she answered, staring straight ahead.

'Ambulance?'

'No, I'm booking a taxi.'

The bus pulled away and they sat in silence for a minute.

'I'll fetch her home if you like,' Gareth suddenly said.

'What, on the back of your bike?'

'No, you wally. Courtesy car.'

'Oh, I see.' Judith was horrified by the prospect. Uncertain as to whether she could handle the stress of Patricia being rude to Gareth, or Gareth reacting to Patricia. 'Maybe.'

'Blimey, Lana's right about you, isn't she?' Gareth said with a smile.

'What?' asked Judith, trying to hide her annoyance.

'That you hate being helped.'

'That's completely . . . that's totally unfair,' Judith said indignantly, feeling slightly betrayed by her best friend for discussing her like that. 'I just didn't want to inflict my mother on you, that's all.'

'Why?' asked Gareth. 'Does she bite?' And he looked at her in all seriousness. The image of Patricia snapping like a Yorkshire terrier made her spontaneously laugh. 'I'll take that as a yes,' he said, unwrapping a piece of pink bubble gum and chucking it into his mouth. 'Wanna bit?' He offered her the packet.

'How old are you, twelve?'

'Suit yourself,' he said. And they didn't speak for the rest of the journey.

16

Lana

Applause. The most beautiful sound in the world, she'd often joke. And if there was ever a chance for an encore, then even better. She knew roughly where the gang were all sitting – she'd got them great seats in the middle of the stalls: Judith and Catrin and Gareth and Sol. Looking out into the audience as she took another bow, she tried to catch their eye. But the blinding lights and the dust of the auditorium kept them hidden from view. The important thing was that they were out there. Somewhere. And she knew she'd done a cracker of a performance. She'd smashed it. The buzz was intoxicating.

'*That the guy's only doing it for some doll!*' And bow and smile. And bow again. And blackout. The show was over.

Lana rushed into the wings and headed for the dressing room, pulling out the hair pins that had secured her little 1940s wedding hat, the crowning glory of her character Adelaide's costume. All she wanted to do was get changed, get to the bar and meet the gang.

When she walked in, they applauded her again. She

saw Catrin first – who rushed forward and hugged her. 'Oh my God, Larn, you were amazin'!'

'You made it! Thank you! Thank you!'

'So proud of you, babes,' said Gareth, kissing her. And he handed her a glass of wine.

She hesitated, then mumbled, 'Couldn't get me a vodka, could you, babe? With soda?'

Gareth looked confused. 'Since when did you start drinking vodka?'

'Couple of weeks ago,' she smiled. 'Less calories.'

He shrugged and obediently headed off to the bar.

'Lana, you remember Solomon?' said Catrin shyly, and Sol stepped forward.

'Hi!'

'Let's have a look at you then,' said Lana, beaming. 'Yep, he'll do!' And she gave him a big hug and planted a smacker on his lips.

'Aw, don't embarrass him,' laughed Catrin.

'That was a brilliant show,' said Sol. 'I don't know how you do it! All those words – the songs!'

'Not exactly saving lives though, is it? Like you two medical whizz kids.' Lana turned to take the vodka from Gareth. 'Thanks, babe,' she said and kissed him on the cheek.

'I couldn't get over the dancing! All those moves!' Judith was clearly impressed.

'But you saw me in the school shows!' Lana laughed.

'Yeah, I know, but this was like *so* professional! You are gonna be such a star.'

'Stop it!' Lana said, laughing, quickly checking that no one from the cast was in earshot. Bit uncool to talk like that, she thought, though she knew Judith meant well.

'Talking of stars,' said Gareth, 'shall we give her the present?'

'Ooh yes,' said Judith, reaching behind her chair for a black bin-liner she'd brought with her, containing something spiky and flat wrapped in tissue paper.

Lana looked intrigued, put down her drink and began unwrapping.

'I should point out,' said Catrin, 'that me and Sol contributed absolutely nothing to this. We are such bad friends.'

'Though to be fair,' added Sol, 'we did get you a large bag of pick 'n' mix.' And they all laughed.

'What's this?' said Lana, pulling back the paper to reveal a large home-made golden star, with a photograph of Lana stuck in the middle surrounded by the words *LANA LLOYD SUPERSTAR EXTRAOR-DINAIRE! WE ARE SO PROUD!*

'Gareth made it, and I sort of painted it.'

Lana smiled and did her best to sound grateful. 'Aw, that's fantastic – thank you!' she said.

'You can stick it on your dressing-room door or whatever,' said Gareth. 'When you do your next show.'

'Yeah!'

They were interrupted by some of Lana's fellow cast on their way to the bar and Lana surreptitiously hid the gift back under the tissue. 'You coming to Juno's, aren't you?' asked Kiki, the girl playing Sarah Brown.

'Yeah, maybe, we'll see,' said Lana coolly, avoiding any introductions. 'May just stay here.'

Kiki nodded and moved off with the others.

'You were really good, Sarah Brown!' Gareth called clumsily after her. But Kiki didn't hear and the compliment was left hanging in the air. Lana felt simultaneously sorry for Gareth and embarrassed by him.

'Don't think she heard you, mate,' said Judith, laughing at him.

'Or maybe she didn't understand my ridiculously thick Welsh accent,' he laughed back. 'So who's for another drink then?'

'Good God!' shouted Judith, clearly in good spirits. 'Make the most of it, folks. Gareth Metcalf is buying a *round*!'

It had been Lana's idea for Judith to move in with Gareth. She'd received a letter from Catrin a few weeks previously, desperately appealing for help. 'I think it's really bad for her, living with Patricia,' Catrin had written. 'The woman's poisonous. And without George there any more it must be unbearable.' So setting them up as flatmates seemed like the obvious solution. Gareth had a spare room, after all – surely Judith would leap at the chance to be free. But her reaction to Lana's suggestion was far from positive.

'No, Larn, I don't think so, do you?'

'Just hear me out,' Lana'd said, unfazed by her

response. 'You can't stay at your mother's, you'll go insane. Me and Cat are worried about you.'

'I'm fine,' Judith nodded. She obviously wasn't.

'And anyway, I've already asked Gar and he's cool with it.'

This wasn't strictly true. When Lana had first asked him, he'd refused outright. 'You're kiddin', aren' you?'

'But she's one of my—'

'Even if she *is* your best friend. I mean, what happens when you come home for the weekend and I want to . . . y'know?'

'Shag me up against the bathroom wall wearing nothing but my black stilettos? *Me*, that is, not you.'

'Well yeah, that kinda thing.'

'We'll stick a lock on the door!'

'No, sorry, Larn. I just couldn't handle it.'

So she'd left it a couple of days and then resorted to emotional blackmail. She knew she'd have to play her trump card and aim for his Achilles heel: Gareth had not had a great upbringing himself. He and his sister had been pretty much raised by their grandparents, their mother being 'otherwise occupied' and their dad never having been on the scene.

'Thing is, you'll know more than anyone what it feels like to be rejected,' she'd said earnestly one evening during an overnight visit, persuasively stroking his arm as they lay in her single student bed. He paused. And in that pause she knew she'd won.

'Oh for God's sake, OK!' he'd finally relented. 'But

she'll have to pay me something – and I can't be feeding her as well.'

'Well, I can't pay him much,' Judith had said to Lana when she'd reluctantly agreed.

'I know!'

'Sorry if I sound ungrateful. It's just, y'know, me and Gareth, we're ... well, we're not exactly each other's cup of tea. And at least at Patricia's I don't pay rent.'

'Oh, it'll be fine. You'll both be at work in the day, doin' your own thing at night – you'll hardly see each other.'

However, despite Lana's optimistic outlook, she did wonder if she'd made a terrible mistake. After all, Judith was right. She and Gareth *weren't* each other's cup of tea. Judith thought *he* was a bit common (even though she denied it) and Gareth thought *she* was a bit up herself.

So the weekend that Judith moved in, Lana had come home, just to smooth things over as the new flat-mates grew accustomed to each other. The atmosphere was far from harmonious: Judith and Gareth barely spoke to one another or remained in the same room for more than a couple of minutes, and Lana found herself overcompensating with hysterical, meaningless conversation. It was then that she had the lightbulb moment.

Lana had never played pool in her life, but both Judith and Gareth were top-notch players, Judith having been taught to play by George and Gareth having learnt from his granddad. So the night before Lana headed back to Guildford she suggested a game in the Coach and Horses. At first they both said no, so Lana goaded Gareth that he was scared of being beaten by a woman, and teased Judith that she'd probably forgotten how to play. Their innate competitiveness saved the day. After six games, Lana was yawning with boredom and declared the tournament a draw, grateful to get out of the dingy, smoky pool room, but even more grateful that the two new flatmates seemed to have found some common ground and developed a grudging tolerance of one other.

Which since then had blossomed into a friendship of sorts. Lana was glad of this, of course. It made life so much easier. Now she and Catrin could stop worrying about Jude, and secretly Lana felt she herself could stop worrying about Gareth too. Nothing had been said, but things between the two of them had been more than a little tense since she'd been in Guildford. At least now Judith could keep an eye on things for her at home, and let her know if Gareth started complaining that he didn't see enough of her or questioning the state of their relationship.

Spooning in bed that night after the performance – Judith was asleep on the sofa downstairs and Cat and Sol were in a nearby B&B – Lana asked Gareth how the new flat-share was going.

'Yeah, she's all right once you get to know her a bit,' he conceded. And within two minutes was fast asleep.

*

At lunchtime the next day, Lana, Gareth and Judith met up with Sol and Catrin for a half-price curry lunch and Lana felt so full of love for her two best friends, and for Gareth and for newbie Solomon. 'Do you have to go?' she whined, when they all started getting their things together, ready to leave. 'Why don't you all stay up another night? There's this brilliant club we could all go to. Come on, let's live a little!'

'Sorry, Larn,' said Catrin. 'We've got a nine o'clock lecture tomorrow.'

'And it's bio-chem,' said Sol, taking Catrin's hand, 'with Prof. Chambers, who is vicious if you're late or miss it.'

'And some of us normal mortals have got work to go to!' Gareth chipped in.

'Yeah, we can't all live this showbiz lifestyle, you know,' added Judith.

It was a flash. A tiny spark of resentment. Over before she knew it. But it was there, and a voice in her head said, *Oh, you boring bastards!*

She felt herself blush for even thinking it. But she'd thought it nonetheless.

Was she growing away from them? Were they becoming less and less her tribe?

To dispel the unwelcome feeling, she gave them all big, ostentatious hugs and kissed Gareth long and hard, until he pulled away, embarrassed.

'Hey, all right, woman! People will start talking!' And she laughed.

'Go on then, bugger off, the lot of you!'

She watched Catrin and Sol, all loved up, as they got into their car, tooting the horn and waving madly out of the window with promises for a big catch-up at Christmas. And she smiled as she watched Judith clumsily clamber on to the back of Gareth's bike.

'There's an art to it, babe!' shouted Lana over the roar of the engine. 'You'll get used to it.' And she waved them off. Smiling all the while until they were out of sight, the growling of the bike's exhaust fading to a whisper.

She stood alone for a moment, staring into the road.

This inability to articulate what it was she was feeling completely stumped her.

It was like she'd been *unplugged* from something.

It was like she'd been *liberated* from something.

She was still feeling out of sorts on Monday morning when she went into college for her Shakespeare tutorial. Passing her pigeonhole, she saw an envelope sticking out. She didn't recognize the writing and it had been hand-delivered. She tore it open, expecting it to be from one of the tutors.

Hi Lana – blast from the past. You said to get in touch when I was working over here. So here I am, getting in touch. Am staying at the Collingwood Guest House on Westbourne Road. There most nights. Or the Fox and Vivian pub. Come and see me! Let's reminisce.

See ya!

Damian Magill (Damo)

Lana stood stuck to the spot. Jesus. The builder from Belfast.

It all came flooding back. That night in Athens. A memory she'd hoped to erase, now brought sharply into focus.

'I'm working over in Guildford later in the year! Big new shopping mall,' he'd shouted over the music in the club.

'Brilliant. Come and see me!' she'd shouted back. *'I'll be wafting around drama school being an unbearable luvvie. I'll need a bit of rough to remind me of my roots.'* And she'd laughed and they'd carried on dancing.

She folded the note and put it inside her pocket, disturbed by the thrill it had given her to read.

17
Catrin

They'd waited. For six weeks. They hadn't needed to, but seeing as it was going to be Catrin's first time, she wanted to make it memorable. *'We've only really done kissing so far. And a bit of boobs an' stuff . . .'* she'd written to Judith in a letter, followed swiftly by *'don't tell my mother'* in brackets.

'Take as long as you like!' Judith had written back. 'It's not a race. And to be honest, the whole thing's a bit over-rated if you ask me, though I'm sure our dear Lady Lloyd would disagree!'

In the same way that Catrin approached most things in life, she built up to losing her virginity with a positive outlook and a one hundred per cent cast-iron level of preparation. Sol teased her that the amount of research she'd put into it would put an Arctic expedition to shame. But she said she just wanted all the boxes ticked, the i's dotted and the t's crossed, so that 'I can properly enjoy myself'. She'd been to her GP and asked to be put on the Pill, not wanting to rely entirely on condoms 'just in case'. She took it bang on eight o'clock every morning without fail and stuck with it, even though it made her feel a bit sick at first. She wasn't sure if this was something to do with the old Catholic guilt plaguing her for using contraception. But either way, she knew that removing the risk of getting pregnant was worth any amount of conscience attack. And anyway, she reminded herself, she wasn't a practising Catholic any more! She couldn't afford to buy sexy underwear, but dug out the best pair of pants she could find, and the bra that looked least tired.

And when they'd decided to see Lana in her show, Sol had booked a room at the Collingwood Guest House in Guildford, run by the ultra-efficient Mrs Daniels.

'I've given you the Sid James suite!' she announced as she showed them to their room. 'Named after Sid James. *Carry On*? All my rooms are named after famous *Carry On* actors. I find it makes people feel special. Breakfast is eight till ten, no dogs, no curries, and please limit use of the toilet flush to once during the night. Enjoy!' And she'd opened the door to the Sid James suite with a flourish, standing back to let them pass and shutting it behind them.

They stood for a few moments till they heard the creak of the stairs as Mrs Daniels withdrew, then fell on to the bed, laughing.

Eventually they stopped, turned and looked at each other. Neither saying anything, both thinking the same.

'Shall we get it over with?' whispered Catrin.

'You're such a romantic,' he smiled back, running his finger along her cheek.

'You know what I mean . . . I just don't want to make it a *thing*.'

'D'you mean you want it to be . . .' and he started kissing her neck, '. . . uneventful?'

Catrin giggled. 'No, but just, y'know . . .'

'No?' The kisses went lower, and her breathing speeded up. Sensations she'd never felt before began flooding through her entire body. Did she feel sick? Or dizzy? What did she feel, exactly?

'I'm scared, to be honest, Sol.'

He stopped for a moment, hid his face in the crook of her neck and whispered, 'Would it help at all to know that it's my first time too?'

She sat bolt upright in the bed.

'Is it? But you never said!'

'Well, you never asked.' He smiled back awkwardly. 'And I wanted you to think I knew what I was doing – like, the guy is *meant* to know, isn't he . . . ? And I'm half Jamaican! I'm meant to be cool . . . but in truth, I haven't the first idea.'

'Oh, well that makes me feel *loads* better!' She beamed, as if she'd just solved a complicated puzzle. ''Cos if I get it wrong you'll be none the wiser, and the same goes for me!'

'Great!' Sol laughed. 'So let's both mess it up together!' And they kissed and laughed some more. And then stopped laughing and just kissed. And then . . . did everything. Apart from mess it up.

18

Lana

She'd spent the whole day thinking about the note. And it had distracted her. To such an extent that her Shakespeare tutor had had to take her to one side in the sonnet class and ask if everything was all right.

'Yeah, fine,' she'd lied, 'just winding down after *Guys and Dolls*, y'know.'

'Look, Lana, we may be near the end of term,' said the tutor, 'but you've still got a fully timetabled fortnight of classes, remember. You're not in school any more, we don't *wind down*. So concentrate and start again.'

She was working on Sonnet 64 and had stumbled over two of the lines:

Ruin hath taught me thus to ruminate,
That Time will come and take my love away.

Ruin. Was that where she was heading? Sometimes Lana wondered whether she knew herself at all. She knew she was attracted to danger and to risk, but why? Why jeopardize what she had? What was it inside her that drew her towards this weird kind of self-sabotage? Was she in some sort of tantrum with Gareth and Jude for being such good mates these days? For pushing her out? Did she resent it – was she in some way, indirectly, unjustifiably, looking for someone to make *her* feel special? Or was she simply bored? Hundreds of thoughts chased each other around her head – she'd met this guy just once! And she'd been drunk, for God's sake! She couldn't even remember what he looked like – so even if she *did* meet up with him, which she wasn't going to, how would she recognize him? The whole thing was ludicrous.

She would throw the note from this Damo fella straight into the bin. And focus on going home in two weeks' time for Christmas. It was going to be brilliant. A whole month with Gareth – sleeping in Gareth's bed, being in the flat with Gareth, just hanging out. Judith would be there too, of course, but that was OK, it'd be *fun*! Of course it would. And being with Gareth properly would make everything better.

'I knew you'd come,' he said, handing her half a lager and laughing in a way that she found both irritating and irresistible. 'Cheers!'

She took several gulps to allay her nerves.

She was standing in the bar of a busy pub down the road from the Collingwood Guest House. Half an hour earlier she'd been at the reception desk there, asking if Damian Magill was available. Just as the *Carry On*-obsessed Mrs Daniels was informing her that the contractors didn't usually get home till about seven, she heard a voice behind her. 'Ah now, what took you so long?'

Damian Magill was stood in the doorway, dusty in his work clothes, flask and Tupperware in hand, a copy of the *Sun* under his arm and a Bensons behind his ear. *What a cliché*, Lana thought. Whilst at the same time noticing the breadth of him and the height of him and his confident jaw-line and laughing green eyes. His complexion was ruddy, his hair was thick and sandy, and she realized straight away that she was in trouble. Struggling for something to say, all she could come out with was, 'Well, I was just passing, y'know . . .'

He looked at her and grinned as if he was eyeing up his dinner. And Lana hated him in an instant. He was a bit older than she remembered. Thirty, maybe?

'Give me those old things, Damian, and I'll get them washed,' interrupted Mrs Daniels as she took his flask and sandwich box.

'Oh you're a star, Mrs D, so you are,' he said, twinkling at her. 'Damo' was clearly a charmer. And his gruff Ulster brogue embellished his rock-solid air of self-assurance. No wonder Mrs D was putty in his hands. Eugh, perish the thought.

'And will you be wanting any laundry done?' Mrs Daniels asked with a smile. 'I'll put a load on tonight.'

'No, you're all right, sweetheart, I'm just taking my cousin here out for a cup of tea and I'll be home and tucked up in bed before ten. Been a long day. Come on then, Lana, let's hear all your news.'

Cousin? Christ.

Within three minutes they were waiting to be served at the bar of the Fox and Vivian, now teeming with pre-Christmas revellers.

'I wasn't going to bother. I was just a bit intrigued,' she said. 'To be honest, I had difficulty remembering who you were.'

'Shagged a lot of fellas in Athens, did you?' he smirked.

'No, that's not what I meant, I—'

'Hey, makes no odds to me, sweetheart,' he said. 'I like a woman who knows what she's doing.' And he looked at her intently over the rim of his beer glass.

She held her own and stared back, refusing to be intimidated.

Go home, Lana, she said to herself. Shouted to herself, even. *Go home now!*

'Right, well, I've got lines to learn. Nice to see you again.' Lana finished her beer and put the glass down on the table. 'Thanks for the drink.'

'Any time. You know where I am.' And he didn't even look at her as she left, just headed to the fruit machine and fed it with a few coins.

Outside in the cold air, Lana could hear the muted music filtering out from the pub and the punters singing that they wished it could be Christmas every day. Lighting a cigarette, she leant back against the wall and thought of a woman she'd read about in a magazine, who really did try to make Christmas a daily event. Ate turkey every day an' everything. Utter madness. But wasn't she, Lana, just as mad herself? What on earth had she been thinking, coming here tonight? She closed her eyes and blew out the smoke, willing her nerves to calm down with every drag.

And suddenly he was there, with that stupid grin again. 'Couldn't quite bring yourself to leave, I see.'

She stubbed out her cigarette, and didn't grin back. 'Yeah, looks that way, doesn't it?'

He nodded – an implicit agreement made silently between the two of them.

And that was that.

Ten minutes later, they'd locked the door of his room at the Collingwood Guest House and were pulling off each other's clothes in frenzied desperation.

Downstairs in her private quarters, Mrs Daniels was oblivious to the reunion taking place in the Kenneth Williams suite above her, currently occupied by the charming Damian Magill, whose flask and Tupperware container she'd just washed and dried ready for re-use tomorrow.

Lana had seen him the following night and the night after that. And on all three occasions it had just been about the sex – they hardly even spoke. As she silently got dressed on the third night, he sat up in bed watching her, smoking, an ashtray balanced in his lap. She waited for him to ask her if she'd be visiting the next night. But he didn't. And in her head she reconciled herself to the fact that this was going to have been three mad nights in her life where she'd lost her footing, lost her mind, and given in to the insanity of this sordid, lust-driven force.

She was almost at the door when he said, 'So you're off home soon then?'

'A week tomorrow, yes.'

'Y'know I'm only back to Belfast for three days over Christmas. Holiday overtime here's too good to turn down.'

'And you're telling me that because . . . ?' She knew exactly why, but she didn't want to give him anything more.

'I'm just sayin'. If you change your mind about going back to your wee fella for the festive season . . .'

'He's not "wee" – and he could give you a run for your money!'

She instantly reddened and was filled with regret, especially when he answered with a patronizing, 'Oh. Sweet.' Then he chuckled before saying softly, 'Hey, come here.'

'No.'

'Come here!' Firmer, but still smiling. And she felt herself being drawn to him again, like a steel pin to a magnet. She walked slowly over to the bed.

'Closer,' he whispered and she obeyed. He put his hand behind her neck and gently pulled her face towards his, kissing her delectably. His kiss, she hated to admit it, was out of this world. Then he took another drag of his cigarette and slapped her on the arse. 'Now run along home and I'll see you tomorrow.'

She stood her ground for a moment. Wanting to tell him where to go, wanting to tell him that this was the last time he would ever see her.

But she knew it wasn't.

And so did he.

19

Catrin

When term had finished she'd agreed to go up to Northumbria and meet Sol's parents for the first time. It was a terrifying prospect – she'd been putting it off for as long as possible, but now she knew there was no escape.

'You *know* why, Sol!' she'd said. 'They'll still be blaming me for Cambridge, won't they!'

'Cat, I promise you, they're fine,' he said, but Cat thought his voice faltered on the word 'fine'.

'Look, you're not going to believe me till you meet them in person, are you? So let's get on and do just that.'

Catrin's own parents hadn't helped put her mind at rest either. When they'd heard the full story about Solomon giving up a medical degree at Cambridge just to be with Catrin, Huw had made that annoying long whistling sound through his teeth and Liz had laughed and said, 'That's a *hell* of a sacrifice, love. I hope you're worth it!'

'Cheers, Mum,' Catrin replied, hurt.

'No, you know what I mean.'

'Hey, we think Sol's a crackin' fella. You know we

do!' her dad chipped in. 'We're *very* happy with him, and your grandmother absolutely idolizes him. But will *his* mum and dad feel the same about *you*, that's all.'

Sometimes Catrin wondered whether her parents were 'the full shilling' as her grandmother used to say. Liz and Huw Kelly were certainly very different from Edward and Amelia Blythe. She'd seen a few framed photos of them in Sol's room, and she knew from what he had told her that they were both quite quiet.

'D'you mean quiet in a shy kind of a way? Or in a sitting-in-judgement-on-me kind of a way?'

'Don't be silly.'

'You can't blame me for being a bit scared, Sol. I don't even think *you're* that convinced yourself,' she said as they sat in his car driving towards Bayfield village and the Blythe family home. He squeezed her hand, but it didn't go unnoticed that he hadn't actually disagreed.

Twenty minutes later, they pulled into the gravel driveway of the double bay-fronted detached Georgian house, and Sol turned off the engine. Without looking at her he said, 'Cat, I didn't want to say this before, because it would've freaked you out and you probably wouldn't have come . . .'

'What? . . .' She looked anxious. 'Sol! What?'

'Well, it's just my mum . . . she can be really shy when she meets new people and sometimes it comes over the wrong way. Like you might think she's ignoring you or being rude.'

'She's going to *ignore* me?'

'It's nothing to worry about. Just, y'know, let her get used to you a bit. She'll come round in the end.' And he got out of the car to avoid discussing it further.

'You make her sound like a rescue puppy!' She struggled with her seatbelt and clambered out of the passenger seat. 'What does "in the end" mean?'

But it was too late. The front door had opened and Dr Edward Blythe stepped out – fifty-two years old, dressed in crisp navy chinos and expensive shoes, his hair thick and silver, his face handsome and clean-shaven. 'You made it!' he said, with what Catrin decided was an air of fake jollity.

'Hi Dad!'

Instead of turning and running like she wanted to, Catrin rustled up a smile, and followed Sol to the porch, waiting whilst he and his father embraced. Catrin was about to follow suit when Edward held out his hand to shake hers, greeting her with a formal 'Delighted to finally meet you, Catrin.'

'Oh yes, hello. Thanks.' *What am I thanking him for?* she thought. And they went inside.

'Your mother's in the kitchen. MEEL?' It was a bit of a shock to hear him shout and Catrin jumped. 'THEY'RE HERE!'

There was no answer.

'You'd better go and see her,' Edward said, motioning down the tastefully decorated hallway to the kitchen, from where several loud bangs were emanating.

Sol rolled his eyes affectionately. 'What's *today*'s project?'

They stopped in the doorway to take in the sight. Doctor Amelia Blythe, her long Jamaican hair in braids tied back in a practical band, looking a decade younger than her fifty-one years, was bent over the kitchen table, sweating profusely, hammer in hand. Spread out over the table was a deconstructed set of drawers. Catrin thought they looked antique and quite fragile. But this didn't seem to bother Amelia, who was bashing the living daylights out of one of the side panels.

'Been bothering me for months. Damn thing's not flush with the rest!' She gave it one more big bang and stood back to admire her work. 'There. That should do it.' Putting the hammer down, Amelia wiped her forehead with a tea towel, before promptly bursting into tears and turning to welcome her youngest son. 'Solomon, Solomon – why d'you stay away so long!'

'Hi Mum!'

And she opened her arms and wrapped him in a big, warm and loving Mama hug. Not once did she look at Catrin.

So Catrin just stood there, mute, nervously twisting the toggle on her anorak until the stupid thing came off and went flying across the room.

'Sorry . . . I'll find it later,' she mumbled to no one in particular.

But Amelia didn't so much as glance in her direction, so intent was she on staring at the beautiful face of her boy, as if she was seeing him for the first time.

Sol didn't seem bothered in the least. *He must be used to it*, Catrin thought.

She hadn't noticed that Edward was standing right behind her, so when he spoke, she jumped again.

'Right, enough of the maternals – let's have a catch-up and some tea.'

Amelia wiped her eyes and headed to the cupboard to take out the cups and saucers.

'Catrin – Indian or China?' asked Edward as he filled the kettle.

'Sorry?'

'Your tea,' he said with a smile. 'Do you prefer Indian or China?'

Catrin was really confused. In her house they just had PG Tips. 'Umm . . .'

'She'll have Indian, Dad. Stop showing off,' said Sol, laughing.

'With lemon or milk?'

'*Dad!*' Sol looked sternly at his father. 'Come on, Cat, let's take our stuff upstairs.'

Once they were on their own in the guest bedroom, Catrin found her voice. 'Sol! This is awful! They hate me!'

'They don't *hate* you, you wally. They're just nervous. Like you are!'

'But your mother has literally not spoken a word to me yet.'

'Look, the thing you've got to understand about my mother is that she is one hundred per cent lioness. She may be a grown-up doctor in the week, saving lives and diagnosing illnesses, but when it comes to her boys she's a freak. She would literally kill to protect us.'

'This isn't helping, Sol.'

Sol cupped her face in his hands. 'You love me, don't you?'

'Stupid question.'

'Well, that's the only qualification you need, in my mother's eyes. And I've never had a proper girlfriend before, so from her point of view she's no longer the only woman in her baby boy's life. Ask my brother Tom – my mother's hated all his girlfriends.'

'Great!'

'For the first hour, that's all,' he laughed and kissed her. 'Now, you know we'll have to sleep in separate rooms, don't you?'

'God, of course! There's no way I could sleep in the same bed as you in this house – even if they didn't mind. And don't be sneaking in at night – I'll have a heart attack!'

'Can't promise that, I'm afraid,' and he started kissing her neck.

'SOLOMON! TEA!' yelled his mother from downstairs, and Catrin froze, firmly believing that she and Sol would never have sex ever again.

She need not have worried, of course. Sol was right. They'd been drinking tea in the little lounge – or breakfast room as the Blythes referred to it – and Catrin had been so nervous that the saucer rattled every time she put her cup back down. She was busting for a wee but was too scared to ask, since Sol was deep in conversation with both his parents, answering a slew of questions about the course, chatting in a flurry of medical jargon. She couldn't find a suitable time to interrupt, but knew she had to.

'So sorry, but can I use the toilet?' she burst out, and all three turned to look at her.

'The lavatory? Of course,' said Edward. 'Second door on the left.'

Catrin clumsily put down her cup and saucer, thinking it was the worst cup of tea she'd ever tasted, and headed out to the loo.

As she sat there, she wondered whether she'd made a big mistake in coming, but decided to trust Sol. After all, they were his parents. He knew what they were like. She washed and dried her hands, noticing the expensive hand wash and the pristine, neatly folded towel. This place was a world away from what she'd grown up with and she suddenly felt overwhelmingly homesick. Fighting back an unexpected desire to cry, she opened the toilet door and nearly jumped out of her skin. Standing there, arms folded and waiting, was Amelia.

'So,' she said, and Catrin wondered what she could possibly have done wrong.

'Sorry?'

'My son tells me you are the love of his life.'

'Oh . . . did he?'

'Is he the love of yours?'

'Gosh, yes. I mean, I . . . I love the absolute bones of him, Mrs . . . Dr Blythe. And his face and his hands and his soul and everything! And his heart and, well, *all* of him. Every last drop.'

Amelia stared for a moment, which felt to Catrin like an hour, then she narrowed her eyes. 'Anyone who hurts my boy hurts me a hundred times more. You understand that?'

'But I don't want to hurt Solomon,' she said, confused. 'Why would I want to hurt Solomon?'

And suddenly Amelia was laughing – the glorious Jamaican cackle that Sol had gone on about so much. And Catrin was laughing too, and before she knew it, she was enveloped in Amelia's arms and being rocked back and forth. 'Welcome to the family, little Cat.'

20
Judith

Patricia answered the door wearing an ill-fitting nylon dress in emerald green, her hands and neck bedecked with costume jewellery. *She looks like a Christmas tree*, thought Judith. They gave each other an awkward, unenthusiastic gesture of a hug – *because it's Christmas*. But seeing as Judith and Patricia never did hugs, it was more of a feeble tap on the back.

Inside, they exchanged gifts. Judith had bought Patricia a wooden banana tree and a yoghurt maker – in the hope that she might embrace some healthy living in the New Year. Not that she'd ever seen her mother eat either a banana *or* a yoghurt, but there was always a first time. Patricia, on the other hand, had bought her daughter a highly inappropriate T-shirt that said *Get your hands on this hot pair* and a Boots voucher for twenty quid, which was at least useful, if uninspired.

An hour later, they were sat eating Christmas lunch in Montgomery Hall – a hotel considered to be the poshest in Coed Celyn. This had been a family tradition of sorts, since Judith was ten. Of course, last year there'd been three of them. And Judith felt a lump in her throat when she wondered where George was eating *his* Christmas lunch this year. She entertained a secret fantasy that he'd gone back to Cyprus and was spending the day with his family, eating *kourabiedes* and playing *Kounga*, but she'd spoken to Sofia only last week, and depressingly, predictably, she confirmed she'd still not heard from her elusive brother.

'Fetch me some more gravy, darlin',' said Patricia to the young waitress in an oversized Santa hat, 'there's a good girl.'

'Yes, Mrs Harris.'

Watching her go, Patricia's smile dropped and she leant across the table to Judith. 'They don't train them properly any more, you know. In my day, you had to learn silver service.'

Judith looked puzzled, chewing a difficult sprout. '*You?* Trained in silver service?'

'Piece of cake,' said Patricia as another forkful of turkey and mashed potato headed mouthwards, followed by a few more glugs of Blue Nun.

'Go on then, show me,' said Judith, whose relationship with her mother had recalibrated since leaving home. She was no longer intimidated by her and in fact often relished winding her up, catching her out in little fibs and tall tales, such as claiming she could speak Welsh or that she'd once met Princess Margaret.

'Don't be ridiculous! What d'you think I am, a performing duck?'

'It's *seal*, Mother – performing *seal*.'

The waitress returned and began ladling gravy over Patricia's overcooked turkey.

'Don't hold back, kid.'

Judith watched the glee on Patricia's face as she eyed up the meal before her. *She's like a child, really*, she thought.

When Mr Perry the hotel manager approached their table on his rounds, Patricia launched immediately into flirtation mode, fazing him with double entendres and unashamed sycophancy, all the while unaware that a piece of sage and onion stuffing was hanging from her chin.

Once they'd eaten their Christmas pudding, Judith sought an appropriate moment to suggest it was time to leave. Having long since learned the pattern of her mother's drinking, and judging by how much Blue Nun she'd already consumed, Judith knew that Patricia would soon revert to type and start to snipe, to pick, to luxuriate in sarcasm. The default Patricia would begin to emerge. The great thing these days, though, was that once the switch had been flicked, Judith could walk away. She didn't have to put up with it any more.

So she ordered a taxi and dropped her mother back home. Duty done. She made sure Patricia was OK, poured her a large whisky and selected something on the telly from the *Radio Times*, knowing that in half an hour's time her mother would be snoring away to the soundtrack of a family favourite.

It was nearly three o'clock when she shut the door

behind her and headed out into the Christmas Day quiet of the Coed Celyn streets. It would soon start getting dark, but the cloudless sky and winter sun yielded more light than was usual for the time of year. She headed for Griffin Park, to sit on the swings until it was time to wander over to wait outside Lipton's, where she'd arranged to meet Lyndon at four thirty.

They'd had five dates so far, including the office party a month previously. Carol, the office manager at Stats Services, had chosen the Travellers Rest as the venue for their annual bash because she'd left it too late to book anywhere else, and the only available date was November 25th. The whole place was geared up for big numbers, putting on a Christmas 'night out to remember' for a hundred office workers, few of whom actually knew each other or even shared the same employer. But hey, what did it matter? *It's Christmas!*

Judith had decided to stay sober that night. So she couldn't even blame the drink when 'Three Times A Lady' came on and she found herself slow-dancing with Lyndon the trombonist. She'd kissed him at the end of the night – a perfectly nice, perfunctory kiss that didn't send her pulse racing or leave her desperate for more. Nonetheless, when he'd asked if he could see her again, she'd agreed. Because, why not? She liked him, he was clever and funny and not bad looking and, who knows, maybe the fireworks were poised, ready to go off, and were just waiting for someone to set them alight.

He'd invited her to his sister's for Christmas tea and,

although she really liked Lyndon, she felt guilty that she'd only agreed to this out of desperation for somewhere to stay. She'd much rather cwtch up on the sofa at the flat and read a good book, or watch some crappy video, but that was out of the question: Lana was only home for two days, and Judith had thought it best to give her and Gareth some privacy. So she'd taken up Catrin's offer to stay at the Kellys' on Christmas Eve, and Lyndon's invitation for Christmas night.

On the previous morning, as she'd packed her bag in readiness for the sleepovers, Gareth had teased her about her new boyfriend. 'I just didn't realize you and him were, y'know . . .'

'We're not.'

'Yet . . . ?' He grinned.

Judith zipped up her bag and looked at her watch. 'Anyway, I better get on, still got a few presents to wrap . . . I've left yours under the tree,' she said. 'It's nothing special.' And she wasn't lying. What should she buy the boyfriend of her best friend, who she wouldn't normally buy anything for, but felt obliged to because they'd both been unexpectedly thrown together as flatmates? She'd settled for socks. And a king-size Toblerone.

'Got me anything nice then, Judi-moo?' It was an innocent, playful remark, but it stopped her in her tracks.

'What d'you call me?' she stammered.

'Judi-moo . . .' His smile faltered. 'Sorry, I was only messin' . . .'

'No, it's fine. It's just that's what my dad used to call me.'

'Never! Great minds, eh?!' he replied, trying to make light. 'You must've told me that sometime, I suppose.'

'No. No, I didn't.' And she smiled. 'But it's fine. I don't mind.'

'Here y'go!' he said, disturbing her reverie and handing her a large, badly wrapped box. 'You may as well open it now. Save you carrying it round everywhere.'

She stood gawping, completely blindsided.

'Go on then, you fool!' he said with a grin.

She did as she was told, ripping off the cheap paper, getting ready to laugh at some daft present he'd bought her.

Except the gift inside was far from daft.

'It's secondhand, but it's a good one. And the guy said any problems you can take it back and he'll sort it.'

Judith was lost for words. She opened up the box, removed the polystyrene packing and gently lifted out the contents: an Olympus OM10 camera, cold and weighty in her hands, accompanied by a proper leather case and strap.

'There's a couple of films in there too. Get you started.'

Judith kept looking down. She knew if she looked up, or if she spoke, she would cry. The camera was beautiful. But that's not what touched her, not even the generosity of such a gift – despite it being second-hand, it would not have been cheap. No, it was the thoughtfulness that had gone into choosing it – thinking about something that *she* would have loved.

A little thrown by Judith's lack of response, Gareth carried on, 'Lana mentioned you used to take photos. But your camera got nicked on a ferry or something?'

Judith nodded. It was all she could manage, focusing all her energy on handling the camera in her hands, feeling its heft and textures and the craftsmanship that had gone into this small yet substantial apparatus. But no matter how hard she blinked, she couldn't hold back the tears.

'It's from Lana too, by the way,' he added, unaware that she was crying. 'Not that she's seen it, just said she'd go halves, like – Hey! You all right, mate?'

A big fat teardrop had landed on the lens cap.

'Sorry, sorry . . .' she mumbled, choking on emotion. 'It's just so . . . Sorry.' She tried clearing her throat and ended up having a coughing fit, resulting in Gareth having to pound her back three times and fetch her water. Which was so humiliating, but at least it was a diversion.

Eventually, when she'd gathered herself together, she was able to thank him properly and tell him what a brilliant present it was and to please thank Lana, though she would do it herself, of course, when she saw her next.

'When will that be, by the way?' asked Judith, glad of the change of subject.

'Well, unless you catch her tomorrow, who knows?' said Gareth with a laugh. 'She promised she's gonna make it down for New Year's Eve after the show, but we all know what Lana's promises are like.'

Two weeks previously, Lana had suddenly announced that she'd found herself a last-minute job in Guildford and would only manage a flying visit home at Christmas. Judith was aware there'd been a few heated phone calls between her and Gareth since. Understandably Gareth was hurt by Lana's change of plans, but then Lana *was* incredibly ambitious – *and* she liked earning cash, so it all made sense on a practical level, just not on an emotional one. Judith secretly vowed to remain neutral in the whole thing – not so much because she didn't want to take sides, but because she was worried that she would. And the last thing she wanted was to jeopardize her friendship. With either of them.

Once inside Griffin Park, she watched the sun heading for bed, its rays bathing all they touched in a diminishing tangerine light. It was a stunning evening. And here she was, alone, on Christmas Day, sitting on a swing in the deserted playground where she'd spent many hours as a child.

Cut the self-pity, Judith Harris, she said to herself, and reached inside her bag to take out her fabulous, deeply cherished camera. She'd already taken a few photos that morning – Catrin and Sol making Christmas pancakes and mess in the Kellys' kitchen. She'd got a fabulous shot of them both, faces covered in flour and Cat in hysterics.

Over on the park railings, a robin was singing his heart out now, his chest all puffed out and brave. Judith smiled to herself as she lined him up in her viewfinder, zooming in tight on his bright little eyes and the magical violet line that ran between his red breast and brown feathered body. *Click*. She loved the sensation of pushing down on the chrome button and activating the shutter. She loved the sound and feel of the heavy, velvety action, as it slowly released beneath the pressure of her finger. And there it was. A moment captured in time, never to be revisited.

'Judith?'

The voice startled her – so unexpected in the solitude of the empty park. And yet the ring of familiarity in its tone made her heart want to leap out from her chest.

She turned around.

And there he was.

She could barely say his name.

'Dad?'

The only place open at four o'clock on Christmas Day in Coed Celyn was, ironically, Montgomery Hall. How Patricia would seethe, would *explode*, if she could see them now, huddled in the corner of the residents' lounge on two big armchairs, sharing a pot of tea.

It had taken a good couple of minutes' worth of staring before Judith could believe her eyes. She kept squeezing his arms, checking he was really there. He'd grown a beard, and he was thinner, but yes, this was definitely, most certainly, without doubt, her beloved dad, Georgios Andreas Charalambos.

'I didn't buy you anything,' he said. 'I thought you prefer money.' And he took out a wad of notes, which he thrust at her.

'Dad, I don't want money from you – *this* is the best Christmas present I could ever have! Seeing you!'

'Take it. Please.'

Reluctantly she took it. Two hundred pounds. 'It's too much,' she said.

'No. It's nowhere near enough. For what I've put you through. It's nothing.'

Judith shook her head, 'Dad – I'm *glad* you went, don't you see? Of course I miss you – but I want you to be happy.' She hesitated. 'You *are* happier, aren't you?'

And George just smiled in response.

He'd driven down from Scotland early Christmas Eve, and was staying in a cheap motel five miles away. When he'd seen her leave Patricia's house on her own, he'd followed her to the park.

'I was frightened you would be angry. Tell me to go away,' he said.

'You're mad. Why on earth would I do that?'

He smiled and took a big gulp of tea, as if seeking courage in its warmth. He paused for a moment and gathered his thoughts. 'Judi-moo, there's something I need to tell you. Something you don't know about me,' he said, unable to look her in the eye.

She couldn't bear to see him suffer and quickly

interrupted him. 'No, Daddy, *I* need to tell *you* something first,' she said quietly.

But George was so focused on getting his words out that he didn't really hear what she said. He'd been gearing up to telling her, to facing this moment, for months – for years, in fact – and he carried on talking, determined to confess.

'You see, when I was young, when I lived in Cyprus—'

She took his hand. 'You lived in a little village called Kakopetria, in the Troodos Mountains . . .'

'Yes . . .' George's confusion grew as she continued.

'And you had a sister called Sofia and *proxenia* with Cleoniki who you were betrothed to, but you came to Wales for work and you met Patricia, and you fell in love, and so you couldn't go back.'

She paused for a moment, letting him absorb her words. 'I saw your letter. Sofia showed me,' she said, tears now hurtling down her cheeks. 'It's OK, Dad,' she said gently, taking his hand. 'I know your story.'

He wiped his eyes on his jacket sleeve and cleared his throat. 'No, Judi-moo. I'm afraid you don't know all of it.'

21
George

The boarding house had been recommended by Louis, one of the boys on the site. A four-storey, fifteen-bedroom terraced house, Ty Marshfield had in its day been home to a wealthy coal magnate; now patched up and badly maintained, it was a shadow of its former glory.

'Cheap and cheerful, mate, and they do a cracking full English,' said Louis.

It was certainly cheap – which was fine by him. The more he saved, the quicker he'd be on that flight back home. To Cleo. To his family. To daily sunshine and olive groves, souvlakia and backgammon, which all seemed now like a lifetime away.

The house was a stone's throw from Newport's east bank of the River Usk, with its thick swathes of black mud always threatening to swallow him up, and a sky that seemed permanently overcast. He had the smallest and cheapest room in the house (his choice), up on the top floor with a little window that didn't shut properly. His single, utilitarian bed was made up with Bri-Nylon sheets. A chest of drawers and a chair were the only other furnishings, apart from a small electric fan heater that yielded little warmth. The bathroom was a cold walk down the linoleum-covered landing and was shared with three others. Downstairs at the back of the house was an optimistically described 'residents' lounge' – a small living area comprising a tired three-seater sofa, a red Formica fold-up table for card games, two hard-backed chairs and an ancient black and white television, which was chained to the wall to prevent theft.

During the week several other contractors from the building site stayed there too, and George had formed a couple of lightweight acquaintances – had even been to the pub on a few occasions to play darts with Jim from Leicester and Mike from Lytham St Annes. But on Friday nights they all scuttled back to their various homes scattered around the country, leaving him alone at Ty Marshfield. So on Saturday and Sunday mornings, he'd often be the only resident taking breakfast in the gloomy basement dining room.

And that's when they'd first started talking.

Her name was Patricia. He'd watched the other men flirt their way through their bacon and eggs, and he'd noticed the confidence with which she handled them – giving as good as she got, enjoying the attention and cutting it dead whenever it went too far. Louis said he 'wouldn't mind a bit of that' if the opportunity came his way, but the wedding ring she wore on her left hand warded off even the most blatant attempts at seduction.

Although he never joined in with their lads' humour,

he wasn't blind to what they saw in her: the brunette hair whisked up into a carefully constructed beehive, her plump crimson lips and feline brown eyes, the sexy gap between her teeth and her throaty laugh that always made anyone she spoke to feel like she was their closest friend. She was older than him – early thirties, maybe. And she knew she had a good figure, wearing impractical but elegant skirts and stiletto heels that showed off her slender ankles and tiny waist, and blouses that hugged her glorious bust. He'd only made polite conversation with her in the three weeks since he'd arrived, but on this particular Saturday morning he'd looked her in the eye for the first time.

Because he was the only resident that day, she'd cooked for him herself – giving Len the owner and breakfast chef a much-wanted day off. It was certainly a bigger feast than the usual weekday fare, with double egg and bacon and a hefty slice of black pudding.

But he wasn't alone in the breakfast room.

A small girl – aged about five or six – was sitting quietly at a corner table with a colouring book and crayons. She didn't look at him when he came in, engrossed in finishing her picture of an elephant, a small frown on her forehead all the while.

When Patricia breezed in with a pot of tea and milk jug, the little girl looked up.

'Don't be bothering Mr Harris now, you. Let him eat his breakfast in peace.'

She put down the tea. 'She's mine,' she said. 'Name's Judith. Had to bring her with me today.'

George smiled at the little girl, who didn't smile back.

That afternoon, the three of them were sat on the Eastern Promenade at Porthcawl, eating ice-creams and staring out across the Bristol Channel. *She's just a friend,* he thought. A friend with a small child. He wouldn't have agreed to go on this outing had she not explained that she was widowed. Her husband had died when she was expecting little Judith, she said, but she kept the wedding ring on 'to ward off unwelcome attention'.

'Am I unwelcome attention?' he asked, the words tumbling out before he'd had a chance to think. *Was he actually flirting?*

'I'm not sure yet,' she replied. And winked at him.

After that their days out became a regular occurrence. Judith always tagged along, and quickly began to warm to George with his 'funny voice'. He took them to St Fagans folk museum in Cardiff, where Judith played in the gypsy caravan and marvelled with him at the little row of terraced miners' cottages 'through the ages'. Patricia was happy for him to entertain her young charge whilst she took the weight off her feet and enjoyed a ciggy break. Butlin's at Barry Island was another special treat, as were Penscynor Bird Gardens and Dan-yr-Ogof Caves. And these trips were mutually beneficial: George had company at weekends, and Patricia enjoyed free childcare, along with the companionship of a handsome Greek Cypriot.

One Sunday morning, as she served him his porridge, she said, 'Would you like to come for afternoon tea today? Me and Judi'll bake some scones.'

He thought a baked stone might be hard to digest but he said yes anyway – he'd not seen the inside of anyone's actual home since arriving in the country that summer, and being November it was getting too cold for excursions.

Patricia and Judith lived a twenty-minute bus ride away in a strangely named town called Coed Celyn. 'It's Welsh for Holly Wood!' she'd told him with a throaty laugh as he'd written down her instructions for getting there.

When she opened the front door, he noticed she was dressed up more than usual, wearing fishnet stockings under a knee-length crepe dress. Her lipstick looked darker, her hair seemed fuller, and instead of her usual stilettos, she wore fluffy kitten-heel slippers.

'Welcome!' she said, and invited him to follow her along the dark corridor and down the steps that led to her basement flat. 'This is us!' she declared as she pushed open the door.

The bay window at the end of the room looked out on to a wall three feet away and steps that led up to the pavement. Only a meagre amount of outside gloom crept in, hindered even further by the sad grey nets.

Patricia switched on a standard lamp and said, 'Take your coat off, make yourself at home.'

The room was modestly furnished but it was cosy at least, and the two-bar heater in the fireplace radiated some warmth. In the corner a small round table had been covered in a crisp white cloth and adorned with three large doily-covered plates piled high with sandwiches, a jam sponge and a pyramid of scones.

Patricia headed to the kitchen to put the kettle on, shouting to Judith on her way, 'Don't be hiding in the bedroom, young lady! Come and say hello to George.'

Feeling out of place, he perched on the edge of the sofa as if he was in a dentist's waiting room.

'I'm wearing my best dress,' said a little voice, and he turned to see Judith in the doorway, resplendent in a fuchsia party frock tied in a bow at the back.

'My! A princess!' he said.

There was silence for a moment, and from the kitchen the shrill whistle of the kettle pierced the air.

'I've brought you a present,' he said. 'It's a jigsaw.'

Judith had never seen one before, and he tipped the contents of the box out on to the floor.

'We have to put this pieces together, see, and make picture of this roundabout. It's a magic roundabout!'

Judith was delighted, and set about the task immediately.

'We start with the corners.'

When Patricia came back in with tea on a tray, Judith and George were silently and industriously piecing the jigsaw together.

'Right, tuck in!' she said in a jolly voice that didn't quite suit her, and he helped himself to a salmon paste sandwich.

*

Later on, Patricia told him that Maisie upstairs had offered to babysit so that they could go to the pictures. 'If you fancy it, that is?'

He was thrown by the sudden change of dynamic: two of them, not three.

Before he had a chance to answer, Judith said, 'I want to come.'

'Well, you can't,' her mother snapped.

'I want to see *Digby: The Biggest Dog in the World*!'

'Well, you can't!' Patricia repeated. 'George is taking Momma to see a film about spies, aren't you, George?'

He felt torn. He hated to upset the child, but how could he say otherwise? 'Maybe we all three see *Digby* next week?'

Little Judith wasn't a sulker. Even aged six she'd learned to live with disappointment and she simply nodded. 'OK.'

Despite the fact that he'd seen the film before, they went to the ABC and watched *Live and Let Die*. On the way out of the cinema, Patricia took his arm and bombarded him with chat – mainly about Roger Moore and how much better he was than Sean Connery and how creepy that voodoo funeral scene was. She only stopped chatting when they reached her doorstep. They'd never had a farewell like this before – there'd always been an unacknowledged chaperone in the form of little Judith.

'Well, goodnight then!' he said as he watched her walk up the steps to the front door.

She turned to him, her voice quieter now. 'Judith's staying the night at Maisie's. We won't be disturbed.'

'Oh.'

Half an hour later she was sat astride him on the sofa, her crepe dress hoisted up over her stocking tops and the suspenders that held them in place. He was out of his depth, falling, unable to resist and common sense failing to prevail.

'I have no . . . I have nothing with me for . . .'

'Don't worry, Georgie,' she whispered in his ear. 'Everything's taken care of.'

The sensation of her breath on his skin made him shudder. She was clearly more experienced than him, grabbing his hands and running them along her fleshy thighs. 'You like?' she asked breathlessly.

'I like,' he whispered back, concentrating hard, willing himself not to surrender. This was only the third time he'd ever had sex in his life and her prowess made him feel even more unworldly. She undid the buttons at the front of her dress, releasing her fulsome breasts, barely contained by her well-upholstered bra. Leaning forward, she put her hand beneath his chin and kissed him fully on the mouth. It was all too much for him and he gave in, shivering, and cursing himself in Greek. He couldn't look at her. Felt ashamed. For what he'd done and for what he'd failed to do.

Patricia smiled at him, leant over and took a cigarette from the packet. 'Don't worry,' she said, lighting up. 'We'll have a little ciggy break and go in for round two!'

It wasn't a love affair. He was mesmerized by her, drawn to her, but he didn't love her. Even though in the throes of their regular sex she'd say, 'Do you love me, Georgie?' and he'd always reply, 'Yes,' which only added to his guilt. The image of Cleo would creep into his mind and he'd shut his eyes in shame. *What was he doing?*

Now that the status of their relationship had changed, the dynamic between them in public was also different. Whereas Patricia had previously been jolly and friendly to him, treating him like all the other contractors in the breakfast room, she'd recently taken to mocking him, or blatantly ignoring him, leaving him wondering what he'd done to annoy her. It could be the smallest thing, like failing to tell her she'd looked nice the night before, or yawning in her company. It was exhausting. And soul-destroying. George was on rocky, uncertain ground and continually stumbling.

She took it for granted that he'd spend Christmas Day with them at the flat. After lunch he played *Mousetrap* with Judith, before settling down to watch the Queen's speech, Patricia curled up next to him on the sofa. To all intents and purposes, the three of them looked like the perfect family unit. But she was steadily getting more drunk on whisky, and by the time *Billy Smart's Circus* started she was a little worse for wear. A chance remark he'd made about the Queen and

British rule in Cyprus seemed to have riled her. 'You don't like our head of state, Sonny Jim, sod off home!'

Like a puppy sensing negative energy, Judith got up quietly and left the room to lie on her bed. George, in turn, realized that his presence was only going to annoy Patricia even more, so he got up too.

'Where d'you think you're going?' she said.

'I'm sorry,' he stammered. 'Thank you for lovely day.'

He felt helpless leaving Judith behind when Patricia was in this mood, but it was the lesser of two evils. As he headed out of the front door, a barrage of insults followed in his wake.

Nothing was open. Not even a pub. And it was getting dark. He had no option other than to head back to Newport by foot along the deathly quiet streets. There were no buses and barely a passing car to offer him a lift. Any that *did* go past didn't stop.

Three hours later, he arrived back at Ty Marshfield, let himself into his tiny room, lay on his bed and wept. By the time dawn broke on Boxing Day morning, George had made the decision. He was going home.

He expected there to be tears when he broke the news. But he didn't expect so many.

And then she told him.

She was eight weeks gone. There was no doubt.

As he stood in front of the registrar, listening to him spout forth a stream of words he didn't really understand, all

George could think about was Cleoniki. And what *their* wedding would have been like – exchanging the *stefana*, dancing, flowers, delicious Greek food, sunshine and love. Love. There was no love in this room. And it was his fault entirely. He was a weak man. A weak, weak man.

He turned and looked at Patricia. She knew nothing of Cleo or his life in Cyprus. He'd wanted to keep it secret, keep it sacred and unsullied. But now it didn't matter anyway. Because he would never be going back there. He'd made his choice and sealed his fate the day he gave in to his sordid desires. Once the letter to his sister Sofia was written and posted to Cyprus, he erased the past from his mind and accepted that this life was his new life.

'I do,' Patricia said and gave him the most winning of smiles. She was blooming. The blushing bride, in a fur-trimmed velvet suit she'd hired from a shop in Cardiff, with little Judith standing next to her, a confused but willing bridesmaid who had no idea of what was really going on. Maisie from upstairs was a witness, along with Len from the boarding house, and afterwards they all went to a Berni Inn for lunch. George paid.

There was no honeymoon. Patricia wanted to spend their money (*his* money, his savings for Cyprus) on a deposit for a small house she'd seen in Victoria Road. She'd already found herself a new job in a nearby hotel, as well as a job for George on an assembly line in the local factory. She seemed to have it all worked out.

When George handed in his notice at the site, the foreman was sorry to see him go. 'You're a good worker, George,' he said. The boys had all clubbed together and given him ten quid as a wedding present. 'You'll be needing it to pay for the nappies,' they'd laughed. And he'd laughed too. But inside he was crushed. He walked around in a daze, unable to process the speed with which everything was happening. It was a living nightmare and he felt permanently sick.

They moved in quickly. Patricia, glad to see the back of her dingy little flat, had splashed out on new furniture, all bought 'on tick'. George became more and more subsumed by the horror of it all. Sinking into debt, sinking into infinite sorrow. His only saving grace was little Judi-moo, who he'd grown to love as his own, who kept sharing her excitement about their new house with its little back yard and the hills in the distance. And how much she loved her new, bigger bedroom and how she wanted to invite her little school friends Lana Lloyd and Catrin Kelly over to the house to play. It was a fresh start for them all. Their little family of three, soon to be four.

When she told him she'd miscarried, all he could think was, *So I did not need to marry you. I did not need to marry you.* But it was too late. Because now he'd promised, till death did them part, to remain by her side. Shackled to a woman he didn't love.

He felt ill. Ashamed and trapped.

Serves you right, Georgios, he thought.

*

It was five more years before he learned the truth. A chance remark, a lazy mistake, a friend of a friend passing comment on past events and there it was – the revelation. That there never had been a baby in the first place.

He'd always questioned her honesty. Little examples of little white lies, which built and grew until he was witness to her downright deceit. So when he discovered she'd lied about the pregnancy, it didn't surprise him. He'd grown to hate her, then grown to be indifferent. And yet still he stayed. As if he must pay the price, endure his penance, be punished for his sins. For all these years.

It was only when Judith had confirmed the date she was leaving for her travels that he knew – instantly – that that was when he would finally go. He applied for a job in Aberdeen, handed in his notice and swore his boss to secrecy; stashing his cash in his locker at work, he put together a small holdall of essentials along with a change of clothes. And on 5 August 1986, George Andrew Harris walked out through the factory gates of BDE Electronics, never to return. He wrote a short note to Patricia, which he put in the post on his way to the bus stop. It simply said:

Patricia
I cannot live with you any more.
I wish you well.
I am starting a new life in Scotland.
Please be kind to the cats and tell Judith I am sorry.
Best wishes
George

He left Coed Celyn and didn't look back.

The next morning a postcard from Crete arrived for him at the factory office signed by someone called Judimoo. George's old boss glanced at it briefly, before throwing it into the wastepaper bin.

22

Lana

She'd *said* the job was a great opportunity, something solid to put on her CV for when she left college. In truth, she was no more than a second-rate kids' entertainer, selling ice-creams and sweets in the interval and silly hats and glow-in-the-dark wands, whilst dressed up as a space alien. Hardly a foot on the West End theatre ladder. But she knew Gareth would know no different, nor would anyone else back home, and if she accepted the job it would mean she could stay in Guildford longer and see *him* every night.

She couldn't bear saying his name. That made it sound like a relationship. He was an addiction. A compulsion. Sex with him was exceptional. It was angry, powerful, insanely erotic and so, so shamefully good. What's more, it was available to her nightly. Try as she might to say no, to promise herself every morning that today would be different, she would still find herself turning up at the pub every evening, to be barely acknowledged and taken back to his room to fuck, not speak – other than the commands he firmly issued during sex – and then leave again. Her dignity was shattered, destroyed by this burning, inexplicable need that ran riot inside her.

On the one occasion when she'd opened up to him, complaining that she couldn't go on like this – that the guilt was too much – he'd just brushed it aside with his usual disinterest and unemotional nonchalance. 'Makes no odds to me, sweetheart. You want out? There's the door.'

It's a stupid fling, it'll pass, she kept telling herself, and focused on seeing Gareth again. But when she came home for her two nights off at Christmas, they spent most of the time either arguing or not speaking, which made the prospect of returning to Guildford even more attractive than it was already.

The worst row was on Christmas night, when Gareth accused *her* of being miserable and up herself, and she accused *him* of being parochial and unambitious. He told her he wasn't ashamed of being unambitious, and had no idea what 'parochial' even meant – and that using words like that just proved his point about her being a poncey actress. They didn't speak for half an hour, separated from each other in different rooms, until eventually Gareth came and sat next to her, took her hand and said softly, 'It's Christmas Day, for God's sake. Let's go to bed.' And she relented.

They made love that night, the first time in weeks – gentle and faltering and sweet, so different from sex with Damian Magill. And Lana loathed herself for making comparisons, but the truth was that she yearned for the Belfast builder to be fucking her instead. *What had happened to her?* When she shut her eyes she couldn't get him out of her head, so she kept them open and stared at Gareth the entire time.

And when it was over Lana cried silently. 'I'm sorry I'm such a God-awful bitch,' she whispered, turning away from him in bed so he couldn't see her tears.

'Hey, bit heavy, isn't it, babe?' he said, stroking her hair.

'It'll be all right once I've got through my first year,' she lied.

'You work too hard, y'know. You shouldn't have taken this job.'

'I know. I really wish I hadn't.'

They lay in silence for a while and then he said, 'Don't go back tomorrow. Stay.'

She felt herself go cold inside. 'I can't.'

'Why not?'

She didn't answer him. She daren't.

'OK, then I'll come back with you. I'm off till third of Jan. I could.'

'*No!*' she snapped.

'Larn?'

'It's just it would be pointless,' she said, desperate to calm the giveaway agitation in her voice. 'I do three shows a day, Gar, I'd be at the theatre all the time!'

'I know, but we'd get to sleep together,' he whispered, snuggling into her neck.

She had to stop this in its tracks. 'Look, I've messed up. You're absolutely right, I shouldn't have taken the job, but I did, and it's a lesson learned, and I promise you, come Easter, I won't be taking any stupid holiday jobs in Guildford, OK?'

'If this is just a stupid holiday job, why go back?'

And over the edge she went, pushing him away and clambering out of bed. 'That attitude is exactly the difference between you and me, Gareth – I'm committed to my career, you haven't even got one.' And she grabbed her things and headed for Judith's room, which was thankfully vacant.

Gareth shouted after her, 'You're pathetic!'

She lay there, in Judith's bed, staring at the ceiling, contemplating how this sordid mess had affected not only her relationship with Gareth, but also her friendship with the girls. They'd barely been in touch since the *Guys and Dolls* weekend and this Christmas she wasn't going to see them once. That hadn't happened in all the years they'd known each other. And it was entirely her fault. Drifting off to sleep that night, she was full of remorse and shame and anger.

An hour later, she was woken by a short scream and the glare of the overhead light, brutal in its brightness.

'Oh my God! What are you doin' there?' exclaimed Judith, standing in the doorway.

Lana shielded her eyes. 'I could ask you the same thing,' she mumbled, still half asleep.

'I'm so sorry, Larn. I know I said I'd stay away tonight, but . . .' Judith's voice petered out and Lana could tell her friend had been crying.

'Hey, babe! What's up?' she said, her voice dry and raspy. 'Come here.'

Judith sat on the bed, forlorn, and Lana put her arm around her shoulders.

'Is it Lyndon the trombonist?'

A quiver of a smile flickered on Judith's lips and she shook her head.

'I've just spent the last three hours with my dad.'

Judith went on to tell Lana all about her surprise meeting with George earlier that day and how he'd told her everything: how his marriage to Patricia was a sham, how she'd conned him into marrying her all those years ago. 'My parents have been lying to me, Larn. For, like, *years*. Both of them! They've *never* loved each other. I mean, I thought Cyprus was bad enough, finding out about Sofia and Cleoniki an' all that. But this? *This?* I've got no fucking idea who I am any more.' And with that she broke down in fresh tears, sobbing like a child as Lana held her tight. She kissed the top of her head and soothed her with gentle words until Judith cried herself to sleep.

That night they topped and tailed like they used to when they were seven, and in the morning Lana brought Judith a cup of tea.

'You look absolutely crap,' said Lana, smiling and smoothing her friend's hair.

'Cheers, mate,' Judith croaked, her voice bashed with emotion. She sipped her tea. 'Hey, you never told me, by the way. How come you were sleeping in my bed?'

'Doing a character study on Goldilocks,' Lana joked, hoping to avoid the inevitable explanation.

But Judith was one step ahead of her. 'What d'you row about this time?' she asked.

'Oh I dunno, Jude. This an' that.' She couldn't face talking about her relationship with Gareth right now. 'Listen, I've got a show at two o'clock. What you gonna do? Will you go to Cat's?'

Judith took the hint. 'Yeah, maybe. I thought about goin' there last night, but I couldn't face the inquisition. And Lyndon is . . . Well, I don't really know him, to be honest. I wasn't about to start confiding in him about my dysfunctional parents.'

'Fair enough,' said Lana. And she hugged her friend. 'Hey, but nice to know George is OK.'

'Yeah. I just can't bear thinking what he must've gone through. Living a lie like that.'

'Wasn't all bad though, was it, babe?' said Lana gently. 'He ended up getting you as a daughter. And that's immense.'

Judith smiled faintly as Lana headed for the door. 'Thanks for being here, Larn. I don't know what I'd do without you and Cat.'

'Best mates, aren't we?' said Lana. 'All part of the job description.'

Outside the room, Lana hesitated, listening to see if Gareth was up and about. Silence. She thought about waking him, telling him Judith's sorry tale. But she couldn't guarantee he'd give her much of a reception, and right now she didn't have the energy for more arguments.

Back in Guildford twelve hours later, she finished the last of the Boxing Day shows and headed back to her deserted student house. On any other day she'd have found it depressing to be there alone, but today she was grateful for the solitude. A chance to just take some time for herself, nurse her wounds and regroup.

She lay in the bath for an hour, topping it up with hot water every now and again, and luxuriating in the Opium bath oil Gareth had bought her.

Christ, what a Christmas.

Everything felt such a mess. Such a bombsite. She could feel tears encroaching but refused to let them come, promptly pulling out the plug and sitting with her arms wrapped around her bent knees till the water drained with one final, adamant gurgle. And then silence. She ought to get dressed and go to the phone box to call home. Check on Jude, make up with Gareth . . . But maybe not tonight. No. She'd do it tomorrow.

Soon the chill on her exposed wet skin prompted her to climb out of the bath. She dried herself and put on her favourite brushed-cotton pyjamas, thick stripy socks and a well-loved cardigan with holes in it. She wanted to feel cosy, wrapped up. Reaching under the bed for her seen-better-days slippers, she found the big painted star given to her by Gareth and Jude when they'd been to see her show. She'd stuffed it away that night, embarrassed by the silliness of the gift. And now she couldn't face looking at it, the guilt was too much.

Padding down to the kitchen, she was relieved that she'd had the foresight to buy butter and a loaf of bread on her way home. This evening was definitely a hot-chocolate-and-toast-in-front-of-the-TV night; a Damian Magill-free night. She felt a wave of relief knowing that he'd still be in Belfast. Maybe going cold turkey for a couple of days would make her stronger. Maybe if she built up enough resistance she could finally knock this whole thing on the head. A tiny spark inside her ignited a small flame of optimism. Tonight was the first night she'd not had a drink in months. And tonight was the first time she'd felt she might be able to give up this awful addiction to this awful man. She smiled and changed channels, hugging her hot-water bottle and taking a big bite of buttered toast.

Five minutes into *EastEnders*, the doorbell rang.

One of her housemates come home early, no doubt. But then why didn't they use their key?

She heaved herself up from the sofa and ambled into the hallway. Still clutching her hot-water bottle, she reached out for the latch and opened the door. Standing there smoking, with a six-pack of beer under his arm, was Damian Magill.

'Nice pyjamas,' he said, smiling.

23

Catrin

'Happy New Year!'

'Yes, Happy New Year!'

'*Blwyddyn Newydd Dda!*'

It was the seventh couple they'd passed coming down the mountain as they were making their way up. And the obligatory New Year's greeting was politely exchanged every time. They thought they'd be the only ones mad enough to climb Pen y Fan on the first morning of 1987, but clearly plenty of others had had the same idea. And they all shared a knowing smile – as if they were part of an elite club, who'd not got drunk the night before and were starting the New Year as they meant to go on, with robust enthusiasm and a spirit of *carpe diem*.

It had been the best Christmas Catrin had ever had. With Edward and Amelia on a cruise to celebrate their silver wedding, Liz and Huw had *insisted* that Solomon join them for the holidays. Sol didn't need asking twice – he loved the Kelly household and had slotted in very easily from the word go. He was quite at home sharing chores with Cat, picking up Grandma Kelly from bingo or the church party, sitting and chatting with Catrin's brother Tom, who described Sol as 'solid'. When it came to sleeping arrangements, Liz and Huw had been surprisingly – and disturbingly – laid back about it. 'You're in a committed relationship!' Huw had said, as if quoting from some self-help manual. 'And we weren't born yesterday, y'know. Me and your mother know a thing or two about rumpy-pumpy, don't we, Liz?' And he'd winked at his wife, and Cat had thought she was going to be sick.

'Well, exactly. You think we don't know what you must be getting up to in Cardiff all term?' said Liz.

'Mum! Stop it! You're so embarrassing!' Though Sol seemed to find the whole thing hilarious.

'But we won't discuss contraception,' continued Liz.

'*No we won't!*' Cat was dying.

'Because, y'know, being Catholic an' all that – well, it's a sin, isn't it? So we'll leave it up to your own consciences.'

'On the other hand,' Huw interjected, 'we don't want to hear the patter of tiny feet *just* yet, do we?'

'Right. Stop it. Subject well and truly closed!' said Catrin, her face burning with humiliation, and she headed upstairs to make up the little sofa bed in the tiny box room, ambitiously referred to as the study.

On Christmas Eve they'd all gone to Midnight Mass, which had been so magical. And despite her best efforts to remain a committed agnostic, Catrin couldn't help but feel an inexplicable euphoria as she queued up to take communion in St Theodore's Church, with the boy she loved alongside her mad but lovely family. She thought how much her friends loved him too. Not that she'd seen much of them over Christmas.

There'd been a couple of festive flies in the seasonal ointment, of course: one was the shocking discovery made by Judith about George, and the other was the tension between Lana and Gareth, especially evident at the Kelly house on New Year's Eve when the couple had spent the whole evening not speaking to each other. Lana had only stayed a few hours, announcing she had to leave early to get back to Guildford for the matinée the next day.

It was still dark outside when Catrin and Sol got up for their New Year's hike and the house was hangover-silent. They packed their rucksack picnic, donned as many warm clothes as they could and headed off, the faint winter sun doing its best to brighten up the icy January morning.

After walking for two miles, they reached the summit. The three-hundred-and-sixty-degree view took their breath away – as did the frost-filled air and the fact that they'd been climbing for over an hour. Sol reached out his hand for Cat's and they stood there in the heavy quiet, taking it all in, the view that stretched for ever all around them. There was no one else there. Just the two of them, snuggled up in woolly hats and gloves and scarves and love.

'Come on,' said Sol, and he led her over to a rock

where they could sit and ponder. 'Shall we have some coffee?' he asked.

'No, I'm OK actually,' she answered, mesmerized by the view.

'A biscuit then,' he carried on, opening the rucksack.

'No, let's wait till we've walked back down, shall we?' she said, as she gazed into the distance.

But Sol had taken out a Tupperware box containing some home-made Welsh cakes. 'Please have one, Cat.'

She looked at him as if he was having a funny turn. 'You OK?'

'Yeah, I just . . . I just want you to have one.'

'But I don't want one, Sol . . .'

He thrust the Tupperware at her again. 'Just, please, for me, just *look* at the bloody Welsh cakes then!' He seemed hugely disappointed. 'Jeez, this is a disaster.'

'What is?' Confused, Cat took the Tupperware and peeled back the lid. Inside, surrounded by half a dozen of the sugar-dusted cakes, lay a small square box loosely attached to the base with some Sellotape. Catrin caught her breath and barely whispered, 'Sol. No!'

'What? Oh my God, how could I have got this all so wrong?'

But Cat was now opening the box. Inside, nestled on a tiny bed of velvet, was the most beautiful ring she'd ever seen – plain silver, adorned with three tiny sapphires. 'No, I meant, *No. I don't believe what you're doing* . . . I think I'm going to be sick.'

'Oh please don't be! Don't be sick!' he panicked, and

took the ring from its little bed. 'Please just say we can get married instead?'

Catrin's vision was blurred from tears and the cold, but inside she was burning with joy. She just wasn't able to speak, that was all.

Sol interpreted this as uncertainty, so on he ploughed, trying to convince her. 'I mean, I know they'll all say we're too young and that we don't know what we're doing and that it's just infatuation and there are so many other people out there still to meet and what about our degrees? But it doesn't need to affect that. We'd just carry on as normal, only we'd be married, we'd be together properly for ever, and we don't need to buy a house or anything and we don't need, well, *anything*, just each other, and oh Cat, I love you so, so much that it . . . look, I . . .'

She waited patiently till his loving rant petered out, then said, 'Oh yes, let's absolutely get married,' and immediately tried taking off her glove so that she could put on the ring. Easier said than done, because it had one of those strap thingies around the wrist which was quite difficult to undo.

'Hang on a minute,' said Sol, helping her remove it – practical now, not romantic. 'That's it.'

Once her hand was free, they both looked down as he slid the ring on to her finger, before staring at each other in disbelief.

'They'll all be so cross,' he whispered, suddenly gripped with uncertainty.

'Yes, they will,' said Cat, reassuring him. 'But that's OK. It won't change my mind.'

'Really?'

'Really.'

They sealed the moment with a gentle, timid kiss.

Then, pulling away from him, Cat said, 'So are we engaged then, Solomon?'

'We're engaged, Catrin.'

And the two of them promptly found their feet, jumped up and down and shouted as loudly as they could to the silent horizon, 'WE'RE ENGAGED! WE'RE ENGAGED!!' And the panorama of hills and fields twinkled back in congratulation.

24

Gareth

Since Lana had gone back to Guildford on New Year's Day, he'd received three silly postcards from her and a handful of phone calls. These contained more silences than conversation, and on two occasions she'd only rung to cancel coming home for the night. It was now early February, and Gareth had started to wonder whether long-distance relationships were always doomed to fail. One evening over a game of pool he tentatively asked Judith for her advice. He worried that she might feel compromised, but she'd insisted she was glad to be a sympathetic ear. 'Least I can do, Gar – the hours you've had to listen to me drone on . . . 'bout my self-centred mother, my non-existent love life . . .'

He laughed. 'It's not non-existent, you idiot.'

'If you're referring to Lyndon the trombonist, well, it transpires he doesn't actually bat for my side, after all.'

'You're kidding!' said Gareth.

'Yep. Told me today in work. One of his New Year's resolutions had been to be honest with everyone, so he finally fessed up. Didn't go down too well with his parents, mind. They haven't spoken to him for a month.'

'Poor bloke.' He took another shot and missed. 'Bollocks. Right, so, what'm I gonna do then? About Lana.'

Judith sighed. 'Oh, I dunno. I reckon you just need to spend more than five minutes together. Why don't you drive up there tomorrow and see her. Take the bull by the horns,' she laughed. 'Not that Lana's a bull.'

'No, and she's not a fan of surprises, neither,' Gareth mumbled.

'Likes a bit of romance though.' Judith smiled back. 'All girls like a bit of romance, Gar. Deep down.' And she struck her cue forcefully against the white, which in turn smashed the red into a corner pocket, exploding a tiny cloud of chalk dust into the air.

The next day, he decided to take Judith's advice and, getting on his bike straight after work, headed for Guildford.

The traffic wasn't too bad and he arrived at her front door just after seven, with a box of orange Matchmakers and a smile. Ringing the doorbell, he felt nervous for some reason. So hyped up he was about seeing her that his heart sank a little when Gerard opened the door, eating a Pot Noodle.

'She's not in,' he said.

'Oh. Rehearsals, is it?' asked Gareth.

'I don't *think* so,' said Gerard sarcastically. 'Otherwise *I* wouldn't be standing here, would I?'

Gareth wanted to grab the Pot Noodle and pour it over Gerard's supercilious head. 'Umm, I don't know,' he said. 'Why not?'

'Because I'm stage managing the show? Evening rehearsals don't start till next week,' sighed Gerard. 'You coming in or what?' And without waiting for an answer he wandered off down the corridor, wolfing down his beef-flavoured rehydrated vegetables as he went and shutting the living-room door behind him.

Which Gareth took as a cue that *he* was meant to go upstairs and wait.

Lana's bedroom was a mess. It didn't surprise him and it made him smile. Gareth himself wasn't the most domesticated, but seeing as he had nothing else to do, he thought he'd tidy up a bit whilst he waited. He made her bed and collected up the dirty mugs, emptied her ashtray and gathered the clothes that she'd dropped all over the room.

By the time he'd finished, an hour had passed and the room looked a lot better. But still no sign of Lana. So he lay on the bed and started flicking through one of her theatre books. He may as well have been reading Japanese, it made no sense to him whatever. He turned his attention to the black and white portable TV he'd found during the clear-up hidden under a coat. Switching it on, he fiddled with the tuner till he found a grainy repeat of *Fawlty Towers*.

By now he was starving. It was getting on for nine o'clock and he daren't disturb Gerard again to ask if he could spare a Pot Noodle, so his only option was to rip into the cellophane and feast on the Matchmakers.

He must have dropped off soon after that, only to

be awoken by a loud scream. Lana had finally arrived home.

'Jesus! Gareth! What the actual fuck!'

'Sorry, babe,' he said, smiling. 'I didn't mean to frighten you.'

'Well, you failed,' she said, catching her breath.

'Didn't Gerard tell you I was here?'

'What? No, he's asleep.' She lit a cigarette, shaking from the shock, and sat on the bed.

'Came to surprise you,' he said, venturing a smile.

'Well, *that* you *did* succeed in doing.'

His plan hadn't had the happy, romantic outcome he'd hoped for. They hardly talked at all other than about college stuff and how full-on this term was turning out to be with rehearsals for *Carousel*. The weird thing was that she never seemed to get over her irritation about him frightening her like that. But even weirder was that she didn't offer an explanation for where she'd been that evening. It felt odd having to ask her, but when he did, she brushed it off.

'Sorry, didn't I say?' she asked vaguely as she got undressed for bed. 'Rehearsals.'

'Oh.'

'What?' She sounded annoyed.

'Well, Gerard said you didn't start the evening rehearsals till next week or something.'

Was there a flicker of doubt in her eyes or did he imagine it?

'Gerard's a bloody prat,' she said, irritated. 'We do back-up singing rehearsals in the evenings. He thinks

205

the world revolves around him – if he's not needed, then it can't be happening. Now shift up and show me what you really came to Guildford for.'

They had sex, but it was quick and uninspiring.

'Sorry, babe,' said Lana. 'I'm just absolutely knackered.'

'Never mind, there's always tomorrow,' he said as they spooned cosily in the single bed. 'I took the day off work so we could spend some time together.'

'Great,' said Lana.

And he decided that the lack of enthusiasm in her voice was another figment of his imagination.

In the morning he took her to college on his bike. She seemed in a better mood than the night before and for the first time in a long while he felt that things might get back on track. He hung around the town centre after he'd dropped her off, visiting a bike shop and a record store. It had been such a long time since he'd taken a day off, he'd forgotten how relaxing it was to just potter.

As arranged, he met Lana for lunch and they went to a new vegetarian café she'd discovered. He hated the food, but loved the company, and by the time he'd taken her back to college, he felt the warm glow that he used to feel whenever he was with her.

They planned to see a film that evening, have hot dogs for tea at the cinema and then an early night. Gareth would have to leave at five the next morning to get back in time for work. He had an hour to kill before picking her up from college at seven, so he headed to the pub for a swift half. *I could get used to this!* he thought, smiling, as he walked through the doors of the Fox and Vivian.

'Finished with the paper, lads?' he asked the two men sitting at the corner table.

'Help yourself,' said one of them, before turning back to his pint and chat.

Gareth looked through the sports pages, disappointed there was no news of Cardiff City's latest away game. Hardly surprising – he was in England, after all. He looked for the crossword and made a start on it. He'd never done crosswords until Judith had moved in. She was addicted to them, and it hadn't been long before he too caught the bug.

The two guys next to him were deep in conversation. He tried not to listen in, but couldn't help being drawn to their accents. One of them sounded a bit like Sol – north-east? – only stronger. And the other – was that Glasgow? No, it was Northern Ireland somewhere. Sounded like Dennis Taylor the snooker guy.

Gareth had been on a roll with the crossword, but was now struggling with one of the clues. *Six down, eleven letters, 'double trouble' – D, blank, blank, L-I-C blank blank blank U-S*. As he pondered the answer, the conversation filtered over from the next table.

'You watch, fella, come seven fifteen she'll be walking through that door. Like clockwork,' the Ulster man was saying. 'She just can't stay away.'

'But night after fuckin' night, man!' said the Geordie. 'It'll drop off, the way you carry on!' And they both laughed.

Gareth looked up for a moment, catching the Irishman's eye and smiling back politely, as if partially in on the joke.

And then it struck him.

The word he was looking for: DUPLICITOUS.

He filled in the blanks, then looked at his watch. He ought to get going, really. He reached for his biker's jacket and got up. 'See you, lads,' he said.

Damian Magill raised his pint glass back at him and carried on talking to his friend.

'She was a bit of a nutter though, Larn, you have to admit. 'Specially that bit with the fork.' They'd been to see *Betty Blue* at the local art-house cinema and were making hot chocolate in the kitchen.

'She wasn't a *nutter*, Gar. Blimey, where's your sympathy? The woman was in emotional turmoil. You want toast?'

'Aye, go on then.' He snuggled up behind her. 'And we'll eat it in bed, is it?'

She turned to him and kissed him softly. 'Thanks for coming, Gar. It's been nice.'

'Yeah.'

There was a knock at the front door.

'I'll go,' he said.

'If it's someone called Zoe, tell her I'm in the bath and don't invite her in. We'll never get rid of her.'

He wandered down the hallway, smiling. When he opened the door, it took a moment for his brain to compute what he saw. The guy on the doorstep looked equally stumped. They both stood in silence for a moment.

Then Damian Magill spoke. 'I was looking for Lana,' he said. 'She didn't show up tonight.'

Gareth's breathing accelerated and he could hear his heart beating in his ears. He stared at the Northern Irishman from the pub, and without dropping his gaze, shouted behind him, 'Lana! Someone to see you!'

He heard her approach but didn't turn round, painfully putting two and two together.

A smile crept slowly across Damian Magill's face. 'Well, this is interesting,' he said, looking over Gareth's shoulder to where Lana was now standing, rooted to the spot.

It was excruciating to hear her desperately try to right the situation unfolding before her, forcing jollity and nonchalance into her shaking voice as she said, 'Oh *hi*, Damo. Have you come for the book?'

'What book?' said Damian Magill, faking confusion.

'This is Damian, Gar,' said Lana, ploughing on and attempting to edge her way past Gareth. 'He's a friend from college and—'

Gareth put up his arm, gently easing Lana back behind him. His voice remained level, despite the adrenalin that was now racing around his system at a pace of knots.

'You fucking my girlfriend, mate?'

Damian Magill stared back at him, grinning.

Behind him Lana carried on, fruitlessly attempting to sustain the lie. 'Gareth! What you talking about? I told you—'

'You gonna answer me, *Damo*?' said Gareth, ignoring her.

'What do you think, Taffy boy?' Damian Magill replied, his grin unfaltering.

Gareth stepped out of the house towards him.

'Gareth, stop it!' shouted Lana, but still he continued.

'I think,' he said calmly, 'that the answer is yes – that you *are* fucking my girlfriend.' And he jabbed hard at Damian Magill's shoulders.

The builder's smile dropped. 'You don't wanna do that, fella.'

'Don't I?' And Gareth pushed him again.

This time Damian Magill responded, taking a swing at Gareth, who ducked in time, coming back himself with a punch, hard in the builder's gut. Damian Magill doubled over and Gareth swung at him again.

'She who you were talking about in the pub, you fucking Paddy bastard? Been seein' her night after night . . . ?'

'GARETH!!' Lana screamed at them both to stop, but her plea went unheeded.

'Yeah, that's right, mate,' said Damian Magill, blood now running from the corner of his mouth, which had curled into a sickening smile. 'And I tell you what, it's true what they say about Welsh girls – absolutely fucking gagging for it!'

Gareth lunged at him again, the rage in his veins spurring him on. But suddenly Damian Magill got the better of him, and within the blink of an eye he'd got Gareth on to the ground.

'She was pretty fucking hot in Athens, you know, but she seems to have got better with time!' And he delivered another punch.

Gareth cried out in agony, 'FUCK!' and the builder took aim again, only to be caught out by a blow to the back from Lana, who was brandishing a golfing umbrella she'd grabbed from inside the front door.

It wasn't so much that it hurt, but it knocked him to the ground, giving Gareth the chance to scramble to his feet.

Lana stood in front of him, watching Damian Magill get up, his energy slightly diminished. He wiped the blood from his mouth and checked his head. 'Right, well, good to meet you, Gareth,' he said. 'I'll be seeing you tomorrow, Lana.'

'Fuck off, Damo!' she screamed.

'Ah, you'll be back,' he replied, and swaggered off down the street.

Gareth made to follow him but Lana pulled him away.

'Let me see to your eye,' she said quietly.

But he brushed her off and stared at her for what felt like a full five minutes. So much information was running round his brain and he tried desperately to make sense of it all: the job over Christmas, the moodiness, not wanting him to visit her in Guildford . . . All of it made sense, apart from one thing.

'Athens?' he said. 'You met him in Athens?'

She didn't try to deny it. She didn't try to stop him leaving either.

Three hours later, back in Coed Celyn, when he let himself into the flat Judith was still awake, sat in her pyjamas reading.

'Jesus, Gar, what happened to you?' she said, looking terrified and going to him.

And only then, when he was home and safe, could he finally give his body permission to acknowledge what had happened. Every limb ached and his head throbbed. But it was his dignity and heart that hurt the most. No physical injury could be worse than that pain.

'Oh Jude,' he whispered.

'Hey! Come here!' she said softly, and she wrapped her arms around her friend, letting him crumple and silently cry. 'It's all right,' she soothed. 'It's gonna be all right.'

25

Catrin

'The whole thing's getting out of hand,' she said. 'We're not getting married till December, but the way my mother's behaving you'd swear it was next week!'

On the other end of the phone, Sol was laughing at her. It was the Easter holidays and he'd gone home to Bayfield to revise. 'She won't leave me alone,' Catrin moaned. 'Follows me round the house with questions about serviettes or Uncle Glan or sugared bloody almonds! I'm meant to be studying undisturbed, for God's sake. This morning she barged into my room with a picture of this horrible wedding dress she likes. Honestly, it'd make me look like a lampshade.'

'Well, if it's any consolation, I'm getting exactly the same thing at my end. Be thankful you don't have to deal with a whole load of relatives in Jamaica and all their travel arrangements. My father's losing his marbles trying to book flights, and then my mother keeps ringing Montgomery Hall every five minutes to check the hotel rooms have got face flannels or tea-making facilities.'

'Oh, Sol. Shall we just run away to Gretna Green?'

'They'd never speak to us again. Plus, I want all my friends to hear Father O'Leary's accent. It's superb,' laughed Sol.

'He's not a bloody cabaret act,' Catrin replied, trying to sound stern. Though she had to admit, when they'd gone to see Father O'Leary to organize reading the banns of marriage and receive their pre-nuptial instruction, it had been hard to remain straight-faced.

'Marriage is like a multinational business,' he'd said, high-pitched and with Cardiffian rapidity. 'You have to keep investin' in it to reap the rewards. Solomon, you and Caitlin here—'

'Catrin,' Sol had corrected him.

'. . . sorry, Catherine,' the priest had continued, 'you're both like the managing directors of this business, y'know? The CEOs, if you will, and you have to, like, keep an eye on the accounts, y'know?' Father O'Leary had seemed really pleased with his analogy, one which Cat and Sol suspected he thrust upon every couple planning their wedding at his church. They also wondered if it would feature in his sermon on the big day.

'I miss you,' she said now quietly, hugging the receiver.

'Yeah, I miss you too,' he replied. 'How's Histology?'

'You old romantic! Not bad, actually. It's Neuroanatomy I've been struggling with. Keep getting my corpus callosum mixed up with my caudate nucleus. Still, I'm having a night off tonight. Lana's home for a few days, so the three of us are having pizza at mine.'

'Good luck with that one!'

'Oh, it'll be all right. They just need to spend a couple of hours together.'

Things between Lana and Judith had turned decidedly frosty since *the night of the fight*. Judith hadn't actually *said* anything to Lana, but it was obvious that she'd taken Gareth's side.

'I don't get why you're so annoyed, Jude,' Catrin had said when she'd seen her a week later.

'It's the lying!' Judith said, incredulous. 'After finding out all that stuff about my mother and how she lied to my dad, I'm not a massive fan of deceit.'

'Of course,' said Catrin, who knew how much Judith had suffered since discovering the truth about her parents' marriage.

'And honestly, Cat, if you'd seen Gareth that night. I've never seen anyone so broken. It was awful.'

Catrin didn't know what to do. She was torn. She could see Judith's point of view – and poor Gareth: what had taken place was horrible. But at the end of the day, *Lana* was their friend, and even though she'd been an idiot, it was Lana they ought to be supporting. 'She'd do the same for you, Jude. You *know* she would.'

But Judith had just shrugged it off and Catrin gave up trying to persuade her.

Since then there had been little contact between the three girls – partly because of the whole Gareth/Lana debacle, but also because they were all bogged down with work. Judith had opted to take some Civil Service exams and spent most evenings with her head in her books, Catrin had been gearing up for her first-year assessments on top of wedding preparations, and Lana had been deep in rehearsals.

At the end of the spring term, Catrin went to see Lana in her college production of *West Side Story*. Judith didn't go. She blamed it on revision but all three of them knew this was just an excuse.

'She's still pissed off with me, isn't she?' Lana said sadly.

Catrin tried to reassure her, but was aware that she had no conviction in her voice. 'You know Jude,' she said, 'she can never stay cross with anyone for long.'

'When I ring the flat, *she* always answers, not Gareth. And she's never unfriendly or anything, but there's just this . . . *tension*. And if I ask to speak to Gar she says he's out, or on a couple of occasions that he simply won't come to the phone. So humiliating,' Lana sighed. 'I've really messed up, haven't I?'

Catrin couldn't disagree, so she just squeezed her friend's arm.

'Did you ever see him again? The builder fella?' she asked Lana when they were topping and tailing in Lana's bed that night. In the darkness, Lana didn't respond. 'Oh my God, Larn, you're not *still* seeing him?'

'I can't explain it . . . He's just—'

Catrin interrupted, shocked. 'Please don't say you're in love with him.'

Lana sat bolt upright and switched on the light. '*What?* No! If anything, I hate him. He's a completely dreadful person.'

'So I don't understand,' said Catrin, genuinely puzzled.

'Look, I tried to put an end to it, I really did – Can I smoke?'

'No.'

'But sex with him is . . . it's addictive. I don't want to keep doing it, but I *have* to keep doing it . . . I can't stop.'

'Flippin' heck, Lana,' Catrin whispered, trying not to show the loss of respect she was feeling for her friend.

They fell silent for a moment, then Catrin offered a solution. 'Remember when we all gave up chocolate for Lent?' she said. 'And sometimes it was really hard to say no, but we did it – all three of us – didn't we? Well, why don't you just treat it like that? Learn to resist, to say no to the builder.'

'He's not a fucking Mars bar!' snapped Lana. 'Sorry.'

'It's OK. I'm just worried about you, that's all.'

'Look, his contract is coming to an end soon and he'll be gone. And then I'll *have* to stop seeing him. I'll have no choice.'

'Sure.'

'Right, enough of the sad stuff,' Lana said with forced jollity. 'Let's talk about your hen party!'

'Oh Larn, it's ages away yet,' yawned Catrin, feeling guilty for nipping her friend's enthusiasm so brutally in the bud. 'D'you mind if we don't?'

Lana hesitated. 'Course not! 'Night, babe,' she said.

But they both knew that the real reason why Catrin's wedding was off the agenda was because it was strictly a subject for when the three of them were together. Two out of three was no good.

Tonight, though, at last, the three of them *were* all together. Huddled round two big pizza boxes in the middle of Catrin's bedroom floor, pyjama'd and free of make-up. It reminded Catrin of the sleepover nights they'd enjoyed when they were younger.

At first it had been tense. Frosty, monosyllabic conversation between Judith and Lana made the atmosphere unbearable. It was like they didn't know each other any more. Catrin tried to navigate the choppy waters of disdain that kept her two best friends apart, but it was Huw who eventually broke the ice. Whether unwittingly or not, he came bounding into the room, singing at the top of his voice:

> *Catrin Kelly, Judith Harris, Lana Lloyd!*
> *Fell into a muddy ditch and got annoyed*
> *All their clothes they were a-smellin'*
> *So they went back to Coed Celyn*
> *Catrin Kelly, Judith Harris, Lana Lloyd!*

And the three of them couldn't help but laugh. *Good old Dad*, thought Cat.

After that, things got easier. Gareth wasn't mentioned, other than Lana awkwardly asking Judith if he ever talked about her. Judith had to admit that no, he didn't. And then they had to agree not to talk about him at all.

Desperate to get things back into shallow but benign territory, Catrin resorted to the one thing she knew would help. 'OK,' she said, producing a bridal magazine. 'Who wants to see the dress I like?'

It was like waving a magic wand. They squealed with delight and excitement as the clock whizzed back a decade, transforming three sensitive young women into eight-year-old princesses again. And Catrin felt that things might finally be returning to normal.

26
Judith

'Why don't you come with me?' she asked. 'Get a bit of sunshine on your old bones, bit of Cypriot vitamin D.'

Gareth laughed. 'Hey, less of the old!'

'You're tempted though, Gareth, I can tell,' said Judith as she packed her summer clothes into a rucksack.

'Well yeah, who wouldn't be? Your aunty's cooking sounds immense.'

'There's more to Cyprus than lamb kebabs!' she laughed.

In celebration of being promoted up one rung of a very tall ladder to the post of administrative officer, Judith was treating herself to a holiday. It was thrilling – the thought of seeing her dad again, along with her recently discovered family, whilst spending seven days in the sun. Her flight was at three o'clock and George was due to meet her at Nicosia airport that evening. He'd been living back in Kakopetria now for nearly six months and, according to his letters, it was like he'd never been away.

After their Christmas reunion, Judith had persuaded

him – no, *commanded* him – to return to Cyprus and pick up his life from where he'd left it in 1973. 'You owe it to yourself, Dad,' she'd said to him gently. 'And to Sofia and to me – to all of us!'

He'd been welcomed home – predictably – with very open arms, found work at the local government offices and settled back into Cypriot life with astonishing speed. He'd even been reconciled with his former sweetheart, Cleoniki, though this had taken time. She'd never married. Too hurt and humiliated by George's abandonment to risk it happening again, she had made the decision to stay single for the rest of her life. George had been determined to change her mind and didn't give up trying until finally he succeeded, though it came at a price: Cleo's brother refused to forgive him and frequently threatened to hit him. 'I think we just have to be patient,' George had said in one of his letters to Judith. But apart from that, life in Cyprus was good, and George wanted more than anything to share it with his beloved stepdaughter.

Predictably, Patricia hadn't been as enthusiastic about Judith's forthcoming trip. 'Don't know why you're bothering. He's not even your real father!' she'd said. But Judith had just smiled back: she'd long since grown immune to her mother's cruel jibes. And she hadn't felt this content in a long, long time.

'What time d'you want to leave?' Gareth asked her, eating his daily staple of three Weetabix and hot milk. She was flying from Cardiff airport and he'd offered to take her on the bike. She knew he was being kind, but

221

she also knew he loved any excuse to go on the motorway and accelerate for a few brief, exhilarating seconds.

'Half twelve? Just in case there's traffic?'

'Yep,' he answered through a mouthful of cereal, wandering back to his room. She smiled to herself and continued packing.

The radio was on, the theme music for *Our Tune* was playing and Simon Bates had begun telling another tale of woe. About 'Leanne' – *That's not her real name, folks* – who had been really happy for a long time with 'Greg' – *That's not his real name either, folks*. Simon Bates went on to describe this apparently idyllic relationship and how well things were going until Leanne went on holiday to Greece last year, got drunk and made a stupid mistake with a guy she met in a bar. Changing gear, the DJ launched into melodrama mode, drawing out his sentences and punctuating the story with meaningful silences as the theme tune filled in the gaps. *And that mistake would cost her dearly . . .*

Judith sat there in shock. This was Lana's story! 'Leanne' was Lana. And Simon Bates was telling the whole sorry tale of infidelity, remorse and heartbreak. On national radio, for all to hear!

She was so glued to the spot she didn't hear Gareth marching into her room. 'You listening to this crap?' he said, his hand shaking as he turned up the volume, not even waiting for a reply. Simon Bates was concluding the tale. *So Greg, if you're out there, Leanne wants*

you to know that hurting you was the biggest mistake
of her life . . . and she'll regret it till the day she dies.

'Oh, for God's sake,' mumbled Judith, appalled by the melodrama.

Gareth turned to her, staring in disbelief. *And so this is for you, Greg. From Leanne, who's hoping, just hoping, that you'll forgive her . . .*

Neither moved as the opening bars of Jim Diamond's 'I Should Have Known Better' filtered through the airwaves, the lyrics piercing the atmosphere.

> *It's true, I took our love for granted all along.*
> *And trying to explain where I went wrong,*
> *   I just don't know.*

Gareth leant across to the radio and switched it off.

'What you gonna do, mate?' Judith ventured to ask.

But he didn't answer, and went back to his room. She knew it would be unwise to follow him.

Shortly afterwards, she heard Gareth go out, shouting, 'I'll be back to pick you up.'

When he returned, she asked him if he was OK and he said yes he was, but more than that Judith daren't ask. There's no way he could have driven to Guildford and back to see Lana in such a short space of time, but where *had* he been? He barely said a word as he helped her with her rucksack and settled her on to the bike.

When they arrived at the airport she told him not to

worry about coming in with her, she was fine on her own.

'Try and enjoy it,' he said. 'You deserve a break.'

'Thanks. What about you? You've got the place to yourself for a whole week. Planning any parties?' she asked, knowing that the last thing on Gareth's mind right now would be a party. He'd more likely be heading east on the M4 for a showdown or a reunion with Lana.

He gave a sad laugh in response. 'Sorry I've been a bit . . . y'know. Just wasn't expecting it, that's all.'

She wanted to comfort him, but didn't know how. 'Come here,' she said, and reached her arms around him for a hug.

'Be fuckin' lost without you, Jude,' he said quietly, emotion cracking his voice.

Embarrassed by this rare show of vulnerability, she quickly changed the subject. 'Right. See you in a week's time!' And she headed towards Departures, Gareth shouting after her, 'I'll pick you up!' She turned round once, but he had already gone.

Over two thousand miles and twelve hours later, she was sat at Sofia's homely kitchen table in Kakopetria, surrounded by her family, the warm June air outside alive with an orchestra of busy crickets. The children had long since fallen asleep, but the adults were still in full flow. Iannis, Sofia's husband, offered to top up her Metaxa, but she yawned and said she really had to get to sleep.

Lying in bed, she thought back over the day – the excitement of meeting George at the airport, the constant chat with him all the way to Kakopetria as he told her his plans for the week ahead, the emotional welcome she'd been given by Sofia and Iannis and the kids. Even the goats and chickens had seemed pleased to see her again. She was so happy to be there. It really did feel more of a home to her than Coed Celyn and she'd already successfully tried out the Greek she'd been learning. They applauded every slow sentence she attempted. She should be feeling over the moon to be here – and she *was*! There was just this niggling doubt in her mind about Gareth and it wouldn't go away.

The next morning she was awoken by Danoulla and Andreas, who wanted another look at their funny-sounding cousin before they went to school. They brought her some coffee and tried out their broken English on her. 'Goot morrrrnink,' they said and giggled, rushing out of the room as Judith laughed, yelling '*Kalimera!*'

At breakfast, Sofia had laid on another feast, akin to those she'd prepared for the girls when they'd visited the year before. Judith munched her way through two large slices of watermelon, enjoying the sensation of the sweet juice running down her chin and dribbling over her fingers.

George was like an excited puppy, clean-shaven now and tanned. He wore a smart shirt and chinos and Judith thought how different he looked from the sad factory worker he'd been in Coed Celyn and the bearded Scottish-oil-rig worker she'd met at Christmas. George was a new man.

After their daytrip through the mountains and their picnic in a shady grove, they headed back to Kakopetria and the house of Cleoniki Kyriacou. She was a petite, slender woman in her early forties, with pretty lips and shiny, bright brown eyes, dressed plainly but elegantly. Judith was touched by how respectful George was of his sweetheart, kissing her politely on each cheek and greeting her with a formal salutation.

When he turned to introduce her to Judith, Cleo's eyes filled with tears. She opened her arms wide and embraced her, as if welcoming a long-lost relative back from the war. Judith could pick out a couple of Greek words, but George translated. 'She says you are beautiful, like a small deer.'

Judith wasn't sure if this was a compliment or not, but decided to take it as such. '*Efcharisto poli*,' she timidly attempted, and Cleo seemed to love her even more.

They stayed for tea and Cleo showed Judith her little garden, in which she took such pride. Beautiful blooming geranium plants in pots, and cyclamen and peonies.

'I am building her a garden seat, to go there in the corner by the olive trees,' said George, bursting with pride. And Judith noticed the couple share a secret smile.

On their way home, they called into the little churchyard to lay flowers at the grave of George's mother. It was a happy occasion this time, both Judith and George buoyed up by the sheer joy of being there together. Because who'd have thought this could possibly have ever happened?

As they walked back to the car, George said he had something to tell her, and they sat on a little stone seat in the shade.

She'd already guessed what he wanted to say, but didn't want to take the wind out of her father's very full sails. She could tell he'd been rehearsing it, and, after he'd gathered his thoughts, out it came in a loud and definite declaration.

'I have asked Cleoniki Kyriacou to be my wife and she has consented.'

Judith tried to keep a straight face, his formality was so sweet. 'Oh, I see,' she teased.

'I understand if you feel uncomfortable about this, but—'

'Dad—'

'But I love her and I'm afraid I will marry her with or without—'

'Dad!'

He stopped and she held his hand.

'It's wonderful news. I could not be happier for you.'

George beamed, and hugged her. 'Oh my little Judi-moo!' He went on to explain that they were hoping to be married as soon as the decree absolute was through.

'Yes, Patricia made a big point of telling me about that,' said Judith, and George looked concerned. 'Oh, don't worry. No offence, Dad, but I don't think she's that bothered. She went out with the rat-catcher last week.'

'Rat-catcher?'

'You remember Norman Protheroe from Pickard Road? He's the pest-control fella. But we've always called him the rat-catcher. He seems all right, to be fair.' And she and George shared a smile.

'I had thought,' said George, 'that Cleo and I wouldn't be allowed to marry in church, due to my being divorced. But because my marriage to your mother was not in this country, the Church of Cyprus does not recognize it!'

'Convenient prejudice!' said Judith.

'Yes. Exactly.' He paused for a moment. 'There's one other thing,' he said cautiously.

'Go on,' Judith urged him.

'Well, I've decided to give your mother the house. I'm not going to make her sell it to give me my share.'

'What?' she said, a little too loudly. 'Why can't you make her buy you out?'

'Judi-moo,' he said, stroking her hand, 'we all know that's impossible with what she earns. And if I insisted on selling it, where would she live? And how would she manage? No, for all her faults, for all she's done and for all the insults she still throws my way, I feel I owe it to her as some compensation for agreeing to the divorce.'

'Well, you've got a kinder heart than most, Dad, that's for sure.'

George smiled. 'Your mother isn't all bad, you know.'

Judith held her tongue.

They arrived back at the house shortly afterwards, and as they pulled into the yard at the front of the small-holding Sofia came running out to greet them, wiping her hands on her apron and looking very excited. She said something in Greek to George, who turned to Judith and translated. 'Apparently, we have a visitor!'

Judith thought maybe it was Cleo's brother, come to make amends – or to make trouble. Walking through the door, her eyes took a few seconds to adjust to the darkness after being outside in the sunshine. But eventually she could see him.

'Gareth,' she whispered.

'Alrigh' mate?' he replied, grinning. 'Decided I needed a holiday, after all.'

27

Gareth

The trip to Cyprus had been a mad, spur-of-the-moment decision. He *had* intended spending his week pottering at home, enjoying his time off and tinkering with the bike. But hearing *Our Tune* had thrown a different spanner in the works. And all his plans for a laid-back, chilled-out week at the flat had turned into something very unexpected indeed. He'd gone out on his bike, speeding along the A470 as it snaked through the Brecon hills. It was the only way for him to clear his head.

More than four months had passed since the fight with the Irish guy, and more than four months since he'd seen or spoken to Lana. Disturbingly quickly, he'd grown accustomed to her not being in his life. It wasn't that he hadn't thought about her. It's just that when he did, he felt nothing. So much so that he wondered if he'd been under some hypnotic spell all along, and the *real* Lana was the one he saw on that awful night in February. The hurt he'd felt then, and the humiliation, were so overwhelming that he'd spent the following week in a complete daze. How could he have been so stupid? So duped?

Over time, he'd started to feel better. And then he'd heard *Our Tune*.

Had he been subconsciously waiting for it? Was this the big romantic gesture he'd secretly been hoping for to make everything OK again – the missing piece? Did he even know there *was* a missing piece? Had he just got used to a Lana-less life and suppressed any notion that they could get back together? Or had he in fact finally mended his broken heart?

Revelations, he'd realized, could come at the most unexpected of moments. There he was, sat on his bike at Cardiff airport, the engine ticking over, the planes taking off and landing, watching Judith walk towards Departures, and it couldn't have been clearer.

He'd enjoyed the excitement of it all. Getting the flight from the little travel agent the next day on Coed Celyn high street, packing his rucksack and heading off. He never doubted he was doing the right thing. He meant it about the holiday – he needed one. And Judith had invited him, after all. He was right not to doubt: the shock and thrill on his friend's face when she saw him in Sofia's kitchen was priceless.

And he couldn't have been made to feel more welcome. Sofia made up a bed for him in the living room, and he ate everything she put in front of him and more.

'Oh man,' he said, rubbing his tummy after yet another spectacular Greek meal. 'Jude wasn't lying about your cooking,' he said to Sofia. 'It's ace!' And George translated, laughing.

It had been good getting to know George.

On their final evening there, he'd sat out on the terrace sharing a Metaxa with him and smoking one of his rollies. He was waiting for Judith to get changed. They were off to see a local band playing in the village square, keen to try some authentic Cypriot nightlife.

'This is Kakopetria, remember,' George had smiled, 'not Limassol. Don't get your hopes up!'

The evening was balmy and peaceful, with a cool breeze from the mountains freshening the air. They sat in silence for a while, both lost in their own thoughts.

'Ready?' said Judith, interrupting. She was wearing a cream cheesecloth top, a gypsy skirt and strappy espadrilles. Her hair in glossy brown curls was loose around her shoulders – different from its usual style, scraped back into a modest ponytail.

Gareth was thrown for a moment. 'You look . . .' He struggled to find the right word.

'Is it weird?' she asked, alarmed, looking down at her clothes. 'I borrowed the top off Sofia.'

'No! No. It's cool.'

'Right.' But still he didn't move. 'Come on then,' she said.

The band was strange. And that was being kind. A mix of traditional Cypriot instruments playing current pop tunes, and fronted by a lead singer who was a cross between Sid Vicious and the guy from Bucks Fizz. But despite this, the atmosphere was joyous and buoyant and they spent most of the evening dancing or laughing.

Gareth hadn't had such a good night in a long time and they weren't even drunk – they'd stuck to home-made lemonade, neither wanting a hangover the next morning at five a.m. when they would have to leave for Nicosia airport.

'I've had an immense few days, Jude,' said Gareth as they began the amble back to the house.

'Aw, me too,' she said. 'Thanks for coming. I still can't believe you're here!'

And there was an easy silence between them as they walked along – alone save for an occasional hooting owl and a multitude of stars to keep them company.

When they arrived home, the others had gone to bed and they talked in whispers as they made hot milk and honey in Sofia's well-organized kitchen. She'd left them a plate of delicious almond cookies, still irresistibly oven-warm. They sank down into the vast sofa, sitting at opposite ends and dipping their cookies into their steaming drinks. Gareth slouched, just like he did at home. And Judith sat with her legs tucked in beneath her – just like she did at home. Both so comfortable in each other's company.

He was aware she hadn't asked him about Lana for the whole time he'd been there. She was so considerate like that, was Jude. But he felt he owed her some kind of explanation now.

'You don't need to talk about it if you don't want to,' she said.

'I know that.' And he paused for a moment, gathering

his thoughts. 'It's over, Jude,' he said gently. 'Well and truly. I owe her a favour really, her doing that *Our Tune* thing – it put it all in perspective.'

'It was a pretty spectacular gesture, Gar,' she said, blowing on her milk to cool it down. 'Incredibly romantic.'

'D'you think? I found it all a bit . . . cheesy. Didn't you? Be honest now.'

He could see Judith struggle. He was testing her loyalty, which wasn't really fair.

'Oh I dunno, it was very *Lana*,' she replied diplomatically.

'Yeah, maybe that's the problem. Lana's not very *me* any more. Don't get me wrong, I wish her all the best an' that, but life's moved on.'

'I see.'

'And there's something else,' he said, unable to look her in the eye.

'Go on,' said Jude, taking little sips of milk like a thirsty cat.

How could he tell her? He had no choice now other than to dive in, throw a grenade and smash the status quo. Say it. *Say it!*

'Well, I've . . . You see, there's . . . someone else now.'

Judith choked a little on her milk. 'Sorry,' she said, spluttering. 'Is there?'

'I know this is difficult for you, because Lana's your best friend and, y'know, of course I'll be straight with her, like, I *will* tell her . . . I just wanted to talk to you first.'

'Why me?' she asked, frowning.

This wasn't going well at all. He tried a different tack.

'You've been so good to me, Jude, so kind and, y'know, just *there* for me, and we're sort of . . . well, we're good friends now, aren't we? Despite a rocky start, like.'

'Er, yes,' she replied cautiously.

'Thing is, I kind of . . . well, I kind of love you,' he said, his nerves strangling any emotion and making it sound like he was informing her that the kettle had just boiled.

'I love you too, mate,' she replied.

And he knew straight away that he'd misjudged the whole situation.

'No, I mean . . . I love you. I'm *in love* with you.' He was desperate now and he wished he'd never started.

She stopped drinking, holding the cup tightly in her hands, staring at him.

He found the courage to look back up, squirming inside as he realized that his confession had horrified her.

'No you're not,' she said firmly.

He was confused. 'Umm, but yes, I *am*!'

'You're deluded, that's what you are. And talking absolute bollocks.' She stood up and grabbed his unfinished drink from his hands.

'I was hoping you might say you felt the same way!'

'Gareth!' She turned on him, trying to suppress her annoyance and keep the volume down. 'Have you smoked weed tonight or something? You are *not* in love with me, and I am *not* in love with you. We are friends. We are flatmates. And that's that! Now we both need sleep if we're gonna get that flight tomorrow. So will you lock the back door, please?'

'Sure,' he answered her, a bit stumped as to what to say next.

She rinsed the mugs in silence, dried her hands and headed to the stairs, passing him where he stood, eaten up with embarrassment.

'Jude, I'm sorry. I got it really wrong, didn't I?'

'Yeah, you did,' she said, then relented with a little smile. 'But don't worry about it, OK?' And she disappeared up to bed.

The next morning, despite the early hour, she'd been full of energy and bonhomie, as if compensating for the gaping hole that his confession had left in their friendship the night before. Her overzealous friendliness sent a silent message to him not to dare bring it up in conversation again. And so he didn't. And to all intents and purposes, the journey home together had been civilized and friendly, and to any outsider they would have seemed like the best of mates. But once they were back home, it was as if they were just strangers sharing a property. Polite deference and a sense of unfamiliarity had created a difficult atmosphere in the flat.

Gareth was lying on the sofa, listening to The Clash and wondering how long they could continue avoiding each other like this. It'd been three days now. Judith had gone out every evening – Greek class or swimming or some other excuse. Would they ever return to how they once were, or had they crossed some kind of relationship Rubicon? Had he ruined what had up till now been a lovely, easy friendship – just because he'd completely misread the signs? He couldn't unsay what he'd said on Saturday night. And nor did he really want to – it was the truth, after all.

Jude was probably going to tell Lana, which would make things between *them* even more awkward. And yes. This was a complete fucking mess.

Faintly, under the music, he heard her key in the door at the bottom of the stairs and the familiar sound of her feet climbing each step. When she reached the landing he waited to hear her go into her room and shut the door behind her, like she'd done every night since they'd come home from Cyprus. But tonight her footsteps took a different direction and within seconds she was standing in the doorway of the living room, the frown he knew so well furrowing her brow.

He stood up and waited for the words to come. *Gareth, I think it's best if I found somewhere else to live . . .*

But she said nothing. Just stared at him, biting her bottom lip.

Time stood still.

The song filled the room, seeming to grow louder as if an invisible hand were turning up the volume. '*Should I stay or should I go now?*' Joe Strummer was belting out the lyrics from the stereo.

Eventually he had to speak. 'You OK?'

Still nothing, she just nodded back.

And then she did it. She walked steadily over to him, determined and decisive. He wondered for one bizarre moment whether she was going to hit him.

But far from that, she reached her hands up to his face, closed her eyes and slowly kissed him. It took a couple of seconds for him to shut his eyes too and respond.

'I just wanted to tell you,' she whispered, 'that no, you didn't get it wrong.'

And she kissed him again, as The Clash continued singing in the background.

'So come on and let me know, should I stay or should I go?'

28
Judith

That very first night they'd slept together was so intense she actually thought her entire body would expire with pleasure. She couldn't even speak afterwards. Neither of them could. They just lay there, in a tangle of tired limbs, inhaling the sweet scent of each other's skin, their breathing blissful and deep, and their eyes wide open, waiting for the sun to come tiptoeing in through the window. And she just *knew* that something gloriously irrevocable had happened to her. There was no going back.

'What do we do now?' she'd whispered eventually, breaking the silence.

'Put the kettle on,' he'd replied, and kissed her head before sliding out of bed.

He stretched – a contented stretch, like a sated cat – and she'd marvelled at the fact that what had taken place between them now gave her licence to blatantly stare at his body, and to take in the whole beauty of him. Because he was hers. And she was his. And they were each other's.

They'd sat in bed sipping their tea, still dumbstruck, holding hands and staring ahead of them.

'Jude, last night . . . that was . . .' he struggled. 'Well, I don't think the words exist. It has never, *ever* felt like that before.'

'I'm still buzzing,' she said. 'Like there's this . . . I dunno, this . . . current running through me or something. A kind of deeply pleasant and continuous electric shock.'

They'd both had to go to work an hour later, and neither of them could concentrate, desperate just to get home, to see each other and repeat exactly what they'd done the night before. Almost to confirm that it had really happened. And this carried on for days and days. And all of it in secret. In fact, apart from work colleagues and the postman and the woman in the corner shop, they didn't see another soul for weeks on end, hungering only for each other's company and lost in the hedonistic, inward-looking world of new-found love. Catrin phoned and Lana wrote, but Judith ignored them both. The London School of Economics contacted her, asking if she intended taking up her place again in the autumn. She ignored them too, letting the time pass by, luxuriating in the heady haze of loved-upness. Only Gareth mattered, no one and nothing else.

But she was pulled out of her secret little love cocoon one September night after work. Gareth had promised to make them a curry and do the washing-up if she bought all the ingredients. Letting herself into the door next to the launderette, a big smile on her face for several reasons, she hauled two carrier bags full of groceries up the stairs, calling out as she went.

'Right, Metcalf! You ready to woo me with your vindaloo?'

But instead of answering her, Gareth was standing at the top of the stairs, still in his work overalls, his manner agitated and nervous. 'We've got a visitor!' he said with forced jollity. 'Catrin's here.'

Judith's stomach flipped as reality came crashing into their private little world. She painted on a smile and headed to the kitchen. 'Cat!' she said, hoping she didn't sound too false, and dropping the shopping on to the table, ready to hug her friend.

'Where've *you* been, stranger?' asked Cat, and over her shoulder Judith and Gareth exchanged glances. This was a close call.

'Oh babe! I'm so sorry. I've been up to my eyes in work!'

She caught sight of the chalk message board hanging at the side of the fridge, blatantly emblazoned with Judith's own handwriting: *I completely adore you GM xxx see you tonight.* As surreptitiously as she could, Judith headed towards it and subtly wiped the board with her sleeve. Whilst praying that Catrin didn't notice.

'I got your postcard from Cyprus,' said Cat. 'How brilliant that you went out there, Gar!'

'Yes!' said Judith and Gareth simultaneously, both desperate to sound normal and flatmatey.

'You want some more tea, Cat?' asked Gareth.

'No, you're OK. It's only a flying visit. I've got a meeting with the florists. Honestly, the amount of organizing this wedding is taking is nuts.'

Judith was suddenly aware of her and Gareth's body language. That they couldn't be standing further apart if they tried.

'Thing is, because you never got back to me . . .'

'Sorry!' sighed Judith.

'. . . I've had to go ahead and organize my own hen party.'

'Oh shit,' said Judith. It was something that she and Lana had always said they'd sort out.

'I think Larn's been trying to get hold of you, y'know.'

'Has she?' said Judith, lying through her teeth. 'Oh God, I'm useless. It's just we . . . I was in Cyprus after my Civil Service exams, and then the promotion . . . Sorry.'

'Nearly three months, Jude!' said Catrin, but she couldn't be cross if she tried. 'Still, never mind,' she went on. 'Here's the plan. I'm keeping it simple. Just you, me, Lana and my mum. She insisted, I'm afraid. And I've booked us into the Angel Hotel in Cardiff, afternoon tea, then a night out on the town – my mum has even said she'll come to the Taurus Steakhouse and Kiwi's!'

'Wow.' Judith stole a glance at Gareth, but his eyes were firmly fixed on Catrin, an unflinching smile on his face.

'And I've booked it for the end of October. I know that's still a few weeks away, but you'll be back at LSE next month and I want to get it in the diary.'

There was a momentary silence. How could Judith tell her she wasn't going back to uni?

'You think it's a terrible idea, don't you?' said Catrin, misinterpreting her friend's lack of response.

'What? No! Don't be daft!'

'Good. Well I've told Lana, and she's up for it. Saturday the twenty-fourth, OK?'

'Brilliant!' said Judith, swallowing before she asked, 'How is Lana, by the way?'

Catrin glanced awkwardly at Gareth. 'She's fine. You know Lana, throws herself into everything. Always on the go.'

Gareth looked at the floor and Judith nodded, smiling, trying her hardest to act normal.

'Anyway,' said Catrin, full of forced jollity, 'you'll see her at the hen, won't you? And we can all have a proper catch-up. It's been too long.'

'Yes, it has,' said Judith.

There was a beat and then Catrin was on her feet. 'Right, can I just use the loo before I go?'

''Course!'

Catrin headed out of the kitchen, chatting back to them as she went, telling them about how her father had already written his father-of-the-bride speech and kept laughing at his own jokes whilst rehearsing it in the garden shed. Judith and Gareth stared at each other, fearful, hysterical, saying nothing.

And then Catrin's jolly chatter suddenly stopped. And they were struck with a simultaneous realization.

Judith closed her eyes and sighed.

'Fuck,' whispered Gareth.

And as they held their breath, Catrin came back and stood in the doorway. 'Your bedroom, Jude . . .'

Judith could only look at her.

'It doesn't seem to be a bedroom any more.'

'No,' said Judith, struggling to find her voice. 'It's a study . . . kinda thing.'

'So in that case,' asked Catrin, already knowing the answer, 'where do you sleep?'

Later that evening, Judith and Gareth cwtched up on the sofa, dealing with the after-effects of Catrin discovering their secret. Earlier they'd watched her weigh up the situation, absorb the information and calculate the fallout. She'd been torn between thinking Judith and Gareth were being hugely disloyal to Lana, and thinking the two of them made a lovely couple who were really well suited to each other. The one thing she was certain of, though, was that she wouldn't breathe a word to Lana.

'It's up to you to do that, Jude,' was her parting shot. 'But please do it soon. Otherwise the whole thing's gonna just drag on and the hen night, let alone the wedding, will be unbearable. 'Cos we've never had secrets from each other, have we?'

Catrin was right, of course. They couldn't just pretend Lana didn't exist. 'She's still one of my best friends,' she said to Gareth as he massaged her feet. 'And for as long as I'm in your life, *she*'s gonna be in your life. We can't get around that.'

'I know,' he said quietly. 'So, d'you want me to tell her?'

'No. It should be me. I mean, I've known her longer than you. I reckon *I*'m the one who's being the most disloyal.'

'First off, nobody's being disloyal,' he said, irritated. 'Me and her finished months ago, remember? And *also*, remember that *she* was the one who was shagging around.'

'Right, well, on that subject . . .'

'Oh Christ, don't tell me *you*'ve been shaggin' around too,' he laughed.

'You laugh because you know that that is something I will *never* do.'

He stopped and took her hand and kissed it. 'Yeah, I do know that, as it goes. Anyway, carry on.'

But Judith didn't answer immediately, steeling herself for what she had to say.

'Jude?' Gareth looked confused.

'Well, first of all I'm sorry for not telling you this sooner, OK?'

'OK . . .' said Gareth quietly.

And Judith took a deep breath, closed her eyes and said the words.

29
Lana

Three months later

Remember this moment, she kept thinking. She wanted to capture it for ever, engrave it in her memory, the day one of her two best friends got married. Standing there in St Theodore's with the frosty December sunshine streaming in through the stained-glass window behind the altar and the smell of incense making it all feel so holy. Catrin and Solomon were kneeling down before Father O'Leary, receiving his blessing and the blessing of every person in that church. She wasn't religious herself, but today she felt something akin to a spirituality she'd not experienced before, a joyousness that filled her to the brim.

She glanced at her other best friend, standing next to her in an identical Empire-line gown of royal-blue velvet. Poor Jude. She hated the dress. And Lana could see why – she looked so bloody uncomfortable in it and was clearly glad to be able to hide under the pretty wrap that not only accessorized the dress but also kept out the December cold. Lana tried smiling at her, keen to inspire a shared moment, a moment of *Isn't this amazing?* But her enthusiasm wasn't returned. Still, she wouldn't be put off. Today was special. And nothing was going to spoil it.

Apart, possibly, from Gareth.

Of course, it wasn't ideal that he'd been invited to the evening party. When Lana first discovered this, she'd protested. 'What d'you have to do that for, Cat? It's gonna ruin my night having him there!'

Catrin was uncharacteristically tetchy in her response. 'Yeah, well it's not your wedding, is it? And he's our friend, after all.'

'Suppose so,' said Lana, realizing she was being a bit selfish.

Over the past ten months she'd thought about Gareth a lot – mainly with guilt over how she'd behaved. She'd tried talking to Catrin and Judith about it on the rare occasions she'd seen them recently, but neither of them had been much help. In fact, neither of them had been much *anything* of late: Catrin's hen night in October had been a bit of a damp squib – thank God for Liz Kelly, who had joined in with the tequila slammers and generally been up for a fun night, because Jude and Cat had been like two boring old women. Lana had asked them several times what was wrong – but they'd both clammed up.

'Right, have you two had a falling-out or something?' she'd finally asked, exasperated.

Nothing. It didn't help that neither of them were drinking. 'It's a bloody hen night, for God's sake!' But

Jude was on another of her stupid diets and Cat had decided to forego booze until the big day. Which was finally here and actually happening. And Gareth didn't matter for now. Nor did whatever had gone on between her two best friends.

'Okey doke,' said Father O'Leary, checking his notes, 'I'm gonna ask Lara Loin to come up the front now, alrigh'? An' sing a little song for the lot of us? Crackin'.' And he waved at Lana to join them.

Despite being used to performing, she was surprised to feel her throat contract with nerves and emotion as the guitarist they'd hired began gently strumming the introduction. She stumbled at first, missing the cue, and the guitarist started again. What was happening to her? She'd never felt so vulnerable, so exposed. She was out of her comfort zone. Because this wasn't bold, brash show-time – this was time for heartfelt singing, and lyrics about the beautiful bond of unshakeable love between Catrin and Solomon. Lana focused all her energy on them. It was the only way she could get through it.

The reception at Montgomery Hall was superb. Lana, being from a big family, had been to lots of weddings in her twenty years, and this was by far the best.

When Huw made his father-of-the-bride speech, he had to keep stopping to gather himself, and each time Catrin would squeeze his hand, which would start him off crying again. In the end, Liz took over, taking his prompt cards from him and saying, 'This is what my husband would like to say . . .' She was far more controlled, and the jokes that Huw had written in there were met with appreciative laughter and cheers. When she came to the final few lines, though, she too crumpled, and this time Edward Blythe took the speech from Liz. It was like some sort of parental relay race, with the speech baton being handed from one parent to the next. 'This is what Solomon's father-in-law would finally like to say,' said Edward. And being of a more serious disposition than Huw, he delivered the closing line in a monotone that lacked any attempt at humour. 'Sol-she's-my-only-daughter-and-without-her-I-am-lost-I'm-not-in-the-Mafia-nor-nothing-so-I-won't-wreak-any-revenge-or-have-you-disappeared-but-if-you-hurt-her-in-brackets-DeNiro-accent-I-will-have-to-chase-you-the-hell-out-of-town-in-brackets-laugh.'

There was an awkward silence, before Edward added, 'I think that's meant to be a joke,' and everyone clapped and laughed with relief.

'Better behave myself then, hadn't I?' Sol whispered, before standing up to give his own speech.

And when he spoke, Lana could see exactly why Catrin had fallen in love with him. He'd ended with the words of e. e. cummings, which had everyone in floods:

here is the deepest secret nobody knows
(here is the root of the root and the bud of the bud
and the sky of the sky of a tree called life; which
*   grows*
higher than soul can hope or mind can hide)

and this is the wonder that's keeping the stars apart

i carry your heart (i carry it in my heart)

'Some people are just *meant* to be together, aren't they, Jude?' Lana said to her fellow bridesmaid once the wedding breakfast was over and the tables were being cleared in readiness for the disco.

'I guess so,' said Jude.

Lana was drunk now, having taken advantage of all the free champagne laid on by Edward and Amelia Blythe. Judith, it seemed though, was entirely sober.

'Lana, can we talk?' Judith said. 'I need to tell you something.'

'Of course! Let's get some fresh air.'

Sat outside in the cold December night on the seen-better-days garden furniture, they watched as two of Catrin's little cousins chased each other round the tables, before one fell over and started crying.

'Too much excitement for one day!' their mother shouted.

'Why do adults *always* say that?' Lana asked, smiling. 'When I have kids, I'm gonna let them run wild like feral dogs!'

They sat in silence for a few minutes and watched the evening guests arriving with presents under their arms, looking brighter and shinier than some of the day guests, upon whom the lunchtime drinking had taken its toll.

'So what's up, mate?' asked Lana.

'Not sure where to start, to be honest.'

'Is it your weight? 'Cos I know you've put on, but honestly, Jude, you still look so beautiful and—'

'No, it's not that,' said Judith, cutting her off.

'Go on then, what?' Lana asked gently, and reached in her bag for a cigarette.

'Actually, d'you mind not smoking? Makes me feel a bit, y'know . . .'

This slightly irritated Lana, who felt she was already being very patient and indulgent of Judith's strange mood. 'Never bothered you before, me smoking.'

'I know.'

'And your *flatmate*'s a smoker. Gareth smokes. So how does that work?'

'He doesn't, actually. He's given up. A couple of months back.'

'Blimey.' There was more silence, then Lana said, 'And how *is* the delightful Gareth Metcalf?' She laughed. 'Does he still hate my guts?' She'd promised herself that she wouldn't mention him, but champagne-fuelled curiosity had got the better of her.

'I don't know,' Judith sighed.

'You know the *Our Tune* thing . . . I was drunk when I sent the letter off. I didn't mean any of it. I hope he knows that?'

The truth was that Lana had been completely sober when she wrote to the Simon Bates show. But she'd felt so humiliated by Gareth's lack of response to what she thought was a romantic gesture that her self-defence mechanism had kicked in and she'd turned it into one big drunken mistake.

'Lana,' Judith blurted it out. 'I'm pregnant.'

In the background they could hear the evening DJ introducing himself.

'What?' Lana locked eyes with her, unable to process what she'd just been told. 'You can't be. *Oh my God – Jude!* Shit!'

So let's have everyone on to the dance floor now as the bride and groom take their first dance . . . the DJ was saying as everyone applauded them on to the dance floor – Mr and Mrs Solomon Blythe.

'Does Catrin know?'

'What? No – yes, I had to tell her. Look, I've wanted to tell you about it for a while, but it was never the right time . . .'

'But I don't understand,' Lana interrupted. 'I didn't even know you were seeing anyone.'

'Come on, you two! You'll miss it!' shouted Huw Kelly, who'd come out looking for them, panicking that his daughter's bridesmaids would miss her first dance. He reached out and grabbed them both by the hand, before leading them back through the French windows of the function room, where Catrin and Sol had begun moving awkwardly to the sound of Minnie Riperton's 'Lovin' You'.

'Aw, will you look at the pair of them?' sighed Huw. 'And the song says it all, doesn't it? You simply cannot beat a bit of Riperton, all them screechy high notes.'

Judith and Lana stood either side of him, both fixing their gaze on Sol and Cat, and attempted to join in with the general *oohs* and *aahs* of admiration coming from the crowd that encircled the happy couple.

As the song approached its conclusion, the guests applauded the newlyweds and, in return, Sol and Cat invited the others to join them on the dance floor as the strains of the first dance segued into Rick Astley's upbeat number 'Never Gonna Give You Up'.

'Come on now, Amelia! Let's show 'em how it's done!' shouted Huw as he took the hand of Solomon's mother, who in turn squealed with delight.

'Right,' said Lana, her eyes shining with intrigue, and eager to finish the conversation. 'So who's this mystery fella? And how comes Catrin Kelly – sorry, Catrin *Blythe* – knew about him before *me*, you traitor!' She laughed, trying to hide the fact that she was a bit hurt. 'And oh my God, you're *pregnant*, Jude!'

Judith stared back at her friend. Only with sorrow in *her* eyes, at what she was about to do.

'Jude?' said Lana, confused and frowning.

But then another voice came from behind her. 'Jude!'

Lana followed Judith's gaze and turned around to see Gareth, standing in clothes she'd never seen before, his hair shorter, clean-shaven, wearing a shirt and tie. Clothes so alien to him.

'Alrigh' Lana? How's it goin', alrigh'?' said Gareth quickly, unrecognizably polite and avoiding eye contact.

She barely recognized him or his nervous demeanour. 'Gareth! There's nice! How you doin'?'

He looked gorgeous and she felt herself blush; it was impossible not to find him attractive. This was the first time they'd seen each other since that terrible night in February.

He didn't answer her, but turned instead to address Judith with disturbing familiarity.

'Where do I put the present?' he asked her quietly.

And without needing any further explanation, without even needing to hear Judith's reply, Lana knew.

She knew.

'Fuck me, Jude, please don't say it's Gareth,' she shouted over the strains of Rick Astley.

But Judith didn't answer, just looked down at the floor.

'I said,' Lana shouted, louder this time, and peering into Judith's face, 'is it Gareth? Is he the father? HAVE YOU BEEN SLEEPING WITH GARETH?'

Gareth reached out to put his hand on Lana's shoulder. 'Can we go somewhere quieter to talk?'

Lana pushed him away. 'Mind your own fucking business. This is to do with me and my friend.'

'Let's go outside,' said Judith, and began making her way across the dance floor.

Lana, fired up, furious, followed hard on her heels, knocking past dancing guests as she went, her sense of balance compromised by the alcohol she'd consumed. 'Don't walk away from me, Jude. You tell me to my face!!'

But still Judith kept walking.

Lana caught up with her and grabbed her by the shoulder, pulling her round. 'TELL ME!!' she screamed. By now people had stopped dancing and were trying to find out what was going on.

Catrin had broken away from her dance with Sol's brother and run over to stand between them. 'Girls, don't do this now. Please.'

'Don't *you* speak to me, Catrin Kelly. Little Miss Fucking Butter Wouldn't Melt!'

An audible and collective gasp filled the room in shock.

'You *knew*!'

Catrin began sobbing. 'I'm sorry, Larn, but it wasn't my place to say! I begged Jude to tell you, but—'

'Yeah, well, at least we know where *your* loyalties lie now, don't we?'

'You don't understand . . .'

'Oh shut up, Catrin,' Lana hissed.

'Leave her alone,' shouted Judith. 'I wanted to tell you myself!'

'So do it then! TELL ME. I'm still waiting.'

Everyone was watching now as Rick Astley still warbled in the background.

'Yeah, OK. I'm with Gareth. I love Gareth. OK? And I'm sorry for not telling you sooner, I really am.'

Lana stared at her, chewing her lip, struggling to focus, fighting the effects of the champagne, aware that everyone was awaiting her reaction. She should just walk away, of course.

'You didn't need to find out like this,' said Gareth quietly. 'But you have now, so—'

And then it struck her – the intense humiliation. Not just that her best friend was in love with her ex-boyfriend, not just that they were having a baby together, but that her two best friends had kept this a secret from her, they'd colluded and excluded her. She felt like an abandoned five-year-old.

'*Bitch*,' she hissed quietly, before exploding into a terrifying rage. 'YOU FUCKING TREACHEROUS BITCH!' And with that, Lana lunged forward and pushed Judith as hard as she could.

Judith lost her balance and fell backward, reaching for something to grab in the process. The only option was the linen-covered table on which was placed the three-tier wedding cake. It seemed to happen in slow motion – Gareth reaching and failing to break her fall, and the white-iced cherry-sponge tower flying through the air, dismantling into three separate parts and landing like wet clay with an undignified triple splat on the floor.

Amelia and Liz screamed the loudest.

'Lana! It's my wedding day!' cried Catrin, held back by Sol.

Gareth helped Judith slowly to her feet, confusion on her face.

'You OK?'

She said nothing at first.

'JUDE!' Gareth shouted.

And she nodded, numb, blasted.

Gareth turned once more to Lana. 'You sick in the head or something?'

And everyone watched as Lana ran out of the room, Rick Astley ringing in her ears.

'Inside we both know what's been going on . . .'

30

Catrin

'Are you sure we can postpone?' she asked him again. 'I mean, she's got Gareth. And my mum and dad, of course.' Catrin was sitting on a hard plastic seat in the waiting room of Coed Celyn General.

'Ssh,' comforted Sol, his arm firmly around the shoulders of his new wife. 'My dad's taken care of it. We can go on Thursday. And that's only if you feel you can leave her.'

They were meant to be heading to the airport the next day, to fly to Kingston, Jamaica for their two-week honeymoon. But since ten a.m. that morning Catrin and Sol had spent most of their time at the hospital, waiting to see Jude again. Endlessly waiting.

At first they'd thought she was all right. She certainly did a good job of convincing them and once the shock of Lana's walk-out had receded, the guests slowly returned to their celebrations. It wasn't until an hour later that Judith was taken ill. Catrin had been talking to Father O'Leary at the time.

'I've called an ambulance,' said Gareth, rushing up to them. 'There's something wrong.'

Edward and Amelia Blythe were at Judith's side in an instant, making her comfortable, reassuring her with the well-practised calm of two doctors long used to navigating a health crisis.

When the ambulance arrived, Catrin had wanted to go with them, but Judith and Gareth both refused.

'It's your bloody wedding, Cat,' said Judith, her breath shallow and her face white. 'I'd never forgive myself if you abandoned it just for me. I'm gonna be fine. Don't be an idiot.'

And with that they'd left.

Later that night as she lay with Sol in the honeymoon suite of Montgomery Hall, Catrin called the hospital, asking for news.

'She's stable now and sleeping,' said a kind nurse on the end of the line.

'And the baby?'

'I'm afraid I can't divulge anything over the phone, but be assured your friend is being looked after.'

Catrin asked the nurse to pass on a message to Gareth, asking him to phone as soon as he knew anything.

But they didn't hear from him until the following morning.

'Will you come and see her?' was all he said.

On their way to the hospital, Catrin thought again about what had happened. Could she have stopped it? Probably not.

Since finding out about Judith and Gareth's relation-ship, and the *huge* subsequent revelation that Judith was pregnant, Catrin had been in turmoil. She had asked Judith over and over to tell Lana. And each time, Judith would say she was waiting for *the right time*.

'Why on earth she thought our wedding day was *the right time*, Sol, I will never understand,' she said as she looked out of the car window.

'Yeah, me neither,' he replied.

It was an amazing feat of friendship that the invisible triangle connecting Lana, Judith and Catrin had always been balanced, always equilateral. In all the time they'd known each other, the dynamic had never been two against one. But that lovely equilibrium had been lost the day Judith shared her secret with Catrin alone. It would've been easier, of course, if Judith had never confided in her, though ultimately she realized her friend had had no choice. For one thing, the bridesmaid's dress had needed to be altered; being six months gone by the time of the wedding, Judith's bump would not have been easy to hide. Thankfully, it was a winter wedding, so the design of the dress and the wrap-around shawl would help hide the pregnancy.

At the hen weekend, and again at the final dress fitting, both Lana *and* Liz had privately commented to Catrin on Judith's weight gain. She tried to brush it off with a nonchalant response about Judith being stuck at her desk all day in a sedentary job, eating too many cakes off the tea trolley. And they had seemed to buy that.

Catrin knew Judith had also confided in her because

she would need moral support when she finally *did* break the news to Lana. But never in a million years could she have predicted such a violent reaction.

'What if it's broken us three up for good, Sol?' she sobbed now, the emotions of the past twenty-four hours finally catching up with her. 'Lana wasn't just furious with Jude, she was furious with me as well.'

This time Sol stayed silent, no longer sure that things *would* work out.

When they arrived at the hospital, Gareth was outside smoking. Still in his crumpled wedding suit, he looked tired and raw and dishevelled and was sucking the life out of a cigarette. 'I've started again,' he said, with a shock-tainted smile.

'Don't blame you, mate,' said Sol, putting his hand on Gareth's arm.

They stood there in silence for a moment, lost for words, in a fug of irreverent and sour tobacco fumes.

'Oh, and I'm a dad, by the way,' added Gareth, as if such momentous news was a minor afterthought.

'What?'

'And Judith's a mum. Weird, huh?' His voice was shaking, broken.

Catrin tried to process what she was hearing, 'Oh my God—'

But Gareth ploughed on. 'Yeah, little boy. Callin' him Jack, we are. Only three and a half pound at the moment, like . . .' The words were tumbling out of him, punctuated by the drags on his cigarette. He didn't look at Sol and Catrin as he spoke, as if he was afraid to connect in case it made him collapse. 'He's in one of them incubators—'

'Jesus,' whispered Sol, and Catrin's hands covered her face in shock.

'Yeah, still a bit touch and go, like, but I reckon he's a fighter.' He tried smiling. 'The other one didn't make it though.'

'The . . . other one?' stammered Catrin, exchanging looks with Sol.

'There were . . . twins?'

'Yeah. We'd wanted to keep it a secret for a while. That there were two of them, like.'

'Oh Gareth,' whispered Catrin, wrapping her arms around him.

He seemed unmoved, his body rigid. 'It was a little girl,' he said. 'And she was smaller. Than Jack.'

'Oh God,' sobbed Catrin.

They stood in silence, each deep in their own thoughts.

'I need to see her,' said Catrin quietly. 'I need to see Jude.'

'D'you want me to wait here with you, Gar?' asked Sol.

'No, you're all right. There's something I've got to do.' And he stubbed out his cigarette.

'Can't *we* help? With whatever it is . . . ? I mean, wouldn't you rather stay put?'

'No. Tell Jude I'll be back in an hour,' Gareth said,

and he took a few steps before suddenly stopping in his tracks.

'We called her Georgia, by the way.'

His voice finally breaking when he uttered her name, wiping away tears of rage.

31

Lana

Her mother had knocked twice on her door that morning and both times she'd shouted out to be left alone, that she was still sleeping. She didn't want to talk to anyone. Luckily her sister Jess was away for a sleepover at a friend's, otherwise she'd have had no peace. Since Lana had left for college, Jess had commandeered the room they'd once shared, pushing Lana well and truly out of the nest. She lay on the bed with her back to the door, staring at the wall, feeling utterly bereft, hungover and alone.

How could she? Lana asked herself over and over again.

How could Judith, her best friend since they were five, do this to her? It must have been going on for months – Judith and Gareth, Jude and Gar, playing the happy couple in secret, sleeping in the bed that *she*'d slept in with him, having sex, sharing jokes, making dinner, making a *baby* . . .

Looking back, it all made sense, of course. All these months when Judith had cold-shouldered her, even when things were apparently OK again with them – the pizza night at Cat's, the hen night in Cardiff – she'd obviously been sleeping with him all that time.

Thief.

Traitor.

Disloyal, two-faced, backstabbing bitch.

It hurt her, despite everything, to call her best friend a bitch. But she was in so much pain. And what made the pain so much worse was that Catrin knew too. A double disloyalty. A double deception. A double loss.

Sleep had eluded her. All night, thoughts of Judith and Gareth had swirled around her head in a taunting maelstrom. She was the hard-done-by one. The wronged woman. The spurned girlfriend.

Except she wasn't his girlfriend any more, was she? She'd relinquished that title the moment she'd invited Damian Magill back to her room. So what right did she have to be upset? And yet it wasn't *Gareth* she was most upset with – it had long been over between the two of them, after all.

No.

It was Judith's betrayal that stung the most. And thinking back to last night, the two best friends of the bride standing there in their bridesmaid dresses, surrounded by nuptial frills and floral arrangements and delicate decorations . . . she had no regrets.

She only wished she'd pushed her harder.

*

Downstairs in the distance she'd vaguely heard the doorbell go and her mother answer it. Lana pulled the duvet over her head, willing the world to go away.

Seconds later, footsteps on the stairs, her mother's voice raised – *She's still asleep, love, she won't thank you for waking her* – and then the door burst open.

'Lana.'

She struggled to focus on the figure in the room. Taut with intimidating rage and staring directly at her.

Gareth.

'Get out!' she yelled, retreating back under the duvet. But no sooner had she done so than she felt it pulled back off again by Gareth, who was staring down at her, wild-eyed and hauntingly calm.

'The baby died,' he said, his voice steady. 'Happy now?'

'W-what?' she stammered, trying to process what he'd said.

He ignored her and carried on, choosing not to tell her there'd been twins – she'd find out soon enough, and for now he just wanted her to suffer like he was suffering. He was there to deliver a single clear message. 'You don't contact Judith ever again, d'you hear me? You stay out of her life. And mine. And you never see her again, understand?'

'Gareth,' she whispered, shock inhibiting her speech. 'I am so, so sorry.'

But he'd already turned and was marching towards the door.

'Gareth, please!'

And with the hard December rain bashing against her curtained bedroom windows, Lana was left sobbing, friendless and utterly alone.

PART TWO
2005

Eighteen years later

32

Catrin

When she arrived at her parents' house after morning surgery, Catrin found her mother at it again, this time in the living room.

'Mum! How many times? Romy is not wearing the gown!'

Liz Kelly stared back at her, mortified, like a schoolgirl caught in the act.

'Look! It's digging in . . . oh, bless her,' she said, removing the ill-fitting dress. 'Honestly, stop it, will you?' Catrin picked up her baby girl, who gurgled delightedly, eyes wide in wonder.

'What if I take the seams out a little and put a panel in . . .' pleaded Liz.

'No,' interrupted Catrin firmly, as if scolding an unruly dog.

Ever since they'd set a date for the christening, Liz Kelly had persisted in attempting to persuade Catrin that her little granddaughter should wear this hideous heirloom – a baptism gown passed down from Great-Granny Wilson and worn at generations' worth of family christenings. Including Catrin's own. And her brother Tom's.

'You're wearing a girl's dress,' she used to tease him whenever they perused the family albums and he'd answer her with a pinch.

Catrin completely understood the need to preserve tradition, she really did. But not at the expense of her baby girl's comfort. Romy was eleven months old now. The gown was evidently made for a newborn.

'If you hadn't waited so long to get the poor mite christened it would've been a perfect fit,' Liz had told her numerous times.

Catrin knew her mother had a point, but she hadn't delayed on purpose. It'd just been an organizational nightmare trying to find a date that everyone could make. Sol's parents spent half the year in Jamaica these days, so that didn't help. Then on top of that there was the question of Romy's godparents. Sol's brother Tom had been really flexible, saying he'd move heaven and earth to be there fulfilling his role as godfather. It was the god*mothers* who were the problem.

The choice was obvious, of course.

But seeing as they'd not been in the same room together for eighteen years, persuading Judith and Lana to stand side by side in front of a font, jointly vowing to fight Beelzebub on their god-daughter's behalf, had been far from a walk in the park.

The initial response from both of them had been an emphatic no. At least, no to actually *sharing* the honour. Individually, of course, they'd both be delighted. But

Lana wouldn't do it if Judith was doing it and vice versa.

'You'd think by now they could have a swift word with themselves and move on,' Sol had said.

'I know!' she'd replied in frustration. '*We're thirty-seven, for God's sake!*'

Catrin, of course, had wanted more than anything to share the day with *both* of her best friends there as god-mothers, not just one or the other. It wasn't fair on Romy to be stuck in the middle of this ridiculous feud. Surely eighteen years was long enough to bury hatchets, mend bridges and finally reconcile? And for what better reason than the celebration of the arrival of her beautiful daughter into the world? But each attempt at persuading her friends was met with a rock-solid negative response.

'Well, maybe I won't have either of you then!' she'd announced. This ultimatum unsurprisingly set the cat amongst the baptismal pigeons.

'Why should *I* miss out just because of Judith bloody Harris?' Lana had said when she was home, visiting. 'It's not fair. I haven't got any kids . . .'

'You're hardly menopausal!' interrupted Catrin, but Lana ignored her and ploughed on.

'She steals my boyfriend and now she wants to steal my only opportunity for a mothering role?'

'Don't be so dramatic, Larn,' said Catrin.

'I'm an actress,' she muttered. 'I'm meant to be dramatic.'

'By the way, Judith didn't *steal* your boyfriend. And in case you've forgotten, we were only *nineteen*!'

'Yeah, nearly two decades ago and still the woman blames me for what happened. It was an accident, for God's sake.'

Catrin was fighting a losing battle.

So she'd turned her attentions to Judith, going with Sol to visit her and the family in Richmond. Catrin pleaded with her one more time to change her mind or else forego the chance to become Romy's godmother.

'That's blackmail,' Judith complained.

'Exactly,' retorted Catrin. 'Needs must.'

'Yeah, well I won't do it. So you're gonna have to choose,' declared Judith. 'It's either me or her.'

Several weeks went by and nothing changed. Catrin's threat of having neither best friend as godmother had had no effect whatsoever. So it left her with only one choice: she'd have to invite both Lana *and* Jude and fail to inform either that the other was coming.

'You're taking a massive risk!' Sol told her – though he was smiling at the time.

'Only time will tell.'

The christening plans were in place: two o'clock on Sunday the tenth – at St Theodore's Church, of course, with the service to be taken by Father O'Leary, of course, who'd said he'd be *delighted to welcome little Rosy into the family of Christ*.

The reception afterwards was to be held at the Kelly home. 'Your father wanted caterers,' Liz told Catrin. 'I said, "*Who d'you think we are, Huw Kelly – Madonna and Guy Ritchie? We'll have a finger buffet up the house and be done with it."'*

Judith intended to come down early, visiting Patricia en route. And Lana had promised to get the train first thing from London. Catrin made the whole of her family swear not to mention her plan. Because she knew that if Jude found out that Lana was coming, she'd be off back to Richmond before the booing of a goose. And vice bloody versa.

She snuggled up to Romy, resplendent now in a comfy all-in-one.

'That's better, isn't it, darling?' she whispered, inhaling the luscious aroma of her baby skin.

Catrin still marvelled at her existence, this child who had eluded them for so long, held safely in her arms, warm and milky, smiling and soft: without doubt their little miracle.

'You'll be the star of the show on Sunday,' she said.

Romy gurgled back at her, kicking her chubby legs, excited by life: this little soul smiled at *everyone*, making them feel they had a magic touch when it came to babies. And Catrin was confident that when her two best friends turned up at that church on Sunday, there was no way they'd be able to walk out. Romy was going to have them both well and truly under her spell.

33

Judith

She hated it when he went quiet on her. He'd been like it since the night before. She knew he'd come round eventually, because he always did. But she found it so boring having to wait.

'D'you want a fruit pastille?' she asked, desperate to defuse the atmosphere.

But he kept his eyes firmly on the road. 'No, ta.'

She waited a few minutes, then suggested stopping at the next services. Bit of fresh air and a stretch of the legs might encourage him to talk, she thought.

Once inside, they ordered two cappuccinos and found a table away from everyone. She watched as he tore open the sugar sachets, poured them in and stirred.

'Gareth, for God's sake, we have to talk about it,' she insisted.

'How come we didn't know? Are you sure *you* didn't know?'

'We've been through this.'

She knew he didn't believe her. But it was true.

*

When Jack had come home the night before and told them he'd met someone, they were both understandably excited. Their boy. Their seventeen-year-old, handsome son, Jack Andreas Harris Metcalf, straight-A student and recently passed his driving test, had finally got a girlfriend! *Don't go over the top,* she had to tell herself. *Play it cool.*

'Oh that's nice,' she said. 'Anyone we know?' And she glanced over at Gareth, who smiled and winked at her. This was one of those parental milestones.

'Yes, it is.'

'Let me guess,' she said. Completely disobeying her own rule to underplay. 'Is it Charlotte?'

'No.'

'OK, the girl from youth orchestra you're always giving lifts to?'

'Er, no, not her.'

'Let him speak, Jude, for God's sake,' said Gareth gently.

Jack cleared his throat and looked down, clearly awkward at the prospect of discussing his love life with his ancient parents.

And then he said it.

'It's Dan.'

Everything stopped. The cuckoo clock in the hall declared it was eight o'clock.

'What?' asked Gareth eventually, still smiling.

'Dan. Y'know, Dan Barker.'

'Rugby Dan?' Judith asked. A lot of Jack's friends' names had a prefix.

'Yes,' Jack said, his voice steady, ready for a row.

'Oh.'

'But Dan's a boy,' she said.

'Ten out of ten for observation, Mother.'

She hated it when he called her 'Mother'. So patronizing. As if she knew nothing about life or the world.

Gareth stood up. 'I'm going out for a bit,' he mumbled.

'Where?' she asked, louder than she'd intended.

'Just out.'

And he went. Leaving Judith and Jack shrouded in embarrassed silence.

'Well, that went down better than I'd expected!' he said, trying to cover up the nerves that were catching in his voice.

'I don't know what to say.'

One of Jack's many brilliant qualities, Judith believed, was his considerate nature. He'd always been like that. When he was little she'd often find him rescuing a stranded worm, or a trapped bee. Or if he caught Gareth looking sad or Judith looking tired, he'd always offer them a hug or a glass of squash. In school the teachers loved him, not just because he was such an academic whizz, but because he was so kind to the other pupils. Whenever a new kid started, he or she was automatically consigned to Jack's care. And now he'd grown into a self-assured, quietly confident and exceptionally thoughtful young man. Even last night, having made what must have been such a difficult confession for him, his focus was solely on Judith. He sat next to her on the settee, where, try as she might to stop the tears, they just kept coming.

'How come I didn't know?' she whispered.

'Maybe because I didn't tell you?'

'But I'm your mother. I *should* know things like that. I should be able to tell.'

'We've all got to have secrets, Mum. You haven't done anything wrong.'

She'd always believed this inherent compassion was born out of being a solitary twin. Jack was the baby who'd won the fight for life – a fight which his sister Georgia had so catastrophically lost. Did he suffer some kind of subconscious survivor's guilt? Is that what drove him to compensate? Putting out fires wherever he saw them to somehow make up for the death of his sibling, to pay some karmic price for winning the race.

She had once suggested this to Gareth, who told her it was cod psychology and that the reason Jack was so remarkable was ''Cos we brought him up proper, like, nothing more than that, babe.' Maybe he was right. But whatever the reason, Jack was undoubtedly a beautiful soul.

Even Judith's mother, who'd never shown any interest in children, especially her own, had completely fallen in love with her grandson. It had taken a while for her to come round, but hard-hearted Patricia was helpless in the face of Jack's tenderness. Seeing him bring out this softer, previously unseen side of her mother was disturbing for Judith, who couldn't remember ever experiencing anything akin to maternal love when she herself was growing up.

The day before Cat and Sol's wedding, she'd finally plucked up the courage to tell her mother about the pregnancy.

Unsurprisingly, Patricia had reacted badly to the news that her nineteen-year-old unmarried daughter was 'with child'. She told Judith she was ashamed and wanted nothing to do with her or her 'bastard' offspring. Although she'd been expecting it, it still hit Judith like a slap in the face.

Then after the loss of Georgia and Jack's premature birth, Judith was too blasted to even contemplate telling Patricia what had happened. It felt fragile and private, and she suspected her mother would merely try to make the tragedy her own. So she said nothing, presuming the gossip network of Coed Celyn would do its job and Patricia would eventually deign to get in touch. But she didn't.

It was Gareth who had eventually poured oil on troubled waters. When Jack was just three months old, he took him for a walk in his stroller and knocked on Patricia's door. She opened it, scowling. Gareth responded with a big smile. 'Look who's come to meet you!' he said, and on cue, Jack had gurgled at her and wriggled in excitement.

It was love at first sight, and Patricia had instantly morphed into a doting grandma. Judith could never work out why her mother was able to love her grandson more than her own daughter, but Gareth merely put it down to her 'getting soft in her old age'.

When they still lived in Coed Celyn, Patricia would take Jack for walks at least twice a week, dressing him up in some ridiculous outfit that she'd bought from a dusty catalogue. She doted on him, and so when Judith announced they were moving to Surrey in 2001 it broke Patricia's heart.

'God knows what your grandmother will say when she finds out her beloved grandson is gay,' Judith had whispered to Jack the night before as he sat next to her, rubbing her back.

'Aw, Nana Pat will be OK. I can do no wrong as far as she's concerned,' he'd said, and Judith had managed a small smile.

She looked at Gareth now, sitting opposite her, staring at his cup and scooping the froth from his coffee with a spoon.

'I'm really happy for him,' she said. 'I mean Dan's a nice boy, isn't he? We like Dan, don't we?' She knew she was pushing him, but she needed a reaction.

'It's easy for you,' he said. 'You're a woman!'

'How in God's name does my being a woman make any difference?'

But he couldn't answer her.

She held his hand.

Sometimes she felt poor Gareth had been just swept up in the whirlwind of *her* life and had never been allowed to find his feet again. He'd always been completely supportive of her: of that there was no doubt. When she'd been promoted at the Welsh Office four years ago, he was dead proud, and they had both welcomed the hefty pay rise. At first she'd tried commuting, but it wasn't long before travelling to London at least four times a week began to take its toll. She was on the verge of packing it all in when Gareth suggested they relocate. Good old salt-of-the-earth Gareth, Welsh to his very bones, who'd never travelled much beyond the Principality, was prepared to up sticks and turn English.

'As long as my son still supports Wales in the rugby,' he'd joked. 'I'll disown him he starts supporting England!'

'But what about *your* job?' she'd asked. 'And Jack's school?'

'Me and Jack will be fine. *He*'ll make friends with anyone and my job's like hairdressing – I can do it anywhere.'

She'd laughed at the thought of Gareth cutting hair and blue-rinsing old ladies, but really she was touched that he was prepared to make the sacrifice.

Within two months they'd moved over the Severn Bridge and landed in deepest, leafiest Surrey, where he'd set himself up in a little one-man business. Today, four years later, he was the proprietor of Metcalf's Autos in Richmond, and the employer of two mechanics and a receptionist. He'd made friends on the way, of sorts, and he was adamant that he didn't miss Coed Celyn. But, deep down, Judith wasn't so sure.

Sometimes he *did* go back, of course. On his own. Just to visit that special, quiet place. But those visits were private and necessary for him to do alone.

'I'll be all right,' he smiled, and kissed her hand. 'Just takes a bit of getting used to, that's all. And, of course, we'll never become grandparents.'

Judith knew that now was not the time to point out that just because their son was gay didn't mean he couldn't have babies. She decided to save that one for another day. If there was one thing she'd learned about Gareth, it was that he wasn't good with an information overload.

'Come on,' she said gently. 'Let's get going.'

34

Lana

Adam Pride the photographer was getting on her bloody wick. They'd been there four hours and her mouth had begun to ache from smiling. He was obsessed with the wind machine, and the make-up artist wouldn't leave her alone, fussing with her hair after every shot, it seemed.

'OK, now I really want to see the sex in your eyes,' he said. 'I need you to connect with me through the lens.'

Tosser, she thought.

'Let's try some sitting down.'

She obeyed without complaint, though her patience was wearing thin. She was desperate for a drink, but Frankie the publicist had had 'a quiet word' with her before the shoot.

'Just so you know, Adam is . . . he's in recovery,' she'd said, her voice sombre and serious. 'So it's strictly no booze in the studio, I'm afraid.'

Frankie'd done several of these publicity sessions with her and had quickly learned that Lana needed wine to make it all bearable.

'Oh, OK. Well, you can always sneak a bit of vodka into my orange juice!' she'd said jauntily.

But Frankie had clearly thought she was joking. Lana sighed. It was going to be a very long day.

Four outfits, three make-up changes and another hour later and the photo shoot was finished. Next was the interview. The *Sunday Edition* had sent their 'top' celebrity interviewer Ryan Pearman to sit with her for an in-depth profile piece. She was always wary when it came to these things, but it had to be done – it was part of her contract with any acting job to engage in press and publicity.

She joined him in the chill-out area of the vast white studio. He was already armed with two Dictaphones ('Just in case!'), a battered notebook, on which she glimpsed a list of scribbled questions, and a glossy publicity pack that the PR team had sent out to all the press. The new flagship series she was promoting had garnered massive media interest. Not because of Lana. And she knew this. But because of her co-star – American film goddess Katya Molenski.

The show was Katya's comeback after a dark period of drug addiction and a spell in rehab. She had gone straight to LA once filming finished, so the British press in the main had had to settle for Lana when it came to the interviews. She was very much taking one for the team. Ryan would rather be sitting opposite Katya right now, and they both knew this. But still they played the game.

'So!' he launched in. 'You're playing a sex addict with a score to settle.'

The Dictaphones pointed defensively in her direction, ensuring everything she said was captured on tape.

'Yeah, she's a great character,' she replied.

Lana had done so many of these promotional interviews by now, she knew the answers by rote.

'I knew as soon as I read the script that I simply *had* to play the part,' she lied. Truth be told, she'd have settled for anything when her agent called with the offer. Work was a bit thin on the ground last year and the only reason she got the job was because Carrie Heath had dropped out. Carrie was Lana's nemesis. She actually liked her a lot: they'd worked on a couple of films together. But she always got the parts Lana would love, leaving her to scavenge for the leftovers.

'I was looking at your IMDb. Would you say your big break was playing Myfanwy in *Still Waters*?'

'Most definitely. I was on it for five years and I'll always be eternally grateful for the opportunity. People can be scathing about soap operas – they think they're somehow second-rate. But that's just snobbery. I learned my craft on that show. It was bloody hard work.'

Lana always said this when asked about *Still Waters*. But the real reason they'd kept her on for so long was because she was sleeping with the Executive Producer. And the reason they sacked her was because she stopped. Sleeping with him.

'Now I heard a rumour . . .' said Ryan with a sly grin.

Uh-oh, here we go, she thought.

'. . . that you were having an affair with Paul Durrant, the top guy.'

She was always prepared for this one, and she smiled her effervescent, charming and well-practised smile. 'Oh Ryan, y'know you really shouldn't listen to gossip.'

'But I'm a gossip columnist!' he retorted, laughing. He wasn't giving up.

'Really? And there's me thinking you were a highly professional, highly trained and intelligent journalist.'

Touché. He was letting this one go. For now.

'So d'you ever go back to your homeland, Lana? Ogi ogi ogi an' all that boyo?'

Dear God, she thought, and smiled.

'Yes, as often as I can. I'm going back on Sunday, as it goes. For my god-daughter's christening.'

Why did she tell him that? Never talk personal life, Lana!

'Really? You don't strike me as the religious type.'

'She's the daughter of my best friend. It's an honour to be asked, don't you think?'

That's right, push it back on to him.

'Of course. And how d'you handle those kinds of events back home? Is everyone clamouring for a photo? Must be so difficult being the famous friend!'

'Nah, no one's bothered about all that stuff. They just think of me as good old Lana. I'm pretty ordinary when it comes down to it.'

'Ordinary like the people back home?'

She hesitated. *God, this guy's a prick*, she thought.

'What d'you mean?' she asked, still smiling. But Ryan Pearman had moved on.

'Do you ever regret not having children yourself?'

The fucking nerve of this man. 'Well, I'm only thirty-seven, Ryan, still a spring chicken.'

'Ah! And do you have someone in mind? To be Daddy, as it were? Seeing as you're single again . . . ?'

She sighed inwardly, and smiled at him again. 'Shall we talk more about the show?'

'Of course!' he said smoothly. 'So, this part you're playing in *Devil May Care* . . .'

'It's *share*. Devil May *Share*.'

'Sorry. So this part you're playing, this sex-addicted bad ass – how much of the real Lana Lloyd is in the role?'

'Well, nothing. Because she's a fictitious character.'

'So you don't enjoy sex then?' he laughed.

And she laughed too, to disguise how pissed off she was. 'Ryan, you're starting to get on my tits now, babe!'

'Chance would be a fine thing,' he smiled back.

Perv.

'I'm sorry to hear about your divorce,' he said, attempting a sympathetic smile.

'Are you?'

'Yes. Of course. I've been through it myself, I wouldn't wish it on anyone.'

'Right,' she replied, suspicious of where he was going.

'But to go through it twice like you have, Lana, I mean that's horrendous. Your first marriage lasted . . . what was it . . . nine months?'

'Eight. I was very young.'

'And your second . . . ?'

She stared at him, determined not to answer.

'Just five years, I was told . . . ?'

Mind your own fucking business, you creep.

'Yes, Ryan, I obviously have terrible character judgement when it comes to men.' And then she laughed. 'I mean, I always used to think that *you* were a decent bloke, for example!'

He didn't know how to take this and so he moved on again.

They talked some more about the fun she'd had filming, what Katya Molenski was *really* like, and was it true she could be a bit of a diva? Lana told him she was a peach and he asked her for some amusing anecdotes.

'Well, there was this one time when I had to eat a bowl of spaghetti and I put too much on my fork and it was just falling out of my mouth when I spoke, and Katya got the giggles, which started me off, and suddenly there was spaghetti actually coming out of my nose. It was gross but absolutely hilarious.'

The whole story was entirely made up, but by now Lana was bored and just wanted to get away from the creepy journo.

Before he started packing up, he asked her for a photo. 'My wife's a big fan,' he said. So Lana obediently stood next to him, his arm around her shoulders a tad too tight, whilst the stylist took a quick snap on his mobile phone.

'OK, we done?' she said brightly.

'For sure, that was brilliant. It'll be out in time for the first episode.'

'Great. Thanks, Ryan. The pleasure was all mine.' And she turned to go and get changed.

As she headed over to the dressing area, the stylist asked her if she needed a hand.

'No, you're all right,' she called back cheerily, ducking behind the curtain.

'That's a wrap, everyone!' called the assistant, and they all went about their business of packing up for the day.

Lana began undressing, eager to be out of her alien clothes at last. She was down to her knickers and bra when her mobile rang.

Catrin.

'I'm just getting changed,' she said, putting the phone on to speaker.

'How did it go?'

'Oh you know, same old same old.' Lana leant into the handset and whispered, 'The journalist was a dickhead and so was the photographer, but it's done now.'

'Your life is ridiculous.'

'I know.'

'So what time you arriving Sunday?'

'Well, I'll probably get there just before the service starts. It's two o'clock, right? Sorry I can't get down sooner, but I've got this charity thing the night before.'

'No worries,' said Catrin. 'But when you get to the church, come in the side door, otherwise everyone will hassle you. We'll keep you a seat down the front.'

'Sure.' She was into her jeans by now and struggling to pull on her top.

'And Larn?' asked Catrin from the other end of the line.

'Yeah?'

'I just want to check. Is there absolutely no way you'll come if Judith's there?'

'I can't believe you're even asking me that,' she said irritably. But Catrin wasn't giving up.

'It was eighteen years ago!' she yelled.

'I wouldn't care if it was a hundred years ago!' Lana yelled back. 'Look, if you want to invite Judith, I'll bow out. But please stop asking me about this, Cat.'

'Sorry,' she said. 'Can't blame a girl for trying though, can you?'

Lana grabbed the rest of her things and headed out of the changing area. When she pulled back the curtain she could see Ryan Pearman loitering like a ravenous seagull on the scrounge. He smiled at her – a guilty smile. And Lana realized he must've been eavesdropping.

Tosser, she thought.

35

Catrin

'God, I love you, Catrin Blythe,' Sol whispered, his eyes closed as he kissed her. The final throes of orgasm made him judder, and, exhausted, he freed himself from their tangle of limbs.

She wanted him to stay there longer, but she didn't tell him this. He still had his socks on. She was only wearing a bra. They didn't have sex as much as they used to – and when they *did* do it, it was perfunctory, no room or inclination for foreplay. Like any couple with a baby, she supposed. *Grab it whilst you can!* Though compared to some of her similarly aged patients, Catrin was positively nymphomaniacal.

'They're definitely bringing the cake in the morning, aren't they?' she asked him in the darkness of bedtime.

'Yes,' he mumbled, and she could tell he was dropping off. 'That's the third time you've asked me now, you nutter,' he said lazily, but there was kindness in his voice.

'I'm sorry I'm such a handful,' she said. And she struggled to keep the tears from creeping into her voice.

He turned to her then and kissed her on the nose. 'You always get like this before a party,' he said gently.

'Do I?'

'Yes.' He stroked her hair. 'I think there's a term for it – "social engagement anxiety" or something.'

'Serious?'

'Nooo!' He laughed. 'God, you're gullible! Now roll over and let's get some kip. You're gonna need to be on form tomorrow when Judith and Lana start pulling each other's hair out.'

He was asleep within minutes, leaving Catrin to lie there, eyes open. It wasn't just Judith and Lana she was worrying about: there was something more pressing that she had to confront. Because time was running out.

Over the past ten years, she had cursed herself relentlessly for ever going on the Pill. All the planning, the prevention – born from a fear of getting pregnant; a fear that would later transform into an all-consuming need. An obsession. Which had nearly cost her their marriage. Catrin had simply *assumed* she would have babies. Never for one minute did she think it might be a problem. *Golden rule in life,* Lana used to say, *never assume Fuck All.* And she was right.

Once Catrin and Sol had settled into their joint practice for a couple of years, they'd thought the time had come to start a family. So she'd done everything by the book: came off the Pill, stopped drinking, started taking folic acid, even took up running! They were only thirty when they began 'trying'. Which was great fun. Neither of them would deny that. They'd make charts and take temperatures, sometimes rushing home in the lunch hour for quick sex – they even did it once in the surgery, which was so tense and risky they laughed throughout the entire process.

But despite their commitment and determination, nothing happened. Month after month they'd both wait, Catrin praying to her recently rediscovered Catholic God to ward off that familiar dull throb at the base of her abdomen that heralded yet another unwelcome period.

'You can't have the sunshine if you don't have the rain,' her dad would whisper during those sad times, when he'd engulf her in a big fatherly hug and kiss the top of her head, just like he had when she was little. But the rain fell torrentially and the sun remained absent from her sky. She waited and waited for it to come back, only to be defeated by disappointment again and again.

After three years of trying everything – strange diets, uncomfortable sex positions, meditation and more prayers – they'd finally surrendered to the idea of IVF. And once she'd come to terms with the fact that IVF didn't mean they'd failed, only that they needed a helping hand, Catrin's optimism was renewed.

But the first attempt was unsuccessful.

And so was the second.

And then the third attempt failed too.

So Solomon took over, sitting her down and gently saying it was time for them both to stop trying. They'd used up all three NHS opportunities – now they had to think about other options.

But Catrin wouldn't hear of it and was undeterred in her mission. And it *was* a mission. Becoming a mother was all she lived for – she was obsessed. She went ahead with making appointments, applying for loans, pressing Sol's parents, as well as her own, for financial help, despite Sol asking her not to. Edward and Amelia were the only ones who *could* afford to help, but they gently turned them down for religious reasons, which Catrin found offensive, flying off the handle when they said no and refusing to speak to them ever again.

'They're scientists, for fuck's sake! Doctors!' she screamed.

Sol saw a side to his wife he'd never before witnessed and moved out for a month. Even this did not stop her. Undeterred and in desperation, she asked Judith and Lana both separately if they could help. Knowing that they had less money than she did, but having lost all dignity, Catrin cared nothing for the embarrassment caused when both friends declined. More IVF was all she could talk about or think about, to the point where she stopped looking after herself, sometimes going days without washing, calling in sick to work, wearing the same stained shellsuit every day and barely leaving the house – spending hours on the phone to clinics and loan companies, ordering hundreds of books and magazines, arming herself with knowledge and shutting out the rest of the world. Until her energy finally fizzled to a standstill and she gave up all hope. She sank into a deep, dark pit of despondency. No longer manically determined to pursue her quest, she simply lost the will to go on.

Sol moved back home and turned to his friends for help. Judith arrived with leaflets and tried talking about adoption with her. Catrin refused to discuss the subject. Then, a week later, Lana turned up with a bottle of tequila in hand, telling Cat what she needed was a night on the razz to pull her out of herself and that having children wasn't the be-all and end-all. Catrin screamed at her and Lana scuttled off with her tail between her legs.

That night, Catrin broke down in Sol's arms and wept herself into a weary state of acceptance. It was over. It was time to stop. And despite being couched in a blanket of sorrow, to surrender felt strangely liberating. It brought the two of them closer together than they'd been in a very long while. They made love that night for the first time in months.

She took six weeks off work and promised her family and friends that she would start to look after herself again. She cleaned the house from top to bottom and brought brochures back from the travel agent – she and Sol needed a holiday. She shopped for healthy, wholesome foods and even made bread in her long-abandoned breadmaker. She knew she needed to gain a few pounds – she'd lost so much weight through sadness and self-neglect. So much so that when her period didn't come that month, she presumed weight loss was the reason. Sol had taken to making hearty cooked breakfasts in an attempt to coax back Catrin's appetite. And then one Wednesday morning, she sat and looked at the plate in front of her, oozing bacon, eggs and mushrooms, little rivulets of butter running between them all . . .

. . . and she leapt up and ran for the bathroom. It had been such a long, long time coming, but when they were least expecting it, the rain had stopped and the sun had finally peeped out from behind the clouds, just like her dad had said it would.

Three tests later they were rewarded with the news they'd come to believe they'd never receive: Catrin was pregnant.

They didn't tell a soul until they'd had the sixteen-week scan, too terrified to jinx things. But when Catrin's increasing waistline could no longer be hidden under smock tops and XXL T-shirts, they decided to take the plunge and announce it. Even then they didn't dare get too excited, and Catrin forbade her mother to even think about knitting bootees.

And then, on 26 August 2004, Romy Amelia Eliza Blythe came bouncing into their world. This precious, precious cargo – too precious for Catrin to allow any-one else to hold, except Sol and their parents. For weeks after she was born, Catrin would stand over the cot, watching every breath and checking the rise and fall of her daughter's tiny chest. But gradually she learned to let go and let Romy grow, and to accept that she could never protect her from every challenge life would throw her way. And she was better at it now – another reason she'd agreed to the christening. She knew she should have done it sooner, but better late than never.

*

The next morning, Sol was up and dressed before her. Catrin came downstairs in her pyjamas, sleepy headed and toasty, to find him in his best suit protected by a Spice Girls apron, making scrambled eggs. Romy was sat in her baby chair chatting away to her banana and yoghurt.

'Blimey, you're eager beavers,' she said, kissing Romy on her soft downy hair.

'I didn't risk putting her christening dress on,' said Sol, scooping up the creamy eggs on to thick buttered toast and handing it to her. 'Thought we ought to leave it till the last minute. Don't want her all covered in breakfast when Father O'Leary's holding her over the font.'

'Very wise,' said Catrin, grinding black pepper on to her eggs. She watched as Sol poured them both coffee then came to sit next to her at the breakfast bar. Romy gurgled at them both and Catrin sighed, contented – inwardly offering up a short prayer of gratitude for her beautiful little family. 'You look so gorgeous,' she said to Sol.

'So do you,' he laughed back, 'in a sort of crumpled, slept-in kind of a way . . .'

They munched on their toast and eggs. He was such a good cook. One of his many, many qualities. How blessed was she? She couldn't shatter all this now, could she? Now wasn't the right time to pose the question.

As if reading her mind, he looked at her and smiled. 'Nervous?'

She was thrown off balance. 'What? Er, no.'

'Good. 'Cos you've got absolutely nothing to worry about.'

He was talking about the encroaching potential clash between Lana and Judith at the christening. She wished he was talking about babies. More babies.

No. This wasn't the right time. She didn't know when would be, but it certainly wasn't now. And once again Catrin chickened out, swallowing her nerves with a big gulp of coffee.

36
Judith

They arrived at her mother's house at midday. They'd planned it this way so they wouldn't have to spend more than an hour there before going to the church. It took a while for Patricia to answer the door, and when she did she looked a bit ragged.

'Late night, Mother?' Judith asked.

'Don't start,' growled Patricia, leaving the door open for them to follow her inside.

Judith shared a smile with Gareth. Her mother no longer scared her. If anything, she found her entertaining. She'd long since let go of the catalogue of hurt inflicted by Patricia as she was growing up. And she'd long since forgiven the more palpable blots on her mother's pitiful copy-book, such as trapping George into marriage, or rejecting her daughter when she was pregnant. In fact, she'd long since stopped indulging the self-pity of trawling through Patricia's list of parenting failures. Because happiness was the best revenge: and Judith had found happiness in her own life now, as a mother and a wife and a woman with a highly successful career. These days, she viewed Patricia as a sad, lonely relative, more like an ageing aunt than a mother, to whom she and Gareth would always be connected through a duty of care and no more. And, of course, she was still Jack's grandmother, and that counted for something.

The room was a mess. Overflowing ashtrays and empty lager cans. 'Looks like you've had a bit of a party,' said Gareth, and he started clearing up as Patricia settled herself on the settee. She couldn't have been less pleased to see them.

'Jack sends his love,' Judith said. The mention of her boy was always guaranteed to warm even Patricia's ice-cold cockles.

'He not with you then?'

'No, the thing is he—' Judith started to say, but Gareth got in before her.

'He's got rugby,' he interrupted, niftily heading off a discussion about Jack's recent revelation. 'Shall I put the kettle on?'

These visits were always the same. Duty visits, Gareth called them. Judith found her mother's attitude to life to be unrelentingly negative. Two years previously, when Patricia had turned sixty-five, they'd sorted out a bus pass for her. She'd never used it once. And whenever they called, they always ran through exactly the same conversation:

How is your hip? *Makes my life a living hell.*

How is work? *They pay me a pittance and I work like a dog. I'm sixty-seven, for Christ's sake.*

How's *insert name*? *He's gone back to his wife*, or *Christ knows, the man's a fool.*

She never asked them anything about their lives except for Jack, the one-who-could-do-no-wrong.

Judith watched as Patricia hauled herself up on to her feet, noticing a tomato-ketchup stain on her mother's dressing gown.

Reaching over to the mantelpiece, Patricia took out two crisp twenty-pound notes. 'Give this to my boy,' she said. 'Tell him to come and see his Nana.'

'Will do. Thanks.' Judith glanced at the clock. 'We better get going, the service starts in half an hour.'

And then, without warning, Patricia went off script. 'So you're going to Cyprus next week, I hear?'

'Er, yeah . . . did Jack tell you?' Judith was thrown by this, because she made a point of never mentioning her father to her mother, and although Patricia was aware of their trips to Kakopetria, it was never ever discussed.

'No. George Harris did.' On the very rare occasions when Patricia uttered the name of her ex-husband, it was always in full.

Judith couldn't believe what she was hearing. 'Really?'

Patricia ignored her as she rifled in the drawer of her tiny bureau and took out a sealed envelope. 'He wants this. Give it to him when you see him. And tell him he owes me ninety pound.'

All the way to the church, Judith wondered what on earth her father could possibly have asked her mother to give him. 'I don't get it, Gar. They've not been in touch for years!'

'You're not thinking of looking inside it, are you?' asked Gareth, his voice loaded with caution.

'Well, I could steam it open,' she said.

'No, Jude. It's private.'

'You're too honest for your own good,' she said.

They arrived at St Theodore's, Judith having to put the whole thing out of her mind as they were swept up in the general mêlée of christening guests. Hanging around the church door and patently not dressed for the service were a few familiar faces from her school-days. Camera phones at the ready, they appeared to have come to watch. Judith guessed that, being local GPs, Catrin and Sol were local celebrities of sorts. She recognized Becky Williams amongst the throng – still as mouthy as she was when she was fourteen. She had a tattoo on her arm that read *Serenity* in a Gothic font, and Judith contemplated the different paths their lives had all taken. 'What a sight!' she whispered to Gareth, who told her she was being a snob.

They followed everyone inside and found their seats.

'Godparents down the front,' said one of the sides-men, so they obliged.

She noticed that Catrin was looking exceptionally nervous. She couldn't work out why – it wasn't like it was a wedding or anything. She put it down to anxiety at having so many friends and family gathered in the same place at the same time.

Father O'Leary began the service. Catrin, she observed, kept looking over her shoulder. Was she checking that everyone was there?

'And now may I ask members of the family, along with the godparents, to make their way to the font at the back of the church.'

Judith caught the eye of Sol's brother Tom and smiled – today they were sharing a solemn promise to bring up Romy in the name of Jesus Christ. *Blimey*, she thought.

As they settled into their positions, Father O'Leary handed out several laminated A5 cards that bore the words of the Sacrament of Baptism. He gently lifted Romy from the comfortable nest of her father's firm hold and ascended the two steps of the font. With Romy tucked into the crook of his left arm, his right hand was free to bless the water. 'In the name of the Father, the Son and the Holy Ghost—'

But he didn't get any further, interrupted by a disturbance at the side door. All heads turned to locate the source of the kerfuffle, and Judith caught the sound of urgent, whispered apologies. A flurry of 'Sorry, sorry . . . Can I just . . . Where's the . . . So sorry I'm late.' And suddenly a woman was rushing down the aisle towards the font. Judith saw *her* before *she* saw Judith.

It was Lana.

Judith grabbed hold of Tom's arm, steadying herself. Shocked at the impact of seeing her one-time friend again after all this time. She looked at Catrin, gobsmacked. But her gaze wasn't returned.

'Are you one of the guests?' asked Father O'Leary.

People began whispering.

'Yes, I'm the godmother,' Lana said breathlessly as someone handed her an order of service.

But then *she* saw *Judith*. And stopped in her tracks.

'What the . . . ?'

Catrin interrupted before Lana could finish. 'Shall we carry on?' she said to Father O'Leary, her voice quivering.

'Right. Now then' – he indicated to Lana – 'if you'd like to take your place with the other godparents . . . ?'

Everything stood still.

Lana stared at Judith.

Judith stared at Lana.

'Larn?' whispered Catrin, and she beckoned her over to join them.

With the pressure of thirty pairs of eyes upon her, Lana seemingly had no option other than to do what Catrin asked. She looked down as she settled next to Judith, who was aware of the strong smell of perfume mixed with cigarettes.

She still smokes, then, Judith thought.

The service continued.

Judith couldn't take any of it in, focusing hard on not making eye contact with Lana. Romy started crying when the holy water was audaciously poured over her head three times.

'That's the Devil coming out of her,' whispered Cat's Nana Kelly, who was a big fan of fire and brimstone.

When that part of the service was over, Father O'Leary brought the baby over to where they were all standing. 'Now, if one of the godparents would like to hold this little one while we light the votive candles?' he said.

There was a hiatus. No one knew what to do. If Judith offered or declined in favour of the others, it meant engaging with Lana. She sensed the feeling was mutual.

Luckily Sol's brother stepped in. 'Come to your Uncle Tom, pet,' he said, taking her from Father O'Leary's arms.

The two godmothers were each given a candle to hold and a little card certificate bearing the date and place of Romy's christening. Judith's name was on there, along with Tom's. And Lana's. This whole thing had obviously been pre-planned and she couldn't wait for it to be over. She was furious with Cat, and gutted that she'd not been able to enjoy a single moment of what should have been a special event.

They all made their way back to the other end of the church and Father O'Leary concluded the service. The second it finished, Judith headed straight for the side entrance of the church, swiftly followed by Gareth.

'D'you think she knew?' asked Gareth. 'Catrin, I mean. Or d'you think Lana just turned up without warning?'

'Of course she knew! Her bloody name was on the certificate.'

Over at the main entrance the other guests began pouring out of the church, full of joy and celebration, unaware of the enforced and reluctant reunion that'd just taken place in their presence. Lana was laughing with some of Sol's relatives and Judith felt shocked by how much she resented it. Lana's irritating nonchalance. She also resented how good Lana looked. Occasionally over the years Judith had caught sight of her on TV, so she knew what she looked like these days. But seeing her in the flesh was different. She glanced at Gareth to see if he was looking at Lana too. He was. And she was instantly struck by a flash of jealousy – *Does he think she's more attractive than me?* she wondered. Or was he just being curious? She cursed herself for being so immature and then noticed that Becky Williams had got her camera out. *So that's why she and her cronies are here! To catch sight of Lana Lloyd! Jesus.* When the camera was turned on her and Gareth, Judith looked away.

'A couple of Mum's friends need a lift back to the house,' Catrin called out, walking towards them now, with no reference to what had just happened in the church. 'I'm afraid I offered your services.'

'So you knew,' said Gareth, ignoring the request. 'That she was coming?'

Catrin blushed. 'Well, I invited all of you, didn't I?' she said, attempting and failing to sound blasé.

'Right, well we'll drop your mum's friends off, but then we're heading back,' said Gareth, clearly annoyed.

'Don't be ridiculous. You've come all this way!' said Catrin, panicking.

'Cat, what were you thinking?' Judith finally found her voice. 'This is so out of order.'

'I had to do *something*,' she said. Judith shook her head. 'And Lana's just as pissed off with me as you are.'

They looked over to where Lana was now having photos taken with some of the guests. She seemed to Judith to be lording it all over the place with her un-ashamed showbiz ego.

'She looks anything *but* pissed off, you ask me, Cat.'

'Please come,' said Catrin. 'For Romy, if not for me.'

Judith hesitated and Gareth shrugged. 'It's up to you,' he said. 'Sorry, Cat, but I'm not going anywhere near that woman. Jude, if you want to go I'll pick you up later.'

She was torn. It felt churlish not to go.

'I'll come for an hour,' she said at last. 'But do not think for one minute I'm going to speak to her.'

'God forbid,' muttered Catrin.

And Judith thought how rare it was to catch a sarcastic tone in the voice of her lovely friend.

37
Gareth

It had been a secluded plot seventeen years ago. And back then he'd welcomed the privacy. Out at the edge. In the shade of a magnolia that was too shy to blossom except in April, for one glorious, brief, blink-and-you-miss-it fortnight. He always tried to visit during those magical two weeks if he could, to witness the spectacle: the majesty of the confident white blooms, standing to attention like a naturally forming candelabra. And he'd think the same thing every time he saw it: that the tree should bear a sign saying, *Come see the flowers! For a limited period only!* There were no blooms today, of course. Being July, it was too late in the year. And this was an unplanned visit. But it just seemed the best place to hide whilst Judith did her bit at the party. Normally he brought flowers with him. And a hip flask of whisky to drink a little private toast. He began clearing away the dead flowers from last time, all dried up now and faded.

As the years had gone by, new plots appeared with every visit. A sad indictment of the cycle of life, the wheels of mortality that kept relentlessly turning:

headstones bearing names and dates, declaring never-ending love, promises of eternal remembrance, quotes from the Bible and a hundred poems. It was a double-edged sword – he was glad now that her little grave was no longer alone, but sad at the reason for it being so. Headstones always looked brand new, he thought. Even those that dated back to the 1960s looked pristine and newly hewn. Hers was white marble, guarded by a pretty cherub atop the words they'd chosen back then in a fug of confused despair.

In loving memory of
Georgia Metcalf
born and died
December 13th, 1987
cherished daughter of Judith and Gareth
twin sister of Jack
Sleep safe in heaven, angel
Until we meet again.

They'd always regretted not giving her a middle name. As if she was even more short-changed by that somehow. Had they given themselves more time to think, to breathe, they'd have called her Georgia May after Gareth's grandmother. But it was all so rushed and they were so numb.

Gareth had gone alone to register both the birth and death of his daughter. Judith had wanted to come with him, but his heart was being wrenched apart and he couldn't bear her to feel the same pain.

She needed the little strength that she had for the funeral. Which was almost non-existent. Just him and Jude and Catrin and Sol and the Anglican vicar from All Saints. They didn't want anyone else there. Patricia hadn't even been told of the birth, let alone the death. They wanted to keep it tiny and unassuming, like the tiny, unassuming life of their little girl. And forever etched in his memory was the image of Georgia's tiny white coffin as they placed it gently and carefully into the ground.

Six weeks later, Gareth and Judith *did* go to the register office together – this time for happier reasons. Firstly to record the birth of their baby boy, who, after a precarious start in life, had begun to blossom. Taking the little man himself with them for company and wrapped up warm against the January cold, they gave him two compensatory middle names – *Jack Andreas Harris Metcalf*. His tiny fist grasped Judith's thumb all the while, and his big, wonder-filled eyes, bright and inquisitive, took in his surroundings as if he knew he was being formally acknowledged as a member of the human race. *I wonder if he'll remember her?* Gareth often wondered. Would he hang on to some subconscious memory of the twin with whom he'd shared the safety of their mother's womb for six whole months?

They'd also decided to do something else that day.

They'd decided to marry.

It felt right. To commit to each other even in the depths of such overbearing sorrow, to find a small glimmer of joy that might encourage them, along with the gift of their baby, to look to the future with hope. They invited Sol and Catrin to be their witnesses, with no other guests apart from little Jack. And although the ceremony was quiet and small, it endorsed the vast and boundless love they felt for each other.

Coming here now, almost two decades after Georgia's death, no longer broke Gareth's heart. In fact, as he'd grown older, he'd begun to look forward to his trips back to this pretty little graveyard in Coed Celyn – at least twice a year, around the time of her birthday and during magnolia fortnight. Sometimes Jack came with him. Never Jude. But it made no difference whether he was alone or not. For him it was a chance to stand quietly and contemplate. It brought him peace.

Seeing Lana at the christening had been a strange sensation. It had become second nature to him to avoid any contact whatsoever with her – quite an achievement, given that he and Judith shared the mutual close friendship of Sol and Catrin. But they'd fallen into a routine – that any meet-ups they had with the Blythes would be guaranteed to be Lana-free. And they'd all got used to living like this. To such an extent that Lana's name was never mentioned.

He'd often wondered how he'd react if he *did* ever

meet her again. Whether the anger would have lessened, the resentment diminished. But no. Seeing her standing in that church made him realize he still felt exactly the same. And he was oddly glad about that. Gareth liked to know where he was. He relished certainty.

He just wished he could feel so sure about Jack.

About what he'd told them the night before.

Could it be a phase, or was he being naïve? What were people going to say? What were they going to think? That he wasn't a good enough father – that he hadn't brought his son up to be a proper man? Jesus, what was he turning into – one of those parents who couldn't handle their kid being gay? They didn't even use the word 'gay' when he was younger. Horrible words they'd used – poofter, Nancy boy, and worse – all bandied around like a joke. He felt ashamed of that, thinking back. Nasty. That's what he was. And small-minded, and deeply disloyal. To his own boy. He sighed.

And ran his fingers along the lettering on Georgia's headstone.

Love.

That's all that mattered really.

That Jack found love.

With whoever he chose.

Deep breaths. He watched as a goldfinch flitted around the gravestones in search of food. It landed on the hand of the little marble cherub and rested there, before fluttering its wings and taking off again.

It was time to head off himself. Time to collect Judith and go home. Back to their wonderful son.

38
Judith

At the Kellys' house, Judith found a corner in Huw's conservatory and spent the time talking mainly to Cat's Nana. Occasionally she looked up and did a quick sweep of the room to ensure that Lana hadn't wandered in by accident. Though if she had, Judith wasn't entirely sure what she'd do about it. She'd been on edge since she arrived and couldn't wait for Gareth to come back and collect her. At least she could say she'd done her bit.

Liz Kelly approached, carrying two plates piled high with crustless sandwiches, and thrust them at her, daring Judith to refuse.

'Well now, isn't this grand?' she said. 'What a super day.'

Judith nodded back, not wanting to dampen her enthusiasm.

'It's all about Romy, of course,' Liz went on. 'But I was just saying to Huw, what a treat to have you and Lana and Catrin together again. What a treat.'

Judith was unsure how to react, but didn't want to be rude. 'I can't remember the last time I went to a christening,' she said feebly, taking a huge bite of sand-wich. 'Mm, these ham and egg are delicious, Liz.'

Please don't make me start talking about it.

'Oh, there you are!' said Catrin as she bustled into the conservatory holding a very contented Romy in her arms. 'You haven't had a photo with the star of the show yet!' And she handed Romy to her godmother, who was suddenly all ham, egg and baby with nowhere to hide. 'Come out the front. Dad's got the camera ready.'

She could hardly say no.

'OK, but Gareth'll be here in a minute. We need to get back on the road,' she said to Mrs Kelly Senior.

There was a little bench in the front garden partly shaded by two potted olive trees. It'd been there as long as Judith could remember. When they were fourteen, she, Lana and Catrin all carved their initials into the back of it. Liz Kelly had told them off when she found out, calling the three of them 'mindless vandals'. Though, as ever, she did it with a smile.

'Sit yourself down there, now,' instructed Huw Kelly. 'In the middle, with her highness.' Romy sat comfort-ably on Judith's lap, happily playing with the coloured beads that hung around her neck. 'And Tom,' he said to Sol's brother, 'you stand behind with Catrin.'

'Make sure it's in focus, Dad,' said Catrin, watching as her father fiddled with the camera.

With her free hand, Judith reached back and ran her fingers along the ageing wood. Fainter now after years' worth of Welsh weather-battering, but still there – *CK,*

LL, JH and the date *1982*. Just when the Falklands War began. She recalled how they'd all panicked that the world was coming to an end and they wanted somehow to make their mark on history. To be remembered. Even if it was just on the back of an old garden bench.

Huw Kelly disturbed her reverie. 'Ah, and now we have a full complement!' he said, and Judith realized he was talking about Lana, who was walking towards them. Her stomach lurched. If it wasn't for Romy sat firmly on her lap, she would probably have bolted.

Neither Judith nor Lana could possibly ignore each other now.

'Judith,' Lana nodded, unable to look her in the eye.

'All right?' she mumbled in reply, aware that she sounded like a petulant teenager.

Clearly aware of the tension, the others went out of their way to compensate for the awkwardness with forced jollity.

'Right, Lana, let's have you sat on the bench next to Jude. Godmothers together, isn't it?'

This is awful, thought Judith.

She sat politely and obediently as Huw took a series of photos, but inside she was squirming. Thankfully, Catrin finally intervened. 'OK, Dad, that's enough for now!'

'For sure,' he smiled. 'Now, Tom, how about you and me go and round up the two families so we can get a nice group shot.'

'Aye, good idea.'

'I'll go,' said Lana.

'I don't mind getting them,' Judith simultaneously offered.

'Sit,' ordered Catrin, with an authority Judith seldom heard in her.

She watched as Huw and Tom Blythe disappeared into the house, leaving the three of them in excruciating silence. *Thank God for Romy and her obliviousness*, she thought.

Eventually Catrin spoke.

'So.'

No one responded.

'I've been trying to engineer this for eighteen years.'

'You shouldn't have bothered,' said Lana, focusing all her concentration on Romy. 'You had no right.'

'Hey Lana,' said Catrin. 'Guess what? *You* don't get to tell me what I can and can't do at my own daughter's christening. Now at least do me the courtesy of acknowledging each other's existence.'

Nothing.

From the house came the gentle hum of polite chat, over one of Huw Kelly's Perry Como albums.

And suddenly Romy giggled, then stuck out her little pink tongue and blew an extraordinarily long, triumphant raspberry.

All three tried to ignore it, but it was impossible. Judith cracked first, then Catrin, then Lana. The laughter quickly faded, but at least it'd broken some of the iceberg.

'Look – see? Nothing's happened, has it?' said Catrin, exasperated. 'Neither of you has died.'

Judith shrugged. Catrin was right, of course.

'I want you to be civil to each other, that's all. And I want to be able to invite you both to things from now on. Jude, what d'you say?'

'Why you asking me first?' Judith replied irritably.

'Oh grow up,' said Lana, infuriating Judith even more.

'*Me* grow up? Me?' she demanded. 'You're the one who can't get over a stupid fling you had with Gareth nearly two decades ago.'

'It was not a stupid fling. *You* were seeing him behind my back . . .'

'I bloody wasn't!' Judith shouted. 'And you – you pushed me when I was pregnant! If it wasn't for you we'd—'

But Catrin interrupted her. 'No, Jude. Now stop it. We all know that's not true. *Don't* we.' It was a statement, not a question.

And Judith sighed, because once again, she knew Catrin was right.

It seemed an age ago that the doctors had explained it to them: told them there was no evidence to suggest that Judith's fall had caused the miscarriage; no evidence to suggest that Lana should be blamed. They said it had been *just one of those things*. At the time, Catrin had seized upon this revelation as a way through for reconciliation, and with that in mind, she and Sol had suggested a quiet get-together at their student flat in Cardiff, inviting Lana along with Judith and Gareth, to see if they could mend the broken bridges. But Judith and Gareth had refused the invitation point blank. No matter how hard Catrin or Sol tried persuading them, they wanted nothing to do with Lana ever again, regardless of what the doctors or their friends told them.

It was etched on her brain now: this thing between herself and Lana. This schism. She'd taught herself to believe her own story about what had happened. And as well, the passage of time had gnawed away at the strong bonds that once held their friendship in place. Absence didn't always make the heart grow fonder, she'd long since realized: it could just as easily make the heart shut down. She felt no more for Lana Lloyd these days than she did for the woman in the local dry cleaner's. Their bond was dead. It had died long ago. And she was certain that Lana must feel the same way.

'Yeah, well,' she said. It was the nearest Judith could get to backing down.

'Look,' said Lana quietly. 'I tried apologizing back then, over and over, and you and Gareth just ignored me.'

Judith nodded, because what Lana was saying was true.

They carried on sitting in silence.

God, I wish I wasn't here, she thought.

'Jude?' said Catrin.

This was so painfully awkward. She felt like she was seven, not thirty-seven, being told off by a teacher.

'Right, I'm sorry, OK? About me and Gareth. I mean, obviously I'm not sorry me and him got together, but I'm sorry for not being straight with you from the start.'

'Yeah, so you should be.'

'Lana,' Catrin chastised.

'But we were nineteen, for God's sake!'

'Jude!' Catrin chastised again. And her two friends sat in sulky silence.

Interrupted by Romy, who hiccupped in support.

Struck by a thought, Catrin continued, 'Incidentally, seein' as we're bringing up old resentments, *neither* of you ever apologized for wrecking my wedding day. My father-in-law spent weeks making that cake and neither of you has ever mentioned it!'

Judith looked sheepish. 'Oh Cat, look . . .'

But Catrin was on a roll. 'Plus – *I'm* the one who's had to play piggy-in-the-middle for the past eighteen years, and what about me and Sol? Never allowed to mention the unmentionable friend, depending on who we're with at the time. Can you imagine what it's been like? For all these years. As far as you're concerned, Jude, Lana no longer existed, and vice bloody versa . . .'

'I'm sorry, Cat, I really—' Lana tried to apologize but was railroaded by Catrin.

'Look, it doesn't matter. What's happened has happened, but can we call this a truce? Or a ceasefire, at least? Please?'

And with Romy merrily gurgling on her lap, Judith held out her hand to Lana to shake.

'A handshake? Jesus, Jude. Have a hug, for God's sake!'

'Don't push it, Cat,' said Lana, and Judith felt the strangest sensation of being in agreement with her ex-friend when she spoke, grateful even.

The handshake was brief, clumsy, half-hearted and enforced. But it was a handshake nonetheless.

'That's a start,' said Catrin, looking incredibly relieved.

As was Judith when Gareth's car pulled up outside the house, preventing the conversation from continuing. She could see the confusion on his face as she quickly climbed in, but it was a good ten minutes before she could tell him what had just happened. Because she couldn't quite believe it herself.

39
Lana

This was the worst time of night for her – three thirty a.m. When there was nothing on telly, no one was awake, and the thoughts were running riot in her head. Admittedly the wine didn't help.

On the rare occasions when she'd managed to abstain from booze for a few weeks, life had been a joy – no parched mouth in the morning, no pounding head, no fluid retention and flabby thighs. But most of all, none of this middle-of-the-night anxiety.

Six weeks had passed since the christening. It was evident that because Lana and Judith had actually spent five minutes in each other's company, Catrin believed everything could now return to how it used to be. That was the thing about Catrin – she was unrealistically optimistic. Or away with the sodding fairies, as Lana preferred to call it.

Seeing Judith again hadn't been as bad as she'd expected. And certainly she'd spent years *imagining* it. That's what people said, wasn't it? That the anticipation of a dreaded event was often worse than the event itself.

Judith had aged, of course. 'Filled out' as Lana's

grandmother would have called it, but then Judith was always prone to put on – God knows she used to moan about it often enough. Always on some bloody diet or other. And she was much more pompous than Lana remembered. Admittedly she always could be a bit up herself, but now, with her big important government job, she thought she was the bee's bloody knees. It was funny to think they were once so close, and yet, Lana realized, if she'd met her for the first time that day, she'd never have befriended her in a million years. Judith just wasn't Lana's cup of tea.

On the day of the christening, after Judith had left the Kelly house, Lana had proceeded to write her name in a couple of bottles of Cava. She needed it in order to contend with Catrin's unrelenting persuasion tactics.

'So now you and Jude are friends again . . .' she'd said.

'We're *not* friends again, Cat,' Lana replied, but Catrin just ignored her.

'. . . maybe we can arrange a girls' get-together? A weekend away, maybe? Just us three.'

In the end, the only way to put a stop to it had been to go home.

Since then Catrin had been emailing. Copying in both Lana and Judith and making suggestions for a series of elaborate 'catch-ups'. Lana never replied. And nor, quite tellingly, did Judith. Cat was on to a bit of a loser really, and Lana hoped to God she'd just give up on her mission. She didn't want to be harsh – she knew that Catrin meant well. But some friendships had a sell-by date. *And me and Judith Harris? We're like a loaf of old bread that's definitely gone stale.*

Sometimes Lana would go so far as thinking, *Well, I love Catrin. And Catrin loves Judith. So Judith must have something going for her.* And then she'd wonder if they could . . . ? Could they just eradicate all those wasted years of resentment and start again? Was there still a bond between them other than the fact that they had a best friend in common?

It was on sleepless nights like this that Judith Harris really came back to haunt her. She'd forget the deceit, the guilt, the rejection, and remember the better times instead: like when they'd laughed so much a little bit of wee came out; or when they'd tried dying Cat's hair blonde and it went green; the shared angst of teenage years, getting caught for shoplifting three packets of Opal Fruits, putting on a funeral for Judith's goldfish, revising for exams, passing her driving test and taking them all on a road trip to Brecon; how they'd all cried on their last day of school; and, of course, the trip to Greece. It was all couched in a warm haze of sisterly love that still felt as fresh as if it had happened only yesterday.

She'd learned from Catrin that Judith's dad was seriously ill. Poor George. She'd always been so fond of him. And maybe that's why Judith was on her mind tonight. She'd sent a card via Catrin but had heard nothing back. Lana was being ridiculous, she knew this. Why should Judith reply to a poxy card? She must have so much other stuff to worry about. Still Lana couldn't help feeling rejected again. She knew it was childish of her. And self-centred. But part of her wished she'd never sent it.

She tried and failed once more to sleep. It was five a.m. now and she dragged herself out of bed, zombiefied: neither tired enough to sleep nor awake enough to get on with the day. There was no milk, so she made herself a strong black coffee and drank it with the window open whilst smoking her first fag of the day. Upper Street in Islington was already buzzing, even at this hour. She loved her flat. She loved just sitting there, sometimes for hours, and staring out at London life below. There was a kind of voyeuristic anonymity about it which she relished.

Tonight the first episode of *Devil May Share* was due to be broadcast. She'd already seen it at the cast-and-crew screening and it was good. But she daren't jinx it by telling anyone. There'd certainly been a lot of hype around the show, with the publicity machine going into overdrive. She'd got used to seeing her face on magazine fronts and stories online, which would all help with 'upping her profile' as her agent described it. Later that morning she was scheduled to appear as a guest on *Larry Dodge!*, a relaxed magazine chat show that filmed in the presenter's own house. She ought to check her pick-up time, really. Turning on her computer, she waited for the emails to load. Several had arrived overnight, but there was one that leapt out at her from the inbox.

To: Lana Lloyd
From: Judith Metcalf
Date: 20.08.2005
Subject: Hello from me

Dear Lana

I must admit I've started several emails to you since I received your card about my dad and have deleted them all. Because I don't really know what else to say. Other than thank you for your kind words.

It would be easier for me to pretend we hadn't seen each other at Romy's christening. Just carry on like I have done for the past eighteen years. But Dad's not long for this world now. We fly to Cyprus tomorrow to say farewell. And it's made me reassess things – life's priorities and all that. So I thought, if you're willing, that maybe we should meet up. Just you and me. See if we can at least salvage some civility towards one another.

Best wishes
Judith

Lana stared at the email for a solid three minutes, disbelieving at first that it was actually from Judith and for one mad moment wondering if this was Cat's doing. Desperate measures or something. But no, that'd be so out of character for Cat. This was definitely from Jude. And the second she accepted this, instantly and remarkably Lana felt flooded with love for her old best friend.

As if every grain of resentment she'd ever felt had simply never existed. As if all that nonsense had never happened. She couldn't wait to reply.

To: Judith Metcalf
From: Lana Lloyd
Date: 21.08.2005
Subject: Thank you

Dear Jude

I cannot begin to tell you how overflowing with joy my heart is, having received your email. I'm here ready and waiting whenever you want to meet. But I know you've got a lot on your mind right now so let's get in touch when you're back from visiting George.

My love *ALWAYS*
Lana x

Once she'd pressed Send, she threw on some joggers, grabbed some change and headed out to buy milk.

As soon as she was out in the fresh(ish) Islington air, she became aware of how heavily the separation from Judith had been weighing her down. For eighteen years. She'd done a bloody good job of pretending it didn't bother her, but obviously, from the magnitude of her reaction, she'd been kidding herself. And she felt this huge *longing* to see Judith again: to have her lost friend back in her life. This whole thing had been ridiculous, and it made her laugh out loud to think it was finally over.

She was still smiling as she went through the door of Mr Jamali's 24-hour store. He was unpacking the papers.

'Bright and early this mornin', love,' he said, fag in his mouth as he cut through the bundle tape.

Lana headed to the fridge and pulled out a pint of semi-skimmed. 'Well, best time of the day, don't you think?' she chirped back cheerily. 'I'll take one of those, thanks.'

As Mr Jamali pulled out a copy of the *Sunday Edition*, its magazine supplement fell to the floor. 'Sorry, love,' he said and went to pick it up.

But Lana got there first. And staring back at her from the grimy shop floor was her own face: glossy, heavy make-up, hair blowing in the wind machine, dressed in an outfit she'd never normally wear. And the headline beneath it shouted out:

LANA LLOYD – SEX, RELIGION AND AN
EIGHTEEN-YEAR RIFT WITH AN OLD FRIEND
Interview inside by Ryan Pearman

She froze. Fortunately Mr Jamali didn't notice. Hiding the magazine inside the paper, Lana grabbed the milk and left the money, before rushing out again.

Back in the flat, she threw down the magazine and eyed it with fear and contempt. It stared back at her. Lana's face. Lana's name. And no doubt Ryan Pearman's lies. Lighting up a cigarette for courage, she took a deep drag before opening to the centre pages. She couldn't take it all in, scanning the interview and processing single words and phrases, trying to find some cohesion between them.

. . . two failed marriages . . . sleeping her way to the top . . . alleged affair with an executive producer . . . avoids question about sex then immediately makes lewd comment about her breasts . . .

What an absolute wanker, she thought, breathing at a rate of knots. But the torture was far from over.

Describes her hometown as full of 'ordinary' people – though she clearly thinks she's something special herself . . . attending the christening of her god-daughter, even though she doesn't believe in all that 'happy clappy stuff' . . .

What? But those were HIS words!

And then the ultimate blow. A photograph of her taken on the day of the christening. A bit grainy, but it was definitely Lana, smoking and laughing outside the church. And next to it a photo of Jude, looking pretty miserable nearby. *Where in God's name had they come from?*

And then she remembered there was some woman outside the church taking photos of her, *Because you're famous like now, aren' you?* She'd said she was in school with them, though for the life of her, Lana couldn't remember who the woman was – Vicky something? No,

Becky! Becky Williams – that's it! She hadn't thought anything of it at the time, but the bitch had clearly sold her 'story' to the *Sunday Edition*.

And according to a reliable source, Lana Lloyd fell out with Judith Harris, her best friend, eighteen years ago, when Judith stole Lana's boyfriend from under her nose and went on to have his child . . . "Lana has never forgiven her!" said the friend. This makes sense, considering she's never had children of her own. When I bring up the subject I see a sadness in her eyes. It's clearly a sore point and would explain the jealousy she feels towards her one-time friend . . .

Lana felt sick. Surely this wasn't happening. Her phone buzzed. A text from Catrin:

OH MY GOD LARN, HAVE YOU SEEN THE SUNDAY EDITION????

40

Judith

She couldn't believe she was flying to Cyprus for the third time that year. And for the saddest of reasons. This journey, which they took every summer – and sometimes in spring – had always been a joyful one. Ever since that week in 1987 when Gareth had come out, they'd visited Kakopetria as a family. And every time, they'd been welcomed with open Cypriot arms. All three of them adored visiting the beautiful village in the Troodos Mountains and Jack loved nothing more than hanging out with his Pappoús and Giagiá Cleo. Judith had looked forward to every trip. Until this one.

Because now she was sitting there in silence, no excited smiles at the prospect of two weeks in Sofia's beautiful home, spending hour upon happy hour in the company of her father and his wife, playing with her cousins' children, eating splendid feasts of traditional Greek food and soaking up the Cypriot sunshine.

No.

Because this time they were flying there to say goodbye.

*

They'd gone out just after Christmas for a week. And from the moment they'd arrived they could all tell things weren't right. Cleo was so quiet she barely spoke a word; her girlish giggle had disappeared and her smile had become a rarity. And George, poor George – he'd lost so much weight. Cleo was frequently and uncharacteristically cross with him, and Judith often found herself walking in on hushed conversations held in dark corners. George looked pale and withdrawn and he'd stopped smoking. Had Cleo's nagging finally got the better of him? It was a good thing, of course, but did he resent it? Was his relationship with Cleoniki beginning to lose its shine?

One day during their Christmas visit Judith had asked him if this was the case, but he'd just smiled and shaken his head.

'I love her more than ever,' he'd said, 'and she loves me, the silly woman!'

Judith decided to believe him and to ignore any further tensions.

'Probably just the New Year blues,' Gareth had said.

But when they went out there in July, George was looking a lot frailer.

They'd been there less than an hour when he asked her if Patricia had sent something for him. She handed him the sealed envelope that she'd held on to for almost a week, having been desperate to know what was inside. George slowly opened it, unfolded the two-page document and began to read, whilst Judith watched him, hawk-like, the whole time.

'Anything interesting?' she asked, in a poor attempt to hide her burning curiosity.

He drew breath before diving in. 'It's a copy of your mother's will,' he said. 'I asked her to write one.'

'OK,' she said, confused. 'Because . . . ?'

'I want to ensure Patricia leaves the house to you when she dies. I don't want any of her nonsense.'

'Fair enough,' she laughed. 'Though I don't think she's going anywhere fast, is she, Gar? When we saw her last week, she was a bit worse for wear, but in general she's in very good health.'

'Yes, perhaps,' said George, looking down. 'But I'm afraid . . . *I'm* not.'

And then he'd reached out and taken her hand, before clearing his throat. 'Oh my Judi-moo,' he'd whispered. And the rest was a blur.

She'd heard the words *cancer* and *inoperable* and felt Gareth's arm around her shoulders. And she watched Cleo raise her hands as if in slow motion, to cover her face.

It wasn't till later that night, when she was on her own with Gareth, that the news began to sink in. Her father had lung cancer. There were secondaries in his lymph nodes and he was likely to live only a matter of weeks. He'd known for some time, but had kept it from Cleo until he finally had to break the news. She'd wanted to tell the rest of the family, but he'd insisted they keep it a secret for as long as possible. He wanted to put his house in order, literally, and his biggest concern had been that his second wife and his stepdaughter would be cared for, after his days.

'So that's why he got Patricia to make a will. To ensure that she leaves you the house,' Gareth said gently, stroking her hair and kissing her head, 'even if she remarries or something. He wanted to see it in black and white. Poor sod.'

She'd cried herself to sleep that night. And the next night. And the next. Saying goodbye to them all a week later was impossible and Gareth had to virtually drag her away from her father.

She should've stayed out there really. In the weeks that followed she was useless at work. Catrin came up to see her and was her usual kind self, even though she had her own problems to contend with, and she'd brought with her a card from Lana. Not much in it:

To Judith
so sorry to hear about lovely George
best
Lana x

It was brief, but thoughtful nonetheless. Lana must have swallowed a lot of pride to write that. Which is why Judith had emailed her the night before. Death and dying make people do things they might not normally dream of doing. She was learning that. Of course,

Lana's response was predictably melodramatic, but that was the actress in her.

Judith *did* wonder if she'd made a mistake suggesting they meet up. They were such polar opposites now: no longer childhood friends but grown-up women. Was she going to regret it? Her doubts were redoubled when she saw the feature in the *Sunday Edition*. Did she really want to be friends with someone who was such a liability? How could Lana talk about private matters like that so publicly? It was embarrassing.

She'd rung Catrin to rant about the article. Predictably, Catrin had tried to defend Lana, saying that the journalist was a scummy rat who was only out for dishing dirt and had twisted Lana's words to such a degree they were unrecognizable. And then there was Becky Williams sticking her oar in. Catrin reckoned Becky had been heard boasting in the Jolly Sailor that the newspaper had paid her five hundred pounds for her 'story'. And she'd bought a new sofa with it. That may well be the case. Judith didn't think for one minute that Lana would go out of her way to be malicious; it just made her consider how unreliable she was. And made her question whether she needed a friend like Lana in her life. Probably not. But she'd deal with it when she returned from Cyprus. She could always change her mind.

Iannis was at the airport to meet them. This time there were no smiles, no giggling grandchildren, just solemnity and sorrow and an overwhelming respect for an impending family death.

'He is near the end,' he whispered when he hugged her.

All around them, holidaymakers were buzzing like flies – sunhats and suitcases and excitement at the prospect of two weeks of hedonism. And there were they, four sad souls in amongst this throng of celebration, heading towards inevitable bereavement.

When they arrived at her father's house, Judith was surprised to discover he wasn't in bed as she'd expected. He was lying on the couch in the living room. Cleo had made it so pretty for him. And comfortable. Surrounded by soft downy pillows and propped up with cushions so that he could still be part of what was going on. The room was filled with flowers from Cleo's garden, and candles and bunches of herbs. It was like a living shrine. And so eerily quiet.

But it seemed to keep her occupied, and George, bless him, half in this world and half in the next, his eyes barely open, lay there with the faintest of smiles to remind them he'd not quite gone.

Judith sat next to him and held his hand, which was surprisingly warm.

'Judi-moo,' he whispered.

He wasn't agitated for sure. The generous doses of morphine had seen to that.

The hours lost all definition. Only the sunlight outside, or lack of it, gave some kind of structure to the day. They hardly spoke to each other, hardly ate. Friends and family came into the house and left like passing ghosts.

On the fifth day of their visit, Judith was sat with him, reading whilst he slept. Suddenly he moved and awoke. She asked him if he wanted something to drink – she could see he was struggling to speak. She lifted an ice cube from a bowl on the small table next to the couch and gently ran it along his dry lips.

He gathered strength and then he whispered, '*Parakaló proséxte o énas ton állon.*' She knew enough Greek by then to understand that he was asking them to look after each other.

She leant in closer and replied, '*S'agapó Papa,*' as if it was the most natural thing in the world, and she realized it was the first time she'd ever told her father in Greek that she loved him.

He smiled a final smile, breathed a final breath, and peacefully Georgios Andreas Charalambos departed this world.

Cleo emitted a sub-human scream and threw herself upon the couch; Sofia crossed herself, weeping and praying aloud. Gareth hugged Jack, who was crying like a little boy. But Judith remained silent, offering up her own vote of thanks that this good and honest soul, who had touched her own life so significantly, was now no longer in pain.

41

Catrin

'Bye, Dad!' Catrin shouted as she watched her parents get into Lana's car and drive away.

Liz, Huw and Lana had come over for a very small tea to celebrate Romy's first birthday, Lana having come home especially for the occasion.

'You really don't have to,' Sol had said to her on the phone the week before.

'She's my god-daughter. Of course I'm coming to her birthday party. I want her to know she can always rely on her Aunty Larn.'

Sol and Cat had laughed about this – Lana had taken the role of godmother very seriously. Though neither of them were sure how long it would last, and both had the sneaky suspicion that Lana was secretly competing with Judith to out-do her in the godparent stakes.

Seeing as the family had had such a big bash for Romy's christening barely a month before, they'd decided to keep her actual birthday low-key. And Catrin was glad of this. Because she'd made a decision of her own: that today would be the best day to bring up the dreaded subject with Sol of their trying for another baby. She couldn't put it off any longer. And with Romy now falling asleep in her arms, she felt somehow protected by her. So she took a deep breath and said the words, dropping a bombshell bang smash into the middle of their evening.

'*What?*' Sol asked, incredulous. 'You're not serious?'

'Of course I am!' she said, laughing, in a bid to hide the hurt incurred by his question. 'Here's one we made earlier. Why wouldn't you want another?' And she kissed Romy on the head, as if to prove her point. Romy snuffled sleepily in response.

'You talk about it as if you're thinking of getting a new car!' Sol replied angrily.

'I've been wanting to discuss it for a long time. I just didn't know when.'

'Well, let's not talk about it now, eh?' he said, evidently calming himself and firmly shutting down the conversation.

'It's OK, Sol, she's asleep – and even if she wasn't, she couldn't understand what you're saying!' Her tone was unintentionally patronizing.

'I know, but . . . now's not the time.'

'To discuss it, or to have another baby?' she challenged him.

He sighed and went over to her, encircling mother and daughter in a big, loving hug. 'Babe, you know how I feel. We've got our beautiful girl,' he whispered, kissing the top of Cat's hair. 'She's our treasure. We don't need any more treasure. Don't be greedy.'

This infuriated her. '*Greedy?* You think wanting another child is *greedy?*'

'Please, Cat,' he pleaded, clearly regretting his choice of words. 'I can't see you go through all that again. I can't see *myself* go through all that again.'

She'd expected this reaction, of course.

'I'll put her down, and then we can discuss it properly,' she said, and headed upstairs with Romy.

She heard Sol sigh as she left the room, ignoring him when he called after her, 'There's no point! I'm not going to change my mind.'

When she came back downstairs half an hour later, she'd steeled herself, ready for battle. But Sol was wired too. Whilst she'd been gone, he'd obviously had time to think.

'Cat,' he said, and she could tell he was trying to stay calm. 'I cannot, I *will not*, repeat that whole process. There is *nothing* in it for us, except heartache and disappointment . . .' There were tears in his voice now, panic, '. . . and a relentless fucking sense of failure. We're not doing it, OK?'

She knew she was being selfish, but she carried on regardless. 'I'm sorry, Sol, really I am. But I have to try. And I'll do it with or without your support.'

Silence hit the room with a sledgehammer.

'*What?*'

'I've got the funds, I've been saving . . .'

'The *funds?* What the hell are you talking about?'

'For IVF. I've been saving.' She smiled at him. 'I mean I know we had Romy naturally but let's face it,

340

the chances of that happening again are zilch, so I think we should try for IVF again.'

Sol stared at her aghast. 'Have you actually lost your mind?'

'I've got the first appointment with Dr Hartland next week.'

As if on cue, Romy started crying upstairs whilst Catrin's phone began buzzing, a loud and insistent cacophony, interrupting the brewing row.

Her mobile stopped. Romy continued. And then the landline started ringing. And all the time, Catrin and Solomon stared at each other. An impasse.

Eventually Sol broke free. 'I'll see to Romy. You answer that.'

'The machine can get it.' It would probably be her mother, and she didn't want to talk to anyone right now, not with this unfinished business still hanging in the air.

A click and a beep and a crackle came from the answer machine. And then a voice, distant, choked and tearful.

'Hello? Are you there? It's Jude.'

Catrin snapped out of her mood and grabbed the phone. 'Jude? Yes, sorry, are you . . . ?'

'He died,' Judith gasped. 'My dad's gone, Cat.'

And she broke down. Over two thousand miles away, Catrin's best friend was struck by grief and there was nothing she could do except offer words of sympathy down a crackling phone line to Cyprus.

'Oh Jude, no. Poor George, poor lovely George.'

*

'Anything to drink?' the air steward asked.

'Coffee, please,' said Catrin, holding up the small plastic cup. She'd just finished a lunch of ratatouille and rice, accompanied by a rock-hard bread roll, followed by a chocolate mousse, all squashed into compartments on a neat plastic tray. It wasn't the best meal she'd had in her life, but the novelty of being alone on a flight was more important than haute cuisine right now.

It had been Sol's idea that she should fly out for the funeral. Liz and Huw had offered to have Romy, and Sol had arranged for a locum to come into the surgery to cover Cat's appointments. 'You need to be with your friend,' he said and he hugged her, the subject of another baby conveniently pushed aside as they dealt with the more pressing issue of Judith's bereavement.

'And it might do you good, y'know . . . to take yourself away from home for a bit. Give you a bit of thinking time, a bit of perspective maybe.'

'I'm not going to change my mind, Sol,' she said stridently.

'Christ, you've lost it,' he said. And went to bed.

When Catrin left for Cardiff airport two days later, she and Sol had barely spoken since their last row. Just practical exchanges to do with flight times and child-care. So getting on the plane had been a relief. Because she felt like she was running away. And this had secretly thrilled her. For the first time in her adult life, she felt a sense of freedom, of rebellion.

Lana took her to the airport. Having stayed on in Coed Celyn after Romy's birthday to spend some time with her family, she was keen to help.

'Are you sure I can't persuade you to come too?' Catrin said when they'd parked up at Cardiff International.

'Aw babe, I *did* think about it, but I just worry it's early days, y'know?' Lana replied. 'I mean it's not like me an' Jude are full-on friends again, is it?'

'I know, but she emailed you! She seemed to want to get things back on track?' pleaded Catrin.

'Yes, and then she bloody phoned you up and went on about that magazine thing!' said Lana.

'Oh God, how many times! She knows the score. She's fine about it,' said Catrin, though this wasn't strictly true. Yes, Judith had begrudgingly been won round by Catrin and conceded that Lana had no control over what was written about her in magazines, and that it was Becky bloody Williams who'd sent those photos to the *Sunday Edition*. Nonetheless, Judith's initial, cautious enthusiasm for meeting up again with Lana had been considerably quashed by that magazine interview. Catrin had judiciously chosen not to tell Lana this. It'd taken so much effort to get them together in the first place, she wasn't about to uproot the shoots of this fragile little plant before it had had a chance to start growing. And she honestly believed that if Lana came to George's funeral, Judith, broken apart in the tenderness of her grief, would so touched by the gesture that it would open her heart and reunite the two friends once and for all.

But Lana would not be convinced. 'I'll wait till she comes home, Cat,' she said, 'and then I'll arrange to meet up with her. It's all a bit sensitive, isn't it? And I don't want to mess things up.'

'Oh bollocks,' replied Cat, suddenly changing the subject. 'I was meant to call Patricia. To tell her about George.'

'Why hasn't Judith told her?' asked Lana.

'She said she couldn't face it. So I offered. Don't suppose you'd do it, would you?'

That was four hours earlier. Catrin had chosen not to tell Lana about the row with Sol. Because she knew what she'd say. She'd agree with him – she'd tell her she was being selfish and unrealistic. Or worse than that, she might feel sorry for her. And Catrin couldn't bear that. She couldn't bear to be pitied. And so she decided to keep schtum and focus on what mattered right now – which was helping Jude.

At Nicosia airport, Gareth was there to meet her. They hugged for a long time.

'How is she?' she whispered.

'I don't think it's sunk in yet, to be honest,' he sighed. Catrin sensed he might have been relieved to get away from the grief-filled house for a while. 'It's not a bad thing, Cat,' he said as they headed towards Kakopetria in Iannis's car. 'The Cypriots, they wear their hearts on their sleeve, and they have the opposite of the British stiff upper lip – but I find it a bit much, the constant crying and outward displays of grief.'

'That's 'cos you're so butch!' Catrin teased.

Gareth smiled back. 'I just worry for Jude. She's surrounded by all this weeping, yet she's not shed a tear herself.'

'I guess bereavement affects everyone differently.'

They sat in silence for a while, both lost in their own thoughts, with the windows open and the cool Troodos mountain air filling their lungs.

And then out of the blue Gareth said, 'I spoke to Sol, by the way. He told me about the baby thing.'

'What?' Catrin stammered.

'That you want to try for another. He rang me.'

'Well, he had no right talking to you about it, Gar. With respect.'

'Well, *with respect*,' he echoed, 'Sol's my mate. It's not just women who need a heart-to-heart, y'know.'

Catrin sighed. She could feel a sob rising in her throat, threatening to choke her voice. It was horrible not speaking to Sol and she missed him. She wished he'd come with her now, her bravado and excitement at 'running away' having long since vanished.

'Look, let me just say something,' Gareth said. And Catrin was glad his eyes were firmly on the road ahead so he couldn't see her tears creeping out. 'Tell me to shut up if you like, but I do know how it feels, OK?'

Of course he did. But she could only manage to nod, and let him carry on.

'Every day, pretty much, I imagine what it would have been like to have two kids. Every day. And I'll never completely get over that, truth be told.'

She sensed him steal a glance at her, testing the waters, waiting for her to respond. Swallowing back the emotion that was poised to engulf her, she whispered, 'Sometimes it's like I'm suffocating, Gar. With all the finality of it.' And as she spoke, it came – the tidal wave of feelings she'd held stored up inside her for so long, now finding an opportunity to break free. 'It's all so *terminal* – y'know? No more kids. That's that. Accept it. Get on with your life.' Hysteria began creeping into her voice. 'And I suppose I just want to keep the *possibility* alive. To not shut the door on it happening, no matter how tiny the chances are . . .'

Gareth nodded. 'Yeah. I get it.'

'It's not fair, Gareth!' she wailed. 'It's not fucking fair!'

He let her cry, respecting her grief. And then he said quietly, 'But you've got Romy.' And without taking his eyes off the road, he reached out, took her hand and squeezed it in support. She could see he was crying now too. 'She's immense. And me and Jude, we've got Jack, and *he's* immense, and . . . I dunno . . . let's celebrate what we *have* got, is it? Not mourn what we haven't. 'Cos that's the hand that life dealt us, Cat. And it's a good hand.'

'No,' blubbed Catrin, 'it's a bloody wonderful hand.' And she managed to smile at him, finding a sad solidarity in their loss. 'Thanks,' she whispered, as calm descended, and she found herself feeling strangely relieved: relieved that she perhaps no longer had to try, or fight. Just accept and be grateful. Perhaps Gareth was right.

Twenty minutes later they pulled up outside Sofia's house. Checking herself in the visor mirror, Catrin said, 'God, I look a sight,' and she tried to clean up the smudged mascara clogged beneath her puffy eyes.

'Don't worry, you won't look out of place in there,' he said with a sad smile, and Sofia came out to greet them, weeping with open arms.

During the two days before the funeral, Catrin helped out around the house – mainly with childcare, looking after Danoulla's baby boy Haris, who was only a couple of months older than Romy. He had a similar serene nature to Romy and it made Catrin miss her even more. But it also made her appreciate her even more, Gareth's words ringing clear in her head.

Despite the sorrow in the house, there was also an overwhelming air of celebration, a coming-together, perhaps precipitated by the hysteria of bereavement. Judith leant heavily on Catrin for support during those forty-eight hours, often choosing her company over anyone else's, including Jack, who'd grieved openly with his Cypriot family and found the process very healing.

'It's much healthier, Mum,' he'd told her. 'Get it out of your system an' all that.'

'Each to their own, Jack,' Judith had replied. And

Cat could see him gently back away from his mother, letting her stay safe in her own space.

The funeral was at midday, in the little church in Kako-petria, the same church where George and Cleoniki had been married nearly eighteen years previously. Catrin walked with Judith and the rest of the family in a cor-tège behind the coffin, the glorious sunshine attempting to cheer their souls en route. Processing along the little road to the church, they were accompanied by the solemn toll of its bell. Outside, some mourners were waiting, their heads bowed and silent; inside, the church was packed and bursting with sorrow.

Although she couldn't understand the language of the service, Catrin found the beautiful sounds of the Ancient Greek strangely comforting and mesmeric. As part of the ceremony, they were invited to approach and kiss the coffin and the icon held next to it by the priest. Catrin could see that Judith kept her father's backgammon dice in her hand, turning them inces-santly and seeking comfort from the hard edges of the small cubes.

At the conclusion of the service, the family lined up to receive condolences from the mourners. Judith grabbed Catrin's hand and asked her to stand with her.

'But I'm not family, Jude!' Cat whispered urgently.

'I don't care,' Jude said, her voice shaking. 'I need you with me.'

Not wishing to upset her further, but feeling like a cuckoo in the nest, Catrin compromised by standing just behind her, not wanting to displace Jack or Gareth and certainly not wanting to step on the toes of Cleo or Sofia and the rest of the family. The mourners streamed past, shedding more tears, kissing cheeks, offering sympathy and openly, unashamedly weeping. Judith smiled back politely with stateswoman-like dignity and elegance.

And then it happened.

Confusion and shock, as if in slow motion, began to replace the dignity and elegance. It took several seconds for Judith to process the sight before her, to compute what was happening, and when she did, she stood there in utter disbelief.

Lana.

Wearing an expensive dress. Crying. And holding out her arms, inviting embrace and offering condolence.

'Jude, I'm so sorry,' she said, her eyes red and forlorn. 'Your lovely, wonderful dad.' Arms still held out – waiting tentatively, it seemed, for a hug – she continued, 'I had to come.'

Judith began to shake.

'You said you weren't going to!' whispered Catrin, panicking, aware that Judith was becoming breathless at the sight of Lana standing there.

'It was you who told me to!' Lana whispered back, defensive, clearly feeling foolish at how badly her actions were backfiring.

The situation was horrendous. A social faux pas extraordinaire. The gesture was, of course, well meant – and true, Catrin had encouraged it, but this had been a big mistake on her part too. The only thing she could be grateful for in the moment was that Lana hadn't shouted out, 'SURPRISE!'

The queue of mourners was building up behind Lana. A short, plump woman in a black veil was waiting her turn to pay her respects.

Gareth put his arm defensively around Judith's shoulders and, leaning in to Lana, he said calmly, 'You're unbelievable. It's her father's funeral, for God's sake!'

'It's all right, Gar,' said Judith, composing herself, politely shaking hands with Lana and indicating with her body language that she should now move on. 'Thank you for coming. Very kind.' She could have been talking to a complete stranger.

Catrin watched as Judith turned to the widow who was waiting patiently behind Lana. But Lana didn't budge.

'The thing is, Jude,' she mumbled, and Catrin could feel the tension rise. Now was not the time for a discussion, for God's sake!

'Just leave, Lana, will you?' hissed Gareth.

'But I need to explain something . . .'

'Lana, let's you and me talk outside, yeah?' urged Catrin gently.

'It's just I didn't come on my own,' said Lana, 'I came with—'

And Catrin gasped as she registered the sight before her.

'Patricia!' she said a little too loudly.

And sure enough, the veiled woman – no longer

veiled, her face on show for all to see – was indeed Patricia.

She seemed oblivious to the disturbance she was causing. Or was she actually enjoying it?

'My darling child,' Patricia said, forcing Judith into a hug. 'Your poor, poor papa.'

Catrin fought an involuntary desire to laugh. Why was Patricia talking like this? More to the point, why on God's earth was she here?

A flurry of whispering amongst the mourners quickly established that the mystery mourner was indeed George's first wife, and when Cleo understood this, she shouted out in Greek, lunging in Patricia's direction.

Gareth stepped between the two women as the solemnity of the condolences line-up began to spiral into chaos.

And in the centre of it all, overwhelmed by the combination of seeing her estranged friend and her narcissist mother at the funeral of her beloved father, Judith finally surrendered to the excessive emotional pressure.

And walked out of the church.

42

Lana

After waving Catrin off at Cardiff airport, Lana had sighed and put her head on the steering wheel. The thought of calling to see Patricia to break the news of George's death did not fill her with glee. But she'd promised Catrin she would. And the sooner she headed back to Coed Celyn, the sooner she could get it done.

During the journey home, she thought about Sol and Cat. There'd been such a strange tension in the house when she'd called there that morning, an awkwardness she'd never seen between them before. Surely lack of sleep couldn't be the cause – Romy was such a contented baby and they were always boasting how she slept through the night, affording her parents the same luxury. No, they'd obviously rowed about something. Which disturbed Lana. Because it was such a rarity. Even during their dark days when they'd been trying for Romy, they'd managed to come through smiling. Lana had asked Catrin about it in the car but the conversation was rapidly shut down with a *Don't be daft, we're absolutely fine!* They clearly weren't.

Catrin and Solomon's marriage was a constant in Lana's life – and she held it in high regard. Probably because she herself had been divorced twice, so to her, Cat and Sol were the epitome of how to get it right. She still cringed whenever she thought back to her first husband, William, a guest director at college in her final term. He'd been twenty-five years older than her and married. But Lana had sworn to Catrin that he was The One and that the mess and pain of his divorce would be worth it in the end. Their wedding was a small affair held in Guildford register office, attended by Lana's parents, Catrin, Solomon and William's sister. William's only daughter did not approve and did not attend, disgusted that she was the same age as her new stepmother. After the short ceremony, the twenty-two-year-old bride and the forty-seven-year-old groom treated their small group of guests to a pub lunch nearby. Lana swore to Cat it was the happiest day of her life. Until two bottles of wine later, when she cried to her in the ladies' loos that she wished Judith was there too. Two years had passed since the fateful fall-out at Montgomery Hall.

'It's my wedding day, Cat. For God's sake, the three of us should be here together!' she wailed. 'I should've invited her.'

Catrin quietly comforted her friend.

'D'you think she feels the same?' sobbed Lana.

'I don't know, babe,' Catrin said.

'Well, maybe if she and Gareth ever get hitched, she'll invite me to that and we can start again. You an' me could be bridesmaids.' She smiled weakly through her tears. 'You'll have to persuade her.'

And then Catrin made her confession. 'They're already married,' she whispered.

'What?'

'Jude and Gareth. They got married just after Jack was born.'

Lana felt like she'd been punched. The hurt was so palpable and she'd cried so much she soon transformed her bridal beauty into snotty, red-faced, red-eyed sorrow.

Catrin kept apologizing. 'I couldn't tell you, I knew how hurt you'd be. And look at you now! I was right.'

On reflection, Lana felt hugely sympathetic towards Catrin. It must have been awful for her, being stuck between her two best friends like that. But it didn't make her feel any better.

Lana's marriage to William lasted eight months. It ended when she had an affair with a fellow actor on a national tour of *Hello, Dolly!* The divorce was swift and Lana vowed never to marry again. 'I'm allergic to long-term commitment!' she would often joke and embarked on a series of affairs, usually with older, married men such as Paul Durrant, the executive producer of *Still Waters*.

It wasn't until 1999, when she met and fell in love with a TV writer called Archie Osbourne, that Lana finally succumbed to a second wedding. The event was huge. And Lana, by now a minor celebrity, managed to secure a deal with *The Goss* magazine, who photographed the life out of the whole day in exchange for footing the catering bill. This time Lana had felt no inclination to invite Judith, secretly hoping she would read about it in *The Goss* and regret the fact that she was no longer friends with her now famous friend. She wasn't proud of herself for feeling like that, but feel like that she did.

In many respects Archie and Lana's marriage was quite strong, and even when it came to an end in 2004, when Archie admitted to himself and the world that he was gay, they still remained friends.

'I genuinely think,' Lana had said to Catrin, 'that some people, like you and Sol, are made for marriage, whereas others, like me, are simply useless at it! A bit like dancing.' She'd said it with a laugh, her default position when feeling vulnerable. But Catrin and Sol's marriage really was an important foundation in Lana's life and something upon which she was hugely dependent. 'You know that you two can *never* split up, don't you?' she'd continued. 'Not for your sakes, but for mine.' And although she'd been smiling, she'd meant every word.

Pulling up outside Patricia Harris's little terraced house in Victoria Road, Lana was hijacked by nostalgia. It was almost two decades since she'd last been there and the first thing she noticed was that it hadn't changed. The front door, though weather-beaten, was exactly the same, and when she knocked on the brass knocker (remembering that the doorbell had never worked) it was like she was a teenager once again, calling for her friend to go to school.

There was no answer so she knocked again, wondering what to do if Patricia wasn't at home. When the third knock still prompted no response, she turned and headed back to the car. Maybe she could write a card to explain and pop it through the letterbox.

'What d'you want?'

She was stopped in her tracks by the husky voice of Patricia, groggily calling out to her from the doorstep, wearing a dressing gown, cigarette in hand.

'Hello, Mrs Harris,' said Lana, walking back towards the house and once more feeling like she was sixteen. 'It's me, Lana Lloyd.'

'Who?'

Lana was practically back on the doorstep now.

'Lana. Judith's friend from school.' It felt so strange describing herself as Judith's friend when she hadn't been Judith's friend for nearly twenty years. But how else could she explain who she was?

Patricia stared at her, appearing to focus momentarily, to trawl through the files in her brain and make sense of the sight before her. 'You're the one off of the telly,' she stated.

'Er, yes. But do you remember me from before?'

And suddenly Patricia's tired face was transformed with an unexpected smile, her features softening and showing hints of beauty past. She gasped. 'Of course I do! Little Lana Lloyd. Come on in, kid. Excuse the mess. Late night.' And she turned back inside, Lana meekly following.

The living room was just as Lana remembered it, the smell of cigarettes making her want one even though she'd been trying to give up. The curtains were closed and the room was lit by a small lamp in the corner.

'Have a seat,' Patricia commanded. 'Shove that on the floor.' She was referring to an industrial-sized bra that was hanging limply off the arm of the sofa.

Lana perched herself on its edge.

'What'll you have?' asked Patricia as she made her way to the sideboard, bearing two half-full bottles of whisky and gin.

'Oh, nothing for me,' said Lana. 'I'm driving.'

Patricia raised a defiant eyebrow. 'You've not been to see me for twenty-odd years and now you'll not even share a Scotch?'

Lana was gripped by an old fear, the fear she'd once felt in Patricia's formidable presence when she was just a little girl. It was fear, yes. But it was also a weird kind of admiration. 'Oh, go on then. Just a little one, mind.'

Patricia winked. 'That's my girl.'

Much to Judith's consternation growing up, Catrin and Lana had always been a bit in awe of her mother. They found her intriguing and entertaining when she regaled them with stories of her adventurous youth, shocking them both in a way that none of their parents ever could. When they were fifteen, Patricia had produced some very expensive French perfume in a heavy glass bottle. She had treated them all to a dab on their wrists. Its musky scent was exotic and heady, as if it belonged to a world they knew nothing about.

'Of course, you know what good perfume is made from, don't you?' she asked them all.

None of them did.

'Ulk's balls!' Patricia exclaimed.

Lana had burst out laughing, Judith had gone red with embarrassment, and Catrin had just looked confused. 'Ulk?' she'd asked.

'Yes! That's what they make it from. An ulk!'

'Don't you mean . . . an *elk*?' asked Catrin.

And Lana, who had been drinking an Irish coffee (Patricia always liked to force the glamour of alcohol into their teenage Welsh lives), spat it out in an explosive laugh.

'Ulk? Elk? Tomato? Tomayto? – You know what I mean!' said Patricia. 'Big brown bugger with horns.'

'Antlers,' Judith had said, smiling, and it was one of the few occasions when she'd seemed appreciative of her mother's humorous side.

Lana smiled at the memory as Patricia handed her a chipped glass containing far too much whisky.

'So,' Patricia said. 'I take it this is to do with my hard-hearted bitch of a daughter.'

Lana was on uncertain territory here – how much did Patricia know about the fall-out between herself and Judith?

'Erm, don't suppose I could cadge a fag, could I, Mrs H?'

Patricia threw her the packet of Superkings and a lighter that seemed to have taken up residence on the arm of her chair. 'Help yourself,' she said.

Lana lit up, her hand shaking as she held the lighter to the cigarette. 'It's about George,' she said, exhaling. 'I'm afraid he passed away on Friday.'

Lana had expected Patricia's response to be indifference at best and a sneering laugh at worst; what she *hadn't* counted on was for Patricia to cry out, grief-stricken, clutching her hand to her heart, 'My Georgie, my darling, darling Georgie!' And, head bent, she wept, still clutching a lit cigarette in her other hand.

Lana didn't know where to put herself, she was entirely unprepared for this. 'I know,' she mumbled, feeling inadequate in her role as bad-news-breaker. 'I'm so sorry.'

'I was expecting it, of course,' said Patricia through her tears.

'Right,' replied Lana.

'I'm a bit psychic, you see.'

Lana felt an uncontrollable urge to laugh, but was cut short by Patricia's subsequent snideness. 'Shame *Madam* didn't have the guts to come and tell me in person, mind.'

'Well, that's because she's out there. In Cyprus. Catrin was going to come and see you, but she had to catch a plane, so she asked me to let you know instead.'

Patricia nodded and took a big gulp of whisky. Wiping her eyes and looking firmly at Lana, she said, 'So. When's the funeral?'

*

It had seemed like a good idea at the time. A really good and well-intentioned idea. The chance to mend bridges once and for all. The perfect opportunity to show Judith that life was too short for bearing grudges, that in times of grief we all need a friend. Hadn't Judith herself said something along the same lines in her email? Of course, Lana was also influenced by Patricia, who'd plied her with more whisky and poured out her heart about George: how she knew they'd had their differences, but that was because of the passion between them. Patricia claimed – very convincingly – that George was the one and only love of her life, which completely contradicted Judith's story all those years ago, that her parents' marriage was a loveless one. But aided by more whisky and a second packet of Superkings, Lana decided to give Patricia the benefit of the doubt.

A couple of hours later, Patricia had completely won Lana's confidence, so much so that Lana began telling her about the loss of her friendship with Judith nearly twenty years previously. 'I miss her, Trish, that's the truth,' she said, growing maudlin with the Scotch.

'Right then, well, it's time to take action. You an' me, we've both got hatchets to bury.'

Even in the mist of that boozy afternoon, Lana found Patricia's murderous choice of words a bit disconcerting. Nonetheless, she'd gone ahead with Patricia's mad plan, and by six o'clock that night she'd booked them both on to a flight to Nicosia the following day, so that they could attend the funeral of George Harris.

*

Outside the church now, Lana turned to Patricia. 'I think we'd better go.' It seemed only wise to get out of the way, given that the kerfuffle Patricia's presence had caused was now spreading through the church, creating the distinct impression that they were very unwelcome.

Minutes later, as they sat on the little church bench in the Cypriot sun, Lana reflected on the behemoth mistake she'd made. *What the fuck was I thinking?*

'What the fuck were you thinking?' It was Judith, now heading her way with Gareth and Catrin in tow.

Bizarrely, Patricia – Lana's new best friend – came to her defence.

'Ey, now just a minute, lady!' she snapped at her daughter, caring not a jot about the fact that they'd just abandoned a funeral service attended by a hundred grieving Greek Cypriots. 'This was my idea. I wanted to pay my respects. And she said she'd help me do it. So you say sorry to her now, d'you hear?'

Lana was mortified. 'Patricia, it's fine, really . . .' she mumbled. But it was pointless. Judith stood there, defiant.

'All you wanted, Mother, was to cause drama and chaos and upset. Just as you always do. And why the hell you went along with it, Lana, I really don't know. Jesus! Why in God's name would I want *her* at my father's funeral?'

Mourners from the church had started to gather around them now and the atmosphere was becoming slightly menacing. Judith carried on. She was on a roll.

'And more to the point, why would I want *you* here, Lana?'

Lana looked up at her, shock and hurt hurtling through her veins.

Catrin intervened. 'To be fair, Jude, it was me that—'

But Lana spoke over her. 'I'm here because we used to be best friends,' she said quietly. 'And I loved your dad, and I wanted to support you.'

Judith stared back at her – was it disdain or disgust on her face?

'Well, I don't want your support, Lana, and I certainly don't need your friendship,' she said, her voice getting louder and more hysterical. 'I've survived all these years without it, and your antics today have proved more than ever that you don't belong in my life. Now take my joke of a useless mother and leave.'

Patricia objected loudly, 'Ey, listen here . . .'

Lana tried to apologize. 'I'm sorry, it was stupid of me and—'

But Judith was having none of it.

It was done.

Over.

'Just go,' she said. 'GO!!!'

It was weeks before Lana returned any of Catrin's calls. The humiliation she felt after what she'd done was crushing and she couldn't bear to discuss it. Because that would mean reliving the shame.

When she finally found the strength to meet up with Cat, she pre-empted any discussion of the subject.

'Please don't ever mention it, Cat,' she said. 'I need to erase it from my memory. I need to pretend it never happened.'

'Of course,' said Catrin gently. 'I understand.'

And then Lana paused.

'Just tell me this,' she whispered. 'D'you think she'll ever forgive me?'

Catrin looked down and sighed. 'I don't think so, babe,' she said. 'It feels pretty terminal, to be honest.'

And she reached out and held Lana's hand.

PART THREE
2017

Twelve years later

43
Lana

The roar was getting louder. She couldn't place it –
applause from a distant stadium, maybe? Or was
someone rolling an empty metal drum along the road?
So frustrating – what the hell was it? She scanned
her mind's filing system for a familiar reference,
something – anything – to help her find her bearings.
The sound rose to a crescendo and then *be-ee-eep*. Ah
yes. Of course. It was the kettle. Just boiled. And Lana
was waking up.

'I make tea – you want?'

Lana recognized the voice, the accent, but could neither open her eyes to check out who was speaking nor
open her mouth to respond. Matted layers of last
night's mascara had glued her lashes tightly shut. And
her lips were sealed with a film of tacky spit. She attempted a cough, but oh God! Moving her head was a
big mistake – there were a dozen boulders rolling
around inside her skull, heartlessly colliding like dodg-
ems at a fair. The pain was intense.

Slowly, as if it didn't belong to her, Lana lifted her
hand to her face and managed to prise open her right

eye with her fingers. Something was moving towards her. She blinked the fuzzy dark lump into focus. It was Michel – one of the bartenders from the Paradise Lounge – and he was carrying two mugs. Using his elbow, he deftly shifted three empty wine bottles to the edge of the bedside table, making room for the morning brew.

Her hands shaking, her left eye still clamped shut, she sat herself up and reached for her tea, spilling half of it en route to her lips. The scald of the liquid on her chest made her wince, but she didn't care, she just yearned for the wetness of the weak tea to make her mouth start working again.

Finally she found her voice.

'I suppose we had sex,' she croaked.

'I suppose we did,' Michel replied with a grin. 'You tell me I am the best one you have ever made loving with!'

'Oh Christ.'

Michel laughed, drained his tea and checked his watch. 'And now I must leave you. We disembark in . . . thirty-seven minutes.'

And with that he leapt up, kissed Lana on the top of her head and made his way out of the cabin, whistling far too happily as he left.

She didn't move for several minutes. Mainly because she couldn't.

Because this morning's hangover was a Humdinger.

What was it that singled out a Humdinger from any

other common or garden hangover? Well, for starters it wasn't enough merely to suffer the nausea and the pounding head and the dry tongue and the acid reflux; not enough to suffer the discomfort of the previous evening's crusty make-up left unremoved by facial wipes and smeared instead upon the pillowcase or languishing in the corners of her eyes. Nor was it enough to discover her knickers – hurled across the room with such confidence a mere five hours earlier – now dangling limply from a magazine rack. No. To qualify as a Humdinger of a hangover, there had to be an accompanying sense of dread and crippling shame; to qualify for Humdinger status, one had to wake up fearful of what might have happened during the previous evening's blackout, vainly hoping that at the very least it wasn't something illegal.

There had been several Humdingers over the years that had seen Lana wake up confused as to why she was clutching property that was clearly not hers, but which she'd evidently purloined during the previous evening's events: a gents' Rolex one time, a set of car keys another, a squash racquet and a Wedgwood vase . . . the list went on. And then there were the more bizarre items – including a cheese grater, a staple gun and a deerstalker hat. It would be too embarrassing to return all these objects – even if she could remember who owned them – so technically they were stolen. Technically she was a thief! But she justified her actions by citing the Rules of Blackout: what you weren't conscious of, you couldn't be guilty of. What happened in

Blackout stayed in Blackout. She knew this theory didn't make logical sense, but it was the only way she could live with the guilt of her crimes. That and donating all her stashes to charity shops, of course. Yes, even the Rolex.

But thieving wasn't the only potential downside of a booze-fuelled night. There'd been the countless mornings when she'd woken up in alien places – a garden shed, a horse box, even a builder's skip. And times when she'd lost her shoes, her keys or her pants. She'd once woken up wearing someone *else*'s pants – a pair of men's Y-fronts to be exact. And on another occasion she'd come to, sitting bolt upright in an Eisteddfod Bard's Chair clothed in nothing more than a grey plastic mac. Though to be fair, at least it was buttoned up.

And then there were the relationship-wrecking risks she took with drunken texts, or drunken phone calls or emails. Or the dignity-endangering drunken tweets. She couldn't remember contacting anyone last night or going online, but that didn't mean she hadn't. It always took her a few hours into the Humdinger before she could summon the courage to look at her phone. She needed to be strong to learn who exactly she'd offended and how. So many times she'd received an early-morning text saying, 'Never contact me again – you are appalling.' Or 'Hey sexy! You were soooo horny last night . . . !' But there had also been several mornings in her life when Catrin had rung to check she was still alive, because 'You were in a bad way, Larn. I thought you were gonna, y'know, do something stupid. You were weeping, saying you were lonely, saying your life was meaningless!'

'Was I?' she'd say incredulously. 'D'you know, I have absolutely no recollection of that, chick!' And she would laugh it off, promising herself once more that she must, must, *must* switch off her phone before allowing a single fluid ounce of alcohol to pass her lips. Because she talked such bollocks when she was pissed. She wasn't *lonely*, for God's sake! She was a highly successful singer and performer who travelled the world on the most glamorous and high-class cruise liners! Her life wasn't *meaningless*! Honestly. What a drama queen!

Lana glanced anxiously around her cabin, looking for clues that would help piece together last night. Nothing stood out – the red sequined dress she'd worn for the Celine Dion medley lay abandoned on the floor by the en suite and she could see a silver stiletto jutting out of a sleeve. *How did that get there?* Obviously at some point she and Michel had brought the party back to her cabin – she must have got the wine from somewhere – but she had no memory of any discourse with him other than chatting after the show whilst he mixed her a few negronis.

Admittedly she was a tad surprised Michel had wanted to sleep with her – she'd assumed he preferred guys. But hey ho – her gaydar had always been a bit wonky.

Something was digging into the back of her neck – she reached up and dislodged the offending hair-grip, realizing in the same instant that she wasn't wearing her wig. *Bollocks*. Over at her dressing table she noted with horror that it lay abandoned like a small sick mammal, black, furry and frightened. She must've got too hot last night and pulled it off, hurling it across the room in frustration. But was that before or after? Was she wearing the wig when she and Michel had sex? Or is this how she had looked to him – her real hair matted and pinned, flattened and lank and clinging to her scalp. Hmm, attractive!

The *Malaysian Queen* had been docked for two hours and Lana offered up silent thanks for this: no choppy waters to aggravate the nausea building up inside her; but more than that, today marked the first day of her four-week leave.

As soon as she could get it together and climb out of bed, she would shower, dress, pack and get the hell off the ship. She'd been at sea for three months now and a home visit was long overdue. Usually a trip back to her new-build apartment in Cardiff Bay would comprise opening a ton of post and gossiping with Malcolm her lodger. But *this* homecoming was going to be different. Maybe that's why she'd got so drunk last night – to lift the cloud of foreboding that had been hanging over her head ever since she'd received Catrin's email invitation, sent six weeks ago to both herself and Judith.

It had been strange seeing Judith's name along with hers in the list of recipients.

It still made her baulk.

Not because she hadn't seen Judith in the past twelve years. In fact, since Funeral-gate they'd both attended the same Blythe family occasion at least once a year, Catrin persisting in her commitment to be diplomatic and treat them both the same. At these events Lana and Judith were always polite and cordial to one another, in the most minimal of exchanges – *How are you? I'm fine – and you? We're fine.* And then they'd move on, avoiding each other for the rest of the evening. It was just about civilized and just about bearable. None-theless, seeing Judith was never something Lana could look forward to. Because it always felt so fake. At least Gareth completely ignored her on these occasions, which was somehow more honest.

There'd been a couple of times during the past twelve years when Lana had swallowed her pride and attempted to 'reach out' (how she hated that expression) to Judith. Though she always ended up regretting it. In 2012 she'd got married for the third time, to Paul, a meat-pie magnate with a taste for the high life and an insistence on a pre-nup. The marriage had only lasted eighteen months, but they'd gone all out on a wedding in the south of France and Catrin had suggested this might be a great opportunity to build bridges with Judith again. 'Everyone loves a wedding, Larn,' she'd insisted. 'Send her an invite and let's get the ball rolling.'

Lana took her friend's advice and put Judith and Gareth Metcalf on the guest list. But almost by return of post she received Judith's reply.

So sorry but we won't be able to make it. Gareth's off to the Grand Prix that weekend with friends, and I've got a big audit in work so my Saturdays are no longer my own. Anyway, hope you have a lovely day.

Lana hadn't taken the rejection well and she'd offloaded on to Cat. 'This is your fault. Why did you make me invite her? I feel like a right plonker now.'

'Don't blame me. I can't help it if she's busy!'

'Busy my arse,' said Lana. 'That's the last time I make an effort with that woman.'

Although she'd been angry with Catrin, the truth was that inside she was really hurt. Because Lana had always been the one who'd made the effort to repair the rift. Never Judith. Always Lana doing the chasing. Always Lana doing the apologizing. *Well, fuck you, Judith Harris and the horse you rode in on. No more.* It did make her smile, thinking of Judith dressed as a cowboy riding a horse, but the smile soon faded, replaced by the hurt.

Lana reached into her bedside cabinet and found some paracetamol lurking at the back. Downing them with the remainder of her now tepid tea, she tentatively looked at her phone and scrolled through the Sent messages. Phew. None written.

Twitter? Nothing.

Well done, Lana. Maybe at last you're learning to be a good girl.

Finally she checked her emails.

Oh God.

There it was. Lying shamefully in her Sent box.

To: Judith Metcalf
From: Lana Lloyd
Date: 21.05.2017
Subject: I'm Such a Twat

Dear Judith

Okay so i'm pissd – there's a spanish barman in my bathroom and all night i've bin thinkin bout you an'

me an' us an' Cat an' the party in a coupl wks, and look i'm gonna go ok? And cat said you goin too. i want us 2b friens again jude, i miss you – do yu think its tooo late 4 us? i dunno, I jus dont no. one thing I *DO KNOW* is that i am a twot..twut.*TWAT*. i hate myself.

   zBut i love you jude I do do do.
   Lana xxxxxxxxxxxxx

Oh God. Oh God. Oh God.

44

Catrin

They *had* intended to have a party for their twenty-fifth. But Catrin had been 'indisposed' at the time. Her own silly fault.

Seven years ago she'd taken up running again. She did it to counteract the onset of the menopause at the age of forty-three. 'Most women don't get it till they turn fifty!' she'd complained to Judith. 'A patient of mine is still having periods at fifty-*three*, it's not fair!' She tried to make a joke of it, but inside her heart was breaking. Because there was something so cruel about the menopause. Like it wasn't enough to have accepted she'd never have another child: going through this big hormonal change where all her 'equipment', as Lana described it, began to shut down, was an additional and very harsh blow – *In case you thought you weren't a woman any more, here's confirmation of the fact!*

Solomon told her she was being ridiculous. She countered this by pointing out that he couldn't possibly know what it was like, seeing as he was 'not actually a WOMAN!' It was after that that she decided to take the bull by the horns and out-run her frustration. Literally.

She'd started off painfully and slowly. A single jog around the block left her scarlet-faced, gasping for air and vowing never to repeat it. But something urged her to keep going. Until she could manage two circuits, then three. It became a kind of lucky charm, that she had to run three times a week, or else.

'Or else what?' Sol had laughed.

'I don't know. Armageddon? The Apocalypse?'

'OK, well, I can handle that.'

The running had progressed to 4k. Then the park run every Saturday, then her first 10k. A year later she'd run a half marathon, and a year after that a full one.

Then, two weeks before they were due to celebrate their silver wedding anniversary with a big, bold bash, Catrin had signed up for an Iron Woman, competing with a group of girls from the running club. And having managed two years of regular and strenuous activity without injury – apart from the occasional blister – Catrin came off her bike in training, breaking her right arm and her right femur.

'Think I'd have preferred Armageddon,' said Sol gently as they sat in the A&E cubicle waiting for the X-ray results.

They had no option other than to cancel their anniversary party, deciding to have one for their thirtieth instead, in five years' time.

It had seemed like an eternity away back then, and yet here it was upon them. She knew she sounded like her mother, but *didn't time just fly!* In less than a week they would be welcoming eighty friends and family to join them at Montgomery Hall for a posh sit-down dinner, twenty-nine and a half years after they'd celebrated their wedding there.

They'd decided to have it six months early mainly because the weather in June would be more conducive to partying. But also because Montgomery Hall was already booked up right through December with Christmas celebrations.

'Don't worry, I'll whisk you away for our actual anniversary,' Sol said. 'Paris or Rome. For a dirty weekend.'

'Are we allowed to be dirty at our age?'

'I should bloody well hope so,' he said with a laugh.

A party, whenever it was held, would mean facing the usual stress of having Lana and Judith in the same room together, but this was the norm nowadays and had been for years. And, of course, there was always the tiniest possibility that *this* party would be the one; *this* party would be the occasion on which her two best friends finally reconciled.

No time to think about it now though. She had to get on with morning surgery.

Looking down at her patient list, she spotted a name she always dreaded seeing: Patricia Harris.

When Catrin and Solomon had first become Coed Celyn's new GPs, she'd accepted she would sometimes have to treat patients she knew personally, including people she'd grown up with or parents of school friends and the like. But although Patricia Harris was registered at the surgery, she never seemed to require any medical attention apart from the odd prescription for antibiotics, and on those occasions Catrin had always managed to avoid treating her. It wasn't that she held any bad feelings towards Patricia, she just always dreaded seeing her in case she began ranting about Judith.

In the intervening years since Patricia's catastrophic appearance at George's funeral, Catrin had seen Judith's anger towards her mother gradually subside, until their relationship was reduced to a threadbare, needs-must connection. Their only contact comprised an annual visit by Judith and the occasional phone call, neither of which were appreciated by Patricia and which usually resulted in Judith wishing she'd not bothered.

Catrin always treated Patricia with professional courtesy when their paths *did* cross, but age had not mellowed Mrs Harris, and she'd become more dramatic than ever. Whenever she saw Catrin in and around Coed Celyn, she always made such a big, loud show of talking to her, usually about very inappropriate subjects. And then would begin the maligning of Catrin's best friend. Which she just couldn't handle. So avoidance really was the best option.

But two years ago, Patricia had suffered a fall and her health had begun to decline. She rarely left the house due to her failing mobility, and house-calls to the terraced home in Victoria Road became a regular occurrence. Social Services set up twice-daily visits and arranged to have her little breakfast room converted into a bedroom-cum-living room. Patricia proceeded to spend ninety per cent of her time in there, railing against the world with the curtains shut.

Catrin knew that at the heart of it all, Patricia was just a lonely old lady. She had no friends to speak of, having alienated so many people over the years, and her only family – Judith, Gareth and Jack – lived a hundred and fifty miles away in Surrey. There was one friend, Edwina, who Patricia also paid to clean the house once a week. She was kind, but even that relationship was put under strain by Patricia's demanding ways.

The situation was obviously awkward for Judith, but she certainly had no desire to have her mother move in with them, and she relied on Catrin and Sol to 'keep an eye on the ungrateful old goat'.

Every time someone from the practice visited Patricia, she seemed to have declined even more, and there had been talk of her perhaps going into residential care. But then a year ago this had all changed with the arrival on her doorstep of Adrian Oliver.

He was selling Betterware products. Patricia, although lonely, was still flirtatious, and invited him in, insisting he join her for a whisky and a fish-paste sandwich. His visits became more frequent and within a month Adrian had begun to call daily.

Catrin found out about his existence when Social Services mentioned him in one of their update phone calls.

'He's ever so helpful,' said the care worker. 'Puts up shelves for her, changes lightbulbs, paints doors . . .'

When Catrin told Judith this, she was intrigued. 'So is he a pensioner then? Like my mother? Sort of retired . . . ?'

'Er no, actually, Adrian's about thirty-five, thirty-six, apparently.'

'Oh. I see. But why would any self-respecting fella in his thirties want to hang around with my mother?'

'Well, it takes all sorts, I suppose,' said Catrin.

'Jack called her a bloody cougar!' Judith had laughed.

'He's certainly doing her some good,' said Catrin. 'She hasn't requested a house-call in three months now.'

On a whim one afternoon, her curiosity getting the better of her, Catrin decided to 'pop by' to see how Patricia was faring.

The octogenarian opened the door, beaming, and although she was a bit slow on her feet, the improvement in her demeanour was astonishing.

'Come on in, love!'

The house was bright and airy, the curtains open, and there was a freshness about the place that Catrin had never seen before. Patricia even made her a cup of tea, which was unheard of.

Feeling brave, Catrin broached the subject of Adrian Oliver, only to be told, 'Oh, he's just this kid who comes round now and again. Feel a bit sorry for him, to be honest.'

Catrin hadn't been expecting this: she'd clearly been misled by Edwina, who had said Patricia was 'besotted' with him. Her confusion was soon clarified, however, when, as she was leaving, the man himself arrived.

'He was just really . . . *insipid*, Jude,' she said when she phoned her friend that night. 'Like a bit sort of *spooky*, with matted-down greasy hair, fishy whiskers and damp hands.'

'Eeuw,' said Judith. 'And what was he like with my mother?'

'Well, he clearly adores her,' she said, confused. 'He kept telling me what an absolute *dreamboat* she is!'

Judith laughed. 'I can think of a lot of words to describe Patricia, but "dreamboat" isn't one of them.'

They both decided that although Adrian may be deluded and a little strange, he was ultimately harmless. He took Patricia to bingo, and the theatre, and for ice-cream down in Porthcawl, and if he kept her happy then why rock the dreamboat.

'Mrs Harris for you, Doctor,' came the voice of Catrin's receptionist through the intercom.

'Lovely, send her in,' replied Catrin, bracing herself for a ten-minute blast of Patricia-ness.

A few moments later, Adrian Oliver pushed open the door, carefully keeping it ajar with his foot whilst manoeuvring Patricia inside the consultation room in her wheelchair. She was done up to the nines, wearing a lot of make-up and preening like a peacock.

'Hello, my dear,' she said, as if she was the Queen

bestowing a royal visit. 'You've met my Adrian, of course?'

'Yes,' said Catrin. 'How are you both?'

'Oh, don't you be worrying about me, Doc. I'm here for Patsy, aren't I, babe?'

'That's right,' said Patricia. 'Now then, darlin', I need you to do me one of them medical thingies.'

Catrin smiled. 'Ooh, what's this for then, holiday insurance?'

Patricia looked at Adrian and smiled coyly. 'No, it's to say I'm right in the head an' all that.'

'I don't understand,' replied Catrin.

'I'm giving Adie the PA.'

'POA, she means,' corrected Adrian quietly.

'Power of attorney?' asked Catrin, attempting to keep her voice steady. 'You're giving ... *Adrian* ... power of attorney over your affairs?'

'Yes, that's right,' said Patricia, as if it was the most natural thing in the world. 'And don't you go telling that useless daughter of mine.'

'Well, she can't, can you, Doctor?' said Adrian, fixing his triumphant gaze on Catrin. ''Cos that'd be breaking patient–doctor confidentiality.'

And Dr Blythe felt an icy shiver down the back of her neck.

45

Judith

'She's fired me,' Edwina said on the other end of the phone, fighting back the tears. 'Well, actually that's not strictly true. *Adrian* was the one who did the dirty deed.'

It was the night before the anniversary party. Gareth was laid up with a heavy cold, so Jack and Dom had come over to cook dinner, offering to do the driving down to Wales the next morning.

Over the preceding few months, Edwina had been calling Judith a lot, raising concerns about Patricia. Judith would have preferred to keep her head in the sand, hoping it would all go away. But at the end of the day, Patricia was still her mother and she couldn't ignore the fact.

She put Edwina on to speakerphone so they could all hear.

'But *why*?' asked Judith.

'I've no idea!' said Edwina. 'He rang me up half an hour ago and told me that from now on *he* would be sorting out the cleaning and that my services are no longer required.'

This in itself would have been worrying enough, but

two days ago, Edwina had begun divulging information about a whole load of other untoward activity going on in Patricia's house. 'Like, for starters,' Edwina had told Judith, 'Adrian opens all of her bank statements.'

'What?' Judith was gobsmacked. 'But my mother's always kept such a careful eye on her outgoings.'

'Well, not any more. And he keeps hold of her cash-point card—'

'I'm surprised she's even *got* a cashpoint card!' interrupted Judith.

'Adrian persuaded her to sign up for one. Said it was easier. And last month he turned up in a brand-new car. Well, he sells Betterware, for God's sake, so how come he can afford a new Fiesta all of a sudden?'

When George had died, it was revealed that not only had he given Patricia the house, he'd also set up a decent-sized nest-egg in the form of a pension, which would leave his ex-wife financially comfortable for the rest of her days. At the time, Judith had found this frustrating. 'After the way she treated him, Gar! I mean, *why?*'

'Because he was a good bloke,' said Gareth.

Knowing this made Edwina's recent revelation all the more worrying, because if, as they suspected, Adrian Oliver was taking over Patricia's life, then he was probably influencing what she did with her money.

On top of all this, Catrin kept going on and on at Judith to come and see her mother more often.

'Talk to her, Jude. I know she's annoying, but you need to ask her what's going on. You need to communicate!'

Judith had been irritated by this. But probably only because she knew Catrin was right, even if she *was* behaving a tad too zealously about it all.

Admittedly Judith hadn't seen her mother since Christmas, but she'd spoken to her on the phone a month ago and not once had she mentioned any of these developments.

'He describes himself as her carer now,' continued Edwina.

'What – and she's paying him for this?' asked Jack as he grated some cheese on to their French onion soup.

'Well, she says she's not, but he's been on holiday three times in the past year. How's he afforded that? I'm telling you, Judith, that man's a wrong 'un.'

Sat around the dinner table an hour later, they relayed Edwina's information to a bunged-up, runny-nosed Gareth, who did his usual devil's advocate bit.

'Thing is, babes, if your mother wants to splash out on him, then surely it's up to her?'

'Yeah, of course, and if someone's mad enough to want to spend time with my mother, then the least they deserve is a brand-new Ford Fiesta!'

'But here's the worrying bit . . .' interjected Jack.

'Go on,' said Gareth as he slowly fed himself modest mouthfuls of soup.

'Well, apparently Adrian is a bit too fond of the ole whisky, and on one occasion he was seen taking Nana to town in her wheelchair . . .'

'He often takes her out for the day though, doesn't he?' sniffed Gareth.

'Yeah, but get this – so they're out and about in town, and Edwina sees them from the other side of the high street. And she says Adrian is weaving all over the pavement, like he's pissed. Next thing, the wheels of the chair catch on something and Nana goes flying!'

'She ended up on her hands and knees outside Poundland,' added Dom.

Gareth tried not to laugh. 'Sorry, go on.'

'No, I know, it's horrible,' said Judith, 'but also a bit sort of Laurel and Hardy. Anyway, Edwina rushes over to help and Adrian gets really nasty, says he's got the whole thing under control and to back off. She says she could smell the whisky on him from a hundred paces.'

'Blimey!'

'Cut to a couple of days later,' continued Jack, 'and Edwina pops round to visit—'

'I thought she'd been sacked?'

'No, this is *before* the sacking. So Nana's there on her own, which is why Edwina reckons she'll talk a bit more freely. Turns out she had a visit the night before.'

'Who, Edwina?'

'No, Patricia,' replied Dom. 'A visit from Adrian's *mother*! She gives Patricia a dressing-down, telling her to stop feeding her boy whisky, that she's got no right, that he's only a fucking recovering *alcoholic* and has been going to AA for the past two years!'

'Bloody hell!'

'I know, right?' said Jack, incredulous. 'So she's had to hide all the whisky in the house and promise not to let him go near the stuff.'

'And you definitely don't think there's anything, y'know, *romantic* going on?'

'Well, I've always thought *not*,' said Judith, 'but Edwina said on another occasion she called round and Adrian answered the door all a-fluster, and very red in the face . . . and the way they *look* at each other, is like they're teenagers in love, calling each other "babe" and "sweetheart" and stuff.'

'Dear God, no!'

'Gar, it *does* all sound dodgy, doesn't it?'

'You can say that again.'

'Anyway,' said Jack calmly, 'we're gonna leave early tomorrow and pay Nana a visit. I think we need to take this situation in hand, starting with persuading her to grant Mum lasting power of attorney. That way we can rein in any designs this Adrian fellow has on her. And if he's kosher, then great. But better to be safe, eh?'

It was at times like this that Judith was extra glad of her son's invaluable expertise, him being a highly accomplished property lawyer.

'Don't worry, Mum. We all know I can wrap her round my little finger,' he assured her. 'We'll get this sorted.'

And with that, Gareth did a God-almighty sneeze in agreement.

*

The next morning, Gareth decided he was too ill to come. Feeling sorry for himself, he dragged his aching bones back to bed and vowed to spend forty-eight hours under the duvet.

Judith had already phoned Patricia to tell her they'd be calling in en route to the party, because they needed to discuss something in private. Arriving in Coed Celyn around midday, they dropped their bags at the hotel and sent Dominic off in search of flowers and champagne to take to the party later. Judith and Jack made their way to Patricia's house, but were both surprised to find that Judith's key didn't work in the lock.

As Judith knocked tentatively on the door, Jack pointed out a key safe – a new addition that was jutting out of the wall. But they had no time to discuss it, because the door was flamboyantly thrown open by Adrian, who stood there smiling.

'Welcome! Welcome!' he crowed, and made way for them to enter.

Judith was wrongfooted by his being there. She'd specifically told her mother she wanted to see her alone.

'Can I get either of you a cup of tea?' Adrian said brightly, wringing his hands and reminding Judith of Uriah Heep in Dickens' *David Copperfield*.

'I'm fine, thanks. Mum?' asked Jack, ever the height of politeness.

'No thanks, we just had a coffee.'

They made small talk for a while. Catrin and Sol's anniversary party seemed to be the talk of the town.

'My friend Tina works Montgomery Hall,' said Adrian conspiratorially. 'They've pulled out all the stops for it, I'm tellin' you. Champagne, the lot.'

'Right,' said Judith cautiously, feeling uncomfortable discussing her friends' private lives with this comparative stranger.

'Would've been nice to have been invited!' mumbled Patricia. 'I've known the girl since she was five.'

'I think they were a bit tight on numbers. Anyway,' Judith said, changing the subject, 'don't let us hold you up, Adrian.'

'Yeah, we need a little chat with Nana,' smiled Jack. 'It's a private family matter.'

Adrian swallowed nervously, smiling briefly at Patricia before ploughing on. 'Actually, I've been asked to stay.'

'Sorry?' said Jack.

'See, what it is, Mum's got plans of her own.'

Judith didn't know what threw her most – the fact that Adrian was so flagrantly defying their request for privacy, or the fact that he had just referred to Patricia as 'Mum'. She opened her mouth to protest, but Jack interrupted her.

'Just a sec,' he said gently. 'When Adrian says you've got plans, Nana, what does he mean?'

'I've got a friend who's a financial adviser,' Adrian launched in, and again, with cool diplomacy, Jack interrupted.

'Nana, why don't you tell us what you want, rather than other people speaking on your behalf?'

'I want Adrian to sort everything out for me. I trust him lock, stock and barrel. He's like the son I never had.'

'Is that why he's started calling you "Mum"?' asked Judith, unable to hide her sarcasm.

'Sorry,' said Adrian. 'Slip of the tongue. Look, I know this is a bit of a shock, but in all fairness, I see more of your mother than you ever do. I'm on hand twenty-four seven. She knows she can rely on me.'

'Well, she hasn't got much choice,' said Judith, 'seeing as you've fired her cleaner, changed the locks and put a key safe on the door! Incidentally, what's the number for that?'

Adrian looked at Patricia questioningly. 'That's not up to me to divulge, I'm afraid, it's up to Mum . . . I mean, your mum,' he falteringly corrected himself.

Judith glared at him and then at Patricia.

'Nana?' asked Jack politely. 'What's the number for the key safe?'

Patricia looked confused. 'I don't . . . I don't know it.'

'For God's sake!' snapped Judith, and once again Jack touched her gently on the hand to stop her from losing it. 'What if there's a fire? What if someone needs to get in?'

'All they gotta do is call me, I'll be down here in a flash.'

'Nana,' Jack said softly. 'Would you mind if Adrian gave us the number?'

'Go on,' said Patricia, begrudgingly. And Judith

thought she detected a flash of defeat cross Adrian's face.

'It's 5-9-8-2, OK?' he said, smiling. 'My date of birth, actually.'

'Hah!' said Jack, with an innocence Judith knew he was faking. 'You're only five years older than *me*!'

'Look, you may as well know, Mum . . . *your* mum has asked me to have power of attorney—'

'*No!*' Judith exclaimed, not believing her ears.

'. . . and we're in the process of sorting it,' Adrian continued calmly.

'But you need certification by a doctor for this,' said Jack. 'To confirm that Nana's of sound mind.'

'Oh, don't you worry,' Patricia chipped in. 'We've done all that, haven't we, Adie?'

'Yes. In fact, it was your good friend Dr Catrin who did it for us!'

'Catrin?' mumbled Judith. '*Catrin* did it? But why didn't she tell me?'

'Well, she can't, can she? Not allowed!' And there was a look of glee in his eyes as he said it.

'You're entitled to give power of attorney to whoever you choose, Nana, you know that?' Jack intervened, reasonably. 'I'm just not sure why you didn't ask Mum.'

'Why should I give it to *her*?' Patricia snarled. 'She never bothers with me. I'm lucky if she visits once a year!'

'And can you blame me?' shouted Judith.

'Me and Dom have been down a few times, Nana,' said Jack gently.

'Yes, but *this* one comes here every day! Nothing's too much trouble. I'd be dead if it wasn't for him!'

'Oh don't be such a bloody drama queen!' Judith snapped.

'Mum . . .' said Jack, and she knew he was cautioning her. She also knew he was ultimately doing it for her own good.

Judith was about to get up and leave, realizing that once again her mother had succeeded in unceremoniously pulling an emotional rug from under her, when Jack said, 'Nana, I do understand why you'd want to give Adrian power of attorney, and if you don't want to give it to Mum, then that's your prerogative.' Judith glared at him. *What?* He ignored her and carried on. 'But what about if you gave it to *me*? I'm a lawyer, after all, and I deal with this kind of stuff day in, day out.'

Judith saw Patricia flinch and soften, and she knew Jack's words were having an effect. She also saw Adrian redden, and the muscle in his jaw flicker.

'I mean, it seems daft to burden Adrian with all this legal stuff when you could be concentrating on just enjoying each other's company.'

God, he's good, thought Judith as she watched her beautiful son take the hand of his frosty grandmother.

Patricia's inner battle was evident on her face as her eyes darted between Jack and Adrian. 'I don't . . . I'm not sure what . . .'

'I think what Mu— Patricia is trying to say is that

we've talked about this long and hard and it's not been an easy decision to make, but she's made it now and feels happy with it, don't you, love?' said Adrian, who in a counter-move of charm took Patricia's other hand.

The picture was ludicrous – two men of not vastly different ages, each holding the hand of an octogenarian woman who was trying her best to emulate a pious look, something akin to the Virgin Mary.

Jack backed down first.

'Cool,' he said. 'The most important thing, Nana, is that you do what you feel is right.' And he got up to put his jacket back on. 'Just give me a call if you need any help with anything.'

'So that's it?' whispered Judith a few minutes later when they'd got outside. 'We're just going to leave him to take over her life?'

'For now, yes,' said Jack. 'No point in upsetting the apple cart till we need to. If he thinks he's got away with it then we're more likely to catch him out.'

'But what was Catrin playing at? Why didn't she tell me? All that hinting. *Go and see your mother, Jude . . . talk to her, Jude* – she should've just said it. I'm her best friend, for God's sake.'

'Mother – do *not* mention it tonight. It's not fair on Aunty Cat. She must've been in a horrendous situation – patient–doctor confidentiality and all that.'

'Well, I'm hardly going to report her, am I?'

'That's not the point – Adrian would. Now please,

try and put it out of your mind for now, and let's concentrate on enjoying the party.'

Judith reluctantly nodded. Celebrating was the last thing she felt like doing right now.

46

Catrin

'You look so *young*!' said Romy as they peeled off the bubble wrap to reveal an eight-foot-by-six-foot blown-up photograph of her mum and dad in 1986.

'This was taken at a place called the Samaria Gorge,' said Catrin wistfully as she took in the familiar image before her. 'On the first day we ever met.'

'I know, Mum, you *told* me, like, *loads*!' said Romy in the whining tones of a bored teenager who was secretly very proud of her parents' love story.

She'd been enlisted to help with the party preparations for that evening at Montgomery Hall. 'Where we had our wedding reception!' her dad had told her – *again!* – and Romy had rolled her eyes. *Everything* about today was going to be soaked in nostalgia.

'Well, you'd have thought they'd have at least decorated the place since the nineteen eighties!' said a well-known voice and Catrin turned around to see her in-laws strolling in, Edward carrying a large plastic crate and Amelia unimpressed as ever. Though by now, after experiencing years of social awkwardness, Catrin knew only too well that this was just her mother-in-law's way of dealing with her own shyness.

'Nana! Bampeeeee!' Romy screeched and hurtled towards her grandparents like a deranged bowling ball.

'How is my favourite granddaughter now!' laughed Amelia, opening her arms wide for the biggest of hugs. Catrin loved how much her in-laws loved her girl. Sol's brother Tom had three boys who were equally as loved, but Cat glowed with pride that Romy was their only granddaughter.

After they'd said their hellos, they unpacked the Jamaican ginger and caramel cake made by Edward. Since his retirement he had taken up baking, and never let a celebration opportunity pass without making a cake. 'Let's hope none of your friends decide to smash *this* one to pieces!' he laughed and Amelia tutted, having never quite forgiven Judith and Lana for the horrendous incident thirty years previously.

Changing the subject, she offered to help hang the giant photograph of Sol and Cat. 'My God, you look so young!' she said.

'That's what I said, Nana. That's the day they first met!' shouted Romy, only this time with pride.

They hung the picture on two big hooks behind the top table, with a banner beneath it that read, *Catrin and Solomon – 30 Happy Years*. And for the most part that had been true, Cat thought as she watched Sol chatting easily with his dad, and Romy helping Amelia put out the place names according to the table plan. Thirty *mostly* happy years . . . what an achievement.

In a few hours, eighty guests, many journeying from across the country, would be there to help them celebrate. Well over half of them had been there on the day itself, in 1987. Some were no longer with them, of course, like their grandparents and Sol's Uncle Ken – he'd no doubt mention them in the section of his speech entitled *Absent Friends*. She smiled when she thought about Sol's speech – considering he was used to public speaking, especially in his recent work training GPs, he'd been uncharacteristically nervous about the pressure on him to say a few words. She'd heard him mumbling away in his study for the past few evenings, though she'd never made out any actual words.

'We'd better go home and change, babe,' said Sol now, snuggling into her neck.

'Leave the woman alone!' laughed Edward. 'You'd swear you'd just got wed!'

Three hours later, they were suited, booted, frocked, primped and frilled, sipping drinks and mingling with the guests. Choruses of 'Well helloooooo!' and 'You haven't aged one bit!' filled the room as old friends and relatives were reunited, some after a thirty-year interlude. A four-piece jazz band played eighties hits on a makeshift stage, as waiting staff weaved their way in and out with trays of champagne and exquisite canapés. Everyone was buzzing and the atmosphere was big-hearted and nostalgic.

Over at the door Catrin saw Judith arrive, with Jack and his husband Dominic in tow. 'Where's Gareth?'

she shouted, bounding over with Sol and hugging them all in turn.

'Man flu,' said Jack, laughing.

'Aw no, to be fair, he's really rough,' said Judith, who didn't seem very happy. 'Felt a bit bad leaving him, to be honest.'

'Oh bless him,' said Catrin.

'Cat, we called in to see Patricia today . . .'

Catrin sensed where this was going, and prayed that she was wrong. To her relief, she caught a subtle glare from Jack in his mother's direction, and he rapidly changed the subject.

'Anyway, Dad really did want to come, Aunty Cat,' he said, and she watched Judith take the hint.

'Yeah, he thought he'd feel well enough this morning.'

'Well, it takes longer to get better these days,' said Catrin. 'We're none of us getting any younger!'

'Hark at Granny!' Sol laughed, kissing his wife's hair.

'Yes, the way you talk you'd think you were geriatric,' said Jack.

'Well, we are!'

'Speak for yourself – I just had another round of fillers done.'

They all turned. It was Lana. Standing with a magnum of champagne and a huge bouquet of flowers almost too big to hold.

'Plus two nights ago I shagged a guy twenty years my junior. Nothing geriatric about me, mate!'

Judith rolled her eyes and Jack grinned, clearly delighted by the new arrival. 'It's Aunty Lana, isn't it?'

'Less of the "Aunty", young man!' replied Lana with mock disapproval.

'We met once, in Cyprus,' said Jack. 'At my grandfather's funeral . . .' The atmosphere took a dip. 'I'm Jack – Judith and Gareth's son.'

Of course! They'd only ever met once. At the few occasions attended by both Lana *and* Judith over the years, Jack had never been with them, and Catrin was suddenly hijacked by emotion when she realized this.

'Ah, the famous Jack Metcalf,' said Lana, clearly moved and trying desperately to cover up the embarrassing reminder of George's funeral all those years ago. She flicked her eyes quickly in Judith's direction.

'Alrigh', Judith?' she said with a curt smile. 'Fellow bridesmaid!'

'Hello, Lana,' Judith replied, equally as curt, arch politeness searing the air.

Thankfully Solomon came to the rescue, introducing Dominic. 'And this is Jack's husband.'

'Dominic,' he said, beaming.

Lana eyed him up and down with exaggerated lasciviousness. 'What a tremendous bloody loss to us straight ladies!' And they all laughed. Apart from Judith, who Catrin noticed rolling her eyes again.

'Let me take those off you,' said Dominic, relieving Lana of the flowers.

'And I'll find a home for this bad boy,' said Jack,

grabbing the magnum. 'Next to ours! Great minds, eh?'

They headed off, Jack shouting behind him, 'We'll be back!'

There was an awkward pause, thankfully interrupted by the arrival of more guests.

'Sol, it's your Uncle Joe,' Catrin said, grabbing her husband's hand, deciding there and then to let Lana and Judith break their own ice. 'See you in a bit, girls, we'll leave you two to catch up.' And she scuttled off, leaving behind a ticking time bomb.

47

Judith

The waiter approached them, star struck. Obviously he'd recognized Lana from TV and Judith wondered how she could escape what was about to happen. She *had* hoped she could get away with completely avoiding Lana Lloyd tonight, but so far the plan was failing.

'Champagne?' said the waiter, ignoring Judith.

'Ooh, go on!' said Lana, helping herself to two glasses.

For a moment Judith thought she was getting them one each, but within seconds Lana had downed both drinks and replaced the empties on to the tray.

The waiter laughed. 'Me and my mum, we love you. We're addicted to that *Still Waters*! They repeat it all the time they do, on Gold. Your character's wicked,' he said, as Judith helped herself modestly to a glass.

'God, that was years ago, but cheers, babes. D'you want a selfie?'

'Can I?'

'As long as you keep me topped up all night. Deal?'

'Deal,' the impressionable waiter said and Lana winked at him.

God, get me away from here, thought Judith, scanning the nearby guests for someone she recognized.

'Would you mind taking it?' said the waiter, handing his mobile to Judith. 'I'm shaking too much to do a selfie!'

He shoved the mobile in Judith's direction without giving her a second glance, caught up in the allure of celebrity. 'You just tap on the circle down the bottom?' he said, eyes firmly fixed on Lana.

'Yes, I *do* know how to work an iPhone, y'know,' she said. And was again ignored.

She cringed as Lana put her arm around the waiter and planted a big smacker on his cheek. 'Take a couple. One of them's bound to be OK.'

Judith had no choice but to obey. The waiter thanked Lana profusely, leaving with a promise to fetch more champagne. It didn't go unnoticed by Judith that there'd been no thanks to her for taking the photo.

Left alone again, the awkwardness resumed. They both stood there, looking around the room.

'So,' said Lana, without making eye contact. 'Long time, Jude. How've you been?'

'Very well, thanks. You?'

'Yeah, not bad. Knocked the acting on the head, did Cat tell you? I do cruise ships now. Pays really well.'

'Right.'

More silence ensued.

'And what about you?'

'I'm still in local government.' Judith immediately regretted saying it. Could her life have sounded more boring?

'Christ, must be over thirty years now – you're nothing if not consistent, Jude!'

Stop calling me Jude as if you're my best mate.

'Where's Gareth?'

'He couldn't make it.' Somehow Judith didn't feel right telling her that Gareth was ill. It seemed too intimate a piece of information.

'Bollocks. It's 'cos *I'm* here, isn't it?' said Lana.

And Judith snapped.

'Well, firstly that makes no sense, because as you know Gareth has been to several of Catrin and Sol's parties at which you've been in attendance . . .'

'Where he completely ignored me!'

'. . . and secondly, Lana, not *everything* is about you!'

Annoyingly, Lana laughed. 'Easy, tiger! Don't be going all Theresa May on me now.'

Judith took too big a gulp of her drink, the bubbles rushing up her nose in protest. She fought the urge to sneeze.

'Listen,' said Lana, lowering her voice. 'About that email . . .'

'It's fine,' said Judith. 'You explained you were drunk at the time of writing.'

Sometimes, try as she might, Judith couldn't avoid the sneering tone in her voice.

'Yes, I was. You should try it sometime. Loosen you up a bit, y'know?'

Before she had a chance to respond, Jack and Dominic returned.

'So has Mum told you about the baby?'

Judith glared at her son. The thought of sharing any private family information with Lana was a total no-no.

'I thought we were keeping it quiet,' she said, but it was pointless. Lana had grabbed the morsel of news like a ravenous terrier.

'What's this?' she asked, scooping up another champagne from a passing waitress.

'We're having a baby,' said Dominic, smiling at his husband. 'With a surrogate. She's four months pregnant now, so we reckon it's safe to tell people.'

'Wow! That's amazing!' said Lana, tears in her eyes. 'Congratulations, Daddies!' She hugged Jack and Dominic in turn, who both thanked her proudly. And then she turned to Judith, beaming. '*And* to you, Grandmama.'

'I think everyone's heading for their seats,' Judith replied, pointedly ignoring Lana's good wishes. Mean-spirited maybe. But this joyful news wasn't Lana's to feast upon. Judith pretended not to notice the look of hurt on the face of her ex-friend. 'Come on,' she said to her son. 'Nice talking to you, Lana.' And she moved away, in the hope of avoiding any further conversation.

'Judith,' said Lana quietly, catching her by the arm whilst Jack and Dominic walked on ahead, 'there's really no need for you to be so bloody rude. You never used to be this much of a bitch. Presumably it's the menopause.'

Judith stared back. 'Oh give it a rest, Lana,' she said. 'You're just drunk. Again.'

'Yes, but tomorrow I'll be sober and you'll still be a bitch!' replied Lana. And off she floated to find her place at the table.

Judith felt a lump in her throat and fought off the annoying and unexpected desire to cry.

48

Solomon

'And so my mother says, *How are you, Mr Thomas?* and Mr Thomas says, *Not great, this morning I got my cat put down,* to which my mother flings her arms around him and says, *CONGRATULATIONS!* and Mr Thomas looks at her and says, *Why are you congratulating me on getting my cat put down?* And my mother says, *Oh, I thought you said you got your Cap and Gown!*'

The guests laughed and Sol continued, 'Not that my mother is obsessed with academic qualifications or anything . . . I mean, I'm all for power to the pensioner, but Mr Thomas is eighty-three!'

He looked around the room at the laughing faces – he'd nailed it. Everyone was having such a good time, this was such a good party.

'Anyway, I'd like to be serious for a minute,' he said, clearing his throat and focusing on the handwritten white cards in his hands. 'As you all know, five years ago we were meant to have a summer party like this one, for our silver anniversary – the invites went out and everything. But a week before, my intrepid wife decides it'd be a good idea to do an Iron Woman and raise money for her beloved charity. And ends up breaking not just an arm, but a leg. Doing it literally cost her an arm and a leg . . .'

Everyone groaned at his bad joke.

'I know, I know, I milked that one for all it was worth. Anyway,' he continued, 'y'know, during that time, Cat was laid up in plaster and hardly able to move, which as you can imagine knocked her for six. She was pretty down. And on the third week of her being laid low, it happened to be a certain little lady's birthday . . .'

And he turned to look at Romy, who went red with all the room's attention focused on her. 'Dad!' she giggled, hiding behind a heart-shaped lilac balloon that proudly bore the names *Catrin and Solomon*. Everyone giggled with her, delighted by her embarrassed response.

'And Romy came into our room on the day she turned eight and brought all her birthday cards and her cake and balloons, and she put them on the bed and she said, *Mummy, you can have my birthday if you like, because it will make you smile!* And it did. It did make Mummy smile, didn't it, pumpkin? And she's been smiling ever since, pretty much. Except when England beats Wales at rugby.'

The room filled with good-natured booing and Catrin once again looked up at him, beaming.

'And . . . *aagh* . . . sorry!' He cleared his throat, continuing, 'Yeah, and so every day we say a prayer of thanks for this bolshy little angel . . .'

'Hey!' laughed Romy.

'. . . who appeared in our lives twelve years ago – YES, SHE IS TWELVE NOW, FOLKS!' He paused for a moment, then carried on. 'Thing is, it's the people in our lives who make us who we are, don't you think?'

The jollity in the room faded a little, to be replaced by a more pensive atmosphere.

'The parents and the grandparents and godparents and the children and nieces and nephews and uncles and aunties and cousins and friends . . .'

At this point he noticed Judith steal a glance at Lana, who glanced back, before looking away again.

He continued, '. . . basically, *all* you terrible lot. We wouldn't be here without you. So I personally want to say thank you for being such a huge part of our marriage, and for being there for us these past thirty years . . . well, thirty-one, in fact.'

He could hear his voice faltering, and felt his whole body begin to shake uncontrollably, as if the relief of managing to deliver the speech he'd been worrying about for weeks had finally set in.

'*Thirty-one years*, Catrin, since we sat next to each other on that dusty bus to a Cretan gorge.' And he realized how hard he'd been holding on to his prompt cards, and felt the cramp in the fingers of his left hand, attempting to discreetly stretch them out, but failing, and making it worse. 'And look at us now,' he continued, choked with tears, 'my beautiful wife . . . I love you as much today as I did back then, you—'

And he stopped. Too overcome to go on. He knew

what he wanted to say, but the words just wouldn't come out – his mouth just wouldn't work.

People around him started laughing, cheering, banging their glasses with spoons, egging him on to finish the speech. He looked down at the prompt cards, and watched as they fell slowly like big square petals from his hand on to the table before him. And he saw the smiles on the faces of his parents turn into something else – was it terror? And he looked at Catrin, shaking her head, her mouth open, saying something, but he couldn't hear what because of this *hissing*, this incessant *hissing* in his ears, and Romy, who'd been holding her heart-shaped balloon, started crying and panicked and in panicking let go of the thread by which the balloon was held. And he watched as it floated slowly, up and up and up, a big lilac heart, set free, flying heavenwards and out of everyone's reach.

And then all was white.

And then all was nothing.

And on the night he celebrated thirty years of marriage to the only woman he'd ever loved, Solomon Blythe's heart beat for the very last time.

49

Lana

Huw Kelly's apple tree stood proudly in the centre of his lawn, branches outstretched, fruit beginning to ripen in the midsummer sun.

Lana had cried so much this past week her voice was hoarse and her filler-filled cheeks were red and dry. Christ, she must look a right mess. Lighting up another cigarette, she inhaled. And remembered.

The hours they'd spent in this garden.

If she looked hard enough she could almost see the ghosts of their younger selves, playing tag, singing songs, discussing boys. Her heart was heavy with sorrow. It ached.

A week had passed since he'd died. And although they'd all pretended to be grown-ups, pretended to know what to do, none of them really did. They were all engulfed in this haze of raw grief.

She'd cancelled her next cruise and extended her stay at the little B&B around the corner. Her parents were long gone from Coed Celyn now, having emigrated to Majorca ten years previously. She hardly ever saw them any more, and this added to her acutely felt sense of rootlessness. How she longed right now for some security. An anchor. A hub. A home. Because now, more than ever, her disconnection was being shown up in stark relief.

Sol was dead. Her dear old friend was dead.

And Catrin couldn't speak, unintentionally isolating Lana even more.

She just wanted a hug really.

Occasionally at the Kelly house during the past week she'd encountered Judith, who had continued to treat her with polite disdain. *Even in these circumstances. Christ!*

But so be it. Lana had no energy left to persuade her to change. And none of it seemed to matter any more anyway.

Every day she'd head to the Kellys', where Catrin and Romy clung to each other in the eye of the raging grief storm, preparing for Sol's funeral to come at them over the hill. It was all too, too grim to consider. She drifted into the house, awash with sadness and Liz Kelly's constant cups of tea and relentless supply of cake. Lana couldn't touch any of it. She couldn't remember when she'd last eaten. She was surviving on black coffee, cigarettes and gin. People wandered aimlessly in and out and around the house, muttering sorrowful, pointless exchanges.

She looked in on Catrin every day. At least twice. Just lying there in her old bedroom with Romy, her tears dried up, lost for words. Mute and on pause.

Between them all, they somehow persuaded her to wash every day, to eat at least a slice of toast, and to wander into the garden for a few lungfuls of fresh air. They were just keeping her alive really, like a feeble plant, carrying her from the pillar of Sol's death to the post of his funeral service. There were other practicalities to achieve, such as taking Romy out of the house for a change of scene, or going to the chemist for Catrin's sleeping pills and other meds.

That afternoon, Lana had volunteered to go to the shops. Liz needed more bread and milk. In order to function. In order to keep her daughter alive with eternal cups of tea. Not long before, Judith's lovely son had turned up with his lovely husband. And Gareth. Not wanting to create any unhelpful awkwardness by being in the same room as him, she'd seized upon the duty of bread-and-milk-buyer in order to get out of the house. 'I'll come with you,' Jack had said. And Lana thought, *Why not?*

The shop was only five minutes' walk away, but after they'd bought the groceries, Lana wasn't ready to return straight away. She was going stir crazy, if truth be told, and she craved a new environment and new faces.

'Don't suppose you fancy a quick one in the Crown, do you?' she asked Jack. 'You don't have to, I just—'

'Yes, please.'

They ended up having two. He was a lovely guy. Sometimes she found herself staring at him, not really listening to his earnest talk about Catrin and what would become of her without Sol.

Jack looked more like Gareth than Jude. Same eyes and the same-shaped mouth. She zoomed in on it now as it formed words, expressions, opinions that she didn't hear. *Snap out of it, Lana,* she thought, aware that she was in danger of being destructively nostalgic, allowing Jack to remind her of a younger Gareth; a Gareth with whom she'd once been so intimate. She didn't want to go there.

'Can we talk about something else?' she suddenly blurted out. 'Sorry. It's just I'm exhausted with death talk. Selfish, I know.'

Jack smiled. 'Of course. I totally get it . . . Umm, saw our surrogate yesterday. She is blooming.'

'Aw, that's nice. Has she done it before?'

'She's had three babies of her own. And this is her second surrogacy.'

'Such a selfless act.'

'Yeah.'

They sat in silence then, sipping their drinks, lost in their own heads and not wanting to climb out of them.

'And how's your grandmother these days? We lost touch.' Thinking about Patricia always made her flinch, remembering the disastrous trip to Cyprus all those years ago.

'Oh, y'know Nana Pat. Still mad as a box of frogs. Did you hear about the toyboy?'

And for the first time in a week Lana smiled as Jack regaled her with the story of Patricia and Adrian Oliver.

'It's an absolute mess,' he continued. 'Turns out this

guy has enlisted the help of some financial adviser – bloke called Steven Dean who he met at an AA meeting.'

'Blimey,' said Lana, gripped by the story.

'*He* was the one who started the ball rolling with the POA. But he's also managed to convince Patricia that she'd be better off if she put her house in trust so that Social Services "can't get their hands on it". And surprise, surprise, the named trustees on the document are Adrian himself and a friend of his called Tina, who Nana's never even met. The whole thing is dodgy beyond belief. But until they do anything illegal, we're a bit stumped. Plus Nana is compos mentis. She knows what she's doing.'

'But I'm sure when we went to George's funeral Patricia said something about her will . . . that George had asked her to ensure she left the house to Judith? I mean, I know that's a few years ago now, but surely she *can't* put the house into trust?'

'That's what I've been trying to explain to Mum. My Pappoús may have *requested* that Nana left her the house, but she's perfectly within her rights to change her will again. And if that's what she *has* done, Mum won't have a leg to stand on.'

'She's such a piece of work, your gran,' said Lana. 'I mean, she must be eighty-odd now, and she's *still* being a monumental pain in the arse.'

Jack smiled. 'The battle's not over yet.'

They finished their drinks and made to head back.

'It's been really nice getting to know you a bit,' Lana said to Jack as they left the pub.

'Yeah,' he mused, and thought for a moment before saying, 'Such a shame about you and Mum. I reckon she could do with someone like you as a friend. Lighten her up a bit, y'know? She does tend to get a bit serious at times.'

'Well, that's not such a bad thing. Playing the clown hasn't got me very far, if I'm honest,' Lana said ruefully. And then the thought struck her that both Judith and Gareth would be at the Kelly house when they got back – and Lana realized how little resilience she had left to cope with being ignored.

Tomorrow's funeral would require all the strength she could muster.

'Jack, I think I'll have an early night, love.'

'Aw no, are you not coming back?'

She smiled at him and gave him a big hug. 'No, sorry. I'll see you tomorrow at the church. You and your dad are bearers, aren't you?'

'Yeah.'

They both looked down, weary with heartbreak, nothing left to say.

'Night, Aunty Lana,' whispered Jack.

And Lana smiled, willing back tears and turning in the opposite direction towards her B&B.

50

Judith

She wanted to walk to the church. It wasn't as if Catrin didn't have enough loved ones to surround her in the funeral car. Plus she had a thing about hearses.

'You'll sit by us in the service though, won't you?' whispered Huw Kelly before she left. 'You and Lana. We'll need you up there.'

'Yes, of course,' she whispered back.

She hugged Gareth and Jack, both smart in their dark suits and black ties, Jack at ease in his, Gareth like a fish out of water in his. 'You'll do him proud,' she said, trying to smile, and she left the house to head to St Theodore's.

She chose to go the long way round, avoiding the little lane which ran along the side of the church. Decades earlier, the three of them would hide down there, sneaking illicit cider and cigarettes. She couldn't bear any more nostalgia today. Her heart was already too heavy, weighed down with loss and the searing pain of grief.

Approaching the corner where the main street met Bessemer Place, she saw several figures dressed in black heading for the church – some solitary, some in couples, some in groups, all unified in their loss. The service would no doubt be packed and Judith's heart lurched like a stalled engine at the prospect of what lay ahead.

And then she saw her. Unavoidable, of course. There was no point in hiding.

'Lana.'

'Hey Jude,' she replied, and Judith remembered sadly that this used to be a little Beatles-related joke between them. But no one was laughing now. They'd spoken occasionally during the past week, of course, about practicalities and arrangements. Though only when they had to and in short, polite exchanges. The only way they knew how to communicate these days. Even Sol's death hadn't changed that.

Standing a couple of feet apart, uncertainty fizzled between them, and they hesitated on the verge of a hug before both deciding against it.

'Can't believe it's happening, can you?' asked Lana, her voice shaking as she fumbled in her bag for a small bottle of Rescue Remedy and swigged back its contents like whisky.

Hiding her disapproval, Judith said, 'The family wants us down the front.'

'Oh Christ, I'm not sure I can handle that . . .' replied Lana, panicking. 'So close to the coffin and . . . I'm just not very good with—'

'Today's not about you though, is it, Lana?' Judith snapped, a reflex action. 'It's about Catrin.'

Awkwardness cracked between them like a pane of breaking glass. God, how she wished she was somewhere else. Then suddenly Lana pulled off the black silk wrap that was draped over her shoulders and rapidly flapped the neckline of her dress. 'Bloody hot flushes,' she mumbled.

Judith fought the urge to smile, an alien grain of affection for her old friend lodging itself unexpectedly in her heart. She rustled in her bag and took out a Spanish-style fan, mumbling, 'Here y'are, borrow this.'

'Cheers,' said Lana, flicking it open with flamencan flair and cooling herself in its welcome breeze. A minute later the flush had passed.

'Shall we go in then?' asked Judith tentatively.

'Yes,' said Lana as she held Judith's gaze. 'We can do this. Can't we?'

51
Catrin

She noticed irrelevant details. Like the fraying hem on Father O'Leary's cassock. And the foreign wording of the prayers – O Lamb of God, That Takest Away the Sins of the World, Grant Us Thy Peace ... Why do they call Jesus a lamb? she wondered. And is he a Welsh lamb? A spring lamb? A lamb chop?

Lamb.

Lam-B.

Why is there a 'b' at the end of the word 'lamb'?

And for some reason, she found this amusing – and first she smiled, then she tittered, then she giggled, and then she guffawed, and then she was weeping with laughter and people were staring at her and someone was saying something – was it Solomon's brother? he was up there in front of them all, reading out words from pieces of paper ... and everyone carried on staring at her, because she was laughing and this was an inappropriate response and she was being an irresponsible adult at an inappropriate time, and she felt Lana's arms around her and Judith holding her hand, telling her she can say whatever she wants and laugh as loud as she wants and do whatever feels right because they will hold her safe – 'nothing you do is wrong, babe,' Lana said to her and then Judith whispered, 'you can stand up and flash your boobs at Father O'Leary if you want,' and this made her laugh even more, until the laughing flipped over into tears and the tears flipped over into screaming and all the while they held her tight.

Her two best friends in the world.

And the people put him into the ground, and still they held her tight.

And she thought about Gwynnie, her cadaver at med school, and at his graveside she whispered, 'you're a cadaver now, Solomon,' whilst Father O'Leary said something quick and fast about dust and ashes and the Father's house having many rooms, and Solomon's mother was weeping and throwing roses on to the coffin, and everyone looked at her, prompting her to do the same, to throw a rose into the ground, but she couldn't do it, because the rose she was holding was pretty and so she clutched it in her hand.

She'd take it home and give it to Sol.

No, she wouldn't.

Because Sol wasn't there any more.

And still they held her tight.

Her two best friends in the world.

52

Judith

Never had she been so relieved to get home. She'd been away for three weeks and her exhaustion was palpable. Work had been really understanding, but she knew they were struggling without her and in fact she relished the thought of going back the next day and restoring some boring order into her life. She'd also found it difficult being away from Gareth for so long. Although he'd been there for the funeral and the weekend before it, the rest of the time he'd had to stay home and she'd missed his stoicism, his gentle temperament and grounding spirit.

Lying in the bath scented with geranium oil, a Jo Malone candle flickering on the windowsill, she looked up at the ceiling and sighed, allowing the comforting warmth of the water to wash over her and soothe her aching bones.

It wasn't only bereavement that was bruising her soul, not just the loss of their dear, dear Solomon, though that in itself was debilitating enough; and it wasn't only the draining pain of seeing her best friend suffer such catastrophic heartache. No, there was another issue that kept swirling around in her head.

Lana.

After the funeral, back at the Kelly house, Judith had gone for some fresh air, seeking an escape from the suffocating atmosphere of whisky, tears and condolences. Lana had obviously had the same idea, and Judith could see she, too, was alone, smoking on the front garden bench, glass of wine in hand. Lana hadn't seen her, so Judith decided to creep back inside, undetected. But standing in the doorway watching *her* was Jack.

'Don't be such a coward, Mother,' he whispered, handing her an empty glass and a half-full bottle of Malbec. 'Go and say something, for God's sake.'

She felt like a petulant schoolgirl reluctantly obeying instructions.

'When are you heading back to Cardiff?' she asked, and Lana jumped slightly, disturbed from her reverie.

'Oh Christ, Judith . . . Umm . . . tomorrow, I guess. Thursday, maybe.'

'Right.'

Silence.

Judith didn't wait to be invited and sat on the bench next to her, pouring herself some of the wine before filling Lana's glass – a small, tentative gesture.

'Thanks,' said Lana.

'I'd propose a toast, but maybe that's inappropriate.'

Lana shrugged, staring straight ahead, then a few moments later blurted out, 'I know nothing about you, y'know. Catrin doesn't tell me anything.'

'Ditto,' replied Judith with a little smile.

And more awkward silence ensued.

'Christ, it's like being on a Tinder date, this!' Lana drained her glass.

'I wouldn't really know about Tinder,' Judith replied, realizing instantly that she'd sounded frosty. She knew she had a habit of doing that when she was nervous, and understandably Lana reacted defensively.

'No, you wouldn't have needed Tinder, seeing as you've been happily married to my old boyfriend for the past thirty years.'

'Oh, this was a mistake,' said Judith, and she got up to leave, but Lana put out her hand gently to stop her.

'I'm sorry. That was *really* childish of me.'

Judith sighed and sat back down. 'Right, let's start again, shall we?'

But then the strangest, most unexpected thing happened.

'Actually Jude, let's not.'

Judith was thrown. Had she even heard properly?

'Thing is, mate,' Lana continued, 'there was a time when I'd have taken your arm off for an olive branch like that. God only knows over the years I've tried. I've endlessly attempted to apologize, to explain, to make amends, and with each attempt you knock me back . . .'

'I know,' said Judith quietly, her mind blown by this unexpected reversal of their usual dynamic. 'And I'm sorry.'

'Well, I appreciate that, I do,' said Lana. 'But I think it's time to accept defeat, don't you? We're both too old now, too long in the tooth. And we have zilch in common, let's be honest.'

Judith nodded, out of shock more than anything.

'Done and dusted, kippers and custard. No shame in that, yeah?' And she got up, patted Judith on the arm and headed back inside.

Judith remained in the garden for a good half-hour afterwards, taking in what had just happened. But try as she might to dismiss it, her mind kept returning to the fact that *Lana* had rejected *her*. She felt hurt and foolish, but, worst of all, she knew it was only what she deserved.

Reaching forward she let out the water and climbed out of the bath. Her whole body felt heavy – she needed an early night. The ever-growing to-do list would have to wait, despite how much had gone by the wayside during her time in Wales. She made herself a camomile tea, said goodnight to Gareth and headed off to bed.

By the following Thursday she'd started to get her mojo back and had begun to feel more like herself again. But on her way home from work, she received a call from Jack.

'Mum, there's been a bit of an update with Nana.'

The whole matter of Patricia and Adrian had been put on hold when Sol died. Judith had had no room in her head, because it was already filled with Catrin and what was to become of her, as well as her own painful sense of loss.

'Is it good news or bad?'

'I'm not really sure.'

Jack went on to say he'd been looking into the background of Steven Dean, the financial adviser 'friend' of Adrian Oliver, who was arranging to put Patricia's house in trust as well as organizing the power of attorney.

'According to Companies House, he's held quite a few directorships over the years, of businesses purporting to offer various financial services . . .'

'Right,' said Judith.

'Three of them were dissolved,' he added.

'That's not illegal.'

'And he's been made bankrupt twice.'

'Also not illegal.'

'No, but then I found a report by the FSA online.'

'Financial Services . . . ?'

'. . . Authority, yeah. Well, it turns out this Steven Dean – he's only *done time*!'

'What?'

'Yes! Six months for *fraud*. And not just any old fraud – he actually defrauded several beneficiaries out of their inheritance!'

'Fuck! Oh, sorry.'

'Love it when you swear, Mum. It's so, so wrong.'

'What are we going to do?'

'Well, surely Nana can't ignore this, can she? Let's be honest, she's a canny old bird at the end of the day, and she won't be wanting to throw her money away. Can you go down there tomorrow? The sooner you let her know, the better. I've got meetings all day, but you can FaceTime me at lunchtime when you're with her. In the meantime I'll send a letter to the solicitors dealing with the POA. They're in Preston, of all places.'

'Hardly a local firm,' said Judith.

'I've googled them and their office looks like a Nissen hut, only not as classy. They must be in cahoots with this Steven Dean fella.'

'You mean they're dodgy?'

'Looks like it.'

'I was always under the impression that solicitors were such honest folk.'

'You're so naïve, Mother.'

'I've spawned a monster,' she laughed. 'So what will you say?'

'I'll just tell them what we know about Steven Dean's history and express our concern about their being two hundred miles away, and ask how can they possibly vouch for their client's – i.e. Nana's – mental state? It won't legally mean anything, but it might frighten them off. They don't seem to have an email address, which also rings alarm bells, but I'll fax them on headed paper.'

And so twenty-four hours later she found herself in Patricia's little living room, trying to convince her mother that Adrian Oliver was no good, whilst Jack tried acting as peace-keeper from the safety of Judith's smartphone screen.

'We're not lying to you,' she said, finding herself feeling unexpectedly sorry for her mother, who today looked very much her age. 'Jack's got the proof. This friend of his – this Steven Dean – he's a criminal, Mum. And Adrian . . . well, so many things just don't add up. Like the fact that he takes charge of your bank cards, and your statements. Edwina said he put you in a home three times last year so he could go on holiday. I didn't even know.'

'And doesn't that say something?' said Patricia, turning on her daughter. 'You come here, shouting the odds, attacking poor Adrian, who has done nothing but look after me . . . of course he needs holidays!'

'You bought him a car! Please don't tell me he's got his hands on your pension – that money was Dad's gift to you!' And then, following swiftly on the heels of that thought, she had another more frightening one. 'Oh my God, has he made you remortgage the house?'

'Mum? Nana?' Jack's voice, small as his picture, was drowned out as mother and daughter launched into a full-blown row.

'Yes, I did buy him a car! So that he can drive me places. The pictures, the shops, daytrips – what have *you* ever done for me?'

'Can we all just calm down?' said Jack from his office in London.

'I've put up with you, Mum. That's what I've done. I've indulged you. I took the shame of having the worst mother in the school and bore it like a bloody martyr. You didn't give me a childhood, you gave me a job – a lady in fucking waiting, a nursemaid, a prop. And then you got rid of the only decent relative I ever had . . .'

'Oh that's right, bring old Greco-chops into it. He wasn't even your real father . . .'

Judith gasped, incredulous at her mother's cruelty. 'You're pathetic, d'you know that? You're a sad little old lady who's driven away the few people who might have cared for you, and replaced them with some parasitic freak who pretends to be your son and drains you of every penny you've got. Well, d'you know what, Mum? Good luck with that one. You deserve each other. *He* wanted me out of your life and *you* wanted me out of your life, and now you've both got what you wished for.'

And with that she stormed out of the house. As she left, she could hear Patricia calling Adrian on speed dial. 'Adie, come quick. It was awful!'

Judith stood outside and leant against the wall, catching her breath. She'd forgotten that Jack was still on the line and had witnessed the whole showdown.

'Well, that went well,' he said.

And Judith promptly burst into tears.

53
Catrin

People had warned her against it. *It's too soon*, they said, and *You'll regret it*, and *You don't need to make any decisions yet* ... Funny, she thought, how some people were experts on grief. Some people knew the timetable. The schedule, the itinerary of bereavement. Some people acted like they knew best.

Except they didn't.

From the very first night she'd slept in their bed without him, she knew she would have to move house. Actually, she hadn't slept alone in their bed, ever. Because from that first night, Romy had slept in there with her, clinging to her mama like a petrified fawn. And so it had continued, in the days that followed, when they stayed at her parents' house. Catrin was only marginally aware of her daughter's presence during those heavily sedated, emotion-numbing nights. Only marginally aware of the warm snuffling bundle of love that lay next to her, desperate for her assurance, her help, her consolation. But Catrin had no comfort to offer, other than to lie next to her. In fact, she could barely speak. And if breathing had been optional, she really wouldn't have bothered.

It went on around her.

Life.

For weeks it felt like her head was submerged in water – she could hear the voices of the people in the room, discussing *what was best*, but the sounds were smudged and incoherent and muffled, and the smiles that everyone seemed to cast in her direction were tentative, as if they sought permission.

This whole epoch had been saturated with shock and Diazepam. It was the only way she could survive, stay alive – with the help of lots of legal drugs – though she wasn't quite sure what she was staying alive *for* . . . Except the little snuffling fawn.

Except for her child.

Yes.

Except for Romy.

The fog had eventually, and so, so slowly, begun to disperse. But in myriad ways she wished it hadn't. Because when everything *did* begin to clear, everything also began to ache. Her arms, her legs, her chest, her head . . . everything throbbed, and stung, like frostbitten fingers in front of the fire, like ancient, battered trees emerging from the winter snow, near dead, gasping and desperate for the tiniest ray of life-giving light from a watery sun.

Hah. Sun. Sol. There was no Sol any more and there was no sun.

So her world would be eternally, continually,

irredeemably grey. Yes. She knew this. But that was OK. As long as she didn't have to feel the sting any more, the open wound that would not heal – the cut, the burn, the near obliteration of her soul. Yes, as long as she didn't have to feel that, then great! Smiley face, smiley face, smiley face.

It was strange sharing her old bedroom with her little girl, and yet somehow the most natural thing in the world. She would tell her about her own teenage years, how she'd spent hours in there with Aunty Lana and Aunty Judith, sharing secrets, laughing, whispering, quarrelling. And the comfort this gave her was huge. And every now and again she'd go to see a doctor – the locum at their practice (*She must talk to Sol about a permanent replacement for him now – Oh no, she couldn't do that because Sol wasn't there any more*) – yes, the locum, she was sweet. Alice, her name was, soft-voiced and kind-hearted, graduated from Cardiff too, but several years younger than Catrin. And Alice prescribed some lovely anti-depressants, and sent her off to a group every week where she sat on a plastic orange chair in a room full of sad people like her and they'd cry and talk about the dead people they'd known, but then one day she made the mistake of saying that the dead people were all just cadavers really, and the others didn't like that, so it was suggested that she didn't come again.

Lana thought this was hilarious – 'You've been kicked out of a self-help group for the bereaved! And you were always such a goody two-shoes in groups! Recorder group and guitar with Mrs Dent and netball and chess – you were *always* the good girl, Catrin, you *never* got kicked out!'

And she'd smiled at Lana, even though she didn't really know what she was talking about. It was like Lana was speaking in French or something.

So when did things begin to change? Was there a defining moment when her grief decided, like some sort of nomadic chief, to move on to the next stage in the process? To find a less painful bit of land on which to subsist? Elisabeth Kübler-Ross – the five stages of grief. That's right. She remembered it from her college days. But for the life of her she couldn't recall what the stages were . . . was one of them anger, maybe? She didn't feel anger. How could she feel angry towards poor Sol? *He's a cadaver now*, she thought again, and imagined him in the ground and how decayed his body would be two months on, without the help of formaldehyde like poor Gwynnie had had.

No, it was the piece of paper in the silver frame that had done it.

Every week – so she was told – Lana, who lived only half an hour away in Cardiff, had come over to help with the move. Pictures of houses at first. Houses she'd take her and Romy to look at, saying, *We're just gonna rent somewhere first, babe, OK? You can think about buying when you're in a better place* . . . And they'd gone in

Lana's car, sometimes with her parents too, to look at all sorts of possibilities – cottages and flats and new-builds and old-builds – and she would smile at them all, whilst Lana talked to the lady or Huw talked to the man and Romy would run into all the rooms, treating it like one big adventure. And she would smile throughout it all, until at last she must have shown a scintilla more interest in one place than the others, and she said yes, and Romy said yes, and Lana reminded her that it was only for six months and then they could think again.

And so when the time had come for them to move in, Lana and her mum and dad had all fussed around her, unpacking, re-stacking, rejuvenating, enlivening – whilst she stood still, and let them construct this new nest, this fresh start, this home in which Sol had never drawn breath.

She'd asked for a brand-new single bed in her room. A bed that boasted no memory of her dead husband, a soft fabric and feather-filled oblong used solely for sleeping, perfunctory, functional. And on the evening they'd finally moved in, she sat on the brand-new Solomon-free settee, and watched her mother unpack a box of photos and ornaments and knick-knacks that had been carefully packed by the removal men, finding places for them on the soulless, sterile bookshelves, in her soulless, sterile new home.

And it was maybe the eighth, the ninth item that Liz took out of the box which sent the jolt through her body, the shock, the sharp awakening. She watched as her mother carefully peeled back the protective layers of newspaper to reveal a small gift, wrapped in gold paper, with the words *Happy Anniversary, my darling husband* written on an accompanying tag.

Liz stared at it. 'Oh my God, Catrin!' she whispered.

Lana, who was sitting on the draining board of the kitchen sink, smoking out of the window because it was too cold to go outside, said, 'What? What is it?'

Liz hesitated.

'D'you want me to throw it away, sweetheart?' she whispered.

'No,' said Catrin, reaching out for the unopened gift.

She looked at it for a moment, then took a deep breath before unwrapping it.

Mounted in a brand-new silver frame was the thirty-one-year-old sliver of paper on which Solomon had written his phone number and a message . . . the same sliver of paper that had been secreted snugly inside Catrin's purse . . . the same purse that had been stolen from her rucksack somewhere in Athens, breaking her eighteen-year-old heart.

'Didn't I ever tell you?' she said, her voice croaking and weak. 'A year after we got back, my purse – it got returned. I'm sure I told you?'

'Yes, I remember,' said Liz softly.

'No money in there, just my library card, and this . . .' She held up the chunky silver frame. 'I kept it for years in a box. Forgot about it, really. And then . . . I found it. And for our anniversary I had it framed . . . as a present . . .'

'For Dad?' asked Romy, her eyes big with sorrow.

'What does it say?' said Lana quietly.

Catrin paused, gathering her strength before stammering out the words, '*Solomon Blythe, 091 066 5879* . . . And then . . .' She stopped, blinking away the tears that were misting her eyes.

Lana leapt down from the sink and stood behind her friend, reading aloud the words in the frame, held in Catrin's shaking hands.

'*Today when we built our pyramid of pebbles, the wish I made was to see you again. And I think that will happen.*'

Nobody moved.

Catrin stared at the paper in the silver frame.

Romy stared at Catrin.

Liz stared at Romy.

And Lana stared at them all. Till the silence, weighted down with fresh pain, was broken by Catrin.

'*Will* it happen?' she asked them. '*Will* I see him again?'

And then it came. The release that she'd been waiting for, the catharsis of tears that had so far eluded her.

'Oh Sol . . .' she wept, clutching the little frame to her chest. 'My beautiful, beautiful Sol . . .'

54

Judith

They were on their way to Coed Celyn to see Catrin in her new home. Judith felt a tinge of jealousy that Lana had helped her choose it, but one thing she was learning was that petty jealousy and resentment was not a good look. And she didn't want to turn into her mother, who she hadn't spoken to for over a month now.

As they were arriving in Coed Celyn, Jack called to say the Preston solicitors had finally been back in touch and that, due to unforeseen circumstances, they would no longer be pursuing Adrian Oliver's request to be made power of attorney, nor would they be processing Patricia's application to put her house in trust.

'That's brilliant, Jack!' said Judith, who'd put the call on to speakerphone.

'Yeah, well done mate!' said Gareth from behind the steering wheel. 'D'you think that's all down to your posh letterhead and strong words?'

'Seems that way. They must have been up to no good to crumble so easily. And even if they *weren't* up to no good, I reckon they just didn't want the hassle.'

'Blimey,' said Judith. 'Well, hopefully my mother has seen sense and won't pursue it any further.'

Gareth suggested that in the light of this development it might be a good idea to make peace with Patricia, especially seeing as Christmas was only three weeks away. 'Goodwill towards men an' all that?' he'd said.

'Don't mention wills, Gareth Metcalf. Sore point.'

He smiled. He knew she agreed with him. 'Let's take her out for lunch somewhere, and then you've done your festive bit,' he said.

'Fair enough, but *you* can ring her to arrange.'

Gareth thought this a good compromise.

That night at Catrin's new-build they were both heartened to see that she'd started to regain the tiniest glimmer of life in her eyes. Romy had cooked dinner for them all – a vegetarian Bolognese that she'd learned to make in school – and they all tried to be hearty and cheery, avoiding *the* subject.

The only time the conversation came close to mentioning Sol was when Romy told them about the cruise. 'Aunty Lana's taking us away for Christmas!' she announced. 'On a mini-cruise.'

Catrin looked sheepish. 'Well, no, we haven't definitely decided yet, sweetie.'

'What's this?' asked Judith, desperately trying to sound nonchalant.

'Oh, I dunno, Lana thought it might be an idea for

us to get away, and she's working on this Tenerife mini-cruise over Christmas, so she can get us a free cabin.'

'Well, it's an idea, all right. But is it a *good* idea?' said Judith.

'This Bolognese is stunning, Rom,' interrupted Gareth, heading off a best-friend rivalry conversation.

The next morning, on their way to Patricia's, Judith brought the subject up once again. 'I mean seriously, Gar, that woman is *so* irresponsible.'

'Yeah, you said.'

'The last thing Catrin needs right now is to be taken away from home. She needs security around her, familiarity.'

'Yeah, you said that too.'

'Look, I know I'm annoying you, but I think one of us should have a stern word.'

'I'm sure you will,' said Gareth as he pulled up outside Patricia's house and parked the car. 'But for now, let's concentrate on your mother, shall we? And putting out *that* particular fire.'

Judith nodded. He was always such a calming influence, was Gareth.

'And remember,' he said, turning to Judith, 'if you feel like she's winding you up, just breathe deep and remind yourself we'll be away from her in a couple of hours.'

'Yeah, I know.'

She opened the cover of the key safe and punched in the numbers. But the catch didn't give. Thinking she'd made a mistake, she tried again. Still it wouldn't give.

'It's not flippin' working,' she said, and was about to attempt it for the third time when the door opened and Adrian Oliver appeared.

'The number has been changed,' he said solemnly.

'Eh?' said Gareth.

'You'd better come in.'

Judith cautiously went inside, Gareth following behind. Patricia was sitting there in all her finery, hands crossed in her lap. Adrian took up his position next to her, like some sort of bodyguard.

Nobody spoke for a few seconds, then Gareth broke the silence. 'You all right, Pat?' he said, forcing the jollity.

Patricia took a deep breath before launching into what was clearly a rehearsed speech. 'Do you have *any* idea how much trouble you've caused me?'

'What?' asked Judith, confused.

'Don't come the innocent, my girl. You sticking your nose in with my solicitors has cost me a bloody fortune! Why couldn't you have just left things be?'

'Because, Mother,' said Judith, trying to remain calm, 'as I've already told you, Steven Dean has a criminal record for fraud. Which Adrian omitted to tell you! And that's just *one* of the reasons we don't feel it's in your best interests to grant him power of attorney, nor do we think it's in your best interests to put this house in trust. We're looking out for *you*!'

'Absolute codswallop,' answered Patricia. 'You just

don't want me to be happy. I've always come second as far as you're concerned. It was the same with George. You always put each other before me – and he wasn't even your flesh and blood.'

'Oh Pat, let's not go down this road, shall we?' said Gareth.

'Zip it, you!' snapped Patricia.

And Judith noticed a small tight smile from Adrian in response.

'I take it lunch is off, then?' retorted Gareth.

Patricia ignored him, preening herself as she continued, 'You thought you could stand in my way, did you? That you could dictate to me what I can and can't do?'

'No, that's blatantly not true.'

'Don't lie to me, you little rat.'

'Let's go, Jude,' said Gareth, who refused to let his wife be bullied by his vicious mother-in-law. This was not a solvable situation.

As they reached the door, Adrian said, 'Oh, there's one more thing we wanted to tell you.' He looked at Patricia, who picked up his cue.

'Yes,' she said, with a malevolent smile Judith hadn't witnessed in many years. 'I wanted to show you *this*.' And with that, she unclasped her hands, and thrust the left one triumphantly at her daughter, displaying a cheap solitaire ring on her fourth finger, which was too tight and dug into the flesh.

'Jesus,' whispered Gareth.

'Patricia and I are getting married,' said Adrian, jutting out his jaw in defiance.

'Next May!' added Patricia. 'So stick that in your pipe.'

55

Gareth

He'd brought an elegant festive wreath with him today, comprising holly and mistletoe and ivy and fir. With Christmas just two days away now, the magnolia shivered in the frost-tinted sunshine, its unformed buds a twinkle in the eye of its silent branches.

After brushing away a few stray leaves and winter twigs, Gareth laid the arrangement upon the tiny grave before taking out his little whisky flask and drinking a generous, body-warming mouthful. Several rows away from where he stood lay Solomon's grave, and even from this distance he could see it was still bedecked in floral tributes. It'd been six months now and Gareth missed him far more than he could have ever imagined.

When he'd arrived, he'd seen a woman reading Sol's headstone, wearing big sunglasses but wrapped up warm against the biting wind that even the bright sunshine failed to counter. They'd not acknowledged each other, though in fairness they were too far apart to make eye contact, and he was glad of this. Over the years he'd learned that there was a strange respect afforded to fellow mourners attending graves in the same vicinity; if he did ever pass anyone, he usually just nodded, a tacit registering of mutual sorrow. Rarely did anyone make conversation in the cemetery. It felt vulgar somehow.

Gareth took another gulp of whisky, glad of its warmth and cheer.

'So your grandmother is up to her old tricks again, Georgie.' He'd never told Judith about his secret name for their little girl – Georgie – because it felt like cheating, developing a fatherly nickname for a baby he'd only known for a day. 'I've just left your mother now at your Aunty Catrin's, telling her all about it. We've had lawyers and social workers and doctors and all sorts involved, it's been a right pain in the neck, I tell you. And now she's gone and got engaged! To a thirty-six-year-old! She really is a piece of work, that woman. Your grandmother, that is, not your mother.' He smiled. 'I think Cat likes to hear all the details – gives her something else to focus on, I guess. She's a lot better than she was. Time's a healer an' all that.'

He paused for a moment, then said, 'Hey, I wonder if you've met your Uncle Solomon yet? Ha! Listen to me – I'm meant to be an atheist!' He smiled and imagined Georgia's sweet little spirit dancing around him and laughing. 'And your brother's baby is due any day now. They're calling her Ivy 'cos of, y'know, Christmas. She'd have been your niece. Weird that, isn't it? – Aunty Georgia.' And he paused to catch his breath.

He rarely cried during these visits, especially during recent years, but it was the reaching and passing of a milestone that often tripped him up: the realization that here was yet another event or accomplishment that Georgia had missed.

'I love you still,' he whispered. 'Whether you can hear me or no.' And he kissed his cold fingers before touching the letters of his daughter's name engraved upon the headstone. 'Happy Christmas, sweetheart.' It was stupid, he knew that. He was just kissing a piece of stone. But he always found it comforting.

'Gareth?' The voice interrupted his reverie. 'Is that you?'

He turned around to see the woman he'd noticed earlier at Solomon's graveside. She'd removed the sunglasses.

He sighed.

'Lana.'

Gareth's thirty-year-old resentment against Lana had become part of his life's familiar landscape. It no longer burned away at him in the way it once did, and he'd grown accustomed to living with it – rarely did a day go by without his thinking about the blame he would always feel towards her.

But after Sol's death it had become increasingly difficult for Gareth to pretend that Lana didn't exist, and even more so to justify his determination never to forgive her.

What no one realized – and what he could barely

admit even to himself – was that he *wanted* to hold on to that blame.

Because it gave him an actual reason for Georgia dying.

Because if her death *wasn't* caused by Lana pushing Judith at Catrin's wedding, if it really was just an inexplicable, unfortunate accident, then he didn't think he could live with it. He found the whole idea suffocating. *Just one of those things*, a doctor had told him, and he'd wanted to punch their lights out. No. His daughter died because Judith's bitch of a friend had pushed her over when she was pregnant.

And he'd turned this belief into fact. And the fact had become darkly reassuring. There was a *reason* for Georgia's death. And if he were to forgive Lana, then surely this reason would disintegrate.

It helped, of course, that he usually only saw her once a year, and even then from a distance and amongst a crowd of party guests. Because absence makes the blame grow stronger, enhances the myth, makes it all the more manageable. But certainly since Sol's funeral, Lana Lloyd – or whatever her surname was these days – had started creeping back into his mind. Without even trying, she'd made her unwelcome presence very much felt.

And now here she was, standing before him in her expensive winter coat. How strange it felt, to not be shocked. As if he'd been expecting to see her.

'I'm down to pick up Catrin and Romy,' she said, as if small talk between them was the most natural thing in the world. 'Heading to Portsmouth, y'know. For the cruise.'

He nodded, taking in the sight of her. Wisps of high-lighted hair peeped out from beneath the faux fur brim of her Russian-style hat. She wore a thick layer of foundation, sealed in with fine powder that had settled in the crevices around her mouth and crow's feet. The hazel eyes he remembered were less vibrant now, but augmented with dark brown eyeshadow and heavy mascara. Her lips, thinner than in her younger days, were painted – they literally did look painted, he thought – with a deep red gloss, a little of which he noted had seeped on to her front teeth. He didn't find her attractive, but nor did he find her repulsive. If any-thing, he was surprised by how gentle she seemed; her manner, despite the heavy defences of make-up and glamorous clothes, was quite ordinary. Timid, even.

'Coffee?' she said.

56

Lana

She'd gone to pay her respects to Sol before calling in on Liz and Huw Kelly, to reassure them that the Christmas cruise with Catrin and Romy really was a good idea. And there he was. By his beloved baby girl's final resting place, marked by a headstone she couldn't bear to look at. She'd stood behind him for a few moments, just watching, unsure whether to make him aware of her presence or just to creep away undetected.

Gareth Metcalf.

Although she'd seen him from a distance over the years and in June at the funeral, this was the first time she could properly take a look. His broad shoulders of long ago were less confident with age, but still prominent as he stood there in his biker's jacket. It felt intrusive to be there, at such a private place, in such a private moment, and she said his name in a bid to end what felt like something akin to voyeurism. When he turned around she'd instantly wanted to cry, but had swallowed down the urge and waffled on as she always did when she was nervous.

*

Twenty minutes later they were sitting in Milza's café on Coed Celyn high street, drinking coffee, with the buzz of Christmas shoppers all around them, and the hiss and steam of the espresso machine accompanying the good-natured shouts between Giovanni and his customers. They were in the window seat.

'Amazing this place is still going!' said Lana as she stirred in three sugar lumps.

'Still using the same cups and saucers,' said Gareth.

They were making awkward small talk, both looking out of the window on to the high street, distracting themselves and delaying the subject they knew they'd eventually have to address.

Across the road from Milza's was the launderette. 'Looks busy as ever, doesn't it?' said Lana, as they watched a man take two bin-liners full of washing inside. 'I wonder who lives upstairs these days?' she ventured, aware that she was on dangerous old-relationship territory now. *We had so much sex in that place,* she thought. *The things we did!* And she blushed at the memory.

If he'd been thinking the same, Gareth didn't give anything away. 'It was such a long time ago,' he said softly.

And finally he turned to look at her.

'Lana,' he said, and held her gaze.

She jumped in. 'Can I just say first of all that I'm really—'

'Please don't,' he interrupted. 'What's the point? It can't change anything, can it?'

'No,' she replied. 'But it might make me feel the tiniest bit better if you *did* let me say sorry. Because it lives with me, Gareth. Every day. And I'm always gonna feel responsible. No matter how much Catrin tells me otherwise.'

Gareth sighed and shook his head.

'What happened happened, Lana. And you are no more responsible for it than her b'there outside the post office.'

Lana glanced in the direction of a blonde woman on her phone, surrounded by bags of shopping and looking stressed. 'I think that's Geraldine Harper, y'know?'

Gareth put on the glasses which he kept inside his jacket and took a closer look. 'God, yeah, it is! Jude told me she's a great-grandmother now.'

'Doesn't surprise me,' said Lana, watching as Gareth took a mouthful of coffee. 'Dirty mare.'

And Gareth spat out his drink, laughing. Which made Lana laugh. And the ice was broken.

After a few moments he said, 'Anyway, if anyone should apologize, it's me. I just . . . I dunno, we get into a groove in life, we write these stories, don't we? And I'd got used to making you the bad guy. It was stupid . . . senseless . . .'

'No, it wasn't.'

'Yeah, it was. I just think maybe you and Jude might have made up if it wasn't for me.'

'I'm not sure we would, you know,' Lana said wistfully, staring into her coffee cup.

'D'you miss her?' he asked.

The question took her by surprise.

'Not any more.' The words caught in her throat, suggesting this might be a lie. 'Truth is, we've been enemies much longer than we were friends, if you think about it. And we've probably both got used to that now.'

Gareth frowned. 'I think *enemies* is a bit extreme, don't you?'

'Well, y'know me, ever the drama queen.'

He smiled, then she said, 'Oh fuck it, Gar. Today's what matters, isn't it? I mean, it's not like we can say to some big boss person in the sky, *Oh sorry, I made a mistake there, in nineteen eighty whatever, can I go back and re-do it?* We are where we are, aren't we?'

Gareth nodded, taking the cue to change the subject. There was only so much could be said.

'Romy tells me you're a Cher impersonator these days!'

'Yeah, and Celine Dion.'

He smiled. 'Classy.'

'It pays disgustingly well and I get to wear nice wigs.' She laughed, though there was a part of her that felt embarrassed to be saying this in front of the person who'd known her when her eighteen-year-old's ambition was fresh and she hungered for bigger things.

'Catrin said the likeness is uncanny!'

'Well, you've got to take work where you can at my age. This new lookalike agency I've joined, they've already lined me up with four gigs in the New Year, so . . .'

'Excellent,' said Gareth.

He looked at his watch. 'I'd better be getting back. Jude's on granddaughter alert. Arriving any day, she is.'

'Grandchildren. Blimey, Gar, who stole all them years, eh? Bastards.' And she reached across the table and squeezed his hand.

'See you, mate,' he smiled, and squeezed her hand back.

57
Catrin

In the end it hadn't taken much to persuade her to go on the cruise.

'It'll blow away all the cobwebs,' said Lana, 'and stop you dwelling on things.'

But when Catrin told her parents, the suggestion was met with a lot of resistance. How could they possibly be away from home for Christmas? Their first Christmas without Sol? What would *his* parents say?

'He was *your* husband,' said Lana to Catrin. 'And Romy's *your* daughter.'

Surprisingly, Romy needed no persuading. All of Cat's worries about taking her little girl away from home at Christmas had come to nothing. Romy made no complaints about missing family traditions like opening presents under the tree, going to church with Grandma and Grampa Kelly, or the Boxing Day rugby with her friends . . . none of these seemed to bother her.

'Mum! We'll be in the Mediterranean! On CHRIST-MAS DAY!! That's amazing, don't you see?!'

And Catrin had laughed, hugely relieved.

There was a brief shared moment of sorrow when Romy hugged her mum and said quietly, 'Anyway, it wouldn't be the same opening presents without Dad.'

'No, sweetpea, it wouldn't.'

'So, what d'you say?' asked Lana, attempting to change the subject, excited that she'd managed to secure a great deal: in exchange for a posh family cabin with its own private balcony, Lana would work each evening of the five-day mini-cruise, doing a stint as a Cher tribute act.

'We say yes, thank you very much, Aunty Larn!' smiled Catrin.

Snuggling down in her cabin bed on Christmas Eve, Romy announced, 'When I leave school I wanna work on a boat.'

Catrin smiled. 'What, you want to be a cruise singer like your Aunty Lana?'

'Aw, I'm touched,' Lana teased.

'No! I wanna be a captain!' giggled Romy.

Lana and Catrin laughed.

After dining at the captain's table on their first night aboard – a treat organized by her 'fairy godmother' – Romy had asked him if women ever captained cruise liners. He'd told her that he'd heard of only two female Masters of the Ship to date, and that he didn't really know of the reason for this. Romy had told him this wasn't fair. He'd agreed, and asked if she'd like to visit the Bridge and watch him command his ship. She'd ended up staying there for most of Christmas Eve, fascinated by the mechanics and power of the vessel, all governed by a single person at the helm.

'It's amazing, Mum!' she said. 'This ship weighs over two thousand tons and is operated from this one tiny place. Did you know everything is lighter in water?'

'That's Archimedes' principle,' said Catrin.

'You what?'

And suddenly, without warning, Catrin tapped into the archive of her science-trained mind and speedily reeled off the definition she'd learned several decades earlier: *'Archimedes' principle states that the upward buoyant force exerted on a body immersed in a fluid, whether fully or partially submerged, is equal to the weight of the fluid that the body displaces and acts in the upward direction at the centre of mass of the displaced fluid.'*

Lana and Romy sat stunned and open-mouthed for a moment, before Lana began slow-clapping her brainy friend.

'Way to go, Cat, way to go!'

'Mum, you're such a swot!'

'It's why boats stay afloat and why, when you're in the sea, you can carry someone much heavier than you. Don't you remember you used to do it with your dad when you were little?'

'Umm . . .'

'You used to think it was magic that you could lift him up in the swimming pool and carry him around as if he was light as a feather!'

There was a beat of sadness. One of many that had

occurred over the preceding couple of days, and surely there would be more to come – they were unavoidable, of course. But at least on board the *Princess Eugenie* the environment was all shiny and new, and a world that neither Cat nor Romy had ever visited before. It was a zone that was free from memories of Sol.

On Christmas morning, Catrin awoke early. For the first few seconds of consciousness, she forgot that Sol had died. This happened almost every day. She looked round at Lana, who was out for the count, and Romy, who was snoring in her bunk. She sighed, clambered quietly out of bed and wrapped a blanket around her shoulders before heading out on to the balcony, where she sat on the little deck bench and stared out to sea. The morning was fresh and misty but she could just make out the shape of land in the distance. She tried not to cry – she so didn't want to cry. When was the crying ever going to stop?

A few minutes later she heard the door slide open and was joined by Lana, who stumbled out on to the balcony for her early nicotine fix.

'Budge up,' she said, lighting her cigarette and clambering under the blanket with her sad friend.

'You stink,' said Catrin in an attempt to lighten the mood.

'You don't smell so great yourself,' said Lana, puffing away, regardless of how much Cat hated it. 'D'you wanna drag?'

'Lana, you of all people know that I have never smoked in my life. Why on earth would I start now at the age of fifty?'

'Because it's Christmas Day, and your heart is breaking, and I'm trying to distract you by being incredibly irritating.'

'Nothing new there, then.'

They sat in silence, letting the Christmas-morning sea air comfort them both.

'It'll never go,' said Lana as she exhaled the acrid fumes. 'There's always going to be this . . . missing part.'

Catrin nodded, and squeezed her friend's hand as she looked out at the ocean.

'But it's still early days. It *will*, one day, feel better than it does right now.'

'I just don't seem to be able to put one foot in front of the other. Can't think about the future, can only take a day at a time. Sometimes I can only manage an hour before I start crumbling. I mean, I should've gone back to work by now, shouldn't I?'

'There are no rules, Catrin. Stop being such a fucking head girl!' Lana laughed and kissed her friend on the head. 'How d'you eat an elephant?'

'Eh?' said Catrin, confused. 'I dunno . . .'

'One bite at a time. It's all you can do.'

And Catrin broke into a small smile. 'What a revolting thought!'

'We all miss him, babe. There are so many people in this world with a Solomon-shaped hole in their lives. He'll never be forgotten.'

And they sat like that in silence for a good half-hour, their hair dampened by the spray, the gentle movement of the boat soothing them in the solitude of their own thoughts.

Their reverie was interrupted by the door of the cabin sliding open as a sleepy, excited Romy came out in her pyjamas.

'Can we open our presents now?'

And Lana responded with her biggest, loudest Noddy Holder impression, 'IT'S CHRI-I-I-I-ISTMAS!!'

58

Judith

She'd been looking after the baby when she got the call. Sweet little Ivy May, now three months old, born on Boxing Day weighing a healthy nine pounds, and the apple of the entire family's eye. Having both been back at work since the beginning of March, Dominic and Jack relied upon their stalwart nanny for childcare. But today she'd phoned in sick. And they had found themselves turning to Judith and Gareth for help.

'It's no chore, it's a joy!' she'd said to Jack when he dropped off his daughter at his parents' house that morning. 'I just hope me and your father don't fight over who gets to cuddle her the most!' She was trying to put him at ease, knowing that both Jack and Dom felt bad for abandoning their parental duties.

So when Judith's landline rang an hour later, she presumed it would be either one of the nervous new neurotic fathers, checking in on their newborn.

'Don't worry, we're all doing fine!' she said as she answered the phone. But it wasn't Jack. Or Dom.

It was Catrin.

'I've been trying your mobile! Jude – you better get down here as quick as you can.'

Catrin had called her from the surgery, where she'd agreed to do a day's locum – just to see how it felt to go back to work.

'I've just seen Greta Hughes,' she said quickly. 'You remember her, Jude? She was a dinner lady.'

'Used to call her Garbo! Yeah, go on,' said Judith, keen for Catrin to get to the point, the phone nestled in the crook of her neck as she nursed her sleeping grandchild.

'Sorry, right . . . so, just as she was leaving she said she had some gossip to share. Well, I tried to put her off, 'cos, y'know, we're not meant to gossip . . .'

'Oh Cat! Spit it out, for God's sake!' said Judith in a whispered shout so as not to wake Ivy.

'It's your mum,' said Catrin. 'She's getting married.'

'Well, so she claims!' said Jude. 'But she's put it off several times already.'

'No! She's getting married *today*! At two o'clock!'

An hour later, Judith, Gareth and baby Ivy were on the M4, heading for Wales. Gareth was driving and Judith was in the back with her granddaughter.

'What the hell's she playing at, Gar?' demanded Judith for the umpteenth time.

Since Adrian's announcement in December, Jack, Gareth and Judith had all worked tirelessly to persuade Patricia that she was making a mistake. And she had

461

seemed to be relenting, having changed the wedding date twice to later in the year.

Jack had been optimistic. 'I really don't think she'll go through with it, Mum,' he'd said. 'And that social worker agrees. They're keeping a very beady eye on things, y'know.'

So it wasn't that Judith had become nonchalant about the wedding, she'd just come to believe that it was never going to happen; that, true to form, Patricia would keep Adrian well and truly hanging on.

And now here they were, heading for Wales to try to put a stop to a wedding that Patricia clearly had every intention of undertaking.

'She's a sly, manipulative old witch. And so is he,' she said. 'They've obviously been lying to us, planning to do it in secret all along!'

The phone rang. It was Catrin again. 'I can't get hold of my mum or my dad!' she yelled over the speakerphone. 'So they can't help. And I've got a list of patients as long as my arm waiting to be seen. There's no way I can go, Jude! Maybe you're just gonna have to accept you can't stop her.'

'No way.'

In the background they could hear Catrin's receptionist informing her the next patient was on his way in.

'Look, there *is* someone who can help,' Catrin said hurriedly. 'But you're gonna have to make the call. I'll text you the number now. And if I *can* escape after morning surgery, I'll meet you there.'

Catrin hung up. And within seconds Judith's message alert beeped.

CONTACT DETAILS for LANA LLOYD.

Judith sighed.

59

Lana

She was getting ready for a lunchtime event at a gay club in Cardiff. The gay clubs seemed to love her, but she didn't want to take her recent popularity for granted. Who knew when the next brilliant look-and-sound-alike would come along? She'd heard rumours of a *very* convincing Barbra Streisand from Pontycymer taking the scene by storm. So she mustn't let her guard down – or drop her standards.

She was just adding a few more spiral curls to her Cher wig when the phone rang. The number wasn't one she recognized – but that wasn't surprising. It was probably a new club wanting to book her. She answered the call in her best, smooth and silky, Cher sound-alike voice. '*Hi, honey pie! What's up?*'

'Lana?'

There was a hint of familiarity in the way the caller said her name, but she couldn't quite place it. She cleared her throat and tried talking normally.

'Yes, speaking?'

There was a moment's silence, then, 'It's Judith. Metcalf.'

Fuck!

'Oh. Hi.'

A beat, then, 'Look, I'm sorry to call you like this out of the blue, and I wouldn't ask if I wasn't desperate, but I am. I need a big, big favour.'

60

Patricia

The setting was certainly not romantic. Nor majestic nor impressive on any level. Had it been in a town hall, the location would at least have offered some grandeur and solemnity – a few stone pillars on which to tie a ribbon, a bit of 1930s wood panelling maybe, or a stained-glass window here and there. But there was no town hall in Coed Celyn. Its unremarkable register office was housed in a bland brick municipal building, designed and constructed during a particularly un-imaginative period at the end of the 1960s. It had absolutely nothing going for it other than the fact that it was clean and boasted good wheelchair access. In every other regard it was not only ugly but falling apart – the walls were actually crumbling in places. It should really have been put out of its misery several decades earlier.

The smallest of two purpose-built ceremony rooms had been incongruously named the Richard Burton Suite. This had been done in a jocular attempt to cap-italize on the town's tenuous link with the movie world: the English translation of Coed Celyn was, after all,

Holly Wood. The room was functional, sparse and distinctly lacking in personality. Stark neon ceiling strips ensured participants could see clearly when it came to signing the register, but the modest high windows offered little in the way of natural daylight or a pretty vista to accompany the joy of getting married. It was more akin to a mortuary viewing room than a wedding venue. A desk, a pen and five people: Steven the best man, Tina the maid of honour, Alison the registrar, and of course the happy couple.

Patricia wore white and held a demure bouquet of lilies of the valley in her lap – fake, of course. She wouldn't have real flowers: she couldn't risk her sinuses. Not on a day like today. Adrian wore the corduroys she'd bought him and a smart navy jacket – no tie, but Patricia didn't mind. She wanted him to be comfortable and he wasn't a dresser-upper, as he often reminded her.

Admittedly, Patricia would have preferred a little chapel wedding, or even a trip to Vegas. *She*'d have paid! They could've got one of those Elvises to do the service – by God, they'd have had some fun with that! But Adrian had pointed out, gently of course, and sensibly as ever – because *I only ever have your best interests at heart, Patricia* – that the flight would've been too much for her. And even a chapel wedding down the road in Capel Bethesda would have attracted too much attention. *You know what they're like in Coed Celyn, Pat – gobby bitches, the lot of them. They just wouldn't understand.* And, of course, if Judith found out she'd have stuck her oar in too and scuppered the whole thing.

He was right. As ever. Because, like he said, this was *their* day. Their special and *private* day. Better to keep it simple and quiet. And secret.

He was always thinking of her, never of himself. Even today, he'd attached a couple of sprigs of lily of the valley to her wheelchair handles. And as he'd helped her into the car, he'd looked at her and said, 'Remember now, today is *our* day, yeah? There'll be no mention of you-know-who, OK?'

And she'd smiled coyly. She loved it when he took charge. He'd protect her from Judith, make no mistake.

Along the corridor in the Zeta-Jones Hall (renamed after the 1990s success of *The Darling Buds of May*, when Swansea's most famous daughter shot to fame), an Indo-Welsh marriage was being solemnized between a couple from Pontydrueni. That room, by contrast, was drowning in colour. Packed with over one hundred and twenty guests (thirty more than fire regulations permitted), all jostling for space amongst the balloons and flowers and streamers and saris, that wedding could not have been more different. Muted strains of the sitar and tabla drifted down from the Zeta-Jones Hall to the Richard Burton Suite, where the only sound was the heavy tick of the wall clock and the sombre tones of Alison the registrar's voice.

*

She looked up at Adrian now, staring straight ahead, listening intently, with that serious little furrow on his brow that she'd come to know and love so well.

He turned to her and winked, mouthing 'You all right?', and she nodded and smiled. She couldn't have been more all right.

Alison the registrar turned to him and said, 'Do you, Adrian Alan Oliver, take Patricia Mary Harris to be your lawful wedded wife? Will you love her, honour her, cherish and protect her and, forsaking all others, be faithful unto her as long as you both shall live?'

Adrian took a deep breath and glanced momentarily at Steven, his best man. Steven smiled back encouragingly, nodding his approval.

Bless him, thought Patricia. *He's filling up!* Her Adie, always the level-headed one – Adrian the Calm, she called him! – never fazed by anyone or anything, who'd face down any challenge: her Adrian, her beloved Adrian, was now overcome with emotion. She wasn't used to seeing him so vulnerable, so shy – the little boy in him showing his frightened face.

He cleared his throat and she could see him physically pull himself together before answering a little too loudly, 'I do.'

Without looking up, Steven put his hand on Adrian's shoulder and squeezed, whispering, 'Well done, love.'

And then Alison stopped speaking. Her attention was taken by some activity in the doorway, which Patricia couldn't see – she had limited mobility in the wheelchair and was unable to turn around very fast.

Alison's jaw dropped as she stared at the sight before her.

'Good God, are you . . . ?'

'I'm sorry,' said a breathless woman. 'I'm sorry, but this wedding has to stop . . . You have to stop it immediately.'

It took a few seconds for Patricia to process what was going on.

'Jesus!' screamed Tina the maid of honour, who up until now had been quite bored. 'It's Cher! Are you Cher?'

'I'm a big fan of your work,' said Alison meekly.

'Fuckin' hell, *and* me!' Tina reached for her phone to start videoing it all – this would be mega on Instagram.

'No, I'm not Cher! I'm a Cher *impersonator*,' screeched the woman. 'I've come straight from a gig and I didn't have time to change, and I said I'd meet the others here, and they should've arrived by now but . . . Anyway, that's not important.' She was clearly frustrated and embarrassed.

'Sorry, but you do look exactly like her,' said Alison, blushing to her roots.

'That,' announced Patricia, who had managed finally to turn herself round, 'is Lana Lloyd, an acquaintance of my useless lummox of a daughter, who has done nothing but cause me heartache and misery since the day she was born and with whom I no longer wish to be associated.'

'Patricia, listen . . .' Lana said, looking over her

shoulder for back-up. 'I'm not exactly sure what's been going on and I—'

'Get away from me!' screeched Patricia.

'But no, seriously now, *are* you Cher?' Tina persisted. She wasn't the sharpest pencil in the pack. 'Can I get a selfie? What you doin' in Coed Celyn?'

'Shut up, Tina,' hissed Steven.

'Pat, I'm sorry,' spluttered Lana, red in the face from running, 'but you can't go ahead with this! Please – just wait till Judith gets here, is it?'

'GET OUT!' screeched Patricia, only it sounded more like GED than GET. Patricia often Americanized when she wanted to make a point.

'OK, let's all just calm down, shall we?' said Alison, resuming her professional mantle. They had a marriage objector in their midst and she flushed with excitement. In all her twenty years of officiating, Alison had never encountered an objection to marriage. Thankfully she *had* been trained in how to deal with one. She cleared her throat. 'My name is Alison Booth, I'm the senior registrar here today and I am fully aware of the complications regarding Mrs Harris's wish to marry, of her daughter's objection, and now yours.'

'Then you'll know,' said Lana calmly, 'that this seventy-nine-year-old woman is being taken advantage of.'

'Oh my God, Pat!' chirped Tina, who was viewing everyone through the video camera on her phone. 'I never knew you was seventy-nine – I thought you was, like, fifty or somethin', which is still well old, but seventy-nine is, like, *mental*!'

'Tina! I said, shut up!' snapped Steven Dean. 'And turn that bloody thing off!'

Tina ignored him and carried on filming. This was pure gold.

'Mrs Harris has undertaken psychological testing and interviews with Social Services—'

But Lana was no longer looking at the registrar. She was staring instead at Steven Dean.

'I know you, don't I?'

Steven looked irritated. 'I doubt it.'

'Yes, I do. I've seen you a few times down Molinski's. You've had loads of selfies done with me . . .'

'If we could just get on,' said the registrar.

But Lana was on a mission.

'. . . Yes, me, you and your boyfriend – Aden, is it? We had a session on the tequila couple of weeks ago, d'you remember? I was doin' my Celine Dion.'

And then she did a double-take that would have done Mr Bean proud. 'Hang on . . .' she said, as she clocked Adrian. 'It's *you*! You're Aden!'

'His name's Adrian,' said Patricia sternly. 'Now leave us alone.'

'Patricia – you're not marrying *him*, are you?'

'Ignore her, Pat,' said Adrian. Then, turning to Alison the registrar, he hissed, 'Get on with it.'

And just as Alison was about to resume the ceremony, a voice rang out, loud and commanding and very, very in tune, '*If I could turn back time!*'

Lana was singing.

'*If I could find a way . . .*'

They all looked at her.

Then, having gained everyone's attention, Lana Lloyd reconnected with her Coed Celyn roots and launched into a heartfelt plea that would be the envy of any politician.

'Patricia, you cannot marry this man. Because he is gay. And he loves *that* man right there.' She began searching for something on her mobile. 'He told me so two weeks ago in Molinski's gay bar in Cardiff. Look. Here's the proof!' And she showed them a short video, taken at one of Lana's gigs, where Steven Dean was very passionately kissing Adrian Oliver. 'Can't really argue with that, can you, Adrian?'

'Um,' interrupted Alison Booth, 'I should point out that Mr Oliver's sexuality isn't necessarily a bar to his marrying Mrs Harris, as long as Mrs Harris is aware and happy to proceed.'

They all looked at Patricia.

And down the corridor in the Zeta-Jones Hall, a drum roll on the tabla signalled the end of proceedings, whilst momentarily the world stood still.

61

Lana and Judith

Outside the register office, a small crowd had gathered, including Judith, Gareth, baby Ivy and Catrin, standing with Lana and Patricia. They watched in disbelief as the police cars drove away, carrying Adrian Oliver, Steven Dean and Tina Grey to Coed Celyn police station. It was at this stage just 'for questioning', but as Jack explained to them on FaceTime, 'They'll arrest them once they get there – any criminal allegation needs an arrest. I'm not saying they'll charge them, but it's looking like they will.'

'They can't charge them for being gay!' laughed Lana, who despite the cold was baking from a hot flush.

'Of course not, you idiot!' laughed Jack. 'Most likely Conspiracy to Defraud.'

'I'll sue the living daylights out of him!' shouted Patricia. 'The little scheming rat. Fleecing me for every penny I own, taking away my daughter's inheritance. I knew he was a bad 'un from the moment I laid eyes on him.'

Judith and Catrin stared at her for a moment, speechless. Both thinking the same thing.

Only Lana had the guts to say it. 'Christ, Pat, you're a fickle fucker! You were all ready to marry the guy an hour ago.'

'I know, but then you showed him up to be the little shit that he is!'

Lana looked at Judith, and Judith looked back.

Then the two of them burst out laughing.

'Lana, thank you,' said Judith, unsure of how her thanks would be received. 'If it wasn't for you—'

'I'd be married to a monster!' shouted Patricia, who was now tucking into a hip flask of whisky, kept 'for emergencies' inside her bridal bag.

'I didn't really do anything, let's be honest.'

'Yes, you did,' said Catrin. 'You stopped the whole thing! I was about as useful as a chocolate teabag.'

'Teapot!!' shouted Judith and Lana in unison. It'd been years since they'd been able to gang up affectionately on Catrin.

There was a lull in the mood, then Judith took the lead.

'I'm so sorry. For being such a twat,' she said.

'Hey, that's *my* role!' Lana laughed, as usual defaulting to self-effacement.

'Not today,' said Judith, smiling gently.

And Lana smiled back. And the smile went some small way towards reclaiming three decades of mislaid friendship.

62

Catrin-Kelly-Judith-
Harris-Lana-Lloyd

'Right then, who's for a top-up?' asked Huw Kelly, coming into the living room clutching a newly opened bottle of bubbly, slower on his feet these days. 'Twenty nineteen is less than an hour away!'

They were gathered at the Kelly house for Liz and Huw's regular New Year's Eve bash. It was a much smaller, more conservative occasion than in previous times, but no less fun. Catrin sat with Romy, Huw with Liz, Jack with Dominic, Gareth with Catrin's brother Tom and his wife; Lana was holding baby Ivy, who was wide awake and enjoying the party, and sitting next to Judith, relaxed on the sofa and dressed up to the nines, was Patricia.

Nine months had passed since the dramatic events at the Coed Celyn register office, but it somehow felt like decades ago.

After the wedding-day-that-never-was, Patricia had taken a turn for the worse, and ended up staying in hospital for a fortnight, after which it was suggested she should go temporarily into sheltered accommodation. They'd thought she would hate the idea, but it turned out to be the making of her. Far from withering and retreating into her shell, Patricia began to thrive in her new environment, taking part in every activity on offer and becoming known in the communal living room as the life and soul of Coed Celyn. She took up poker and in-chair aerobics, joined a book club and the cinema-goers. She'd often claim that life had never been so good, and despite the fact that she had several male admirers, she'd decided to play the field. 'Treat 'em mean, keep 'em keen!' When the time came for her to return to the house in Victoria Road, she'd responded with a loud and emphatic, 'No way.'

It took several months for Adrian Oliver to be charged and found guilty for his intention to defraud. He was given a two-year jail sentence and Steven Dean, his partner in crime as well as in love, was given five years, due to his previous conviction. Tina Grey was given a three-month community-service order, which she described on her Instagram account as 'cowing disgusting', accompanied by a series of filtered and pouting selfies. If the plan had gone through, Adrian Oliver, as Patricia's husband, would have stood to inherit her house and savings.

'And God knows what sort of life she'd have had,' said Catrin.

'Exactly!' said Lana, who couldn't resist a drama. 'He would probably have spent the next couple of years trying to bump her off. You'd have got a call one day to say she'd mysteriously fallen into her soup and drowned.'

'At least she's safe now,' Jack said, ever the voice of calm.

It was decided that they should sell the house to pay for Patricia's sheltered-accommodation fees, and should any of the capital be left 'after my days', then this was to go to her great-granddaughter Ivy May, with whom Patricia had become obsessed.

'Looks like you've been demoted,' joked Gareth to Jack, who gazed at his daughter with abundant fatherly pride.

In an astonishing private moment between herself and her mother, Judith was almost moved to tears when Patricia thanked her for everything she'd ever done for her. Lana and Catrin were shocked when she told them.

'What, she actually used the words *thank* and *you*?' asked Lana.

'Actually, she said *Thank you, love – really.*'

'Oh my God! So d'you think she's softening in her old age?'

'Jesus, no!' laughed Judith. 'In the next sentence she was telling me to turn the volume down on the TV and was I trying to deafen her?'

'Lepers and spots, I guess,' said Catrin.

And her friends exchanged a look.

'You've *always* got that saying wrong!' said Judith.

'No, I haven't,' objected Catrin.

'Yes, you have! It's leopards, you fool,' laughed Lana.

'But I thought it was to do with leprosy. Y'know, the skin condition, like in the Bible stories – lepers and spots.'

'And she's a bloody doctor!' said Judith to Lana, both sharing a huge moment of affection for their mutual friend.

Over the preceding months, Lana and Judith had slowly and steadily crept back into a camaraderie of sorts. There was an ease between them now which seemed to improve, the more time they spent together. But things weren't back to how they used to be. And both of them had come to accept the possibility that this might always be the case; so disconnected had they been from each other's lives, so uninvolved, for thirty years, that even with Catrin as the glue to hold them together, the closeness they'd once known had become sadly irretrievable.

'Too much water under too many bridges,' said Lana one day.

'I thought mixing metaphors was Catrin's thing?' said Judith.

'Oh shut up, you pompous cow,' retorted Lana with a smile.

It was now just half an hour away from midnight. Patricia was fighting sleep, and Huw was checking he had the TV on the right channel for the fireworks at midnight.

'Ladies,' said Catrin. 'Come upstairs a minute. There's something we all need to do.'

Bemused, Judith and Lana followed their friend upstairs.

When they entered Catrin's old bedroom, they found her sitting there triumphant, holding up a tatty hard-backed notebook.

'I found it the other day, sorting through old boxes in the attic.'

Neatly on its cover, in nine-year-old Catrin's hand-writing, it declared:

THE BOOK OF SECRET PROMISES
by
Catrin Kelly
Judith Harris
&
Lana Lloyd

On the front page, still held in place with yellowing Sellotape, was a faded and fragile Curly Wurly wrapper – the same wrapper upon which they'd sworn an oath in 1976. Every December the thirty-first for several consecutive years, they had each written a resolution. In 1978, Catrin had promised to pass her grade two ballet, Judith had vowed to stop biting her nails and Lana had pledged to learn all the words to every Abba song ever written, as printed in *Smash Hits*.

The last entry was dated 1985, when they'd attempted to predict their A-level results and promised each other they'd have the best time ever in Greece.

'Well, we certainly did that,' said Judith, remembering.

Catrin turned to the first blank page and wrote neatly in big letters:

New Year's Eve, 2018

'Right, who's first?' she said, a bright smile lighting up her face.

'Me!' said Lana. And she took a deep breath, along with the book and a pen. 'In 2019, I resolve . . .' She thought about it for a moment, tapping the biro against her chin before launching forth, 'I resolve to plan a massive joint birthday party for us three. To celebrate turning fifty-two in style! Seeing as we did bugger all for our fiftieths.'

'Bloody hell, do we have to be reminded of how old we are?' said Judith with a sigh.

'Fifty's the new thirty, give or take,' exclaimed Lana as she scribbled. 'Don't be such a whinge-bag.'

Cat laughed, taking the book from Lana and handing it to Judith. 'Come on, Jude – your turn.'

'Right, well, my plan is to get a transfer at work and finally move back to Wales.'

'Seriously? You're gonna move back?' said Lana, shocked.

'Yep. Little cottage in the hills maybe. Gareth's wanted to for years.'

'Yass Queen!' shouted Lana.

The other two shot her a confused look and she shrugged. 'It's what all the young people are sayin' these days, d'yamean?'

'You're ridiculous, you know that?' laughed Judith and Lana poked her tongue out.

'Hey! You know what else we should do?' Lana added. 'Next summer?'

Judith and Catrin shrugged.

'We should go back to Greece. We should go island-hopping again.' Her voice was filled with glee.

'Oh my God!' said Judith. 'What, for like a week or something?'

'Hang on a minute,' said Cat quietly.

'Come on, girls, it's five to!' shouted Huw Kelly from downstairs.

'Be there now,' Cat shouted back, before turning to her friends.

'And Cyprus, of course,' said Lana.

'Well yeah, we'd have to go to Cyprus! So we'd need longer than a week, I suppose . . .' Judith mused.

'Girls, there's something—'

Judith and Lana looked at Cat.

'Look, I think it's the best thing ever that you're moving back, Jude,' she said.

'But what?' asked Lana.

'The thing is . . .' said Catrin, treading carefully.

Suddenly the mood in the room changed.

'What?'

'Thing is . . . I'm not gonna be here,' said Catrin, waiting for the onslaught.

'Christ, you're not dyin', are you?' said Lana.

'Shut up!' snapped Judith. 'What you talking about, Cat?'

Catrin paused. The decision she'd made in secret some time ago was about to be revealed.

'I've been offered a job . . .'

'Right,' said Judith cautiously.

'And it's in New Zealand.'

'You're not serious?'

'Starting end of Jan.'

They were all silent for a moment. The sounds of gentle revelry from downstairs drifted up into the room.

'Why on earth d'you want to go to New Zealand?' asked Judith, confused.

'It's for a year initially, but with the option to extend. A lovely little practice in Tauranga on the East Coast. North Island.'

'Oh, well that makes all the difference if it's the *north* island,' said Lana sarcastically. 'I mean, imagine if it'd been the *south* island, God forbid . . .'

'Oh do be quiet, Lana, honestly,' said Judith irritably.

'No, why should I?' moaned Lana, getting worked up. 'You finally move back, Jude, us three finally get a stab at maybe being proper friends again, after a thirty-something-year gap, and then *she* decides she wants to move to the other side of the sodding world!'

'Calm down, will you?' said Judith. She turned to Catrin. 'What do your parents think?'

'I haven't actually told them yet,' said Catrin sheepishly. 'Look, I know it's a shock.'

'That's an understatement!'

'And I'm sorry I haven't told you about it sooner, but I didn't want you to try and dissuade me.'

'Which we *would* have done,' Lana sulked.

'Lana, for God's sake!' said Judith. 'Stop making it about you! Go on, Cat.'

'Please don't be cross. I just need to do it. To be in a completely different place. Somewhere I never went with Sol.'

'So move to Lampeter then! Or the Pembrokeshire coast,' pleaded Lana.

'Lana,' said Catrin, taking her hand, 'it's not gonna change *us*, is it? Who we are together. Just 'cos we don't see each other as often, doesn't mean the link breaks?'

'But it's so extreme.'

'I want a new adventure for me and Rom, that's all. I want to move our lives forward, y'know? Stop looking over our shoulders at what was or what might have been . . . Living here, there are so many ghosts, so many reminders—'

'I thought you found that comforting?' said Lana.

'I did for a while. Not any more.'

'Yeah, I get that,' said Jude quietly.

And for a moment they sat there in silence, taking in the enormity of Catrin's news.

'One minute to go!' shouted Liz Kelly from the hallway.

Nobody responded.

'Well, I think you're a complete arse for leaving me on my own with *her*,' laughed Lana through her tears.

'Feeling's mutual,' replied Judith, also teary now.

'You'll manage,' laughed Catrin. 'Could even be the making of you both!'

Lana rolled her eyes.

'Look, who knows?' said Catrin. 'I might hate it over there. Might be home in six months.'

She reached out and put her arms around them. 'Come here,' she whispered, brimming with love for her two best friends. And they hugged each other, silently swaying back and forth, as the midnight chimes of Big Ben drifted upstairs from Huw Kelly's television set.

EPILOGUE
1976

Forty-two years earlier

The one thing Miss Taylor loved about playtime duty was being able to smoke in the fresh air. Made no sense, she knew that. But smoking in the staff room was a bit overbearing, especially with Alan Jones and his awful pipe. Of the fourteen teaching staff at Coed Celyn Primary, eight of them were smokers. And it got a bit much at break-time, all crammed into the chair-lined room next to the Headmaster's office, puffing away on Bensons and drinking Mellow Bird's.

Admittedly, standing in the playground and putting up with the constant barrage of 'Miss! Miss! So-and-so did such-and-such!' from 250 junior school pupils was a high price to pay, as was having to repeatedly shout, 'Come away from the fence!' But at least she got to enjoy her cigarette and have five minutes to herself.

She should really stretch her legs a bit before the bell, do a quick circuit of the playground and surrounding grass areas, yellowing now after weeks of dry weather. Twenty-seven days till the end of term and she'd be off to Devon with Jerry. Ooh, she must get some new bathers. The elastic had withered in her red ones.

She headed for the top end of the playing field. In amongst the saplings that stood like sentinels around the perimeter fence, she could see three sets of Ladybird-socked feet peeping out from under three skirts – one denim, one broderie anglaise and one green corduroy – all facing inwards in a tight huddle. She couldn't work out who the feet belonged to at first, the heads of the huddlers hidden under a red pac-a-mac, draped over them like a magician's cape. But as she approached, she could hear the confident voice of eight-year-old Lana Lloyd. 'So you have to say after me . . .'

Miss Taylor smiled to herself. If that was Lana, then the other two must be Judith Harris and Catrin Kelly – the sweet little trio who'd been inseparable since their very first day at Coed Celyn three years previously. She'd taught them herself last year.

'I swear on this Curly Wurly wrapper . . .'

A muffled giggling from the other two stopped Lana in her stride.

'You have to take it seriously or it won't work!'

'Sorry, start again,' said Judith.

'And hold the wrapper straight,' added Catrin.

'Right, say after me: *I swear on this Curly Wurly wrapper . . .*'

The two voices dutifully repeated the words. '*I swear on this Curly Wurly wrapper . . .*'

'*. . . that I will always be a royal friend and true.*'

'It's LOYAL not ROYAL, you narna!' said Judith. 'With an "L"!'

'Is it?' asked Lana, confused.

'Lana's a narna!' giggled Catrin, joined by Judith.

And the eavesdropping Miss Taylor had to stifle her own giggles.

'Aw, look, someone else do it then – Cat, you do it!'

'OK, give it here.'

There was some reshuffling and a rustling of the sacred chocolate paper.

'Hurry up, the bell's gonna go in a minute!' said Judith.

'Right.' Catrin cleared her throat and began. 'Say, "Us three are best friends for ever" . . .'

'Us three are best friends for ever . . .'

'And we swear that we will always be there and true . . .'

'We swear that we will always be there and true . . .'

'Come what bloody may!'

'Catrin!'

'We can't say that!'

Lana and Judith were both simultaneously shocked and delighted. Swearing was not something they ever did, which is what made it all the more deliciously naughty.

'We're swearing an oath, aren't we? So we're allowed to swear. Go on!'

There was a pause and then together, gleefully, they shouted, *'Come what bloody may!'*

Miss Taylor was transfixed and strangely moved by this innocent declaration of loyalty. She thought about Jerry, who she'd known for twenty years since she was five. Twenty years. A lifetime ago. She wondered if the friendship of these three little girls would last as long.

And looking at her watch, she saw that break-time was over. Abandoning her reverie, she reverted to teacher mode and began ringing the hefty iron hand-bell.

The three friends jumped with the shock of the sound, surfacing from beneath the pac-a-mac, their faces flushed with embarrassment.

'Come on then, back inside,' Miss Taylor announced over the bell. 'Playtime's over now!'

They ran back towards the classroom, leaving the Curly Wurly wrapper lying forlornly on the grass.

'Excuse me, Catrin Kelly! We'll have no litterbugs in this school, thank you very much. Now pick that up!'

'Sorry, Miss.'

Catrin did as she was told.

As she passed the rubbish bin by the steps into the junior school, she was about to chuck the wrapper away when something made her change her mind. She folded it up and put it inside the pocket of her green corduroy skirt, before hurrying to catch up with her two best friends.

Song credits

Lyrics on p.26 from 'Against All Odds (Take A Look At Me Now)' written by Phil Collins

Lyrics on p.79 from 'If My Friends Could See Me Now' from the musical *Sweet Charity*, music written by Cy Coleman and lyrics by Dorothy Fields

Lyrics on p.135 from 'Guys And Dolls' from the musical *Guys and Dolls* written by Frank Loesser

Lyrics on p.223 from 'I Should Have Known Better' written by Jim Diamond and Graham Lyle

Lyrics on pp.237–238 from 'Should I Stay Or Should I Go' by The Clash, written by Topper Headon, Mick Jones, Paul Simonon and Joe Strummer

Lyrics on p.257 from 'Never Gonna Give You Up' written by Stock Aitken Waterman and recorded by Rick Astley

Lyrics on p.472 from 'If I Could Turn Back Time' written by Diane Warren and recorded by Cher

Acknowledgements

Since I finished writing *Us Three*, the world has changed immeasurably. And it seems an age ago that I began this second foray into the world of prose fiction. It was a genuine labour of love and I feel that Catrin, Judith and Lana have now become my dear and cherished friends. I hope you enjoyed meeting them too.

There are so many people who helped bring *Us Three* to life:

Firstly there are the readers of *Never Greener*, whose generous and positive response to my first novel spurred me on to write my second. I thank you wholeheartedly. You are all lush.

There's Frankie Gray, my superbly talented editor at Transworld. Frankie, I am so grateful to you for your patience, tenacity, optimism and faith, and for your ability to get the best out of me. You are amazing. And thank you, thank you to the rest of Team Transworld for making the novel-writing experience once again so bloomin' enjoyable. Special thanks to the brilliant Alison Barrow and Vicky Palmer for holding my hand once the book entered the public domain and for dealing so smoothly with the challenges of lockdown. Also huge thanks to Larry Finlay for his kind words when he first read the book, to Bill Scott-Kerr, Hayley Barnes, Kate Samano and Imogen Nelson, and of course to the excellent audio book team, especially Alice Twomey, Chris Thompson and Cranc Studios in Cardiff.

Praise and gratitude must go, of course, to my wonderful agent, Jonny Geller, and to the team at Curtis Brown. Jonny, what a privilege it is to be both your client and old university friend. I am deeply appreciative of your calm and unstinting support, genius insights and wicked sense of humour.

Diolch o galon i Dawn French and Jojo Moyes, for your encouragement, wisdom and awe-inducing talent.

Thank you to Hannah Beckerman, brilliant novelist and writer, for reading an early draft and for giving such invaluable advice. (Thank you also for the *Archers* therapy!)

And a special *efcharisto* to Harry and Georgia Chacholiades for helping me with all things Cypriot and Cretan. I am so grateful to you both.

I dedicated the book to my friends. You know who you are and I am blessed to have you in my life. But I especially want to thank dear Nicola Merrigan, Carrie Grafham and Mairwen Williams for your early reading of *Us Three* and your superb feedback.

Thank you to Fiona Adams-Jones for your help and reminiscences, and to the lovely Ceri Hartland and Liza Milza for sharing your tales of interrailing in the mid-eighties. I'm sorry the Armenians didn't really make it, but maybe in book three . . . ?

Thank you to my cherished family for your continued love and support, especially Fi and Llew, Lula and Andrew, Alex and Selena. To Cerys (*ein chwaer anrhydeddus*), to my fabulous big brothers Mark and Julian, whose kindness floors me on a regular basis, and to my lovely baby sister Maria, for reading an early draft and regaling me with Med School stories.

To my beautiful mother Hannah, who is awesome, in the truest sense of the word. You personify kindness, compassion and gentleness and I love you unfathomably. Here's to our next Welsh road trip!

To my father, Richard. It's been three years and I miss you more than ever – but your cheeky humour and the pride you showed in all your children's achievements live on and still make us smile. I like to think you'd have enjoyed this book, Dad.

And finally to David – my beloved husband, best friend and writing partner. I can never, ever thank you enough. What a gorgeous journey we're on. I'm already relishing our next chapter!

Ruth Jones is best known for her outstanding and award-winning television writing, most notably BBC One's *Gavin and Stacey,* which she co-wrote with James Corden and in which she played the incorrigible Nessa Jenkins. The most recent Christmas Day special of *Gavin and Stacey* gained national critical acclaim, drawing an audience of over 18 million, winning a BAFTA for TV moment of the year and a National Television Award for Impact, and gaining an RTS nomination for Ruth's performance. Ruth also created and co-wrote Sky One's *Stella,* which ran for six series. As well as being BAFTA-nominated for her role as the eponymous Stella, Ruth has starred in several other television comedies and dramas.

Her debut novel *Never Greener* has now sold over a quarter of a million copies. It was chosen as WHSmith Fiction Book of the Year 2018, was a Zoe Ball Book Club pick, and was a *Sunday Times* bestseller for fifteen weeks, three weeks at number one. *Us Three* is Ruth's second novel and was a *Sunday Times* bestseller in hardback.

Also by Ruth Jones

Never Greener

and published by Black Swan

The *Sunday Times* number one bestselling debut from

RUTH JONES

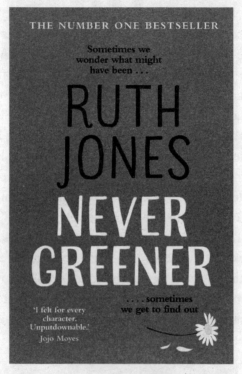

'Ruth Jones is excellent on human nature and why we make the mistakes we do. I felt for every character. Unputdownable.'
JOJO MOYES

'I love books about gnarly, messy relationships and this one kept me gripped from the beginning. A great read.'
JANE FALLON

Out now in paperback, ebook and audio

LOVE UNTOLD

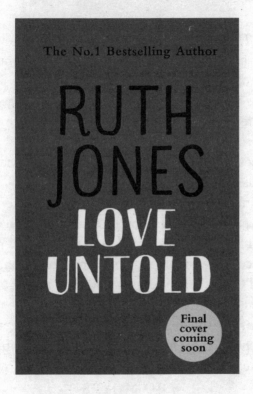

The brand new novel from

RUTH JONES

Coming soon and available to pre-order now

US THREE
A Reading Group Guide

1. *Us Three* is told through several different voices and perspectives. How did this structure affect your reading of the novel?

2. Was there a particular character you identified with? Were there any moments you found surprising or moving?

3. Discuss the ways in which humour is used in the book. Did you find this effective?

4. Think about the ways in which grief and loneliness are portrayed in the novel. Do any of the characters find friendship and comfort in unexpected places?

5. Discuss the events that put strain on Lana, Judith and Catrin's friendship. Could their falling out have been prevented?

6. Consider the final chapters. Did you have any different ideas for how the novel might end whilst you were reading?

Ruth Jones Q & A

1. *Us Three* follows the many highs and lows in Lana, Catrin and Judith's friendship over the years. Did you have a clear idea of where their story would go when you started writing?

   Not really, if I'm honest! I knew I wanted to write about female friendship and I knew I wanted the friends to be very different personalities with a strong shared bond that would need to be challenged in some way – I guess that was my starting point. I also wanted to be able to show how they'd grown from teenagers into young women into older women and what happened to them en route, so splitting the book into three parts gave me the chance to explore their lives at these three different stages. Although Lana, Judith and Catrin get older in the book, they never quite lose that childhood dynamic – so who they are in their fifties is still rooted in who they were as teenagers. I share this with my own friends and I find it compelling.

2. Much of *Us Three* is set in Coed Celyn, a fictional town in Wales. How important was it for you to capture this sense of place and heritage in the book?

   Oh, I really wanted to write something Welsh for my second novel. The Welsh humour and voice and culture are so rich and earthy and they're what I know. I made the town of Coed Celyn a fictional place because I didn't want to set the story anywhere real – if it had been set in the Valleys it would have been impossible and irresponsible to avoid mentioning the Miners' Strike and its devastation in the eighties, so I chose to make the setting fictional but still Welsh. I suppose in my head there were traces of my own upbringing in a small Welsh town at that time – some of the high-street names were nicked from my childhood – but more than anything the novel was a love letter to the female friendship I've enjoyed and been blessed by over the years, in particular my friends in Wales.

3. The scenes set during the girls' Big Trip are wonderfully nostalgic and evocative. How do you go about researching your novels?

Well, I'll confess here and now that I've never been to Cyprus. But a dear friend of mine from uni and his wife are both British Greek and Cypriot so I was able to ask them questions about the two places – food was particularly important. There were dishes I'd never heard of, like mahalepi *and* glyka. *And I discovered that halloumi is more of a Cypriot food than a Greek island one. I'm really chuffed that people loved the Cyprus and Greece chapters and the sunshine inherent in them. I did actually go to Crete with my sister in the early nineties, though we never walked the Samaria Gorge (to my regret), and researching that – watching people's videos of the trek online – was really inspiring. And as well as that, two of my close friends from home went island-hopping in the eighties, so I grilled them about their experiences. In the first draft there was MASSES of stuff about island-hopping, and even interrailing AFTER the island-hopping! But I think I'd reached the word count of a full novel before they'd even come home! So a lot had to go, I'm afraid, but it was a very enjoyable journey.*

4. You are a screenwriter and actor as well as an author. Do you think that your background in film and television has influenced your novels? Where do you find your inspiration when writing?

   I think being an actress, and having written scripts for screen, means I probably have a good handle on dialogue and how a scene would play out, and I think this helps. Also, it's been useful in the creation of characters, because I imagine playing them or how they would come across on screen. I didn't record the audiobook for Never Greener because I was too embarrassed to read out the sex scenes in case my mother ever listened (thank you to Sharon Small, who did an excellent job!) – but I did record the audiobook for Us Three, and I think because of my being an actress the experience was doubly enjoyable and it really brought the book to life for me. So it's certainly been a benefit to my novel writing in lots of ways to have a background in acting and screenwriting. In terms of inspiration – gosh, I really don't know where it comes from. All I know is that it usually finds its root in relationships, rather than a 'hook' of some kind or a plot-driven idea. I wish sometimes that I could be more plot-driven – but maybe that will come with time.

5. After the runaway success of *Never Greener*, what was your experience of writing a second novel like?

   It was completely different. Never Greener had originally been a screenplay, so I had the story all in place (albeit not exactly the same, but in general). So the structure was quite straightforward for me. But with Us Three, I really was starting from scratch. I realized that, like with my screenwriting, I tend to start with the characters and let the story unfold from them. So it took me longer to find out what the narrative drive would be in Us Three. Also, when I conceived Never Greener, I was about twenty years younger than I am now, and I realized that as we grow and change, our writing does too – I think there's maybe more heart in Us Three, it's a gentler story in some ways and not so hedonistic. There are definitely similarities between the two actresses in the novels – Kate Andrews and Lana Lloyd – but Lana is a gentler soul and more comedic than Kate. You have to love your characters though – even if they're not very nice.

6. Where do you think your writing will take you next? Do you have any plans for another book?

   Yes, I'm currently writing book number three, Love Untold, *and really enjoying myself. I don't want to give too much away, but it's about four women (my husband asked me if I was going to call this one* Us Four ☺*) and they're Welsh, but they're from very different generations and they each have a secret.*